SHOOTING THE RIFT

SHOOTING THE RIFT

ALEX STEWART

SHOOTING THE RIFT

A Baen Books Original

Baen Publishing Enterprises
P.O. Box 1403
Riverdale, NY 10471
www.baen.com

ISBN: 978-1-4767-8118-1

Cover art by Stephan Martinière

First Baen printing, April 2016

Distributed by Simon & Schuster
1230 Avenue of the Americas
New York, NY 10020

Printed in the United States of America

10 9 8 7 6 5 4 3 2 1

SHOOTING
THE RIFT

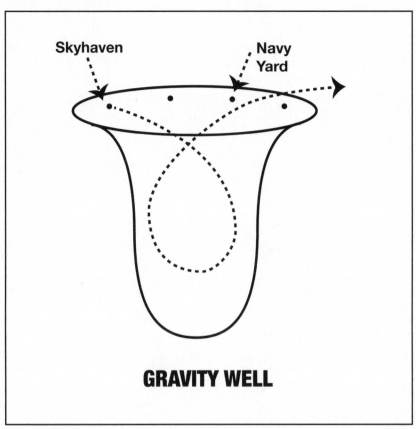

GRAVITY WELL

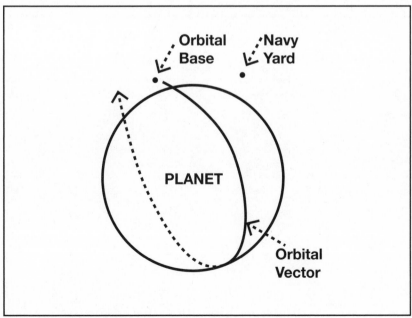

CHAPTER ONE
In which a familial disagreement leads to an impulsive decision.

"I'm extremely disappointed, Simon." My mother paused for emphasis. When I was a lot younger, I'd always assumed she did that to underline the gravity of whatever offence I was supposed to have committed—but these days I had a state-of-the-art neural interface entwined around my synapses, and could easily sense the datacloud surrounding her. Less than half her attention was actually on her wayward son, the rest devoted to the fluctuating datastreams connecting her to her ship.

So I stared past her shoulder, through the window of the dockyard office she'd borrowed from Aunt Jenny, wondering which of the drifting stars beyond was the *Queen Kylie's Revenge*. Typically, I'd been dragged all the way up to the main orbital for this exhibition of parental displeasure, while Mother just hopped a few dozen miles from the outer moorings in the Captain's gig.

Idly, I dipped a probe into the datacurrent, testing its speed and direction. Her ship must be one of those pinpricks of light drifting above the luminescent limb of the night face of Avalon, where the hidden sun was just beginning to catch the edge of the atmosphere. Directly below us the planet of my birth—technically, at least, since I actually entered the universe a few dozen miles above its surface, in the sickbay of HMS *Virago*, mother having left things a little too late to catch the shuttle home once the contractions started—was speckled with the warmly glowing lights of cities and towns. Knowing my mother, I couldn't help wondering if she'd been just as deeply meshed into the *Virago*'s datasphere that morning, more concerned with making a good impression as the new Second Officer than the business of giving birth to me. But that was unfair. Probably.

Before I could fix the *Revenge*'s position any more precisely, Mother's outgoing datastream threw my probe off with a white-hot sting of heavy encryption, far more toxic than the protection I'd breached so easily at the university. If she was aware of my brief attempt to mesh, however, she gave no sign of it, just frowning as she continued the well-worn mantra of her disapproval. Which meant dragging Dad into it, of course. "And so's your father. Aren't you, Harold?"

"Yes, dear. Extremely disappointed." My father nodded, trying to look as though he cared, but a quick dip into his datacloud (civilian neurosuite, blocked as thoroughly as my own from anything up here that might be interesting) showed most of his attention was on a multiway link with his fishing cronies, finalizing the arrangements for a trip they were planning the following weekend. Noticing my presence, he kicked me a virtual of the lodge. Old style, rustic furnishings and a wood-burning stove, which would never be needed with the modern environmental system, but a fire always made a room look cozy. *There's a spare bunk if you want to disappear for a few days.*

Not this time, I sent back. I could hardly think of anything more boring than failing to catch fish with a group of middle-aged fleet widowers. Besides, if Mother found out, she'd give him a hard time for "indulging" me when I was supposed to be in disgrace.

Dad nodded, almost imperceptibly, picking up on the subtext. He was good at that. But then we'd had a lot of practice. Warship captains don't make a habit of taking their families with them on deployment, so he'd brought up my sister and I pretty much single-handed, while Mother was off defending the Commonwealth. If he'd ever had any ambitions or dreams of his own he'd never mentioned the fact to me, abandoning them in favor of marriage and fatherhood as dutifully and uncomplainingly as men of his class were supposed to. Mine too, come to think of it, but I'd always wanted something more out of life.

A reflection which sparked an all too familiar flare of resentment. Maybe if I'd held it in until Mother had finished chewing me out, like I usually did, my life would have resumed its even tenor of suffocating tedium, and I'd have avoided the inconvenience of so many people trying to kill me in the months to come; but I could feel the pressure of innumerable petty slights building into a tidal wave of bile, overriding any attempt at caution and restraint. All those years of my mother's withheld approval, her eloquently unexpressed disappointment that her first-born hadn't been a girl. All the encouragement and support my sister had been given, even after ruffling everyone's feathers by bucking the family tradition and opting for a career in the Marines instead of the Navy, while my own interests had been patronized and ignored. All those times I'd been labeled a problem for showing a bit of initiative, even if I hadn't quite thought through the consequences of acting on it.

"Well perhaps I'm disappointed too," I snapped back without thinking. Mother's eyes focused on me as though her targeting 'ware had just got a positive lock on a fleeing commerce raider, and I suddenly remembered why getting her undivided attention had always been an uncomfortable experience for both of us. Dad shifted uneasily in his chair, and I didn't need his *Bad idea* to tell me he wasn't happy with the way the conversation was going either.

If anything, Mother seemed surprised. I suppose ship captains expect people to just shut up and do as they're told, a principle she'd generally extended to her nearest and dearest, and my flash of defiance had wrong-footed her.

"And what's that supposed to mean?" she asked, in a voice that should have left Aunt Jenny's desk, with its scattering of manifests and requisition forms, coated with ice.

"Exactly what it sounds like," I volleyed back, while Dad tried to become invisible in the corner. "Nothing I've ever done has been good enough for you, has it? When I won silver in the district games, you told me I should have tried harder for gold. I got a college place entirely on my own, without you having to call in any favors like you did for Tinkie, and you just said men don't need to be smart. And the only way you'd let me go at all was if I settled for a course a wife would find useful if I ever find one."

"Of course you'll get a wife," she said dismissively, as though the issue was already settled. Knowing her, she'd have a short list of potential candidates on file somewhere. Then an expression of acute constipation flitted across her face, which was what usually happened on the rare occasion an idea occurred to her. "Good God and all Her angels! You don't prefer men, do you?"

"No." I had to fight the urge to laugh at that point, and I could see Dad trying not to smile too visibly as well. But then he'd seen a great deal more of my social life than Mother ever had.

"Good." Heaven help me, she actually looked relieved for a moment. Then thoughtful again. "Although if you do, Admiral Jollife's got this nephew. Good looking, very poised. Quite a catch."

Which was the real point, of course. Finding a suitable spouse for me wasn't just about continuing the Forrester tradition of supplying generation after generation of cannon fodder to the Royal Navy, I was supposed to marry into the family of someone who could give Mother's career and social status a leg up as well.

"If I ever change my mind, you can introduce us," I said. "But you're missing the point." Which wasn't exactly a surprise; why should she break the habit of a lifetime? "How can you honestly expect me not to resent it when you won't even allow me to pick the college course I want?"

If I'd been able to study something I was actually interested in, like neuroware design or gravitic engineering, instead of a subject my family deemed "suitable for a man" (estate management, in case you were wondering—but I can hear you yawning from here), I might not have been so bored that setting up a lucrative sideline in information brokerage—all right, meshing into the admin system and filching test answers—had been just about the only thing keeping my brain from liquefying and trickling out of my ears. A hobby which had also boosted the meager allowance I got from my family more than enough to let me attend all the right parties, with the cream of campus society: by which, of course, I mean the rich and thick, all of whom were profitably delighted to be in my circle of acquaintances, despite a social gulf so wide I would have been barely visible waving across it in the normal course of events.

Then it all went sour, for which, if I'm honest, I had no one to blame but myself. If I hadn't got overconfident, and sold Rosamund Kearney enough to ace her mid-terms, I'd probably have got away with my little avocation indefinitely. I could have landed a Dame or a Viscountess at some soiree a semester or two before graduating—maybe even

Rosamund herself, who was nice enough in an amiably dim-witted sort of way—and settled into a comfortable life as the pampered husband of an aristo. (Or kept man, anyway—I had no illusions about the sort of welcome I'd get from Rosamund's family if she ever took me home to meet her mother.) The trouble was, Rosamund was one of those students whose acceptance is tacitly understood to be more about funding than academic ability, and her sudden jump from a steady stream of D-minuses to potential valedictorian raised more than a few suspicions.

Which inevitably led to the Proctors finding the ripples my fumbling around had left in the campus datapool, and it was swiftly made clear to me that my presence in the groves of academe was no longer welcome. After a few empty threats of criminal charges had been waved in my direction, despite everyone, including me, being well aware that far too many influential families would be embarrassed by such a thing for the affair ever to be made public, my university education came to an abrupt and ignominious end.

"There's more to life than doing what you want," Mother said, clearly relieved to be able to shoulder-charge the conversation back to topics she understood, like Honor, Duty, and Doing the Right Thing. "And that doesn't excuse you helping your friends to cheat."

"I wasn't helping my friends to cheat!" I protested, indignant at the unfairness of the accusation. "I was helping anyone who was willing to pay me!"

Dad groaned, and buried his head in his hands. Mother's eyes narrowed, and I began to wonder if it was too late to switch places with the commerce raider.

"So, it's come to this." The words fell from her compressed lips like chunks of frozen helium. "Five generations of duty and sacrifice to produce a . . . a . . ." For the first time in my life I heard words fail her. If it hadn't been so alarming, I might have savored the moment. Instead, I concentrated on not looking intimidated, which, considering her years of practice at making underlings squirm, wasn't as easy as it sounds. "A common mountebank," she concluded at last, having bought a few milliseconds to consult a thesaurus somewhere within her datacloud.

"That's right," I rejoined heatedly. "Five generations of Forresters, going back almost as far as the first Rimward settlements. All of them joining the Navy because their mothers and grandmothers did. Did you even think about doing something else with your life?"

"No." Her voice was flat with the unshakable certainty of the imaginatively challenged. "I don't expect you to understand, but it's a proud tradition." Then an unexpectedly wistful note momentarily softened her tone. "I had hoped Katinka would continue it, but she knows her own mind."

"She's her mother's daughter, all right," Dad said fondly, startling us both; locked in our duel of words, Mother and I had practically forgotten he was there. A skill he'd perfected over the years, and one which I strongly suspected contributed greatly to whatever marital harmony was to be found in the Forrester household. "But the Marines *are* technically part of the Naval Service, so—"

"Do you have an actual point to make, Harold?" Mother asked, returning her attention to me. I caught his eye. *Best keep out of it*, I sent, appreciative of his attempt at a diversion, however futile. "I'm the last Forrester in that unbroken line to wear this uniform. There's no one else."

For some reason, that casual aside stung me far more than anything else she'd said so far.

"Of course there isn't," I practically shouted back. "Because Tinkie's the only child you ever had, and if she wants to bugger off and play soldiers instead, that's the Forrester naval line sunk for good and all. It's never even occurred to you that I could enlist instead, has it?" To be fair, it had never occurred to me either, but I didn't see any reason to mention that at the time.

"Don't be ridiculous, Simon." For a moment, it seemed, Mother oscillated between erupting with anger or with laughter, before compromising with an explosive snort of derision. "An officer's son among the enlisted ranks? The idea's preposterous."

"Who said I had to be a swabbie?" I retorted. "Men can be officers too, you know."

"Not on my ship." This time the snort held a note of incredulity. "I don't care what the so-called modernizers in the Admiralty say, men aren't temperamentally suited to positions of command, and there's an end of it. They're too hot-headed to make sound tactical decisions."

Which, I must admit, wasn't just her own view; the numbers spoke for themselves. Fewer than ten percent of the officers in the Royal

Navy were men, and most of those were serving in administrative and support roles. None of the handful actually assigned to ships held positions higher than Third Officer. Strangely enough, though, the further down the chain of command you went the more men you were liable to find, until the bottom tier of enlisted personnel was pretty much a mirror image of the gender balance at the top.

"Are you seriously suggesting applying to the Naval Academy?" Dad asked, looking more surprised than Mother, if that were possible. I was about to laugh it off, admit I was only making a cheap debating point, when I noticed something else in his expression, almost hidden by his astonishment. Pride. And perhaps a little envy.

"Why not?" I said instead. "I got into Summerhall." Which may not have been the most prestigious university on Avalon, but it was well up in the first rank, even attracting academics and research contracts from other worlds in the Rimward Commonwealth. "The entrance exams can't be that much harder. And, as Mother never tires of reminding us, the Forrester name counts for a lot in Naval circles."

"Quite out of the question," Mother said. "I won't see that reputation squandered on an act of the purest folly."

"Anastasia," Dad said quietly, and Mother let go the breath she'd been inhaling. He hardly ever uses her given name, and when he does, she listens. Quite why, I've never worked out; but something changes between them. It's not as though he raises his voice—if anything, it gets quieter—but there's a sort of intensity to it that makes me feel like I'm five years old again, and I've just been caught with my hand in the jar of sherbet lemons. "Perhaps we should consider it. You've often said he'd benefit from having something to think about besides himself."

"I didn't mean he should enlist," Mother said, sounding as though she was just coming round after hitting her head on an unsuspected low beam. "I meant charity work, or something else suitable for a man in his position."

"What could be more suitable than carrying on the family tradition?" Dad said, and I began to wonder if I'd overplayed my hand a bit. But, thinking about it, I supposed I could do a lot worse than follow through on the impulsive suggestion. If I did manage to get a place as an officer cadet, I'd be removed from the orbit of Mother's disapproval for months, if not years, and the salary would make me financially independent for the first time in my life. She might even have a bit more time for me, once the idea that I was adding a sixth generation of Forresters to the roster had managed to percolate though her layers of calcified thinking.

"It certainly couldn't hurt to apply," I said, as persuasively as I could manage. "And you have to admit, something does feel right about the idea of me carrying on the tradition, if Tinkie can't." She was beginning to waver, I could tell, and I added what I thought would be the clincher. "Until, one day, my own daughter perhaps . . ."

"You'll need a wife first," Mother said, returning to the comfort of familiar thought ruts.

"He'd meet a lot of eligible spinsters at the Academy," Dad pointed out archly, "and most of them from good Naval families." He paused, waiting for her to run through the implications for herself.

"I suppose he would," Mother conceded, integrating this new and startling concept with her perennial preoccupation of getting me married off to the greatest advantage. She stood, in response to a sudden flicker of message traffic rippling through her datasphere, and nodded to Dad. "Very well, Harold, we'll discuss this properly at a more opportune moment."

"Of course, dear," Dad said, tilting his face for a perfunctory farewell kiss as she swept from the room. As the door clicked closed behind her he seemed to solidify, and turned to face me looking a good deal less vague and ineffectual. "I hope you know what you're doing, Si. If you screw this up, she'll never forgive you."

"I won't screw it up," I said, and at the time I really meant it.

CHAPTER TWO

In which my sister and I discover something we shouldn't have.

"Where's my brother, and what did you do with him?" Tinkie demanded, striding through the French doors from the terrace and dropping her kit bag. Behind her the muted hum of the rovers trimming the lawn mingled with the buzzing of the flitterbugs swarming around the rose bushes. The scent of the flowers, overlaid with the sinus-tickling odor of new-mown grass, drifted behind her into the conservatory, where I'd settled shortly after breakfast. On the edge of my datasphere the limited AIs of the gardening drones were flickering, barely noticed, just as the whining of their gravitics merged seamlessly into the soundscape of a sunny Southdown afternoon. Engrossed in my studies, I'd completely forgotten my sister was due to visit the family estate on embarkation leave. "Simon never looks that serious."

"Hi, Tinkie." I extricated myself from the dataflow, my personal 'sphere shrinking to the neuroware I normally left running in the background. None of that merited my immediate attention, although there were a number of messages I ought to reply to, mainly from former classmates commiserating with me over my rapid rustication; it seemed I was missed, or at least the service I used to provide was. "Forgot you were coming." If I'd surprised my family with the diligence I was displaying, I was no less surprised by it myself: but now that I'd committed to applying for the Academy, I was determined to make the grade. All right, if I succeeded I'd still have people like Mother telling me what to do all the time, but that would be by my choice, not hers, and once I passed I'd be taking at least some decisions for myself. For the first time in my life I could see a realistic prospect of a measure of independence within reach, and I meant to grab it with both hands.

"Now that sounds more like my brother." Her smile broadened, and I hauled myself off the battered old chaise my father doggedly refused to throw out, into the path of a rib-crushing hug.

"Good to see you too," I said, returning the embrace before I passed out from oxygen deprivation. My sister had inherited Dad's build, short and stocky, while I took after Mother, in that regard at least, which left my chin resting on the crown of her head. We broke apart, and I felt the air rushing back into my lungs. "Where are you off to?"

"Tintagel," Tinkie said. "The briefings are all strictly need-to-know, and junior lieutenants aren't supposed to. But a reliable source told me—"

A phrase I'd heard many times before. "Some clerk in the battalion office you lured into bed—"

"Believe me, he wasn't complaining." Tinkie looked distinctly smug for a moment. "Then again, neither was I. Kind of wish I could remember his name."

"You'd better hope he doesn't remember yours," I said, mindful of the regulations I'd been wading through in preparation for the Academy entrance exam. "Fraternization between officers and other ranks—"

My sister grinned again. "We did a lot more than fraternize. Twice. At least. To be honest it all went a bit hazy after that, but the hangover was definitely worth it." I clearly hadn't kept my doubts off my face, because she reached up to ruffle my hair, something I'd always detested, and which she knew would be a reliable distraction. "Besides, you don't think I was stupid enough to give him my real name, do you?"

"Of course not," I said, a little coldly, as I pulled away. Like rather too many women I'd met, Tinkie's attitude to my own gender could best be summed up as *Of course I like men, I shag them, don't I?* without worrying too much about how the men concerned might feel about that. But she was still my sister, so I swallowed my disapproval as best I could, and tried to return the conversation to safer ground. "And this fraternizee of yours said—"

"We're off to rattle sabers as close to Rockhall as we can get without the Leaguers being able to claim we're fortifying the place ahead of a negotiated settlement."

"I see," I said, hooking the local star charts into my 'sphere from the manor's datanode. The Rimward Commonwealth and the League of Democracies had been squabbling over the sovereignty of the Rockhall system ever since the first Commonwealth colonists turned up there a couple of decades before I was born; which, by now, meant that the place was thoroughly infested with native-born Rockhallers who felt like Commonwealth citizens to their bones, and weren't about to listen to any Leaguers whining "We saw it first." If they wanted the place so badly, they should have left a garrison behind when their own colonization effort collapsed. Most of the time the League just accepted the *fait accompli*, but every now and then they'd get arsey about it, usually just before or after an election; this time round the hardliners had won a majority in both houses of government, so things were unusually tense on both sides. "Which puts the Leaguers in Caprona, if they're playing the same game."

Tactically, that was a no-brainer—you don't grow up in a family like ours without being able to read a rift map, and Caprona was the nearest League system with enough logistical support to mount an invasion from. Like Tintagel, there were only two rifts between it and Rockhall to transit, so if the diplomats on either side fumbled their sessions of verbal rock, paper, scissors it would just come down to which fleet was the quickest off the mark.

Tinkie meshed into my 'sphere, and I felt the tickle of fresh neuroware melding with my own. "You're missing the best bit," she said, directing our attention to one of the two systems connected by a rift directly to Rockhall. I called up the stats for it: Sodallagain, uninhabited, a few rocks devoid of interest orbiting an equally anodyne red dwarf. Two other rifts connected to it; one linking directly to Tintagel, and the other the League outpost at Caprona. "This'll be the flashpoint."

"I can believe it," I said. Unless one of the two fleets was hellishly fast off the mark, and managed to slip through the choke point before the other could mobilize, they'd meet head-on in the Sodallagain system, and things would get ugly as soon as they closed to within firing range. "Could be an uncomfortable ride for you, if you're not first out of the blocks." We'd both heard enough dinner table talk about naval engagements to have few illusions about that. Grandma never tired of reminding us that she first took command of a ship as a midshipwoman ("First cruise, mind, still wet behind the ears") after all the senior officers had been incapacitated by a rift bounce.

"We will be," Tinkie said, with all the confidence I'd come to expect since her enlistment. Royal Marines pride themselves on being able to take the fight to the enemy wherever they are: her cap badge read *Per Inane Per Terram*, and I truly think she barely saw the difference, apart from needing less life support in the latter case. When you came right down to it, though, despite the first part of their motto, Marines in a space battle were just so much perishable cargo unless they were needed for a boarding action.

"What's that?" I asked, indicating a data packet embedded in the Sodallagain stats. It bristled with the same kind of encryption I'd felt when I poked Mother's message traffic back on the orbital, and I was faintly surprised she'd been careless enough to leave something so clearly important lying around in an accessible node. It wasn't as though Dad or I could read it, of course, but it still wasn't like her; then I realized the full significance of the sudden increase in dataflow I'd noticed between the ship and her Captain before Mother's abrupt departure, which, at the time, I'd put down to her feeling irritated at not being able to browbeat me into acquiescence as usual. The *Queen Kylie's Revenge* must have received new orders connected to the deployment, and in the hurry of preparation for that she'd simply forgotten to delete the packet from the node at home. Not that any League spies were likely to find it there, but it was a definite breach of protocol, and I recorded its presence with a sense of gleeful mischief. The next time Mother started in on me, I'd have some potentially career-stalling ammunition to defend myself with.

"Shall we take a look?" Tinkie asked, no doubt with the same idea in mind; though Mother was slowly coming round to the idea of having an air-diver for a daughter she'd made her disappointment all too evident to begin with, and there was still a fair amount of lingering resentment between the two. Nothing like I'd had to put up with over the years, of course, but still enough for Tinkie to relish putting one over on Mother if she got the chance.

"I'm not so sure—" I began, reflecting that it was one thing to know the file was there, and quite another to access the information it contained. Especially as the prosecutor would undoubtedly cite my little college enterprise as evidence that I was a hopeless recidivist, undeserving of the benefit of any doubt, should our nosing around ever come to light.

"Don't be such a willy," Tinkie said, poking at it with a military grade decryption key. The packet's defenses slapped it away, and my sister frowned. "Whatever that is, it's got to be Eyes Only stuff."

"All the more reason to leave it alone," I said, already knowing I wouldn't. I've never been able to resist a challenge, at least where sneaking in somewhere I'm not supposed to be is concerned, and the harder it was to pull off, the more determined I became. Meshing with the university 'pool had started out as nothing more than a puzzle to solve; it was only once I was in there that the idea had come to me to exploit the access I'd gained for money and social connection.

"Course it is," Tinkie agreed, knowing full well I'd be on this like a terrier with a bone from now on. I pulled up the sneakware I'd put together at college and started fiddling with its datanomes, patching in bits I remembered from the sting of Mother's encryption, molding and inverting them to reverse engineer a key. Tinkie's decrypt was still floating in the shared datasphere, and I pinched off a few bits, adding them to the chain I was constructing. "Hey! You're not supposed to be able to do that!"

"Your point being?" I asked, to deflect any questions about how I'd managed to get inside a piece of 'ware she'd fondly imagined was impossible to penetrate, let alone start messing about with.

The truth was, I wasn't all that sure myself. I'd started modifying neuroware about the time I started kindergarten, and I'd just got better and better at it as time went on. It was like Tinkie's perfect pitch—she just tuned her violin with minute twists of the pegs, chatting away the whole time, barely even looking at the instrument, and when she stroked the bow across the strings they all resonated in harmony. She was around seven the only time I ever asked her about it, and I could still remember the almost comical expression of confusion on her face as she asked "Can't everybody?"

"Do you think it'll work?" she asked instead.

I shrugged. "Haven't a clue," I lied, in case my first attempt required some pre-emptive face-saving. In any event, I didn't get fully inside the packet, but managed to rip enough of it open to be able to exploit the breach, and began copying the contents into my personal 'sphere. Once done, I sealed the whole thing up again tighter than a Guilder's purse, making very sure I'd left no traces of my intrusion. Duty, I knew, would always come first with Mother, and if she had the slightest suspicion I'd been breaking into confidential files again she'd report me in a heartbeat.

"Just movement orders," Tinkie said, scanning the contents of the packet with a faint air of disappointment. "For Tintagel."

"Not that much of a surprise," I agreed. The task force assembling there would need warships to escort the troop carriers, and the *Queen Kylie's Revenge* was in the right place at the right time to be roped in. I was about to discard the file I'd broken into so painstakingly, when something else struck me. The orders were for Tintagel all right, but they didn't end there. On arrival, Mother was supposed to report in person to the Commodore in charge of the assembling fleet for a confidential briefing, before "proceeding onwards." And there was only one logical place to proceed to . . .

"What?" My sister knew me well enough to read the surprise on my face before I had a chance to hide it.

For a moment I debated trying to hold back some of what I'd deduced, then thought better of it—she was persistent enough to get round me eventually, and, despite being grownups now (physically at least), I couldn't entirely discount the possibility of wedgies being involved.

"I'm reaching here," I admitted, "but I think she's being sent to Sodallagain." It wouldn't be the first time an escort vessel had been deployed as a tripwire at a choke point in the rift network, but if the League found out it would wreak havoc with the negotiations; the uninhabited system was supposed to be neutral territory, and both powers had pledged to keep their forces within their borders while the diplomats tried to thrash things out. All right, so far as we were concerned Rockhall *was* within the borders of the Commonwealth, which meant Sodallagain was too, but the League didn't see it like that, and if they discovered a Commonwealth warship in the system the shooting would start as sure as a woman's lying when she says "Of course I'll still respect you in the morning." More to the point, the *Revenge*'s chances of surviving longer than the handful of minutes required to transmit a warning would be minimal, and however much I failed to see eye to eye with Mother, I wasn't quite ready to see her committed to the void just yet.

"We never saw this," Tinkie said, joining the dots almost as rapidly as I had once I'd pointed out the first one. "Right?"

"Right," I agreed, wishing I could delete knowledge from my brain as easily as a datafile. If anyone ever had the faintest suspicion we'd stumbled across something so sensitive, Tinkie would spend the rest of her career training civilian auxiliaries to pass muster at the weekends, and I'd . . . My scalp prickled. I didn't really know what would happen to me, but I was damn sure I didn't want to find out.

CHAPTER THREE

In which I find myself in pressing need of a drink.

The rest of Tinkie's visit passed off as uneventfully as they ever did, although for the most part my sister's presence in the house barely registered with me; she spent most of her time roaming the estate in search of small game or young men to amuse herself with, while I was so absorbed in the process of cramming for the Academy that I hardly noticed her periodic returns with a specimen or two of whichever she'd found. Competition for entry was fierce, commissions in the armed forces of the Commonwealth being a traditional means of keeping the daughters of the gentry unsuited by temperament for academe, politics or the church occupied until they were too old to embarrass their families, and I was well aware that there would be three or four candidates competing for every available place.

On the plus side, unlike most other Commonwealth institutions, wealth and social status would have very little bearing on the results: the Armed Forces took their responsibility for the defense of the realm seriously, and competence would be the only criterion considered in an applicant. Which should have worked in my favor, and probably would; but my gender most certainly wouldn't. The Academy might have to accept men these days whether it wanted to or not, but it would certainly take the lowest number it could possibly get away with: to be in with any chance at all, I had to be more than just good enough, I had to be outstanding.

Which meant I spent most of my sister's visit immersed in the
datasphere, memorizing as much as I could, while the best summer
we'd had in years drifted lazily by without me.

"You should go outside," Dad told me, appearing at my shoulder
with a cheese sandwich and a mug of tea, both of which he deposited
carefully on the far end of the chaise. Since embarking on my studies
in earnest, I seemed to have made the conservatory my bolt-hole of
choice without consciously realizing it. Possibly because its glass walls
kept me tenuously connected to the rest of the estate, where life rolled
gently on without me, despite my best efforts to ignore it.

"I'll take a walk later," I said, accepting the snack gratefully. It wasn't
until I took my first sip of tea that I realized how dry my mouth had
become.

Dad sighed, and shook his head. "That's what you said yesterday."

"I meant I'd go today," I lied.

Dad meshed into my 'sphere, his attention glancing off an array of
exercises in orbital dynamics. *I don't see why you have to memorize all
this,* he sent, *when you can just pull it out of the nearest node.*

"Because there might not be a node," I replied verbally. "Data
systems are usually the first things to go down in a rift bounce, and if
you don't already know what to do, you can't look it up."

"I see," he said, in the tones of a man who didn't, and went on
gathering up the handful of mugs surrounding me, the contents of
most having gone cold before I'd even got halfway through them. "Try
not to forget we've got guests coming tonight."

"Have we?" I said, calling up the household social calendar. My
spirits fell. "Oh God, the Devraies are on the list."

"They're not that bad," Dad said, as though contemplating a minor
ailment. "And your mother likes them."

"Likes their connections, more like," I said sourly. From what I'd
gathered over the years, Mother and Alice Devraie had been locked
in quiet but unrelenting competition since their first day as
classmates at the Academy, resenting one another's successes almost
as much as they relished their own. Currently Alice was ahead on
points, having recently been promoted to the command of a capital
ship, which made her a Captain in rank, as well as position. (Though
Mother was Captain of the *Revenge*, and usually addressed as such,
it was merely a courtesy title, her actual rank remaining at

Commander.) But Sherman Devraie, Alice's husband, was the cousin of someone in the Admiralty who was supposed to have influence over the promotions board, and who might, perhaps, be induced to put in a good word on Mother's behalf if Sherman asked nicely. Personally, I doubted that he ever would, even if his wife let him; he was a crashing snob, who thought us jumped-up parvenus because our estates had been purchased with Great-Grandmother's share of the prize money from a Guild privateer her ship had been lucky enough to cut off from the rift point before it could get away with whatever it had been contracted to steal.

"You might very well think that," Dad said, meaning he did too, "but your mother wants them all here, so we'll just have to put up with them."

"All of them?" I checked the invitation list a little more carefully. Sure enough, their daughter was on it too. "If Carenza's coming, I'm having a headache. Or pleurisy. Or gangrene."

Dad sighed. "Please don't be difficult, Si. Your mother wants to give Tinkie a decent send-off."

"Then why hasn't she invited any of Tinkie's friends?" I asked, already knowing the answer to that. Whatever the ostensible reason, these soirees only had one real objective; a Darwinian struggle for social position among everyone who attended. Everyone who mattered, anyway; husbands and offspring were there merely as tactical auxilia.

Dad didn't waste any time answering a rhetorical question. "If Carenza bothers you that much, just ignore her," he said instead. Which wasn't the point at all.

"But she won't ignore *me*, Dad, and she's an octopus. The last time we were on a dance floor together I couldn't sit down for days."

"Then don't dance with her," Dad said, in a "problem solved" voice, which gave me no confidence whatsoever.

I nodded glumly. "I'll do my best," I said, resolving to stick as close to my sister as I could.

The evening got off to a slow start, which was fine by me. The first few grav sleds arrived at dusk, silhouetted against the sunset as they drifted down to hover an inch or so above the lawn, before disgorging family members and a few close friends. These always arrived early, ostensibly to provide help and support to the hostess (although Dad had done most of the actual organizing); I strongly suspected, however, the real reason was to hide the fact that they couldn't afford a chauffeuse from the more well-heeled guests.

"Simon!" My spirits lifted in spite of themselves as Aunt Jenny clambered out of her battered utility sled, easily distinguishable from the highly polished sedans surrounding it by the primered replacement panel over the secondary emitters that she still hadn't got round to getting painted, and plodded towards me. "How's my favorite nephew?"

"A lot better for seeing you," I admitted, bending down for a peck on the cheek. Somehow, I always felt, Aunt Jenny's perception of me had crossed the event horizon over a decade ago, leaving me permanently etched in her mind at the age of eleven.

"Call that a greeting?" She tilted her head back, frowning in mock outrage, and drew me into a hug almost as rib-cracking as one of Tinkie's, heedless of the creases she was adding to her already disheveled dress uniform. She'd obviously tried to smarten up for the occasion, but the plumes on her tricorn were beginning to droop, and a few strands of graying hair hung randomly about her face, escaping from beneath the brim. Breaking free of the embrace, she tried shoving them back for a moment, then tutted impatiently. "Stuff this for a game of dirtsloggers." Whipping the hat from her head, she lobbed it casually through the open side window of her sled. "Where's that good-for-nothing brother of mine?"

"Dad? Trying to smooth things over with the caterers, probably," I said. I'd seen Mother heading for the kitchens about half an hour ago, and if she'd run true to form there'd be ruffled feelings to soothe and gratuities to disburse in her wake.

"More than likely," Aunt Jenny said, knowing Mother of old. They didn't exactly disapprove of one another, but Mother never bothered to hide the fact that she didn't consider her sister-in-law's duties with the Fleet Auxiliary quite Naval enough to be properly associated with the illustrious Forrester name, and Aunt Jenny never bothered to pretend that she gave the proverbial flying one what Mother thought about anything. Pretty much the only thing the two of them had in common was Dad, of whom, so far as I could tell, they were both genuinely fond.

"Let's find the drinks," I said, proffering my arm, and Aunt Jenny grinned, in a way that reminded me strongly of my sister.

"Best idea I've heard all day," she agreed.

As the evening wore on, the number of guests increased, and I did my best to fade into whatever quiet corners I could find. Never for long, though; Mother wanted me on display, in case any suitably connected spinsters happened to mention in passing that they were in desperate need of a spouse, and kept hauling me out for inspection. Which meant that, despite my best intentions, when the Devraies turned up I was still stuck in the entrance hall, balancing a glass of wine and a plate of finger food, neither of which I wanted.

Alice and Mother greeted each other in the slightly overly effusive manner of people determined to mask their mutual antipathy, entirely unaware that they'd only succeeded in drawing attention to it. While they were braying insincere compliments at one another Sherman looked down his nose at me, which was a neat trick for someone almost a head shorter than I was, and Carenza smiled, regarding me the way Tinkie looked at something small and furry when she had a shotgun in her hands. I glanced round, hoping to see some sign of my sister, but she was on the far side of the room, surrounded by the sort of vapid young men whose heads were easily turned by the sight of a well-filled uniform, and was clearly enjoying herself far too much to come to my rescue.

"This is an unexpected pleasure," Carenza said, with a faintly arch smile. "I wasn't expecting to see you before the Christmas vacation."

"Summerhall and I agreed I wasn't cut out for estate management," I said easily, ditching the surplus *vol au vents* behind a convenient aspidistra.

"So we'd gathered," Sherman put in, with a dismissive flap of his delicate lace cuffs. They were the height of fashion among those who cared about such things, which didn't include me, and he took in my plain shirt and cravat with a barely concealed sneer. "But perhaps it's just as well. We men should just stick to what we're good at, and leave all the tedious stuff to the women."

"Remind me again," I said, "just what it is you *are* good at."

Sherman bristled, but before he could come up with an adequate riposte Alice hooked his arm and hauled him away to make disparaging remarks about the array of refreshments on offer.

Which left me alone with Carenza. Not entirely, of course; the hallway was bustling with party-goers heading in towards the dance floor and the buffet, or outside for fresh air and the quiet exchange of confidences. Mother was only a few feet away, but too engrossed in the perpetual game of status chess with her guests to take any notice of me, and Dad had vanished entirely, for which I could hardly blame him.

"So what are your plans now?" Carenza asked, oozing uncomfortably into my personal space, and assaulting my nostrils with her cloyingly floral pomade.

I took a step back. "Get a fresh drink," I said, gulping the contents of my glass, and turning away towards the salon.

"Capital notion," she said, falling into step beside me, disingenuously steadying herself against the flow of the crowd with a hand on my backside as she did so. I twitched away irritably, and she grinned, daring me to comment. "I could do with one too."

"Allow me," I said, hoping the gritting of my teeth hadn't become too audible over the cat-strangling sounds from the ceilidh band currently murdering "The Dashing White Sergeant." The crush around the drinks table was greater than I'd expected, but surely not dense enough to push Carenza quite so close. Don't get me wrong, I enjoy close physical contact with the opposite sex as much as the next man (if he's straight), but damn it all, a fellow likes to be asked first.

"Sparkling wine, if you've got a decent vintage," Carenza said, draping herself around me, which she seemed to think essential to communicate clearly with the caterer standing a handful of inches the other side of my center line. The lad nodded, no doubt used to being addressed like a vending drone, and reached for a bottle. "And another for my companion."

"I'll have an apple brandy," I said, irked at her presumption. And God knew, I could use it then.

"You're not wasting any time," Carenza said, a moue of amusement quirking her lips. She sipped at her wine, managing to convey that it was mildly disappointing but no worse than she'd expected, without saying or doing anything I could plausibly take sufficient offence at to leave.

Then the brownian motion of the circulating guests opened an unexpected gap at my elbow, into which I slipped, momentarily increasing the distance between us to something more comfortable; but a heartbeat later Carenza slithered into the space I'd just vacated, and immediately resumed her impression of a limpet. To hell with subtlety, I decided.

"I need some fresh air," I said, forging my way through the crush towards the open terrace. "If you'll excuse—"

"Good idea." Carenza was one of those people who wouldn't recognize a hint if it came gift-wrapped with HINT embossed on the ribbon. She dumped her suddenly empty glass on an occasional table by the door. "Let's get a little privacy."

At which point I realized I'd made a fundamental tactical error. The terrace was far less crowded than the salon, and full of shadowed corners between the rows of potted shrubs which had been placed out here to afford guests intent on discussing personal affairs (or in some cases conducting them) the privacy they required. No sooner had we gained the cool of the evening air than a tug on my elbow propelled us into a lurking rose arbor, effectively screening us from the house.

"Carenza, stop it." I detached her hands from my posterior, juggling my drink to pry them free one by one, only to feel them clamp back into place again a second later. Her breasts compressed against my chest, and a wine-marinated tongue thrust itself between my teeth, choking off my automatic protest. The biomonitor embedded in my neuroware activated automatically as our saliva mingled, assuring me that she was free of any sexually transmitted diseases or significant genetic defects, but that was hardly the point at the moment.

Almost without conscious volition, my open hand went to the nape of her neck, slipping inside her gown; taking the movement for encouragement she probed harder for a moment, until I poured the contents of my glass down the opening I'd made. Carenza yelped, and I found myself wishing I'd asked for more ice.

"What the hell do you think you're doing?" She broke away, and glared at me. "Have you any idea how much this dress cost?"

"Defending my honor," I said, "and I couldn't give a toss. In that order."

Her expression soured a little more. "This hard-to-get routine's all very cute, Simon, but you're really starting to push it."

"It's not a routine," I retorted. "I'm just not interested." Which wasn't the most tactful thing I could have said, but, as I've already pointed out, subtlety was a long way from being Carenza's strong point.

She flushed. Anyone saying no to her, let alone a man, wasn't something she was used to. "Fine," she snapped. "It's your loss." Then she looked me up and down, in an uncanny echo of her father. "You're nothing special, anyway. And you never will be."

"But you will, I suppose." Stupid of me to rise to it, but I'd had just about enough of her for one evening. Several months worth of evenings, actually.

"Damn right. I'm going to be a naval officer. Probably have my own ship by the time I'm thirty."

I suddenly knew exactly how she'd felt when I dumped my drink down her back.

"You're going to the Academy?" I asked, although when I came to think about it, it wasn't that much of a surprise. The Devraies were Navy through and through, just like the Forresters, and knowing how Mother must have felt about Tinkie choosing a different path for herself, Alice would have jumped at the chance to rub her nose in it by packing her own daughter off to the fleet at the earliest opportunity.

"Isn't that what I just said?" Carenza looked at me scornfully. "If you can't follow a simple conversation, no wonder you flunked out of Summerhall."

"I didn't flunk," I said, without thinking, and a calculating look entered Carenza's eyes. Most of the time she was moderately pretty, if pale skin and too much makeup was your kind of thing, but right then she looked like a war drone deciding which weapon to deploy. I nudged her datasphere with my sneakware, and, sure enough, she was trying to mesh into the house node, looking for correspondence from the college.

That stuff's private! I sent, slapping her connection away with a burst of security protocols. Hardly anything in her 'sphere was protected, and I snagged copies of it all before disengaging: call me a hypocrite if you like, but she started it, and the Forresters have always been big on knowing your enemy.

"You were expelled, then," she said, going straight on the attack. She couldn't have known that for sure, but it was a reasonable deduction, and shifted the focus of the argument away from her attempt to pry; something I'd be equally keen to do in her expensively impractical dance pumps.

"A baseless slander," I said, "which, if you repeat to a living soul, I'll gladly repudiate. Just as soon as I've passed copies of these files to your mother." I kicked the appropriate idents back to her 'sphere, and Carenza went a couple of shades closer to puce. I actually had no idea how Alice would react to the virtuals of pretty boys kissing one another (among other things), but I was pretty sure Carenza wouldn't be keen to find out.

"You wouldn't dare."

I shrugged. "I won't have to. Will I?"

"You're despicable." Carenza glared plasma at me. "I don't know what I ever saw in you."

"That's the whole point," I said. "You never bothered to look past the seat of my pants." *All you saw was a breathing version of this.* I pinged her one of the more anodyne virtuals from her collection, which she instantly deleted in a fit of pique. I braced myself for another onslaught, verbal or physical, but to my inexpressible relief she just turned and stalked off, her fists clenched.

"Nicely handled." Aunt Jenny solidified from the shadows outside the arbor, and I felt my eyes narrowing.

"How long have you been there?"

"Since you spilled your drink." She smiled. "Nice move, by the way. Very inventive."

"If you say so." It may have been the brandy, but I found I was shaking slightly from the aftermath of the confrontation. "Then you know she's applying to the Academy too."

"Certainly sounds like it," my aunt agreed, as though the matter was of no more than casual interest.

"Suppose she gets in?" The thought of two years in Carenza's company, even at the best of times, would be enough to daunt anyone, let alone me. She was hardly the sort to forgive and forget, either.

"And suppose she doesn't? Or you don't?" Aunt Jenny asked reasonably. "Although I'd prefer it if you did. I've a small wager with Anastasia."

So, Mother didn't think I could make the grade. Big surprise there. My feelings must have shown on my face, because my aunt laughed, and took my arm.

"Come on," she said. "Let's get that drink replaced. You might need to defend your honor again." The hint of mischief which reminded me so strongly of my sister sparkled in her eyes. "Better still, you might meet someone who makes you not want to."

CHAPTER FOUR

In which my bright future turns out to be over before it began.

My first impression of the Naval Academy was one of reassuring familiarity: Mother hadn't spent her entire career aboard a warship, although I'm sure neither of her children would have felt unduly deprived if she had, and it seemed pretty much the same as all the other Commonwealth Naval shore establishments I'd seen over the years.

A tranche of barren heathland, unsuited to agriculture, had been enclosed by a sagging chain-link fence, on which dispirited and rusting signs hung every hundred yards or so, warning of dire penalties for anyone contemplating trespass. Since most of the arrivals and departures were by grav sled the barrier served more as a psychological boundary than a physical one, but the array of sensors buried along its length and the constantly patrolling security drones poised to swarm anything not broadcasting the right access codes tended to deter anything airborne and unauthorized from wandering across it. Anything capable of reason, anyway—a thin line of avian bones and carcasses littered the ground just inside the perimeter.

The main buildings of the campus became briefly visible as Aunt Jenny's sled bucked up and over the fence, leaving an appreciable portion of my stomach behind, before the scattering of buildings disappeared again, occulted by the intervening landing pads and servicing facilities. A few glittering motes caught the sun at a more reasonable altitude, probably other potential candidates arriving for assessment, but she'd been having trouble with the emitters again, and didn't trust the sled's stability more than a few feet off the ground. Something I didn't mind too much, as avoiding obstacles had taken up most of her attention during the trip, and I wasn't really in the mood for conversation.

Not that I wasn't grateful for the lift, and the tacit support it represented. Mother was too busy preparing the *Queen Kylie's Revenge* for departure to even pretend any interest in my concerns, Tinkie was back with her unit, and Dad was dealing with the sort of crisis I might have understood if I'd actually listened to any of my lectures in estate management; it seemed to involve a lot of time meshed into the datasphere, and even more wading through mud and nodding to logorrheic agriculturalists, and he'd jumped at his sister's offer to provide transportation for me.

A reflected flash of light from a gleaming metallic pimple in the middle distance suddenly caught my attention, and I couldn't quite suppress a shiver of excitement, despite the number of times I'd seen its like. A spacecraft, whose spherical hull, optimized for rift entry, marked it out unmistakably as a starfarer, was nestled into the open girderwork of its cradle like the Commonwealth's largest breakfast egg. The ground tenders scurrying around it gave me enough sense of scale to identify it as only a small vessel, little more than a cutter or a courier boat; but it was capable of travelling to other stellar systems. Though I'd been in space more often than I could remember, they'd only been local hops to orbitals, or other nearby bodies, and the thought that I might soon be departing for far wider horizons sent a tingle of anticipation down my spine.

Noticing the direction of my gaze, Aunt Jenny smiled at me. "Won't be long before you're aboard something like that. Maybe even the skipper, one day."

"Like that'll ever happen." I snorted at the absurdity of the idea, although I found myself relishing it too.

Aunt Jenny shook her head. "Someone's got to be the first RN Captain with a dick," she pointed out. "Might as well be you."

"Might as well," I agreed, not quite daring to believe it was possible. That'd be a coup for the Forresters, right enough. Possibly even enough of one to gain Mother's grudging approval at last.

"Just need to get you through the screening first," my aunt added, and my good mood evaporated like dew on a sunny morning.

This was going to be tough. I scanned the schedule for the day, which hung conveniently in the overlap of our dataspheres. Orientation. Preliminary testing. Which would boil down to hoping the questions they'd ask were the ones I'd memorized the answers to. Then the one session I was completely confident I could deal with: lunch.

By now we'd reached the campus area, an elegant complex of buildings in *faux* Early Settlement style, surrounded by an untidy sprawl of one- and two-storey structures, many of which had clearly been intended as temporary when first erected a generation or two ago. The main buildings were surrounded by well-tended lawns, across which Aunt Jenny cheerfully skimmed, to the visible consternation of the cadets crisscrossing them on foot. We were at least a head higher than even the tallest, but most of them ducked reflexively anyway, a wake of genuflecting profanity following us as we made our way to the parade ground, where arriving candidates had been directed to park their sleds.

"Good turnout," Aunt Jenny observed, dropping us neatly between a couple of sleek family runabouts, next to which the blocky lines of her utility model stood out like a pig at a cat show. There must have been over a hundred sleds parked there already, most of them relatively new and well cared for, and we drew a few curious glances from other recent arrivals as we clambered out and I began to work the kinks from my back. The majority of candidates were arriving alone, and I felt a surge of self-consciousness at being accompanied by a relative, as though I were being escorted to my first day at kindergarten.

"Yes," I agreed, as a couple of young women, sisters or cousins if the close resemblance between them was anything to go by, glanced in my direction with frank curiosity. There were few other men in sight, and all those I could see were unaccompanied, trying their hardest to project an air of confidence I doubt many of them actually felt as they negotiated the thickets of semi-audible comments from the women around them. At least there was no sign of Carenza . . .

Until a familiar sled swooshed overhead, grounding with a slight bump just where it would most impede our progress across the open expanse between the line of parked vehicles and the building. One of

Carenza's favorite toys, it was as streamlined as the edge of a razor blade, ridiculously overpowered for its size, and sprayed a shade of look-at-me red guaranteed to scorch the retina of anyone incautious enough to do so. Coupled with her level of piloting skill, which was considerably lower than she fondly imagined, the damn thing was a fatal accident looking for someone to happen to; which was the main reason, other than the obvious one, I'd never accepted a lift in it.

"Sorry, didn't see you there," Carenza lied, powering down and glaring at me as though regretting I hadn't ended up underneath the thing. Clearly the incident with the drink still rankled.

"Sorry, *Lieutenant Commander, ma'am*, I didn't see you!" Aunt Jenny barked. "Or did you skip over the section on rank insignia?"

"No, ma'am, sorry, ma'am." Carenza went several different shades of panicky, belatedly registering my aunt's presence. Having been selected for assessment put her under a tacit obligation to abide by the RN's code of conduct, at least while she was on a Naval base. Her hand fluttered indecisively up and down next to her face.

"Have you been sworn in as a cadet already?" Aunt Jenny asked, in patently insincere surprise. Learning fast, Carenza shook her head.

"No, ma'am."

"Then there's no need to salute me, is there?" My aunt watched Carenza scramble out of her open-topped piece of boy bait with narrowed eyes. "Not an auspicious start, young lady. You need to buck your ideas up if you want to stay here any longer than the first cut." She tilted her head towards the trickle of candidates heading towards the main building, several of whom had paused to take in the entertainment. She raised her voice to encompass the loiterers. "What are you lot waiting for, a League invasion? At the double!"

She grinned as the little knot of spectators scattered like pigeons from a shotgun blast. Carenza broke into an unsteady jog, following them, with a last venomous glance in my direction.

"Should I call you 'ma'am' too?" I asked, and Aunt Jenny shook her head.

"Not while there's no one around, anyway." She looked me up and down, and smiled. "Good luck, Simon. I know you'll make us proud."

"No pressure, then," I joked lamely, and strolled away, completely failing to look confident and unconcerned.

⁂

I'd be lying if I said the incident with Carenza hadn't dented my mood at all, but things went pretty smoothly after that. The morning started with a welcoming address consisting mainly of platitudes, after which we were broken up into smaller groups to be shepherded about by upperclasswomen: who, in the manner of their kind, made it patently obvious that they regarded their charges as the social equals of snot. Which was water off a duck's back so far as I was concerned, any Commonwealth citizen with a Y chromosome having met that attitude innumerable times before—although several of my fellow candidates visibly bristled, unconsciously marking themselves out for special treatment should they subsequently find themselves back here as cadets.

A desultory tour of the facilities was interspersed with a variety of assessments, both mental and physical. These included a run through an obstacle course, which I completed a satisfying distance ahead of the pack despite having neglected most of my athletics training during the preceding weeks of sedentary study, a pattern recognition test I felt I'd scored reasonably well on, and some exercises I found completely bizarre (like dropping beans into a bottle with our eyes shut).

The make-or-break one would be the first theory session, though, and as the time to take that drew nearer, my apprehension increased. It wasn't entirely unknown for a candidate to drop out at this stage, once the first batch of assessments were in; even though I knew this hardly ever happened, I couldn't quite shake a nagging sense of disquiet that I might be one of the rare exceptions, and kept picturing my mother's likely reaction if I was. All right, she expected me to fail, Aunt Jenny had let that much slip, but if I crashed and burned at the first hurdle she'd take that not only as confirmation of my uselessness in general, but a slight on the illustrious Forrester name which could only be expunged by changing mine at the earliest opportunity: and once I was married off, I could wave goodbye to any hope of financial or personal independence for the rest of my life (unless fate intervened, in the shape of a fortuitously early widowerhood).

So it's hardly surprising that, as our separate groups reconvened in the main hall, coalescing like drops of mercury, my nervousness almost overwhelmed me. So much so, in fact, that I barely even registered the reappearance of Carenza, who'd fortunately been allocated to a different knot of potential cadets for the morning's activities. Spotting me across the crowded expanse of scuffed parquet, she grinned maliciously as we returned to the seats we'd occupied for the opening address.

Still here? she sent, along with a virtual of a surprised expression.

Perhaps fortunately, I was spared the indignity of failing to come up with an adequate riposte by the swarm of security protocols which suddenly meshed with my personal neuroware, blocking any incoming and outgoing data. The sense of isolation was mildly disturbing for a moment, but I soon got over it: I habitually disconnected from any nodes in the vicinity while messing around with my personal 'ware, to avoid distractions, or anyone else getting a glimpse of what I was up to. If the muttering around me was anything to go by, though, quite a few of my fellow candidates were used to being meshed-in more or less the whole time.

I examined the roadblocks with interest. Some of the datanomes seemed familiar, and I poked them with my homemade sneakware, finding bits of coding I'd encountered breaking into Mother's message packet back home. One patch in particular seemed surprisingly porous, but before I could pick at it, a single channel reopened just long enough to disgorge a datapack before slamming shut again.

Attention, Candidates.

Answer each question in order. If you are unable to do so, move on.

Raise your hand when you have completed the entire test, and the blocks will be removed to enable you to mesh-in for assessment.

Candidates will not be permitted under any circumstances to continue, or modify answers, after re-meshing.

Well, that all seemed clear enough. Stilling a sudden flutter of panic, I slit open the packet and pulled the first question.

My hammering heart slowed. The problem was similar enough to one of the exercises I'd practiced in the conservatory back home to seem easy, and I dashed off the answer with a sudden burst of confidence. So much so that I was on the verge of tagging it complete and moving on before I noticed a subtle error in the starting conditions, which would have completely invalidated the result. I recalculated it, more slowly, checking the answer three times before moving on to the next question, a prickle of cold sweat starting between my shoulder blades.

The next problem was equally tough, and I felt my confidence ebbing away again. This was taking too much time: I'd never complete the test at this rate. I took a deep breath, wrestled my doubts to the floor, and looked at the third question.

This time I felt I'd been punched in the gut. I hadn't a clue what the answer was, or even how to begin to work it out.

I wavered, in an agony of indecision. Skip the whole thing, and accept the massive loss of points that would entail, or waste more time hoping that some kind of solution would occur to me? But what if it didn't? Then I'd have even less time to complete the rest of the test. Or suppose I wrote it off, then found another further down the list I'd be forced to skip?

I could feel the bright future I'd mapped out for myself slipping like sand between my fingers.

Then another solution occurred to me. It was a risk, a huge one, but if I managed to pull it off . . .

Quickly, before conscience or common sense could intervene, I poked at the porous section of the roadblock protocols with my sneakware, scratching away at it, feeling it beginning to give way. Why it was even there I had no idea, but right then I was in no mood to question my good fortune.

Abruptly I broke through, extending a cautious tendril into the wider datasphere, and found the answer. Carenza. She'd been meshed in to my 'sphere when the roadblocks descended, and hadn't broken the connection from her end. After all, why should she, when there was nothing there to connect to? But it had left a hole I could use.

And use it I did. My experience trawling the datapools of Summerhall stood me in excellent stead, and I lost no time in finding the files containing the questions and answers. They were encrypted, of course, but barely more heavily than the ones I'd so cheerfully rifled at the university, and my customized sneakware made short work of that.

I'd have to be careful, I reflected, mindful of my earlier downfall. If I used enough of the purloined data to make a clean sweep of the test I'd be bound to raise suspicions, let alone set up expectations for my future performance I'd struggle to maintain. Somewhere around eighty-five percent should be a high enough mark to ensure my acceptance, without standing out too noticeably from the pack.

Before I could begin to siphon off the information I needed, though, a jolt of heavy-duty counter-intrusion code bit off my tendril, and a pair of invigilators began weaving their way between the seated candidates with an air of grim determination. I cut the link from my end, and focused entirely on the question floating in my personal 'sphere, in a desperate attempt to look innocent. Giving up on the problem I couldn't solve, I skipped it, and began working away at the next, which, thank God, I found a lot more tractable. If I'd broken the connection in time I might still be able to salvage this . . .

"Come with us, please." The leading invigilator spoke quietly, but her voice still carried in the large, quiet space of the hall. I glanced up, my heart hammering, to see her and her colleague flanking Carenza, who was gazing up at them in complete bafflement.

"Excuse me?" She glanced from one to the other, her brow furrowed. "I'm busy at the moment. Can't this wait?"

"No." The senior invigilator reached down, and yanked her unceremoniously to her feet. "Outside, now."

I stared at the drama I'd unwittingly provoked; fortunately I was far from being the only one, or I'd be signaling my guilt to the entire hall by now. I breathed a silent sigh of relief. By using Carenza's open link as a springboard, and cutting the link from my end so quickly, I'd fortuitously pointed the finger at her, rather than myself, when the breach was discovered. All I had to do was sit tight, and wait for the fuss to blow over.

"But I haven't done anything!" Carenza protested, trying and failing to wrench her arm free. Big mistake, as anyone who'd grown up with a sibling could have told her, simply making it easy for the invigilator to apply an arm lock. Expostulating loudly, her feet slipping on the wooden floor, my nemesis was bundled ignominiously towards the nearest exit. "You're making a mistake!"

"If I had a farthing for every time I've heard that . . ." the junior invigilator said, with a sardonic glance at her superior.

Though it does me no credit, I have to admit that my main feeling at that moment was one of vindictive satisfaction. Not only had I got away with it, I'd ensured that Carenza wouldn't be anywhere near the campus during my own tenure. Or ever, come to think of it. Proving her innocence would take a great deal more intelligence and expertise than she possessed, of that I was sure.

But not the Proctors. They'd go over every scrap of data in the nodes I'd penetrated, tracing back the path I'd taken. They'd analyze every crumb of Carenza's datasphere, and it wouldn't take them long to realize she didn't have anything like the sneakware required to access their system, or the knowledge to use it even if she had. They'd find traces of the link she'd left open to me, and draw the obvious conclusion.

I could still brazen it out, though. If I purged my 'ware thoroughly, erased every trace of the sneaker, they could suspect all they liked, but they'd never be able to prove anything . . .

And then I made the mistake of taking a final glance at the scuffle by the door, and found myself looking Carenza full in the face.

I just couldn't do it. However much I detested the woman, I couldn't lay waste to her life, or her future. My conscience wrestled free of the chokehold I'd been trying to put on it, and kneed me in the groin.

"Wait." I watched myself stand as if from a distance, feeling every eye in the hall turn in my direction. *It was me*, I pinged. *Not her.*

Then, without waiting to be asked, I turned and walked numbly to the nearest exit.

CHAPTER FIVE
In which my luggage falls more slowly than usual.

"What were you thinking?" Aunt Jenny asked, not for the first time.

I shrugged. "What can I say? I got stuck on a question, and I panicked. That's all."

"Oh, I get that." My aunt picked up the bag I'd dropped in the hallway on entering her apartment, and slung it through the door of her miniscule guest room, where it teetered for a moment on the edge of the narrow single bed before falling unnaturally slowly towards the carpet. Either her last houseguest had been from somewhere outsystem, and she hadn't got around to adjusting the gravity in there back to Avalonian standard yet, or the household environmentals were as scrupulously maintained as her groundside runabout. "But you had a good chance of getting away with it, and still fessed up. Beats the hell out of me."

"It just seemed like the right thing to do," I said, although I'd spent most of the last week asking myself the same question, with an equal lack of understandable answers.

"If you say so." Aunt Jenny still sounded completely baffled. "You don't even like the girl."

"That's not the point," I said, although to be honest I was some way past wondering what the point actually was by this time.

"I guess not." Aunt Jenny pushed past me into the apartment's kitchen, which was almost large enough for the two of us to stand in together, and began boiling a kettle. "Tea?"

"You're a lifesaver," I said, and mooched into the living room, where the large picture window gave me a heart-stopping view of Avalon rotating gently below, and the curving flank of the orbital itself. Aunt Jenny's skyside *pied a terre* clung to the edge of one of the older docking arms, part of the latest layer of accretion under which the original structure had almost entirely disappeared, like an outcrop of rock lying beneath a coral reef. Skyhaven was the oldest, and by now quite possibly the largest, of the orbital harbors, supporting a population and a range of amenities most cities on the surface of Avalon would be hard pressed to match: which of course made it particularly attractive to anyone wanting a home beyond the atmosphere. My aunt certainly seemed to find it far more congenial than whatever quarters she might be able to find at the navy yard where she worked, and spent a good deal of her time here. (There was also a modest estate dirtside, where she and Dad had grown up, but we seldom visited my paternal grandparents, so I had no idea how often and for how long she resided there.)

"You're family. What else am I supposed to do?" my aunt asked, handing me a steaming mug, which I took absently, still absorbed in the spectacle.

"Shame none of the others felt like that," I retorted. True to form, the Forresters had wasted no time in turning their collective backs on me, in an effort to limit the damage from the scandal. Or, to be more accurate, Mother had turned hers, which meant the others had had little option but to go along with it.

Nevertheless, Dad had done his best to keep up some semblance of awkward conversation while I stuffed what necessities I could salvage from my room into few enough bags to carry away in one go, but his heart clearly hadn't been in it. He'd regarded me throughout with an expression of hurt bafflement, which disinclined me to reply in much beyond monosyllables, and impelled me out of the home I never expected to see again with almost indecent haste. I'd tried pinging Tinkie a few times since the Naval Academy debacle, hoping for a chance to explain things properly to her, but had received no response beyond a terse *Twat* in reply to my first attempt.

Needless to say, I'd made no attempt at all to contact my mother.

Quite apart from the fact that she'd made it perfectly clear she wanted nothing whatever to do with me for the foreseeable future, I was, quite frankly, too scared to even try.

In short, then, thank God for Aunt Jenny, even if I strongly suspected she'd only taken me in as a favor to Dad, and because she knew how much it would wind Mother up. (Even after her real motives had become clear, I was still pretty sure my original guesses had featured in there somewhere.)

"So. Any plans yet?" my aunt asked, sipping her own tea as she settled on the sofa facing the window. The view was undoubtedly spectacular, and ever-changing; from here we could see uncountable lights speckling the surface of the orbital, windows like our own spilling their little firefly flickers of life and warmth into the void from the habitation areas, or larger viewports in the recreational and utility zones. Other motes swirled around the artificial horizon, blurring the boundaries—the unceasing swarm of traffic hopping back and forth between Skyhaven and Avalon, or to the other orbitals, the vessels riding at "anchor" in the distance (easily distinguishable from the stars by their slow, relative drift), and, in a few cases, simply taking a short cut around the hull to avoid the frustrations of the internal transport network. Mingled in and around these were innumerable work pods, maintenance drones, and void-suited hulljacks, too many for all but the most complex informatics to keep track of. When I expanded my datasphere it was almost overwhelmed by the background hum, billions of nuggets of information whirling around like dust in a nebula, which, now I came to think about it, wasn't that unapt a metaphor: perceived in the aggregate, rather than trying to isolate individual elements, it formed elaborate patterns that were both elegant and organic. Order from chaos, fractals of information . . . "Am I boring you?"

"What? No, sorry." Lost in the patterns, I'd missed most of what Aunt Jenny had been saying. I shrank the 'sphere, and refocused on the conversation, seizing on the last remark I'd caught. "No plans."

Which was hardly surprising. All my hopes and ambitions had been reduced to a smoking ruin, which effectively barred the way back to the old life I'd never felt that great about in any case. "Enlisting in any of the services is right out, of course. Even as a ranker."

"Word gets around," Aunt Jenny agreed, sipping her tea. "And it's not as if your mother's family has much pull outside the Navy, so . . ."

"Like she'd lift a finger to help me now anyway," I said. The one truly bright spot I could see in the mess I'd made of things was that the storm front of scandal my actions had unleashed had pretty much swept away any prospect of being married off to get rid of me, at least to anyone Mother would have considered a suitable match. "I suppose I'll just have to do the best I can for myself."

"Just like that." Aunt Jenny chuckled indulgently. "You talk a good fight, I'll say that for you. But you Forresters don't even know you're born. It's dog eat dog out there." Her outflung arm took in the rest of the orbital, the planet beyond, and a fair chunk of the Western Spiral Arm.

"And the Worrickers do, I suppose." So far as I could tell, my aunt's family was cut from much the same cloth as my own, although perhaps a little shabbier. Which made Mother's choice of Dad as a husband faintly surprising, now I came to think about it: perhaps it had been a love match after all. A concept which, knowing her as well as I did, I must confess I struggled with a bit.

"We're not afraid to get our hands dirty if we have to," Aunt Jenny allowed, with a faintly self-satisfied sip at her tea, then she grinned at me unexpectedly. "What couldn't I have done when I was your age with something as neat as that sneakware you put together. Evading a military grade block, even a low level one like that, was a pretty neat trick."

Help yourself, I sent, kicking a copy across to her personal 'ware.

She chuckled again. "I'm a bit too old for hellraising these days. But it's a neat bit of work, right enough." She poked at it, disentangling one of the datanomes I'd helped myself to from Tinkie's decrypt. *I won't ask where you got this.*

"Good," I said.

My aunt nodded, thoughtfully. "So you can be discreet if you have to."

I shrugged. "Never said I couldn't," I said.

"Don't play games, Simon." The bantering tone had slipped out of her voice, and for a moment she seemed hard and businesslike: I had a sudden mental image of her talking like that to a Guilder captain trying to weasel some extra advantage from the small print of a charter agreement, and smiled in spite of myself. It would be a very astute skipper indeed who managed to put one over on Jenny Worricker. "You need to get a lot better at sneaky if you're going to get by in the real galaxy." Then her smile reappeared, as abruptly as it had vanished. "But then you're a good-looking lad. I'm sure you can find some well-off lass who'll take care of you instead, if you'd rather go down that route."

"I'd rather starve," I snapped back.

"No, you wouldn't." My aunt shook her head. "Only people who've never really been hungry say that."

"And only rich people say 'Money isn't everything,' I suppose," I retorted.

She smiled at my naivety. "Mostly the poor ones, in my experience. And it's generally true, too. But I still wouldn't turn down a sack full of guineas if I fell over one."

"Neither would I," I admitted, and laughed, restored to something approaching good humor, much to my surprise. "Don't suppose you know where there's one been left lying around?"

"'Fraid not." Aunt Jenny's expression grew serious again. "You want anything in this life, you have to work for it."

"Which is where it all falls down," I said. My upbringing had left me with no skills worth having, beyond making polite conversation without seeming as bored as I actually was. Which, as I pointed out, was hardly a marketable one, especially since the diplomatic service only accepted women.

"Good God, Simon, surely you don't think diplomacy's only practiced by diplomats?" Aunt Jenny gesticulated for emphasis, discovering in the process that her tea cup wasn't quite as empty as she'd thought it was, and dabbed at the resulting stain on the sofa with her sleeve. "Interworld commerce would completely fall apart without the ability to tell bare-faced lies with conviction." She paused for a moment, and looked at me appraisingly. "If you can keep a muzzle on your conscience, you might do well on a merchant ship."

"A merchant ship?" I sipped at my own drink, finding it had gone cold while we talked, and disposed of it as discreetly as I could on a nearby occasional table. "You mean—as part of the crew?"

"I don't mean as part of the cargo," my aunt said, still rubbing absently at the stain.

I considered this new and startling idea. There was nothing left for me on Avalon, of that I was sure. My reputation was irrevocably tarnished, and with it the family name. Tinkie's grandchildren would still be trying to live down my dishonorable conduct, if she ever had any.

"I suppose it'd get me out-system," I said cautiously, rediscovering a little of the thrill I'd felt at the sight of the starship in its cradle at the Academy. Then I spotted the obvious flaw in the suggestion. "Except Avalon doesn't have much in the way of a merchant fleet." And what there was of it was so intimately entangled with the Fleet Auxiliary that word of my misdeeds would undoubtedly have preceded me, poisoning any chance I might have had of getting taken on.

"That it doesn't," Aunt Jenny conceded, "but there are other options." She looked at me with an air of faint expectancy, as if she was waiting for the coin to drop, but I only shrugged.

"Can't see 'em myself," I said.

"No, you probably can't." My aunt shook her head in a faintly pitying manner, and put her tea cup down next to mine, registering the amount I hadn't actually drunk. "Sod this stuff, I need a proper drink." She stood, and made for the door, leaving me sitting on the sofa in a state of some confusion.

I supposed I could find something to eat in the kitchen if I got hungry while she was out, although just helping myself might be seen as overstepping the bounds of etiquette more than somewhat . . .

Then she glanced back at me with an air of mild surprise. "Coming?"

If I'd known what that seemingly innocuous invitation was going to lead to, I'd probably have—well, done exactly the same thing, I suppose. But I'd definitely have thought about it for a lot longer.

As it was, though, I didn't have a clue, so . . .

"Why not," I said, thereby consigning what little was left of my future to chaos and catastrophe.

CHAPTER SIX
In which I lose sight of my aunt, and find pies.

I'd thought I was reasonably familiar with the layout of Skyhaven in general, and Aunt Jenny's immediate neighborhood in particular, but the walk to her favorite tavern soon made me realize the difference between the superficial local knowledge of the frequent visitor and the innate sense of place possessed by the long-term resident.

For the first ten minutes or so I felt confident enough of finding my way back to her lodgings if I had to, the bland residential thoroughfares we ambled along being laid out on a fairly simple grid of interlocking hexagons. The streets were wide, the tiled sidewalks broken at intervals by brightly-hued mosaics, usually outside the main entrances of apartment blocks, which had been blandly uniform when built; now, however, they'd been personalized by their residents using a variety of pigments, tapestries, and multi-colored flora, which spilled from innumerable terraces and window boxes.

The street above our heads, where the localized gravity pulled the other way, was a mirror image of the one we walked along, many of the larger dwellings in both merging seamlessly into a single block midway between them, like mountains reflected in a placid lake. (The apartments just either side of the center line were particularly sought after, I gathered, as they shared a ceiling, so the residents would never be troubled by the footfalls of their neighbors.)

Traffic hummed busily between the sidewalks; if I stretched my 'sphere a little, I could catch the cicada buzz of the on-board drones, dutifully following the course and speed set for them by the district's traffic control, and watch the sudden flurries of processing as they decided whether or not to brake in response to one of the swarm of bicycles, which wove their way through the larger, slower-moving vehicles with cheerful disdain, cutting across their paths without thought of apology. There were plenty of pedestrians, too, although for the most part they kept to the pavement, only venturing to cross the turbulent stream of traffic at one of the footbridges which had been strategically placed at every intersection.

After a while I became aware that the street-level dwellings on both sides of the road had been replaced by storefronts, selling a bewildering variety of foodstuffs and beverages I'd never heard of (in some cases fortunately, judging by the smell), clothing in unfamiliar cuts, and an astonishing range of curios and artworks. Cafes, bars and restaurants began to appear among them in ever-increasing numbers, too, and I began to salivate, suddenly reminded of how long it had been since I'd last had anything approaching an appetite.

As the buildings had changed around me, so had the people. Many more of them were wearing the unfamiliar garments I'd glimpsed in the shop windows, and not everyone I saw seemed quite . . . well, normal, I suppose. As well as all the usual variations in skin, hair and eye color you'd expect to find on most worlds with a reasonably-sized population, there were one or two which struck me as quite bizarre: a fellow practically naked, apart from sandals and a barely adequate loin cloth, for instance, whose skin had a distinctly greenish hue, and whose breath carried a faint odor of summertime meadows.

"Don't gawp, Simon, it makes you look provincial," Aunt Jenny said, although her words carried more amusement than rebuke.

"I am provincial," I replied, truthfully enough. It began to dawn on me that all my previous visits to Skyhaven had been to the core section, where the passenger flights up from Avalon docked, and nothing in the decor, ambience or services would have seemed out of place in any of the cities on the surface. Same architecture, same businesses, same music in the elevators.

"'Scuse me," a young lady said, brushing past with an apologetic smile. She was wearing something which floated around her, rippling gently, and I felt the hairs on my arms rise briefly, caught in the fringes of the electrostatic field creating the effect. I found myself turning involuntarily to watch her pass, and my jaw dropped.

"Tails are quite a popular tweak with the transgeners," Aunt Jenny said, looking even more amused as she caught sight of my expression. "You'll be seeing a lot more of that sort of thing if you ship outsystem."

"Transgeners," I repeated, as though I'd never heard the word before. Which I had, of course, but seldom spoken so casually. Most Commonwealthers strongly disapproved of altering the human body too much, on the entirely reasonable grounds that God had got it right the first time round, although not everyone in the galaxy agreed with them. Some worlds had entire populations who'd been altered in response to specific local conditions, and whose tweaks bred true down the generations, while on others morphology fluctuated with the fad of the moment, plaid fur giving way to scales pretty much on a whim, the way dandies like Sherman adopted the latest style of cravat.

"You'll get used to it," Aunt Jenny assured me, ogling the green fellow's well-sculpted gluteals as he vanished into the crowd. Then she turned back to me with a mischievous grin. "Always liked the photosynthesisers myself. Don't leave a lot to the imagination."

"I don't suppose they would," I said, trying to sound blasé and utterly failing to do so. The streets were growing narrower and more crowded here, the gridding less regular, and I hurried after my aunt, determined to keep her in sight. I kept expecting her to stop, or slow down, or at least glance behind to make sure I was keeping up, but she never did, gradually opening up the distance between us, slipping through the press of bodies with a speed and dexterity I found faintly surprising in a woman of her age and bulk.

For a moment she vanished as the street suddenly dropped away at a sharp sixty-degree angle, and I felt a stab of panic as I lost sight of her; but a second or two later I felt the surge in my inner ear as I stepped through the intersecting gravity fields, and found myself once again trotting along a subjectively level surface. After a moment of frantic scanning I spotted her again, just disappearing down the mouth of an alleyway half-hidden by the stall of a street vendor, who waved a skewer-full of something greasy resembling meat hopefully in my general direction as I dived down the narrow slot between a tavern and a lingerie emporium.

This was a part of Skyhaven I'd never even suspected of existing before, and I must confess I felt a growing sense of unease. The alley was beginning to feel less like a thoroughfare, and more like a utility conduit into which the population had flowed under pressure from the more affluent regions. There was metal mesh underfoot now, while piping and ductwork had become visible on walls and ceiling, lending the whole place a cramped and furtive air, despite the illumination, which remained as bright as the streets I'd just left. Or would have done, anyway, if all of it was still working.

The people I passed seemed more shabbily dressed than those on the main thoroughfares, or at least in utilitarian garb, with little ornamentation; and a higher proportion of them were transgeners, with whom I was reluctant to make eye contact, for fear of being thought impolite. (Believe me, good manners are important when some of the folk you're mingling with have visible claws or tusks.) Every now and then I could still catch a glimpse of Aunt Jenny in the distance, and tried to pick up my pace, but most of the traffic was moving in the opposite direction. If it hadn't been for my pride, and the fear of marking myself out as someone who didn't belong here, I might have called out to her, but I held my tongue, and bounced a message instead.

Is it far now? If I'm honest, I half hoped that the reminder of my presence would slow her down, but it had no discernable effect that I could see across the distance that now separated us.

No, she sent back, and promptly vanished from sight.

All right, I told myself, that was clearly impossible, so she must have gone somewhere. I had no idea why she seemed to want to turn going out for a drink into a game of hide and seek, but I wasn't so far from childhood, and the wariness I'd learned from Tinkie's habit of changing the rules to hide and ambush, that I'd forgotten how to play.

So, start from the last place I'd seen her. Not difficult: several of the ubiquitous cables converged into a junction box there, emitting a distinctive electromagnetic signature. Not to mention the garish yellow panel warning DANGER OF DEATH, which was kind of hard to miss.

This time there was no obvious alley mouth into which my aunt could have disappeared, but there had to be something—my view further down the tunnel had only been blocked for a moment, and if she'd carried on along it I would have been sure to see her. I glanced up at the tangle of pipework depending from the ceiling—which, as I'd expected, had no room above it to conceal anyone, even if she'd been able to scramble up without attracting the attention of the passersby.

I examined my immediate short-term memories. No one had reacted as though anything out of the ordinary was going on, and in a place this confined, that pretty much guaranteed that nothing had. It would simply have been too noticeable. Which ruled out any trapdoors in the floor, too, although I took a glance at it anyway, just to be sure.

That only left the wall, which clearly concealed a door of some kind. The only question was where.

Adopting as nonchalant an air as I could, though none of the passers-by seemed particularly interested in me, I examined the blank metal carefully. Sure enough, one of the inspection panels seemed a little loose, held in place by only one corner. Before I could reach out a hand to confirm my guess, however, it moved aside, apparently of its own volition, tugged by a rather down-at-heel fellow in early middle age, whose halitosis preceded him like an honor guard.

"Sorry mate, di'n't see yer," he said, ducking through and hoisting a bag to his shoulder, before disappearing down the corridor, whistling. Since no one else seemed in the least bit surprised by his sudden appearance, I surmised that this was a commonly used, though distinctly unofficial, shortcut, and so it proved to be. Lowering my head, I clambered through the gap, finding myself in a narrow space between two walls, stuffed with far too many things festooned with warning decals color-coded by the ways they could kill you. A chink of light showed just ahead of me, however, so after a moment's fumbling I was able to push aside the twin of the panel behind me, and straighten up gratefully in the passageway beyond.

Which was, if anything, even narrower and more wretched than the one I'd just left, though no less densely populated. I glanced up and down it, seeking some clue as to which direction my aunt might have taken. More people seemed to be heading towards my right, and the illumination in that direction seemed a little brighter, so I headed that way, essentially just drifting with the current.

By now, it must be said, I was becoming more than a little irritated. I could, of course, simply have bounced her a message demanding to know where she was and what the hell she thought she was playing at, but I was damned if I'd give her the satisfaction. Besides, she might not tell me. I was beginning to get the feeling that this was some kind of test, and after the Naval Academy debacle, I wasn't about to fail if I could help it.

The lights up ahead were getting brighter, and the ambient noise was growing too: the sort of diffuse assault on the eardrums that comes from a lot of people in a large enclosed space trying to make themselves heard over everyone else's conversation. There seemed to be music, too, quite a lot of it, if you stretched your definition of tonality to the breaking point, competing for attention from a dozen different sources.

Suddenly, the narrow corridor opened out into a wide, high-ceilinged space, roughly the size of a sports stadium. What its original purpose had been, I had no idea, but the number of pipes converging here, many large enough to have driven a sled down, hinted at a storage tank of some sort. These days, however, it seemed to be a marketplace, the stalls of which stretched into the distance, laden down with goods and junk of all kinds. Some served food, and, prompted by my growling stomach, I fished a couple of coins from my pocket and approached the nearest, though not without a sense of trepidation.

"What can I do you for?" the proprietor asked, in professionally friendly tones, taking in the cut of my garments in a single practiced glance. "We got meat pies, cheese pies, veggie pies, cheese an' veggie pies, meat an' veggie pies, cheese an' meat pies, or meat, cheese an' veggie." He paused for a moment, perhaps wondering if he should have added "pies" to the end of the last selection, in case I'd missed that small but vital point. "Or fruit pies," he added as an afterthought, "if you was thinking more along dessert kind of lines."

"What kind of meat?" I asked, and his face furrowed, as he calculated how much honesty would be required to effect a sale.

"Hard to say," he said at last. "They're more of a mixture than anythin', tell you the truth."

In the end it was my stomach that made the decision, rather than my brain, by cramping vigorously in response to the surprisingly appetizing aroma.

"Meat and veggie," I said, feeling I could at least mitigate the damage by spreading it out among the food groups, and the proprietor nodded, his good graces assured by the prospect of imminent money.

"Don't get many groundsiders down here," he said chattily, "this close to the docks. Shippin' out, are you?"

"Maybe," I said, before the first part of his question properly sank in, then nodded as the implications of his opening remark belatedly did so. "Seen any others?"

The stallholder shrugged. "Hard to say," he said, handing me an oblong of warm pastry wrapped in a napkin. "What with all this crowd around."

Unable to resist the importunate growling of my stomach any longer, I bit into the pie, finding it hotter inside than I'd expected, and a great deal more appetizing. Gravy oozed down my chin as I chewed and swallowed, and before I could stop myself I'd taken a second bite, and then a third. Almost before I realized it, the snack had gone. I wiped my face and fingers. "Another one, please," I said, handing over a few more pieces of change. "And a fruit to follow."

"Looks like you needed that," the pie-seller said, distinctly more well-disposed since my evident enthusiasm for his wares had attracted a few more potential customers towards his stall. "Anyone in partic'lar you was keepin' an eye out for? Or just groundsiders in gen'ral?"

"My aunt," I said. "Middle-aged, stocky, brown hair, going grey. Floral print jacket."

"Seen her about," he said, after a moment's thought. "Not today, though. If it's the one I'm thinking of."

"Thanks anyway," I said, wiping the remains of the second pie from my fingers, and accepting my dessert. (Which was sweeter than I'd expected, but still remarkably palatable.) I started to turn away, already scanning the crowds, with a distinct lack of hope.

"You could try down there," the stallholder said, indicating a gap between two nearby pipes, each with the girth of a mature redwood. "She gen'rally comes and goes from that direction."

"Thanks," I said again, with greater warmth, and set off the way he'd indicated.

CHAPTER SEVEN
In which I entertain two offers of employment.

To my relief, the area beyond turned out to be far smaller than the cavernous marketplace, being no larger than the sort of square you might find in a quiet market town; an analogy which struck me as soon as I'd rounded the nearer of the two vast metal cylinders. Every gap and crevice between the excrescences of infrastructure large enough to hold a home or business had been enclosed, using whatever materials had come to hand, to create pockets of living space: sheets of scrap metal, sections of cargo containers, even the odd piece of lumber, which seemed stridently out of place in this defiantly man-made environment. As I tilted my head back, scanning the rising and erratic terraces, I was reminded of the apartment buildings surrounding a central courtyard I'd seen on visits to the cities on the surface.

Most of the buildings, for want of a better word, seemed to be residential; even this far from the more salubrious quarter I was familiar with, plants and banners provided welcome splashes of color in a bewildering variety of hues. The people living here seemed quieter, more domestic, than the ones I'd seen in the streets and market, chatting easily among themselves instead of rushing about on mysterious business of their own. At least the adults were; for the first time since leaving Aunt Jenny's apartment I noticed children, running across the central space or clambering on struts and buttresses, chattering happily under the watchful eyes of their parents and neighbors.

A handful of public spaces were scattered among the living quarters; from the door of one music spilled, the plangent notes of a harp, trailing away in a spatter of applause before resuming after a brief interlude. Others seemed to be selling food, of a far higher quality than the pies I'd guzzled a few moments before, and I felt a pang of regret at having quelled my appetite so comprehensively, before coming to the conclusion that my time would be better spent searching for my aunt in any case.

Feeling uncomfortably conspicuous, I glanced at the nearest shops and taverns, looking for some other clue as to her whereabouts. Given her reason for going out in the first place, bars seemed the most likely place to try, so I concentrated on those, trying to narrow down the possibilities. Not the one with the music; traditional tunes and instruments were decidedly not to her taste. The closest one was crowded enough for its customers to be spilling outside, and I knew she preferred to drink quietly—besides which, nearly half the people milling around the doorway were transgeners, and however blasé Aunt Jenny was about such things, I still found myself a little unnerved by their outlandish appearance.

That left an unassuming frontage, little more than a large banner bearing a cheerful abstract design, which curtained off a shadowy area between a couple of storage tanks. Signs outside promised DRINKS, FOOD, DRINKS, which accorded well with my current priorities, so I strolled over to it, twitched the corner aside, and slipped through the gap I'd created.

I'm not sure quite what I expected to find on the other side; probably a whole bunch of people who'd stop what they were doing and stare at me, in the way far more common in fiction than in real life, but no one seemed even to notice my arrival.

No one, that is, except for Aunt Jenny, who glanced up from a booth at the back, where she had a good view of the billowing pseudo-wall behind me, and nodded an affable greeting. Her companion was less visible from where I was standing, all but a shoulder and upper arm obscured by the corner of the booth, but I got the impression of a large man in the kind of utility garb common among artisans; an impression rapidly confirmed, as he turned in response to the shift in my aunt's posture, and glanced in my direction. His beard was more or less neatly trimmed, and his jacket bore the universally recognized sigil of the Commerce Guild on the left breast pocket: a stylized hand cupping the swirl of the galaxy, symbolizing either the Guild's reach across the entire Human Sphere, or its perpetual readiness to squeeze a profit out of it, depending on your level of cynicism. (Or, quite possibly, given the miniscule fragment of the galaxy humanity actually occupied, the Guild's staggering level of hubris.)

As I made my way between the tables, which had apparently been scattered arbitrarily around the floor, I noticed a number of other Guild sigils, adorning shirts, coats, caps, and at least one evening gown half the hostesses on Avalon would cheerfully have committed murder for. I hesitated a moment, to allow a serving drone to hum past my head and land on an intermediate table with its cargo of drinks, before finally arriving at my aunt's booth.

"That was quick," she greeted me, adding *what do you want to drink?* as our 'spheres interpenetrated.

"Ale," I said verbally, and she kicked the order over to the drone, which had delivered its cargo, and was now aimlessly orbiting the room with its fellows, waiting for another set of instructions. The drink seemed appropriate in this kind of setting, and I wanted something I could make last without seeming to.

Aunt Jenny nodded, and glanced at her guest. "John?"

"Same again." He drained something amber-colored from the bottom of a tumbler, and replaced the glass on the table, as I slid onto the arm of the U-shaped bench directly across from him. He looked at me the way Guilders look at everything, which is to say with a kind of guarded neutrality—at least until they've determined whether you're harmless, dangerous, or likely to be useful to them in some way. "John Remington, of the *Stacked Deck*."

"Simon Forrester," I said, "of nowhere any more." That kind of slipped out, and I mentally bit my tongue, conscious of having revealed some vulnerability he'd certainly exploit if he could. But it seemed to have been the right thing to say: Remington's expression softened, and Aunt Jenny positively beamed.

"Told you he was forthright," she said.

"That you did," Remington agreed, ducking his head as the drone came back, bearing two tumblers of whisky and my tankard of ale, which had been chilled to the point where the last lingering vestige of flavor had been completely expunged—a Skyhaven foible I immediately regretted having forgotten about. The Guilder turned to me. "Jen's just been filling me in on your university career. That doesn't sound like the kind of thing an Avalonian gentleman normally gets up to."

I felt a hot flush of embarrassment rise up my neck.

"That's because most of them haven't got a thought in their heads beyond how they look in tight trousers," I snapped, and took a gulp of the over-cooled beer that made my teeth ache.

"True enough," my aunt agreed. "Though most of them occasionally consider how their actions will affect their reputations and their families."

I must admit that blindsided me; after all her support in the face of familial disapproval, I'd hardly expected her to start expressing the same kind of sentiments.

"I didn't consider it, because I didn't plan on getting caught," I said, feeling I might as well be honest about the affair now she'd brought the whole thing up, even if her motives for doing so baffled me. Clearly she'd been hoping Remington would help to find me a place on a merchant ship, although calling my integrity into question seemed a strange way of going about it. "And even if I was, I knew it would be hushed up," I added, bending the truth a little, though not by much. I had panicked for about five minutes after getting the first summons to the Dean's office, before realizing that my clients' social connections— not to mention their families' financial contributions to the university—would render me pretty much untouchable. Apart from being rusticated, of course, which had brought me back into the orbit of Mother's ire.

Remington smiled. "Sounds like you know how to work an angle," he said, in surprisingly friendly tones. He took a sip of his drink. *And you've a definite talent for sneakware.* Our 'spheres intersected, and I found a copy of the datanomes I'd given my aunt floating in the shared space between us. *You really put this together yourself?*

I shrugged. "Everyone needs a hobby."

Remington laughed. "That they do. Just don't practice on any of the nodes aboard the *Deck*, unless you want to try walking back to Avalon." He spoke so casually, it took a moment for the full import of his words to sink in.

"You're taking me on?" I asked, not quite able to believe my good fortune. "Just like that?"

"I'll give it some thought," he said, although he seemed to be addressing my aunt more than me. "If the deal's right."

"You've got your contract, John." Her tone was casual, but I'd attended enough of my mother's soirees to spot the steel beneath the pleasantries, a knack Remington clearly shared. "It's not up for renegotiation."

"And it doesn't cover babysitting either," the guilder replied, in equally casual tones.

"You won't have to hold his hand, I can assure you." Aunt Jenny took another sip of her whisky.

Remington looked thoughtful for a moment. "Tell you what I'll do," he said, as though it wasn't precisely what he'd been willing to offer all along, "I'll give him one run, out to Numarkut, see how he does. If it all works out, and he's as good as you say, I'll take him on, full Guild apprenticeship. If not, he's on his own. Plenty of opportunities for a smart lad in a system like Numarkut." Abruptly, he turned to me. "What do you say?"

"You're on," I heard my mouth reply, before my brain could catch up with it. If this went wrong, I'd be stranded beyond the borders of the Commonwealth, with only my wits to rely on, and no way home. If I even wanted to return: there certainly wasn't much to come back to, beyond, possibly, Aunt Jenny's guest room, and I wasn't sure even she'd be that happy to see me again.

Remington nodded, appraisingly. "Outer docks, arm seven, bay three, twenty-two hundred tomorrow. Don't hang around, because I won't." He rose, with a courteous inclination of his head to my seated aunt. "Smart lad you've got there, Jen. Not slow to grab an opportunity. One of us is doing well out of this."

"We all are, John. It's just a question of who's doing best."

Remington smiled, with what looked like genuine amusement. "I'm under no illusions on that score. I've known you too long." Then he was gone, weaving his way casually through the slalom of tables.

"What did he mean by that?" I asked.

My aunt smiled, draining her glass and depositing it on the tabletop in front of her with a satisfied clunk. "He's worked for me before. Contract haulage, that kind of thing."

"Right." I took a sip of my forgotten ale, finding that it had warmed up enough in the interim to be almost palatable. "And he's so keen to be shifting dried rations for the Fleet Auxiliary, he'll take on a new apprentice just because you ask."

"Of course he won't." Aunt Jenny signaled for another drink. "He's a Guilder. It's all about what's in it for him."

"Which is?" I asked.

"Initially, just another hand. If he's lucky, which he is in this case, an apprentice who'll learn enough quickly enough to become a real asset. But the main thing is, he'll think I owe him a favor."

"And will you?" I asked.

Pity and amusement mingled on her face. "Of course not. But every time he gets a contract from the Auxiliary that pays a little over the odds from now on, he'll think that's the reason. Which means I can trim the margins a little more on the others without him noticing." She thought for a moment. "For a while, at least."

"Isn't that a bit dishonest?" I asked, trying to sound less shocked and disapproving than I actually felt.

"Of course not." The serving drone arrived again, and my aunt snagged her drink from its back before it had time to settle on the table between us. "It's business. That's just how things work." She took a sip, and regarded me thoughtfully for a moment. "My real job's where the ethically flexible stuff comes in." She looked at me with a faint air of expectation.

"Your real job?" I asked, totally failing to grasp whatever it was she was driving at. Operational logistics seemed enough of a full-time job for anyone.

Aunt Jenny sighed, as though I'd somehow disappointed her. "For Naval Intelligence," she said.

I'd seen and read enough thrillers to have all the usual ideas about what secret agents were like, and my aunt definitely didn't fit the mould. They were supposed to be debonair sophisticates living in luxurious apartments in the most glamorous of locales, not middle-aged middle-rankers in cramped maisonettes with dodgy gravitation, on the fringes of a dormitory suburb. I said as much, in appropriate tones of incredulity, and Aunt Jenny laughed so loudly that several heads turned in our direction.

"I'm afraid the reality's a lot duller than the virts," she said, sipping her drink to recover her composure. "I haven't had a fight on a train roof in years." I must still have been bearing a remarkable resemblance to one of the stuffed fish in Dad's study, because she added, "kidding, Simon," and kicked my ankle under the table.

Which didn't really hurt; but somehow the very banality of the gesture made the whole thing suddenly real to me. Shrugging off my natural surprise I took another mouthful of ale, which was actually beginning to taste like a proper drink at last as it began to approach room temperature, and tried to get my head around the fact that everything I thought I knew about my aunt was completely wrong.

"Of course it isn't," she rejoined briskly, when I spoke the thought aloud. "I'm the same person you always knew. The only thing that's different is my job." She thought for a moment. "One of them, anyway."

"But you don't really work for the Fleet Auxiliary," I persisted, "do you? That was a lie."

"Who says?" She was enjoying this, I could tell, a faint half smile hovering over her face like mist rising from a dew-soaked lawn. "I'm one of the best logisticians we've got. Ask anyone."

"But that's just your cover story, right?" I asked. That was one of the commonest elements of espionage stories. Spies had identities and professions they assumed in order to gain access to the information they wanted. But surely the Commonwealth's intelligence services would have no reason to infiltrate their own Navy's logistics division—they were all on the same side. Or at least they were supposed to be.

"No, it's my job," Aunt Jenny explained, in much the same tone I remembered from her early attempts to teach me the alphabet. "I really am a lieutenant commander in the Fleet Auxiliary, and I put in long hours making sure the Navy has what it needs when and where it needs it."

I could feel my forehead furrowing. "But—" I began.

Aunt Jenny cut me off with a gesture. "While I'm doing that, I'm also talking to merchants, shipping brokers, and Guilders about why they can't get particular items to particular places without more time and money than I'm willing to give them. Conversations which might suggest, for instance, that my opposite numbers in the League are stockpiling supplies in certain systems, which implies in turn that some of their naval assets are likely to arrive there relatively soon. Information our own strategic planners might find interesting."

"I see," I said, finally beginning to feel some firm ground underfoot. "So you're a real logistics officer, who just passes on snippets of intel from time to time." I was quite proud of the abbreviation, which I'd picked up from some thriller or other, and which I felt showed some familiarity with the nuts and bolts of espionage.

"I do nothing of the kind," Aunt Jenny snapped. "I'm a professional intelligence agent, who's been in the field since before you were in diapers. More of which I changed, I might add, than your mother ever did." That, at least, I had no trouble in believing. "I evaluate everything that comes in through my network, and my recommendations are listened to at the highest levels."

I felt as if the floor was dropping away rapidly beneath me, although that might have been at least partially due to the fact that the ale I was drinking seemed less than keen on peaceful coexistence with the pies I'd had earlier. "But you just said your real job was logistics," I protested feebly, feeling more out of my depth than ever.

"So it is," my aunt said, before relenting in the face of my obvious confusion. She smiled, in a slightly condescending way. "They're both my real job. Most people see one of them, a few the other. Me, I see it all mesh together. Couldn't tell you where one ends and the other begins, these days." She drained her glass, and signaled for another. "End of the day, I don't see that it even matters. Shipping boots, or telling 'em where to march, it's all serving the Commonwealth one way or another."

"I suppose it is," I said, still wondering why she'd decided to confide in her double life to me. The one thing I was already certain about was that I was probably not going to appreciate her reasons, whatever they were.

"Would you?" Without warning, she was looking me straight in the eye, the moment of introspection already over.

"Would I what?" I replied, playing for time. If she wanted what I suspected she did, she could damn well ask in so many words.

"Serve the Commonwealth." Her gaze grew more intent. "Given the opportunity."

"I was given the opportunity," I said. "But I screwed it up."

"Yes. You did." My aunt nodded, thoughtfully. "For a principle. Bit worrying, that, but you might still do."

"Do for what?" I asked, still determined to hear her say it.

"A small job for me. The other me, that is. Not the Naval Auxiliary officer."

"You want me to be a spy?" I couldn't help myself: the cool, slightly sardonic tone I'd adopted in my head came out of my mouth as something closer to an excited squeal.

The corner of Aunt Jenny's mouth quirked, in what might have been a hastily suppressed smile. "You won't be getting any exploding toothpaste, or a rifle disguised as a backscratcher, if that's what you're thinking," she said. "But apart from an over-active conscience, you seem to have most of the right skills."

"Which are?" I asked, beginning to find the game of question and frustratingly partial answer more than mildly irritating, but with hindsight I suspect it was simply another test—or, perhaps, a tutorial, in the art of mining information in apparently negligible nuggets.

"You're an opportunist." I opened my mouth reflexively to protest, but found myself nodding in agreement. I wouldn't have put it quite like that myself, but still . . . "You see an opening, and you can't resist exploiting it. Like the weakness in the Academy's block."

"And?" I asked, perhaps a little more brusquely than I'd intended, uncomfortable with the reminder of my own folly. "You said skills. Plural."

You made this, Aunt Jenny sent, indicating the sneakware still floating in our conjoined 'spheres. *A "hobby" that cracked some Navy-grade defenses. Your sister tells me you have a knack for this kind of thing.*

"You've spoken to Tinkie about me?" I asked, unable to conceal my surprise. "What did she say?"

"Nothing complimentary," my aunt assured me, and I felt a kind of numb despair settle heavily into my stomach, where it sat awkwardly, elbowing its way in between the beer and the ill-advised pies. I'd already realized that any kind of reconciliation with my sister was at best unlikely, but having it confirmed so casually still hurt. "But she did confirm your suitability for this kind of work, in a roundabout sort of way."

"Pleased to hear it," I said, conscious of sounding anything but.

She said she's seen you using this, Aunt Jenny continued, then grinned at me conspiratorially. "I didn't ask when or where, but she didn't seem all that surprised that you'd been able to crack the

Academy. Has Anastasia been a bit careless about taking her work home?"

"You're the security expert, you tell me," I replied, and her grin widened fractionally.

"I'll take that as a yes," she said.

"Aren't you going to ask me what it was?" I asked, and she shook her head sadly.

"Now that's disappointing, Simon. You just confirmed you've been somewhere else you shouldn't have. Mistake like that could get you shot in the field." She took a sip of her newly arrived drink. "If I really wanted to know what it was, I wouldn't have to ask you, would I? I'd have found out a long time ago."

"I suppose you would," I said. "Anything else?"

"About what?" For the first time since our conversation began she seemed to be on the back foot, which surprised me a little—unless that was what I was supposed to think. It was beginning to dawn on me that from now on I wouldn't be able to take anything anyone said to me at face value.

"Your little list," I said. "Of things that made you think I'd be good at this."

My aunt shrugged. "You're stubborn. You found this place a lot quicker than I expected. That about covers it."

So I'd been right. Her disappearance had been a test. I shrugged too, and finished my ale, with as much nonchalance as I could manage. "That was luck, more than anything."

"So you're lucky, too. Make the most of it, but don't rely on it. Because the minute you do, it'll bugger off." She drained her own glass, and stood abruptly. "Come on. I'm starving. I'll buy you a pie."

CHAPTER EIGHT

In which I meet a father and daughter, and make friends with one of them.

To my unspoken relief, Aunt Jenny didn't come to the docking arm to see me off. Having her there would have felt too much like my arrival at the Academy, and those were memories I really didn't want to relive. There was also the matter of my cover to consider: Remington thought she was getting rid of me as a favor to the family, and if he saw us apparently on good terms just before embarkation he was smart enough to suspect that there was something else going on we hadn't told him about.

Which, of course, there was. Numarkut, our destination, was one of those rare stellar systems with rift connections to half a dozen others, rather than the mere one or two most stars possessed, which made it a thriving nexus for trade. Which, in turn, made it of great interest to Aunt Jenny, and whoever she reported to. Numarkut had direct links to worlds within both League and Commonwealth, joining each of them to the Rimward Way, a trading route running straight towards the heart of the Human Sphere through a bewildering variety of Federations, Confederations, Alliances, Hegemonies, Dominions, Demesnes, and, for all I knew, a few more Commonwealths and Leagues; not to mention any number of independent and nonaligned worlds, all with their own agendas. What made Numarkut of particular interest at the moment, however, was that one of its open rifts was the second one connecting to Rockhall, bypassing the choke point in the Sodallagain system. It went without saying that if my aunt's counterparts in the League were getting intelligence from their agents on Rockhall, which they were as surely as trying to breathe vacuum was a bad idea, this was the route it was coming through.

"You don't have to do much," Aunt Jenny had told me, "just keep your eyes and ears open, particularly around any crews fresh through the rift from Rockhall." A job I'd thought well within my capabilities.

"And if I hear anything of interest?" I'd asked. Waiting till we got back to Avalon, even if the *Stacked Deck* made a direct return run, which was by no means certain, would render any intelligence I managed to gather so out of date as to be useless.

"I've got an asset in one of the shipping agencies, with access to their riftcom. Anything urgent you can pass on to him."

"Will do," I agreed, trying not to sound too impressed. Though it was possible to send messages across interstellar distances by squirting pulses of modulated gravitons down the right rift and keeping your fingers crossed, it took almost as much energy as sending a ship through, and the kit required would fill a small cargo hold. Which was good news for the Commerce Guild, which kept a tight grip on most of the postal traffic in the Human Sphere, but not so much for everyone else, who had to pay through the nose to keep in touch with the neighboring systems. Only people who really needed to pass messages faster than the time it took for a starship to make its way to and from the rift points at both ends of the journey, and had money to burn besides, bothered to maintain a riftcom: which, in practice, meant the local Guildhalls, most interstellar governments (especially their Navies), and sufficiently prosperous businesses that absolutely had to keep tabs on what was going on elsewhere in more or less real time—like, for instance, a cargo broker with offices on Numarkut and Avalon. "Who do I look for?"

"You don't," Aunt Jenny said. "He'll find you."

Which I supposed was fair enough. And which hadn't stopped me from trawling the 'sphere for any brokers which fit the bill the minute I was close enough to an open node, and immediately narrowing the possibilities down to a short list of half a dozen: there weren't that many with offices in both systems (and a handful of others) big enough to maintain their own riftcom network.

I'd travelled around our home system enough to be familiar with both civilian passenger terminals and, on occasion, the rather more basic facilities the Navy used for personnel transfers, but the cargo docks were a new and bewildering experience for me. Arm 7 was full of docking bays, each hosting between three and a dozen starships, depending on their size: the far walls of the cavernous spaces bulged inwards, matching the curvature of the hulls intended to fit into them, and, for the first time, I really understood why most vessels were built to standardized templates. A freighter forced to wait for an unusually sized cradle to come free would hemorrhage time and money, both of which most skippers were perennially short of.

Between the bulging domes I could see innumerable stevedores and handling drones bustling about like flies on a wall, shifting pallets and cargo containers into and out of the wide doors giving access to the equatorial cargo hatches of the starships beyond, or scooting round the curve between walls and floor, where the gravity shifted direction by ninety degrees.

As I wove my way through the chaos towards the cradle broadcasting the ident code of the *Stacked Deck*, I narrowly missed being mown down by heavily laden trolleys so often I practically became used to it. A quick, and mildly vertigo-inducing, glance upwards was enough to confirm my guess that the ceiling was just as much a hive of activity as the floor around me, although such appellations were entirely subjective in this sort of environment.

I slowed my pace a little as I drew nearer the towering hemisphere into which my new home was nestled, although, of course, I could see nothing of the ship itself—nor would there have been anything particularly interesting about it if I'd been able to. All starships looked pretty much alike, metal spheres completely featureless apart from the outlines of their external hatches, with only their sizes varying. Of course you could tell a lot from the number of hatches, and where they were placed, but you'd have to be a pretty obsessive ship-spotter (or a Navy brat like me) to do so, even if you could get close enough to the hull to take a look.

As I approached the nearest hatch, I found my 'sphere beginning to clutter with data blurts, mostly to, from, and between the steady procession of drones entering the vessel with stacked pallets, or scooting back out again unladen. The nexus of all the activity seemed to be a heavyset man in disheveled coveralls, sporting a Guild patch on one sleeve, and a rough circle of cleaner cloth on the other where a similar badge had been recently ripped away. I sent a brief ident, and he looked across at me just long enough to scowl.

"What do you want?" he snapped, even though the packet I'd just sent had contained all my personal details.

"I'm Simon Forrester," I said, refusing to rise to it. "Captain Remington's expecting me." If anything, the scowl intensified. "This is the *Stacked Deck*?" I added, although the ident still being broadcast in the background left no room for doubt about that.

"It is now." If anything, the question seemed to make matters worse, and the fellow glared at me with undisguised loathing. He jerked a head in the direction of the open hatch. "If he's expecting you, you'd better find the *captain*." The last word contained enough venom to fell an ox. "Some of us have work to do."

"Thanks," I said. One of us could be civil, at least. Leaving him to vent his anger on the uncomplaining drones, I made my way across the threshold of the hatch, and found myself, for the first time in my life, standing on the deck of a starship.

"Hi." I turned, startled. Lost for a moment in the realization of my life's ambition, and trying to orientate myself in the cavernous space of the cargo hold, I'd failed to notice I wasn't alone. My interlocutor smiled at me in a guardedly friendly fashion. "You're going to get squished if you stand there," she added.

"Squished. Right," I said, pirouetting out of the way of a drone cradling something large, heavy, and wrapped in a tarp. "Thanks."

"You're welcome." Her smile spread. "You're a pretty good mover."

"I've done some athletics," I said, conscious as I spoke that it was a lame thing to say.

"I'll bet you have." She was about my own age, quite pretty in a gamine sort of way, and dressed in the same kind of coverall as the fellow outside. In her case, though, there was a crew patch on her left sleeve instead of a patch of bare cloth, newer and cleaner than the rest of the garment: a fanned quintet of cards, with *Stacked Deck* overlaid on what looked to my inexpert eye like an unbeatable hand. (At least in the games I was familiar with—I'd no doubt there were far more variations than I'd ever heard of played out among the stars.) The girl looked me up and down in the appraising fashion I'd long grown used to, but with an easy friendliness that made a welcome and refreshing change. Then she stuck out a hand. "Clio Rennau."

"Simon Forrester." I bowed formally, and began to raise her hand to my lips, as Avalonian etiquette demanded on first meeting a lady. Clio laughed, seized mine in a surprisingly firm grip, and pumped it energetically for a couple of seconds.

"Just a handshake will do." She regarded me from under her fringe. "You're a fast one. I can see I'll have to keep an eye on you."

"My apologies." I felt a warm flush of embarrassment rising up my neck. "No offense was intended, I can assure you."

"Just teasing, Si." She flashed me another smile. "That was just what people do around here when they meet someone new, right?"

"Right." I nodded, relieved not to have offended her. "I can see I've a lot to learn."

"You'll get used to it. Another solar system, another set of customs to get your head around. That's the advantage of being in the Guild, of course. Everyone adjusts to us instead. Saves a lot of time."

"I suppose so," I said, feeling even more out of my depth than ever.

"Good." Her demeanor became suddenly businesslike, and she nodded at my baggage. "Is that all your kit?"

"Yes," I said. Two carryalls and a rucksack. Not much to pack an entire life into. But Clio was nodding approvingly.

"Just the essentials, then. You're off to a good start." The grin surfaced again for a moment. "You won't believe how much some dirtwalkers think they can bring aboard."

"Dirtwalkers?" I asked, and a flicker of embarrassment passed across her face.

"Planet dwellers. It's just an expression. Not disparaging." She paused for a second, tact and candor at war in her features. "Not very, anyway. And besides, you're not one, are you? Not any more."

"I hope not," I said, finding to my vague surprise that it was true. "But Captain Remington said I had to make it to Numarkut before he'd make up his mind about taking me on." I hesitated a second, then decided I might as well ask. "That is the right thing to call him, right? But the guy outside was a real grouch about it."

"I'll bet he was," Clio said, with a sympathetic smile. "But don't mind Dad. He's just still pissed about losing the ship to John."

"What?" I felt as though someone had just switched the gravity in a different direction. "You used to own the *Stacked Deck*?"

"No, Dad used to own the *Sleepy Jean*." She began to lead the way through a labyrinth of cargo containers, exchanging brief greetings with the handful of people we met along the way. A couple were clearly part of the crew, sporting the same hand of cards patch as my self-appointed guide, but how many of the others were among my new shipmates, or just dock workers aboard to help supervise the stowage, I had no idea. "New skipper, new name. It's a Guild thing."

"Right." I hesitated for a moment, before curiosity won out over tact. "What happened?"

Clio shrugged. "Long story. Short version: John paid off some people we owed, and took over the ship as collateral. Good deal for everyone, except Dad's too pig-headed to see it." She led the way up a flight of stairs to a catwalk near the ceiling of the hold, on which my boot soles echoed loudly enough to be heard even above the clamor of the cargo being stowed beneath us. From up here it was easy to see the layout, which, conventionally enough, was a blunt-ended wedge, an eighth the circumference of the vessel: I had no doubt that there were seven more holds identical to it completing the circle. The blank wall at the end, towards which we were now walking, would be one side of an octagon, giving access to the slightly smaller holds above and below, and, higher and lower than them, the crew quarters and utility areas containing the ship's propulsion and life support systems. A large cargo elevator would run between the hold levels, but, glancing down and through the massive open doors, I could just see the platform on the lower tier, locked down, while the handling drones flitted directly up and down the shaft.

"It must have been hard on you both, though," I said. "Losing your ship like that."

Clio shrugged again. "Ships change hands all the time," she said. "He'll get her back, or take on a new one—just got to wait for the right opportunity." Which all sounded astonishingly casual to me, but then Guilders were different: something I supposed I'd get used to in time.

"What did your mother think about it?" I asked, more for

something to say than anything else, and Clio glanced back at me, looking surprised.

"All for it. Who did you think we owed?"

"I see." At least I thought I did. "And I thought my parents didn't get along too well."

"They get along great," Clio said, a faint frost entering her voice. "But a deal's a deal. Can't renege on a contract, whoever it's with." So at least one of my preconceptions about Guilders seemed to be true.

"Do you see much of her?" I asked, conscious of skirting a conversational minefield. I was acutely aware that I was going to be spending a lot of time aboard the *Stacked Deck*, at least if things went as well as I hoped, and I needed to be making friends among her crew. At least Clio seemed to be making allowances for my naivety, although I'd clearly got off on the wrong foot with her dad.

"Whenever we're in the same system." Clio led the way through a doorway at the end of the catwalk, and I found myself in a stairwell, between the inner and outer walls of the central octagon. As she started to climb a few steps ahead of me, I found myself appreciating the view rather more than I suppose I ought to have done. "We'll find you some quarters, then you can officially report to the skipper."

"Sounds good to me," I agreed, as we reached a landing and my field of vision became less distractingly callipygian. Beyond another door was a corridor, painted in some muted shade of not-quite white, which was probably supposed to seem warmer and less harsh in the overhead lighting, but didn't. A strip of carpet, in varying hues of stain, completed the effect, which reminded me of nothing so much as my old student dorm back at Summerhall; certainly the last thing I'd have expected aboard a starship.

"This one's free," Clio said, stopping outside a random door and tugging it open. It slid aside easily, and I stepped through, finding myself in a small stateroom, barely the size of Aunt Jenny's guest quarters. For all that, it was more spacious than I'd expected. "Head's through here." She indicated a door I'd taken for a closet, but which indeed led to a small private bathroom, almost big enough for a grown adult to stand in without banging their elbows on both walls at once. "Okay?"

"More than okay," I assured her. "I'd thought there'd just be a communal one."

"Guilders like their privacy," Clio told me. "Especially on a ship this size. Otherwise things can get . . . tense."

"I guess so," I agreed, happy to take her word for it. "How many people are there aboard?"

"Seventeen, last time I looked," Clio said. "Counting you."

"Seventeen," I said. I was no expert, but that seemed pretty low for a ship this size. The *Queen Kylie's Revenge* had almost two hundred officers and ratings aboard; all right, a lot of them were gunners, or other specialists a civilian cargo barge had no use for, but even so . . .

Clio nodded, clearly reading the doubt on my face. "It is a bit high," she said, "but John's a soft touch. Doesn't like to split families." She shot another appraising glance in my direction. "Or lose the chance of a bit of goodwill from a regular client."

"I'm sure he and my aunt have the measure of each other," I said, trying not to think too hard about our earlier conversation on the subject.

"I'm sure you're right," Clio agreed, with a faint smile. She glanced at my kitbags, still lying on the bunk where I'd dumped them. "Do you want to unpack now, or go see the skipper?"

"Skipper," I said. Stowing my few remaining belongings would only take a handful of minutes, and I didn't want to get off on the wrong foot with the captain. The trip to Numarkut wouldn't take very long, and I felt I'd need every moment of it to make a good enough impression to be allowed to join the crew on a permanent basis.

"Skipper it is," Clio agreed, stepping back into the corridor to make enough room for me to leave.

I followed, and slid the door closed, tripping the latch. "How do you lock it?" I asked, after a moment of fumbling.

"Lock it?" Clio looked surprised. "Why would you want to?" Sure enough, on closer examination, none of the doors in the corridor seemed to have locking plates.

"Security? Privacy?" I ventured.

"No one's going to steal anything," Clio told me, looking faintly offended. "Where would they go afterwards? But if it really matters to you . . ." She pulled a reasonably clean handkerchief from her pocket, and draped it over the handle. "No one'll go in now."

"Really?" I glanced up and down the corridor; sure enough, a few of the other doors had pieces of cloth tied to them, apparently indicating a desire for privacy on the part of the occupants—as we passed one, I heard what sounded like the echoes of energetic carnal congress within, and I picked up my pace a little, trying to look casual.

Clio smirked. "Not many prudes on a starship," she said, reading my embarrassment rather too easily.

"I'll let you know if I find any," I retorted, failing to fool her for a second.

CHAPTER NINE

In which my first voyage commences, and I'm sent to fetch tea.

Captain Remington was, as I'd expected, on the bridge, though not, as I'd expected, barking orders at his subordinates in the way that my mother would have been. I'd half hoped and half expected Clio to accompany me the whole way, but after steering me back to the stairwell she simply meshed our 'spheres for a moment and transferred a schematic of the *Stacked Deck* across to mine.

You can't miss it, she assured me, and clattered back down the stairs to resume whatever job it was in the cargo hold that my arrival had interrupted.

In that, at least, she was right; a couple of flights farther up, and I was in the nerve center of the entire ship. I must admit that, crossing the threshold, I felt a little tingle of excitement—which fizzled out almost immediately, as soon as the realization sank in that actually it was just a room full of stuff not doing anything particularly interesting, including the captain. Unlike the virts, no one was striding purposefully across the middle of the room with an urgent message, or gazing intently at complicated instrument panels. Indeed, there were very few of those, mostly powered down, and the ones that were activated were simply repeating dataflow that was cascading through the fringes of my 'sphere. The ship, it seemed, was flown by neuroware interface, with the physical controls just there for backup.

"You made it, then," Remington greeted me, glancing up from the chair in which he was sprawled, a half-eaten sandwich in his hand. He licked a smear of escaping mayonnaise from his fingers.

"Simon Forrester, reporting for duty," I said, suppressing the urge to bow formally as I spoke. Clio's reaction to my Avalonian greeting had put me on my guard, and I resolved to act a little more casually around my new shipmates, at least until I got a handle on the Guild way of doing things.

"Right." Remington nodded, and slurped from a tea mug. "Found the crew quarters?"

I echoed the gesture. "Clio showed me. I've already picked out a room."

"Good. You meet Rennau on the way in?"

"Her father?" Remington inclined his head in confirmation, still apparently more interested in his snack than in me. "He sent me up here to report in."

"In a few well-chosen words, no doubt." Remington chewed and swallowed the last of his sandwich. "Not one for diplomacy, our Mik. But a good man to have at your back."

I found myself reflecting that if Rennau had Remington's back he'd slip a knife into it as likely as not, but Guilders apparently had their own ways of looking at things, so perhaps the Captain's confidence was justified.

Remington looked at me for a second or two, as though surprised to find me still there. "Cut along, then. Tell him to find you something to do."

"Yes, sir." I hesitated, wondering if I was supposed to salute or something, and Remington sighed.

"Call me Sir if I get a knighthood. Till then, stick to Skipper. Or Captain, if you're feeling formal, or we're trying to impress a dirtwalker."

"Yes, s . . . Skipper."

I left the bridge, and descended the stairs, once again wondering what I'd got myself into.

I'd like to say I found my feet quickly, but I spent most of the next few days getting in the way of people who knew what they were doing, and following the instructions they'd given me in varying tones of tolerance or exasperation. Rennau had started me off by stowing cargo, heaving the pallets the drones had delivered the last few inches into place and securing them, under the direction of Rolf and Lena, a couple of transgeners who'd clearly gone all out for physical strength. Both quite literally bulged with muscle, lugging crates larger than I was with scant sign of visible effort. Despite their intimidating appearance, however, they welcomed me aboard with surprisingly delicate handshakes, and spent their breaks discussing philosophy and literature in terms so abstruse as to leave me floundering within minutes.

On the whole, I felt I did a reasonable job, and the simple physical work seemed to agree with me: by the time we were ready for departure I'd regained the muscle tone I'd been in danger of losing after neglecting my regular training regime for so long, and resolved to continue working out in order to keep it.

Not that lugging boxes around was my sole occupation in the days leading up to our departure. (And days it was: Remington's implied threat to leave me behind having turned out to be either a test of my resolve, or a negotiating tactic to wring some unspecified further concession from my aunt.) If anything needed to be fetched, I went for it. If anyone needed a spare pair of hands, mine were the ones required; I saw a lot of the ship's internal systems while passing tools to people wedged into awkward corners. But cargo stowage took up the greater part of my days for the greater part of a week. It was almost a surprise when Rolf stood back from the containers we'd been securing, and I turned to find the last of the drones humming away towards the hatch.

"That's it," he said, nodding in approval, then smiled in my direction. "Till we shift the whole lot out again at the other end, of course."

"Which you can worry about when we arrive," Lena chided, folding forearms thicker than my thighs across her chest. She smiled at me too. "Not a bad job for a little 'un." Which isn't an appellation I'd have been happy with from most people, but since she and her husband topped me by a head and a half, and two of me could easily have stood in the space either of them normally occupied, I suppose from their perspective she had a point. I'd certainly learned early on that if you met either of them head on in a corridor, the only way forward was back.

Simon, to the bridge. The message dropped into my 'sphere without warning, which at least saved me from having to continue a conversation which was bound to end in embarrassment for one of us.

"Wonder what he wants?" Rolf said, picking the message up too. Remington had simply bounced it off the central node, so anyone in my vicinity could have passed it on if I'd been disconnected or asleep. (Or both. Like most people, I'd found incoming messages didn't always wake me if they arrived while I was sleeping, but they could generally be relied on to induce some disturbing dreams.)

"Only one way to find out," I said, pinging back a brief acknowledgement as I spoke, and went trotting off to do so.

"Thought you might like to see us cast off," Remington greeted me as I entered the bridge. "Seeing as it's your first time." He took in my rumpled, and somewhat breathless, appearance, the inevitable result of taking the stairs two at a time after several hours putting my shoulder to crates heavier than I was. "You didn't have to run."

"You didn't say it wasn't urgent," I said, earning a derisive snort from Rennau, who was watching one of the boards which had been powered down the last time I was in here. In the last few days I'd learned that he was officially the first mate, second in authority only to Remington, but the loss of the top spot clearly still rankled. And, since he regarded me as Remington's protégé, a lot of that resentment was coming my way by default. Clio had assured me it was only a matter of time before he came round, but that looked like it would be a long way off, from where I was standing.

"When I call, it's always urgent," Remington said, with a hint of amusement, though which one of us it was directed at I couldn't have said. He indicated a spare seat. "Sit down, mesh in, and keep quiet."

"Keeping quiet. Right," I responded, and parked myself in the somewhat dilapidated chair he'd waved towards, which turned out to be almost as uncomfortable as it looked. Not that I really noticed, diving headlong into the datasphere and meshing with the *Stacked Deck*'s central node as soon as my buttocks hit the upholstery. (What little there was left of it.)

Don't fiddle with anything, Rennau sent, although I had more sense than to try. Datastreams were blizzarding past to and from the boards ranged around the bridge, and through them to the neuroware 'spheres of the operators. As well as Remington and Rennau, I could make out the distinctive haze of complex algorithms surrounding Sowerby, the chief engineer, who wasn't actually physically present, but meshing in from the power plant on the lower decks, no doubt with her largest wrench poised to deal with any unforeseen difficulties: Sowerby was a great believer in percussive maintenance. One of her assistants was manning the board on the bridge, although I doubted he'd have much to do with his boss on the job.

"Take us out," Remington said, and a virtual image appeared in my 'sphere, apparently being relayed from a vantage point somewhere on the exterior hull. Nothing but pitch darkness at first; then a ring of light appeared, growing rapidly, until it filled the whole field of vision. After a second or two I was able to make out a hemispherical indentation, lined with bright, reflective metal, and realized I was looking at the interior of our cradle on the outer hull of the docking arm, from which we'd just disengaged. As the *Stacked Deck* pulled further away from its starting point, our shadow shrank slowly to an almost imperceptible stain at the bottom of the hollow. A moment later, as the field of vision continued to expand, I was able to make out the domes of other ships, still nestled into their docking ports, and the metallic craters of the nearest unoccupied ones, their smooth, curving sides indented with the outlines of docking hatches and umbilical sockets.

"We're clear," Rennau reported, although that much was obvious from the supplementary data streams; later, I was to be more grateful than I could possibly have imagined for the Guild tradition of reporting verbally and keeping an eye on the manual boards in spite of the instant awareness of all the ship's systems meshing in gave you, but at the time I really couldn't see the point.

Then, unexpectedly, he glanced in my direction. *Enjoying the show?* His expression was still sardonic, and the ping was as devoid of emotional overtones as they always were, but even so it was the first thing he'd done since I came aboard that seemed even remotely affable. So I nodded a reply, determined to take the overture at face value.

Never seen anything like it, I sent back.

"That I can believe." His tone was as dry as ever, but I thought I could detect a hint of amusement beneath it. Besides, it was perfectly true: I hadn't.

I'd seen the exterior of Skyhaven before, of course, but only from viewing ports in the orbital itself, or from a surface to orbit passenger boat. The commercial side, with its array of freight docks, was entirely new to me.

As the image widened still further, the sheer size of the cargo port began to become apparent; the docking arm we'd just disengaged from must have been a good half a mile from end to end all on its own, and there were four more of them jutting from the habitat's main hull in its immediate vicinity, casting shadows across the nearby superstructure that looked curiously like a smudged handprint. And the sky around them was full of ships, over a thousand if the datastream from the sensor array could be relied on. (Which, of course, it could, otherwise we'd never have been able to navigate safely through the swarm.)

I'd been expecting us to continue separating from the habitat along the same vector until we were completely clear of it, but we were still only a few hundred yards from the vast cylinder of the docking arm when Sowerby booted the gravitics (possibly quite literally, knowing her) against the weak gravity field of the orbital, bouncing us into a neat parabola over the curving metal horizon.

Avalon rose into view, and I caught my breath, abruptly conscious for the first time on a truly visceral level that I was leaving my homeworld, and the system of which it was a part, possibly forever. If Remington really decided to dump me on Numarkut, I could be stuck there for good. On the other hand, if I impressed him enough to offer the apprenticeship he'd half promised, there was no telling where the *Stacked Deck* would be heading for next. True, he seemed to do business with Aunt Jenny on a fairly regular basis, but there was no guarantee they always met on Avalon—since she'd revealed her avocation to me, I felt I could take nothing about her for granted any more.

The planet was three quarters full, a lush blue crescent, the muted greens and browns of its land masses veiled by wisps of cloud: white for the most part, though in one or two places its face was marred by the mottled bruising of thunderheads. On the night side, amid the phosphorescent tendrils of cities and roads, I caught a brief flicker of lightning out in the rural hinterlands, and felt a momentary flare of nostalgia—the Forrester estates would be engulfed in the torrential autumn rains now, the drops hammering against the window of my old room, with no one there to listen to it.

"Know why we're not heading straight for the rift point?" Rennau asked, in a tone that made it clear he expected a negative answer.

I nodded. "The planet's got more mass for the gravitics to kick against." We could just have boosted against the orbital, but we'd have accelerated a great deal more slowly that way. "And the sooner we get to the rift point, the sooner we get to Numarkut. The sooner we get to Numarkut, the sooner we get paid for the cargo."

Remington laughed, although whether at my answer or Rennau's expression of surprise I couldn't be sure. "Thinking like a Guilder already," he said.

"Up to a point." Rennau sent an orbital dynamics graphic to my 'sphere. *We can get an additional boost from slingshotting round it before Sowerby powers up.* Which I already knew, of course, from listening to Naval gossip behind the drawing room door as a child, once I was old enough to sneak out of bed during Mother's dinner parties, and the cramming I'd done for the Academy entrance exam. But I'd attended enough soirees as an adult, where I was expected merely to be decorative and laugh at the right people's jokes, to realize that letting on how much you know isn't always a good idea.

"I see," I said, after pretending to study the diagram for a moment. "That way we get to use the planet's mass twice." Then it struck me that was the second time I'd thought of my old home as just "the planet," rather than "Avalon." Perhaps I was beginning to adjust to my new life as a spacefarer faster than I'd thought.

Rennau was looking at me as though calculating how much per pound I'd be worth to a Skyhaven pie merchant. "Quick on the uptake, anyway," he conceded.

Remington grinned. "What did you expect from Jenny Worricker's nephew?"

The mate shrugged. "Same as from everyone else. More than meets the eye, less than they like to think."

I thought about that, trying to fillet an insult from it, but not sure it would be worth the effort. It actually sounded quite astute, if you were a congenital cynic. Though perhaps such a reflection just showed I was already further along that particular road than I liked to think.

"So, how long till we make Numarkut?" I asked, already doing the calculation for myself.

Remington looked thoughtful. "Depends how much speed we've

got on when we shoot the rift," he said. "Couple of days out to the point here, same on the other side—unless we have to slow down for a customs inspection. Once we lose way, there's sod all to push against. Took over a week, once."

Rennau nodded again, sourly. "And we had perishables aboard. Bastard inspector slowed us down to a crawl once he realized there was nothing in the hold worth pilfering."

"Does that happen a lot?" I asked. Sowerby seemed to be running things from the gravitics room at the moment, which gave us more time to talk than I'd anticipated, and I meant to take full advantage of the opportunity.

"Depends on the system," Remington said. "Numarkut, they're all at it. Never find a customs inspector there living the frugal life. On the plus side, it makes them easy to bribe. 'Til they get a better offer."

"League worlds, it varies," Rennau chipped in. "Most of their inspectors are strictly by the book. But you'll find the odd one with his hand out. When you do, they're worth cultivating. 'Til they get found out and shot."

"Shot?" I asked, involuntarily, and Remington shook his head.

"Just that one time. Served him right for resisting arrest."

I nodded, considering this. League law enforcement had a reputation for heavy-handedness, at least according to Commonwealth gossip, and I found it all too easy to believe a corrupt official would be summarily executed.

"What about the Commonwealth?" I asked, hoping my own people would turn out to be relative paragons.

"Pain in the arse," Remington told me. "Want to check the manifest three times before they'll even come aboard. Then they poke about everywhere, expect to be fed and given tea, and complain incessantly about wasting their time. After which, if they can't find anything actually wrong, they'll make up a new regulation they can 'fine' you for infringing anyway."

"Does that happen often?" I asked, trying not to sound shocked.

"Often enough," Remington said, not fooled for a moment. He paused, receiving a message from Sowerby that suddenly dropped into his 'sphere, and nodded once. "Thanks, Sarah. Whenever you're ready." Then he glanced back in my direction. "You'll enjoy this."

If I'm honest, "enjoy" wasn't quite the word that first sprang to mind as I returned my attention to the visual display floating in the center of my 'sphere, which had been quietly getting on with the job of piping an image from the outer hull all the time I'd been distracted with conversation. While we'd been talking, the *Stacked Deck* had sailed serenely around the curve of the orbital, and begun her plunge towards the planet below.

Now Avalon appeared a good deal larger, and more ominous, than it had the last time I'd looked. The wisps of cloud, barely perceptible before, seemed thicker and more solid as we drove in towards the day side limb of the planet. I found myself looking for familiar land masses, as though we were expecting to land, but we were moving far too fast for that ever to be an option: unless, by "land," you mean "leave a crater the size of a city block." I was no expert, but it seemed to me that Sowerby was cutting it a bit fine.

"She'll be skimming air if she's not careful," I said, mildly disconcerted at the realization I'd spoken the thought aloud.

"Not Sarah," Remington said, then hesitated. "Not much, anyway."

It's all a question of balance, see? Rennau added, along with another superfluous diagram. In that, at least, he was right: the closer we got to the planet, the greater the boost to our speed from the slingshot maneuver. On the other hand, the deeper we dipped into the atmosphere, the more velocity would be dissipated as friction.

So far as I could tell, we were slipping just a little bit deeper than we should have been, the first faint wisps of air reaching up like swell on a placid sea to claw at our hull. Temperature readings began to climb, and although they were still a long way from anything approaching dangerous, I felt a faint shiver of apprehension. We began to acquire a visible wake of displaced air, roiling behind us, and a bow wave of condensing vapor, compressed and superheated by the speed of our passage.

"And . . . break!" Sowerby said calmly, her voice slightly attenuated by the node's vocal processor. Another burst of power to the gravitics, and we were suddenly clear, hurtling away into the void.

"Nicely done," Remington said, and turned to me. "Having second thoughts?"

"Bit late for that," I said, with more conviction than I felt, while the world I called home dwindled rapidly in the virtual image. I closed it down: no point watching it diminish into a pinprick, before it vanished altogether in the never-ending night.

"Got that right," Rennau confirmed, glancing in my direction. He stretched, as though the whole thing had been mildly tedious. "While you're up here, you can get us some tea."

CHAPTER TEN
In which I shoot my first rift.

I suppose I'd expected things to settle down a bit now we were on our way, but of course they were no quieter; at least for me. Though there were no crates to manhandle, the *Stacked Deck* was full of systems to check, minor problems to correct, and people needing a gofer *right now*, so there was no shortage of jobs for me to do. In the next couple of days, during which we went very fast through a great deal of nothing, I renewed my acquaintance with the vessel's darkest and dustiest corners, and absorbed a great deal of information from Sowerby and her assistants about which tools were best to hit which pieces of equipment with. I even found myself redistributing the grime on the deck plates of the lower hold level with a broom on one occasion, an implement I'd only ever seen used before in historical virts.

"I thought we had drones for this kind of thing," I grumbled, half-seriously. Clio, who was perched on the catwalk above me, legs swinging, as she applied a molecular bonder to a handrail that had cracked when Lena leaned against it, grinned down at me.

"And what happens if the power goes off?" she asked.

I shrugged. "Life support fails, we all suffocate or freeze, no one gives a stuff about sweeping the decks."

"Well, there's that," she agreed cheerfully. "But the less you rely on the tech, the less there is to go wrong."

"Says the woman who lives on a starship," I said.

"I never said you shouldn't use it." She tested the handrail by swinging from it, and I found myself edging across to stand beneath her. She seemed to know what she was doing, but it was still a good fifteen feet from the catwalk to the deck plates, and I'd tripped often enough while lugging crates about to know just how hard they were. "Just don't rely on anything you don't need to."

"Like you're not relying on that bonder to have worked, so you don't break your neck?" I asked, and she grinned again.

"Exactly. If I didn't know damn well it had worked, I'd never—eek!" She dropped abruptly, and I leapt forward, arms outstretched. One of her hands caught the edge of the catwalk, and she hung there for a moment, looking down at me—then burst out laughing. "Oh, your face. You should see it from this side." She let go, did a neat back flip, and landed on the deck plates next to me, flexing her knees to absorb the impact.

"Very funny," I said, trying to hide how impressed I was. I'd seen sloppier displays in gymnastics competitions. "You didn't tell me you were an athlete too."

"That's cos I'm not," she said, although her face seemed to go a little pinker—probably as a result of the exertion. "I just picked up a few things scrambling round the holds."

"So long as you put them back afterwards," I joked, and she tilted her head, looking at me in the appraising manner I'd quickly come to associate with my new shipmates.

"Suppose I find something I don't want to put back?" she asked.

"Then don't get caught, I suppose," I said, feeling faintly surprised. One thing I'd learned since coming aboard was that, despite the popular cynicism, Guilders were quite genuine in regarding an agreement of any kind as completely binding: I'd heard several stories of crippled ships with cargoes of food whose crews had eked out their rations to the point of starvation before even considering breaking open a hold. The idea of any Guilder, let alone Clio, entertaining the notion of casual pilfering, even in jest, was hard to get my head around.

"I never do," she said, watching my face intently for a reaction. Whatever she saw there seemed to be the wrong thing, however, because she turned away suddenly, heading for the staircase. She paused, and glanced back, with her foot on the lowest tread. "You've missed a bit in the corner."

"Right," I said, but when I went to check it looked fine to me.

As I'd hoped, but never really expected, Remington called me back to the bridge to observe the rift transit. He was just as casual about his reasons as before, saying only that I might find it interesting, but I took it as a hopeful sign that I'd done well enough by now for him to be seriously considering giving me the apprenticeship: after all, if he was planning to leave me behind on Numarkut, I'd never have reason to know what shooting the rift involved.

"Don't say or do anything," Rennau instructed, as I arrived on the bridge, and slipped into the seat I'd occupied before. There was an air of tension about him which hadn't been there during the undocking maneuver a couple of days earlier, and no sign of the suppressed affability I thought I might have detected in him then. "If we screw this up, we're all dead."

"Don't worry." Remington smiled at me, in a way which wasn't quite as reassuring as he clearly hoped. "He always says that. Just so the first thing he can say to me in heaven is 'I told you so.'"

"What makes you think either of us'll end up there?" Rennau said.

"I'm an optimist." Remington shrugged. "God likes those. We make Him laugh."

I meshed in, telling myself there was nothing to worry about, it was just banter between old—well, not friends, exactly, but people who'd known and trusted each other for a very long time. Statistically, the chances of anything going wrong while shooting a rift in a well-maintained ship with a competent crew were vanishingly small: but I couldn't shake the little voice in my head which kept insisting that, in a volume of space the size of the Human Sphere, in which millions of vessels were popping in and out of thousands of rifts every day of the year, it was virtually certain that sooner or later something, somewhere, would go catastrophically wrong. And although the really bad stuff only ever happens to other people, so far as everyone else was concerned, we were the other people. Right?

Time to be thinking about something else. I concentrated on the data blizzarding through the boards and into my 'sphere, half expecting snide comments and simplified diagrams from Rennau to accompany it as before, but he was too intent on whatever he was doing to bother with me. So I just watched the raw data swirling around the system, and interpreted it for myself as best I could.

According to the instruments, if I was reading them right, the space around us was riven with fractures, thousands upon thousands of them, radiating out from the central star in multiple dimensions. Which, for some reason, suddenly reminded me of my kindergarten teacher, Mister Plumridge, dropping a couple of ball bearings onto a sheet of glass to demonstrate the principle, pointing out how the resulting cracks radiated in all directions, and a few of them intersected. I hadn't given him a thought in years, but his earnest, faintly equine face, and soft, diffident voice suddenly came back to me as clearly as if we'd last spoken only a few days before. "Large masses, like stars, create stress fractures in space," he'd said, tracing one of the largest with the tip of his index finger. "Millions of them. But luckily for us, a few of them reach far enough to join up with a crack made by another. That makes a rift a starship can travel down." So far as I knew he'd never even left the province, let alone Avalon, but his simple explanation of the principles of interstellar travel had stayed with me ever since.

There was a lot more to it than that, of course, which I'd only really begun to appreciate when I'd moved on to school, and begun messing about with basic gravitational theory—until Mother had decreed that particular subject superfluous to the education of a gentleman, and its immediate replacement with ballroom dancing. Which hadn't stopped me from reading up on the subject in my own time, to the point where I knew enough to seriously consider taking it as a minor at Summerhall: until she'd stepped in again, put her foot down once more, and consigned me to the tedium of estate management. Anyhow, I felt I understood enough of the theory to follow what was going on around me, even if I couldn't have done anything useful to help.

Basically, to shoot the rift, we had to do two things. Find the right fracture, out of the millions riddling the space-time continuum around us, then increase the ship's mass with the internal gravitics until it broke through. Both of which were a little easier than they sounded.

Systems as long-settled as the Avalonian one had got all their fractures logged and sounded generations ago; a job which began as soon as a new route was discovered to a previously unvisited system, and which usually took decades of painstaking probing with graviton beams to complete (although every now and then a surveyor would luck into a previously unsuspected link with an inhabited system, and become very rich indeed.) All we had to do to find the right one was follow the beacon the nearby customs post maintained, until our own soundings found a fracture which didn't return an echo from a closed end.

The real trick was to increase the ship's mass fast enough to break through at precisely the right time—and into the right fracture. Get it wrong, and you'd bounce off the dead end, sustaining massive systems and structural damage if you were lucky; or being spat back out as a cloud of debris if you weren't. Fail to get the gravity bubble even enough around the ship's hull and you'd tear it open before you even got into the rift. And if the internal field wasn't strong enough to push back, you'd simply implode.

All of a sudden, looked at like that, it seemed a miracle that any ships ever got through a rift unscathed, and it didn't seem nearly so surprising that the *Stacked Deck*'s bridge crew seemed a little nervous, despite having shot hundreds of rifts in their time. (I have to admit, even now, after too many transits to count, I still feel a little dry-mouthed every time we go through one.)

To distract myself I called up the visual feed I'd been looking at during our departure from Skyhaven, earning a brief snort of derision from Rennau, who thereby let slip that he hadn't been ignoring me entirely. For which reaction, in all fairness, I could hardly blame him— it wasn't as though there was actually anything to see. One of the dots in the starfield might possibly have been the customs post, or a picket ship guarding the system from a potential League invasion, but other than that, nothing but the face of infinity, which, to be honest, isn't all that interesting after the first few minutes—or even before. I suppose I could have magnified the image, or overlaid it with the sensor returns, to try and identify the system defense assets, but in all honesty I simply couldn't see the point.

So I returned my attention to the graviton soundings, which rippled around and through mundane three-dimensional space in a virtual display of multidimensional fractals, reminding me in passing of the patterns in the datasphere I'd found so hypnotic in Aunt Jenny's apartment back on Skyhaven.

There. That return was different, a bottomless well into which our probing beam disappeared without an echo.

"Locked on," Sowerby reported, working from the power plant as before, her datastream suddenly spurting with interlocking algorithms. Power readings began to climb, our mass increasing as she fed more energy into the gravitics, carefully balancing the field around our hull. She was good, I had to admit, making minute manual corrections even faster than the automated systems a lesser engineer would have relied on.

According to the soundings we were running parallel to the rift by now, at least in the three dimensions of it relating directly to the universe we normally inhabited, and I found myself tensing involuntarily. But we remained in the physical galaxy, despite the gravitational field around us now being dense enough to warp the light from the stars into a dazzling halo.

Is something wrong? I sent to Clio, who I'd sensed, along with most of the off duty crew, meshed in on the fringes of the node, following the datastreams. She'd seemed a little off-hand with me for the hour or two following our conversation in the hold, but she was still the closest thing I'd found to a friend aboard, so she seemed the best person to ask.

There would be if we went now, she replied, with a brief image of an amused face. A cluster of incoming datanomes from the sounding telemetry suddenly highlighted. *That's a bow wave.*

Abruptly another ship, a gleaming metal sphere essentially identical to our own, popped into existence a couple of miles away, heading in towards Avalon at an impressive turn of speed. The *Repent at Leisure*, a Guild courier boat, according to its ident, laden with mail from Numarkut. I couldn't suppress a shudder. If we'd entered the rift a moment earlier, there would have been no survivors from either vessel.

"Clear," Sowerby reported, and the power levels in the gravitic system almost doubled in an instant. I felt a brief moment of disorientation, as though I'd trodden on a top step that wasn't really there, then the gravitics abruptly shut down—save for the internal emitters, which kept us from floating out of our seats every time we stood up.

For a second or two I felt a flash of panic, wondering what had gone wrong, before realizing that the stars in the visual display had shifted a couple of degrees.

"So, you've shot your first rift," Remington said. "How do you feel?"

I thought about that, but only one honest answer came to mind.

"Hungry," I admitted, disengaging from the torrent of information still cascading through the *Stacked Deck*'s central datanode.

"Good." Rennau glanced up from the board he was manning, his unfocussed eyes giving away the fact that he was still deeply meshed in. Nevertheless, they found me instantly. "You can do the galley run again. Tea and a sandwich." He turned to Remington. "Anything for you, Skip?"

The skipper shrugged. "The same, I guess. How long have we got till the pirates come aboard?"

CHAPTER ELEVEN
In which an error of judgment pays unexpected dividends.

Well, the Numarkut customs inspectors weren't pirates exactly, but once their cutter had matched velocities (using plasma reaction drives, as gravitic repulsion this far from anything big enough to bounce off was pretty close to useless), I could see why Remington seemed unclear about the distinction. A thin, weasely fellow came aboard through one of the personnel locks, his uniform so encrusted with braid and impractical-looking sidearms it seemed a miracle he could walk about in it without getting tangled up in something every time he took a step.

"Inspector Plubek." Remington extended a hand for a perfunctory shake, and withdrew it hastily, surreptitiously checking the number of fingers he had left. "Always a pleasure."

"Likewise, I'm sure." Plubek wiped his hand against the seat of his trousers, leaving a small, greasy stain—knowing the skipper's tastes, I'd been generous with the mayo while making the sandwiches, and, though long gone, they'd left traces of their passing. He favored me with the sort of look normally reserved for squishy surprises on the sole of your shoe. "Who's this?"

"My new deckhand. He'll look after you." So that's why he'd brought me down here from the bridge with him. But I suppose it made sense. My duties were among the least pressing, and while I was fetching and carrying for our unwelcome visitor, everyone else could be getting on with something useful.

"No doubt," Plubek said, in a voice which managed to convey exactly the opposite. He turned to me. "Come on then. First hold."

Just keep him busy, Remington sent, to my faint surprise.

Doing what? I asked.

Remington shrugged. *Doesn't matter,* he responded. *Just so long as he takes his time. Got some stuff to discuss with Sarah.* Then he turned and ambled away, already engrossed in conversation with Sowerby, who'd appeared from a nearby utility conduit while we were greeting the Inspector. Whatever they were talking about, it didn't look like business—their heads were close, and her arm was around his waist before they'd even reached the end of the corridor. I resolved to make sure our tour of inspection skirted around the crew quarters, in case a piece of cloth had appeared on either door in the interim.

"Would you like to see the manifest?" I asked, snagging a copy from the central datanode.

"Might as well take a look at it, I suppose." Plubek shrugged. "Some of it might even be true."

"Of course it's true," I said, perhaps a little more vehemently than I'd intended. In all honesty, the idea simply hadn't occurred to me that it wouldn't be, despite my new avocation of intelligence gatherer, and I resolved to check it through again myself at the earliest opportunity. I shouldn't be taking anything for granted any more.

Plubek snorted. "How long have you been aboard?"

"About a week," I admitted. "Still finding my feet, if I'm honest."

"If you'd found them by now, it'd make you the fastest on record." Plubek stopped walking, and really looked at me for the first time. "You're Commonwealth, right? Not Guild born?"

"What's that got to do with anything?" I asked, a trifle defensively. "I'm hardly the first dirtwalker to sign on with a Guild ship." The slang term slipped out without conscious thought, and it was hard to say which of the two of us was the most surprised.

"Just a piece of advice," Plubek said. "Lot of Commonwealthers on Numarkut. Leaguers too. And people picking sides who aren't either, but see some advantage in it. Watch your step when you get there, that's all."

"I will. Thanks," I said, with about as much sincerity as I thought the thinly veiled warning had been delivered in. (As things turned out, though, perhaps I did the fellow an injustice, and it had been sincerely meant.) I directed the manifest I'd retrieved to Plubek's 'sphere, but, to my surprise, he simply redirected it to a hand-held datapack he'd pulled out of his pocket. I regarded it curiously. "What's that for?"

"What does it look like?" My incomprehension must still have shown on my face, because his own held a faintly condescending expression now. "Making a permanent record."

Can't you just mesh with the datanode back at the customs post? I asked, and the fellow actually smiled.

"You really are a dirtwalker, aren't you? Not everywhere's the same as where you grew up."

"I'm not sure I follow," I said, leading the way out onto the catwalk over Number One hold.

Plubek sighed. "Not everyone uses neuroware. Some places don't trust it. Which means they do things the old-fashioned way, with handhelds, and so do their merchant crews. And don't get me started on the Sanctified Brethren—paper and clipboards. Faugh."

"That must make your job quite difficult," I said, deploying the appearance of polite interest I'd honed to perfection though innumerable social engagements.

"You have no idea," Plubek said. "Especially with the number of trade partners Numarkut has." He began poking at some crates which had preceded me aboard. "So we standardized on the handhelds. What's in here?"

"Apple brandy," I said, reaching into the shared space where our 'spheres overlapped, and filleting out the appropriate item from the manifest.

"Like I've not heard that before," Plubek said skeptically. "Avalon's principal export, if you believe the paperwork. And it just happens to attract the lowest rate of tariff." He gestured to the crate. "Let's see it. And if it's Silverwine in brandy bottles I won't be amused."

"Hang on," I said, rummaging around the tool locker for a crowbar. The little handheld fascinated me, a concentrated mass of data, on the edge of the 'sphere, but walled off from it. This was precisely the kind of thing Aunt Jenny would be interested in, I thought, logging the comings and goings of every ship Plubek had boarded, along with their cargoes, crew complements, and heaven knows what other juicy little nuggets of information. The problem was how to get at it: I might be able to use the direct interface he'd used himself, but unless he was a complete moron, which I rather doubted, he'd be certain to notice me trying to access it.

But there might be another way . . .

"That's odd," I said, handing him the tool, and standing back as he levered the lid off in a shower of splinters and wood shavings: Avalon's distillers believed in traditional methods of packing their wares as well as producing them, although how much of this was genuine reverence for the generations of craftswomen who'd gone before them, and how much was just appreciation of the premium customers were prepared to pay for a sense of history to accompany their intoxication, I couldn't have said without sounding cynical.

"What is?" Plubek asked, lifting a bottle from its nest of shredded wood. He held it up to the light, and shook it suspiciously, listening to the gurgle. Nothing rattled inside, so it contained only liquid; no contraband hoping to escape notice by holding its breath.

"There's one crate too many," I said, poking the manifest with my sneakware. Getting inside was so simple I didn't even have to think about it, beyond a faint sense of unease as I recalled Remington's threat of dire consequences if I started mucking about in the *Stacked Deck*'s datanode. But the prize was worth the risk. I hoped. . . . Reducing the number of crates recorded by one was the work of an instant, and I pulled back from the manifest with the sense of a job well done. If I'd read my man well, he'd only react in one way. "See?"

"So there is." Plubek shrugged, with an eloquent lack of surprise. "Bloody shipping clerks. Couldn't find their own asses with both hands and a map, some of them." He twisted the cork out, and took a mouthful. Swallowed, and sighed with satisfaction.

"Silverwine?" I asked, and he shook his head.

"Not this time." Which didn't stop him taking another mouthful to be sure. I felt a small glow of triumph, which I was careful not to show. Instead, I tried to look indecisive.

"I should tell the skipper," I said. "This is going to make a real mess of the paperwork. Though he'll probably blame me."

"Of course he will," Plubek agreed, taking another swig. This was going even better than I'd hoped. "You're the newbie. That's your job." Then, to my horror, he recorked the bottle, and replaced it in the crate. "That's enough. Against regulations to be drinking on duty."

He smiled at me, in a manner almost entirely devoid of good humor. "You're not trying to get me so drunk I miss whatever you're really smuggling, are you?"

"No," I said, with perhaps a little too much vehemence.

"Shame. It never works, but I don't mind people trying." He shrugged. "Transgene, see; I stop metabolizing the alcohol as soon as there's just enough in my system to enjoy."

"How very nice for you," I said.

"Perk of the job." A calculating look entered his eye. "But I wouldn't want you getting in any trouble with your skipper. Maybe this crate better just disappear."

"Maybe it should," I said. "Stop anyone spotting the discrepancy."

Then my own words struck me like a bucket of ice water. He'd already downloaded a copy of the unmodified manifest to the handheld. If I couldn't find a way in there to make the same adjustment, my meddling would be immediately obvious. Remington would turf me off the ship, and I'd probably find myself on the wrong side of a ton of Numarkut laws and customs regulations to boot.

"Just what I was thinking." He sent a brief signal, and within a couple of minutes a drone emblazoned with the crest of the Numarkut Excise was hoisting the crate and buzzing out of the hold with it. "Now, what else have you got down here?"

As our tour of the holds progressed, I began to understand how the system worked; and, how, gallingly, I'd got myself into potentially serious trouble for no good reason. Anything, it seemed, which caught his fancy, Plubek would decide had been improperly packed, or contravened some local regulation, and impound. And anything impounded would immediately be scooped up by the drone, to be conveyed to the hold of his customs cutter. Which, fortunately, was small enough to have docked comfortably inside only one of ours, or, I suspected, our cargo would simply have been gutted. (A suspicion I was later to discover was entirely unfounded: an elaborate informal, but nonetheless rigidly adhered to, protocol existed between the Guild and the Numarkut Excise, governing precisely how much they could confiscate, and which items that, though technically prohibited, they would regrettably fail to notice.)

At the time, though, I was barely aware of what was going on around me, being completely preoccupied with the problem of cracking Plubek's handheld. Going in through his 'sphere was clearly not going to be an option. However, if it was supposed to interface with old-fashioned technologies, as he'd intimated, there was bound to be a port for that. Not ideal, but if it was my only way in, I'd just have to find a way. In the meantime, I spun things out as long as I could, with a stream of the kind of content-free conversation I'd been perfecting since my first cotillion.

Once again, my gift for improvised data manipulation came to my rescue. Every time the drone removed an item from the hold it sent an update to Plubek's handheld, and once I'd noticed that, I recorded the next exchange. Sure enough, there was an identifiable key at the start of the datablurt, and as soon as I'd got into that, I could set to work. Stripping out the datanomes I needed, and carefully walling off the area of my 'sphere I was working in from the connection Plubek was maintaining, I swapped them into my sneakware and poked cautiously at the handheld's access port.

To my relief, and, I must confess, some degree of surprise, it worked first time. There wasn't any leisure for self-congratulation, though; Plubek could mesh directly with the device again at any moment, and I had to be in and out again before he did.

My first surprise was how little information there was in there. Personal 'spheres tended to be linked to a nearby node most of the time, conferring almost limitless access and storage; but the relatively primitive handheld was constrained by its architecture, unable to spill over into the wider datasphere. Unless that was a deliberate security feature, of course: as that thought occurred to me, I resolved to be even more circumspect.

Fortunately, the *Stacked Deck*'s manifest was the first thing I came across, and repeating my modification to the inventory the work of a nano. After that, I couldn't hang about for long enough to see what else the handheld contained, so I simply grabbed copies of everything and fled. My own 'sphere was too small to contain it all, but I'd been allocated a bit of personal space on the ship's node (with further threats from Remington of dire consequences if I ever misused it), so I simply diverted my digital spoils there, and hoped for the best. I'd walled off the area with some basic privacy protocols (nothing like as sophisticated as I could have done, but I didn't want to advertise just how skilled I was at this sort of thing—which would probably have made my shipmates a little nervous), and I was under no illusions that they'd hold for long if anyone was serious about taking a peek—which was why I hadn't stored anything sensitive there up until now. I briefly considered upgrading the security on the fly, but decided against it, on the grounds that doing so would only draw attention to the fact that there was something worth looking at there now; better just to let sleeping dogs lie.

As the data took a subjectively eternal two or three seconds to copy across I found myself holding my breath in an agony of suspense, convinced that Plubek would notice the transfer; but he remained focused on the cargo, no doubt looking for something else worth filching. As the last few shreds of data slipped out of my 'sphere he straightened up, a bottle of Silverwine in each hand.

"Improperly stamped," he said, shaking his head sorrowfully, although the vintner's impression in the wax seal below the cork seemed clear enough to me. "I'll have to impound it."

"Better safe than sorry," I agreed, colluding in the game. "Where to next?"

"I think we're done," the Inspector said, which came as no surprise. He'd already been through all the other holds by this point, and I had no doubt that his own was so full there wasn't room for any more "contraband" anyway. "Where's Captain Remington?"

"I'm not sure, exactly," I said, truthfully enough, although I was pretty sure I could narrow it down to one of two possible locations. As it was, though, I was spared the potential embarrassment of interrupting his consultation with the chief engineer by the clatter of boot soles on the metal stairway, followed almost at once by the skipper himself. To my pleased surprise Clio was at his elbow, and favored me with a slightly perfunctory nod of greeting.

"All done, are we?" Remington asked cheerfully, and Plubek nodded.

"I believe so, Captain. Everything seems to be in order, although some items in your manifest appear to be unaccounted for. I suggest you adjust it accordingly." The manifest appeared in the datasphere, the items he'd pilfered highlighted.

"Bloody shipping clerks." Remington shook his head ruefully, pretending to believe the bare-faced lie, and not fooling anyone for a second. "Thank you for your diligence."

"And you for your co-operation." The formal words were delivered politely by both, but I'd heard enough superficially civil conversations in Avalonian society to pick up on the mutual antipathy at once.

"Miss Rennau will see you back to the airlock," Remington said.

Clio stepped forward on cue, and nodded to Plubek. "This way."

She turned, and began to lead the way up the stairs without a backward glance, although I had no doubt that the Inspector had seen the inside of enough standard freighters to be able to find his own way back without any trouble at all. The real reason for the apparent courtesy was that Remington didn't trust the man anywhere out of the eyeline of at least one of his crew, and with good reason so far as I could see.

"That went well," Remington said, without much detectable sarcasm, as Plubek disappeared from view. Then he turned to me, his face stern. "Remember what I said about you playing silly buggers with the node on my ship?"

"Yes, skipper." The words forced themselves past a sudden constriction in my throat. It seemed whatever Remington had been up to with Sowerby, clearly not the conclusion I'd jumped to, it hadn't taken his attention off the *Stacked Deck*'s datanode. The sudden inrush of data I'd purloined would have been instantly noticeable to anyone meshing in at an oversight level—which, it belatedly occurred to me, would be precisely what a captain and his chief engineer would have been doing if they were plotting vectors and power consumption for our optimum approach to Numarkut.

Remington nodded soberly. "Good. I have to tell you I've been thinking very hard since you came aboard about whether or not to offer you that apprenticeship, or just dump you as soon as we hit dirtside. But it looks as though you've just made the decision for me."

"Guess it does," I said, feeling all my hopes curdle yet again. Another chance squandered by Simon the screw-up. At least I was consistent, although that was scant consolation at the moment.

Remington slapped me on the back. "God alone knows how you got away with it, but that stuff you siphoned off is pure gold. Can you do it again?"

"I guess so," I said. Now I'd got the trick of it, I should be able to access pretty much any handheld I came across, if the owner wasn't paying sufficient attention. "But if you're putting me off the ship—"

"Off the ship?" Remington was looking at me as though I'd just announced I was taking holy orders and looking forward to a lifetime of celibacy. "Why the hell would I throw away an edge like that? I know what's moving in and out system, how much Plubek's skimming from his supervisor's cut, and which brokers are most desperate for liquidity. All thanks to you." He drew a guild patch, with its hand and galaxy emblem, from his pocket, and handed it to me; I must confess I was so surprised I took it automatically, without any conscious volition. "Get that sewn on when you have a moment."

"Right. Yes. I will." Part of my mind warned me I was beginning to babble, but the rest of it didn't care. "Thanks, skipper. Really. You won't regret this, I promise."

"If I do, you'll regret it a damn sight more than me. *I* promise." Remington grinned, with what looked like honest amusement. "Now go and find something useful to do."

"Useful. Right. I had a broom somewhere . . ." I started up the staircase, feeling his eyes on my back the whole way.

I was an apprentice. Officially a member of the Commerce Guild, at least from the moment Remington logged my induction. But I was under no illusion as to why. He thought I'd be useful, but he'd never really trust me—men like Remington have secrets of their own, and keeping someone close who excelled at uncovering other people's would feel like carrying an unsheathed blade around in his pocket, never quite sure when it would cut his own hand. He'd be watching my every move from now on, and that was going to make my commission from Aunt Jenny even more difficult than it already was.

CHAPTER TWELVE
In which Clio and I decline the offer of a lift.

"How are you planning to celebrate?" Clio asked, as we passed through one of the cargo hatches, and I felt drizzle on my face for the first time in what seemed like forever. Numarkut didn't have much of an orbital infrastructure, which I found slightly odd for such a major trade hub—but apparently the locals didn't like the idea of cargoes being transshipped without hitting dirt first, in case any enterprising merchant crews (in other words, all of them) started cutting private deals instead of going through the local brokers.

"I thought we already had." I pulled my hat a little further down over my face, and raised a farewell hand to Rennau, who was lounging just inside the open cargo hatch, scowling at the low-lying clouds wreathing the aptly-named Dullingham Downs. As far as the eye could see, landing cradles rose from barren heathland and gently rolling hills, interspersed with soggy scrub and bracken. Almost unconsciously, my hand rose to brush a few droplets of moisture from the crisp new Guild patch on my jacket.

"That was just welcoming you aboard," Clio said, narrowing her eyes against the drizzle. The news of my freshly minted apprenticeship had got round the crew as rapidly as you might expect, and one drink had led to another, to the point where I'd started to envy Plubek his tweak; especially if it conferred immunity to hangovers. "Let's find a bar and celebrate properly."

"Just the two of us?" I asked. That didn't sound like much of a party to me, but at least it would be quieter.

"If you like," Clio said, in a casual tone that sounded faintly forced. If I'd heard it in Carenza's voice, or any Avalonian gentlewoman's for that matter, I'd have jumped to the conclusion that she had a lot more than just a quiet drink in mind. But Clio was a Guilder, and played by a different set of rules. Better to remain non-committal, at least for now; if she hadn't been making a pass after all, responding as though she had could lead to all kinds of problems. She raised a hand to her father. "See you later, Dad. I'm just going to show Simon the sights."

And that was another thing. The second most senior man aboard wasn't that keen on me either—a situation offending, or starting a relationship with, his daughter wouldn't exactly help to improve.

"Right." Rennau transferred his scowl from the weather to me. "Mind you watch your step."

"I'll be fine," I assured him. "I've got Clio with me."

"Exactly." For some reason that failed to reassure him, although I was sure I'd be perfectly all right with her as a guide. He nodded to Rolf and Lena, who were heading out arm in arm; both grimaced as the damp air met their faces, and Rolf emitted something which, in a higher register, might have been a squeal of disconcerted surprise.

"How do dirtwalkers manage to live in an environment you can't heat up and dry out?" he asked, with a glance in my direction.

Unsure whether the question was rhetorical or not, I just shrugged. "You get used to it."

"I'll take your word for that." He sounded unconvinced, and looked on the point of turning back, until his wife tugged gently on his upper arm, with enough force to bend a girder.

"It's called 'weather.' If you ever left the ship, you'd find out about it." She steered him firmly onto the rain-slick metal platform surrounding the equator of the *Stacked Deck*, and it suddenly occurred to me that I could see the exterior of our ship for the first time. With a parting nod to Rennau, I hurried after the couple, Clio trotting at my heels.

"They do that every time we hit dirt," Clio said, bumping into me as I stopped suddenly, looking up at the vast, curving bulk of the *Stacked Deck*. She glanced at me, and shrugged. "I guess that sort of thing's bound to happen when shipborns and dirtwalkers hook up. But it works for them."

"They seem very well suited," I agreed absently, my attention still on the exterior of the ship. It was as featureless as I'd expected, the bare metalwork as smooth and unblemished as it had been the day it came out of the shipyard moulds in a system somewhere I'd never even heard of. The equatorial hatches were all level with the platform which surrounded the docking cradle, although the only one open was the one we'd just left by, and which Rennau seemed determined to guard until Remington returned. Not that I could see the point myself—no one was likely to come calling now the formalities were over, and Sowerby's engineering crew weren't going anywhere until all the systems were powered down, checked thoroughly, and walloped with the right sized wrench, so it wasn't as if the ship was exactly being left unattended.

Anyhow, with the skipper away dealing with the Harbormaster, and arranging for the cargo to be discharged, the rest of us had nothing much to do; which meant everyone who could was heading into the town I'd been reliably informed was lurking somewhere in the distance, where the moorland met the lowering sky.

"Do you want a ride?" Lena asked, from the back of an open cargo sled hovering by the edge of the loading platform, the only vehicle for hire which could possibly have accommodated her and her husband. I considered it for a moment, then shook my head. Clio and I would have been jammed in to whatever space the two of them had left, which would hardly be comfortable at the best of times, and the light rain showed no sign of easing off.

"Already called a cab, thanks," I lied, pinging in a request as I spoke. With a cheerful wave, the couple peeled away, and joined the steady stream of sleds and cargo haulers weaving between the forest of cradles like vast metallic insects in search of ferrous nectar.

"Good call," Clio said, apparently sanguine about the prospect of having to wait a few minutes in the wet for our ride to arrive. "Much more fun drinking when your ribs haven't been cracked."

I indicated the open hatch behind us, from which Rennau continued to glower. "We can go back inside, if you like."

"I'm okay." She tilted her head slightly, to let the rain fall full on her face, as if taking a shower. The thought sparked some mental images I pushed firmly to the corner of my mind, for later appreciation, feeling faintly uncomfortable as I did so. I'd already decided my position was precarious enough without adding any further complications to it, and nibbling away at that resolve wasn't exactly going to help. Besides, I couldn't be entirely sure I wasn't misreading the signals I thought she was giving off. "I like the way the weather just does what it wants." She smiled. "The first time I ever felt wind, I was about nine months old. I thought there was a hull breach, and screamed the place down."

"You can remember that?" I asked, faintly surprised.

"No, of course not." She directed the smile at me. "But it's one of Dad's favorite 'embarrass your daughter' stories. Especially if he's talking to a boy I like."

"Are there many of those?" I asked, without thinking, most of my attention still on the arrivals and departures going on around us. From here I could see about thirty cradles, roughly two thirds of them occupied; as I watched, a ship broke free of its girderwork nest and fell upwards, disappearing through the cloud layer in a matter of moments, while another couple drifted over the harbor like bright metal soap bubbles, descending slowly towards their assigned berths.

"A few." Clio seemed disconcerted by the question. "But you know how it is in the Guild. Here today, gone tomorrow. None of them really lasted."

"Lucky you," I said, and her eyes narrowed. "My mother hoarded embarrassing stories about me. Which she trotted out at every opportunity. They lasted a lot longer than I'd have liked."

Her face cleared. "No, I meant . . . Never mind." She pointed at a fast-moving sled, peeling off from the traffic lane to head in our direction, apparently happy to change the subject. "Is that our ride?"

"It is," I confirmed, after meshing briefly with the onboard processor. It seemed manual piloting was prohibited in the docking area, which, considering the number of ships, vehicles and drones in the air, seemed more than sensible. It wasn't much to look at, a basic utility model, sprayed gray beneath the grime, but at least it was enclosed. It drifted into the platform, and popped the passenger door on the side facing us. "Where to?"

"Let me." Clio scrambled in, already meshing with the AI, feeding it a destination as she settled herself on the padded bench seat in the rear. I followed, a little more carefully.

"Seems like you know the city well," I said, as the door closed, sealing us in with the smell of wet hair and damp clothing.

"About as well as I know anywhere dirtside," she agreed. "You can't

do much trade in this part of the Sphere without passing through
Numarkut a lot."

"I guess not," I agreed. The rifts would see to that, funneling trade
through the nexus they created there; an economic advantage which
guaranteed the system's independence, as well as its prosperity. I knew
the Commonwealth had made innumerable diplomatic overtures over
the last few centuries, attempting to convince the authorities there to
abandon its neutrality and join us, just as the League, and probably a
few other local powers, had too: but the Numarkuteers had steadfastly
resisted all blandishments. And who could blame them? Why become
a client state, and watch the bulk of their wealth drain down the nearest
rift?

Of course some states were more belligerent than others, but
Numarkut was as safe from invasion as it was possible to be: not from
the size of its Navy, which was essentially non-existent (customs
cutters like Plubek's were about as close to a warship as the system
possessed), but from the size of everyone else's. Numarkut was too
important to the economies of all the regional powers for any of them
to stand idly by while one of their neighbors attempted to seize it, and
anyone foolish enough to try would be on the wrong end of the gun
ports of every other state in the vicinity. Even the League or the
Commonwealth would be hopelessly outgunned by such an alliance,
let alone the small fry. So, despite the envy of everyone surrounding
them, Numarkut sat comfortably at the center of the local rift network,
getting steadily richer and more corrupt, to the great satisfaction of its
citizens.

"Hang on," Clio warned, as the cab lifted away from the cradle.
"These things can get a little rough to ride in sometimes." As if to
underline her words, it banked abruptly, and dived for the traffic lane
nearest the ground, where most of the passenger vehicles were
congregated. With the greater part of my attention still on the novel
sight of the *Stacked Deck*'s outer hull, I was taken by surprise, and fell
heavily against her. "Oof."

"Sorry." I scrambled back to my half of the seat. "I see what you
mean."

"I did warn you." She grinned, amused at my discomfiture, and
regained her own balance with an easy shrug. Maintaining it seemed
to involve sitting close enough for our thighs to touch, which I must

admit I had no objection to; after half a lifetime of fending off Carenza, and all too many like her, it felt pleasant to be with a woman who seemed to like me for who I was, not just what I looked like.

"Lucky we didn't take that lift with Rolf and Lena," I said. She nodded again. "You weren't really joking about cracking a rib, were you?"

"Not entirely," Clio agreed, settling back against the upholstery.

The cab continued to slalom its way between the towering cradles, surrounded by traffic, and I found myself glancing up at the starships balanced above us. Somehow they seemed a lot bulkier from this angle, looming over us in a manner I couldn't help but find vaguely threatening.

"So you should," Clio agreed, when I spoke the thought aloud. "If the gravitics go off, the cradles would just collapse. We'd be squished like a bug." Which, I must admit, hadn't occurred to me, but was kind of obvious when you came to think about it. Starships were big, and correspondingly heavy. Far too much so to be held aloft by an assemblage of girders, however solid they might appear.

"But Sarah's powering them down," I said, faintly uneasy. Gravitics were like everything else in everyday usage: reliable enough to be used without thinking, but needing maintenance now and again to stay that way. Of course the *Stacked Deck* wasn't about to plummet to the ground, but even so, the image was a worrying one.

"Not ours. The cradle's." Clio meshed into the cab's primitive node, nudging the flight instructions. The little sled began to rise, out of the main stream of the traffic, twisting back and forth as it evaded the heavier commercial vehicles in the higher lanes—which threw Clio and me together again, in a fashion I must admit to finding far from unpleasant. She pointed out of the window. "See?"

"Right." I peered through the murk at the nearest cradle, which was unoccupied, a circle of leaden sky visible through the hole in the loading platform into which a ship would nestle. Ground crew, in garish visibility jackets, were working on platforms and gantries beneath the wide, flat ring, no doubt grateful for the shelter it afforded from the never-ending rain. It was hard to be sure as we swept past, but several of them seemed to be working on gravitic coils embedded in the structure of the tower. "So those units hold the ships in place."

"That's right." Clio nodded, then grinned, in the mischievous fashion with which I was becoming so familiar. "Unless their power fails, of course."

"Of course." But that wouldn't happen. All the port's power systems would be multiply redundant, to prevent just such a catastrophe from occurring.

Override limits reached. Resuming standard course, the sled's AI grumbled, in what could fancifully be taken as an aggrieved tone.

Clio sighed. "Don't you sometimes wish you could just take manual control? We'd be there in half the time."

"Say no more." I don't honestly know where the impulse to show off came from; but I liked the girl, and I suppose I wanted to impress her. It was trivially easy for me to mesh with the guidance system, penetrate it with my sneakware, and override the flight controls while leaving the simple device convinced it was still following the parameters programmed into it. "What would you like to do?"

"I don't know. Something exciting." Clio shrugged.

"Something exciting, coming up." I fed power into the gravitics, pointing the nose skyward. The cab shot up and out of the traffic lanes, the collision avoidance system getting a real workout in the process, which added a few jolts and lurches to our progress.

Clio squealed. "What the hell do you think you're playing at? You'll get us killed!"

"No, I won't," I assured her. She seemed to believe me, too, God knows why, leaning forward eagerly in her seat as the idea sunk in that I was in full control of the hurtling cab.

"Prove it. Shoot the cradle."

For a second or so I wondered what she meant, and then I registered the circle of sky visible beyond the platform I'd been staring at. The idea was irresistible.

"Brilliant." I aimed for the center of the bullseye, and we shot up and through the thick steel ring in a long, smooth parabola, topping out about a hundred feet above it: which was still below the tops of the hulls of the ships in the occupied cradles. Glancing back, I saw several of the maintenance workers shouting and gesticulating in our general direction: I wasn't entirely sure what they were saying, but somehow I doubted that they were complimenting me on my flying ability.

Clio had noticed them too. "Uh oh. We could be in trouble."

"Don't think so." I took us around the nearest freighter, out of their eyeline. "We'd have been past so quick they won't have got a good look at us." This vessel looked a little different from the *Stacked Deck,* its hull less smooth: small metallic blisters ran around it, every thirty degrees, with a larger one on the top. They looked uncannily like the emitters of a warship's offensive graviton beams, although I couldn't for the life of me imagine why a warship would be docked at a commercial starport. Its beacon was transmitting a clear ident, though; the *Eddie Fitz,* non-Guild, registered to a shipping company on Downholm. A League world, a couple of rifts away from Numarkut.

"What about our nav system, though?" Clio fretted. "If Traffic Control mesh in . . ."

"They'll find we're pootling along in the designated passenger lane," I assured her. "It's not the first time I've done this sort of thing, you know." Which was sort of true—we didn't have automated traffic control on Avalon, as the aristocracy felt the odd fatal accident was a small price to pay to avoid the inconvenience of having their movements recorded and restricted, and what was good enough for them bloody well ought to be good enough for the rest of us, but I'd redacted the memories of a fair few trips Mother would have disapproved of from the family runabout's diagnostic systems over the years.

Right about then, though, I was more interested in the *Eddie Fitz.* There wouldn't be anything about her in the hoard of data I'd purloined from Plubek, as she'd have arrived through one of the rifts leading into the League, but the beacon might be informative. I ran quickly through the class and registry details, probing more deeply than the public datacast, to access the additional information she'd passed on to the Harbormaster's office. Former transport for the League fleet auxiliary, mothballed about twelve years ago, sold on to the Toniden Line after a decade or so, and refitted as a civilian freighter. Modifying the hull after stripping out the armament would have been hideously expensive, so the housings had just been left *in situ.* Of course they'd make balancing the grav field around the hull while shooting a rift a bit more tricky, but nothing a halfway decent bit of 'ware couldn't handle, especially with a competent engineer riding herd on it. She seemed to be on a regular run, with three visits to Numarkut recorded in the last six months, but I didn't have time to worm any more out of the system: we were already moving away from the cradle at a rapid clip, and the beacon's power was low, only intended to guide drones and cargo sleds to the right platform once they were in its immediate vicinity.

"If you say so," Clio said, a little dubiously, then glanced at me with a sparkle of mischief in her eyes. "But I guess if you're wrong we're already in trouble, so . . . how fast can you get us to that drink?"

"This fast," I said, overriding the limiter on the power plant, and pinning us back in our seat with another surge of acceleration.

CHAPTER THIRTEEN
In which a small change of plan leads to an unexpected party.

The city of Dullingham lived up to its name just as much as the landing field had. As soon as we crossed the city limits I returned control of the cab to its onboard systems, which remained blissfully unaware that they'd ever been tampered with, and sat back to enjoy the sights, only to discover that there weren't any.

All right, that was a little unfair. According to the city guide I was able to access through the cab's node, Dullingham possessed parks, a cathedral, a municipal art gallery housing several notable works by a renowned Numarkut artist I'd never heard of before, and a botanical garden containing specimens of flora from a dozen different worlds, all of them colorful, and hardly any of which were lethally toxic. Not to mention theatres, music halls, and a fun fair, if your recreational tastes were a little less refined. But the part we were traversing was universally damp and cheerless.

Which, I suppose, was only to be expected. This close to the docks they exerted their own kind of gravitational attraction, pulling in services and utility zones, while the majority of residential areas and their associated amenities drifted to the opposite side of the river dividing the city. Most of the buildings around us were warehouses, ancient and weather-stained, some of them probably dating back as far as the first settlement. Generations of addition and refurbishment had kept them structurally sound, while a few newer structures, like fresh dentures in a gum full of rotting teeth, gave mute testament to those which had given up the battle with the passing of the years. (Or, more prosaically, had proven cheaper to knock down and replace than to keep on repairing.)

"Why did you do that?" Clio asked, as I disengaged from the node, and the cab dropped back to the officially sanctioned pace of an arthritic slug. With good reason, I must admit, the roads between the warehouses being full of big, heavy cargo sleds with a lot of inertia, drone lifters buzzing up and down between the curbside and the higher levels, and people milling around between them, either contributing to the general bustle, or getting somewhere far away from it as quickly as possible. Dusk was coming on by now, accelerated by the looming clouds and the high walls all around us, and lamps were beginning to kindle, spilling puddles of sticky yellow light, which wavered slightly every time a fast-moving cargo sled in the upper traffic lane sent the supporting drones bobbing in the backwash of its passing, across the street below.

"Too much chance of bumping into something," I said, a little regretfully, as our high-speed dash across the landing field had been quite exhilarating. "Besides, if those cradlejacks did get a look at us, we want to look like a sled that's behaving itself in front of all these people."

"Good point." She leaned forward a little, to look out of the window on my side of the cab. "Besides, we're almost there. Don't want to make too big an entrance."

"Quite," I agreed. Even though Guilders seemed to have a fairly flexible relationship with local law enforcement, I was pretty sure entering a tavern without getting out of the sled first would be frowned upon.

The cab hummed round a corner, and most of the commercial traffic disappeared; only a few short-term storage facilities seemed to be on this street, and, beyond the next intersection, a mixture of residential and commercial properties began: low-rent housing for the small army of workers required to keep the dockyard and its cargo handling facilities running smoothly, and the ancillary businesses which would inevitably spring up around them, in an effort to siphon off a portion of their wages. Chief among them, of course, were bars and bordellos, the latter easily distinguished by the number of scantily-clad men and women lounging around in the lobby, eyeing up every passerby with bright smiles and dead eyes. Most were heavily made-up, in an effort to disguise the accelerated aging endemic to their vocation, but without much success. There were a surprising number of transgeners among them too: Aunt Jenny had been right about the popularity of tails, although in this context I found the tweak, and the reasons for its choice I tried hard not to think about, quite profoundly disturbing.

"Anything you like?" Clio asked, and I felt my face flame scarlet.

"Of course not," I said, and she glanced across at me, looking faintly confused: only then did I realize she'd been scanning the diners and food stalls lining the sidewalk on the opposite side of the street. "I mean, I ate before we came out. Thanks."

"Maybe later." She grinned, picking up on the subtext of the exchange. "I said I'd buy you a drink, Si, not a hooker."

"Good," I said, a bit too vehemently, and she snickered quietly, greatly amused by my evident confusion. "Kind as the offer would be, I'm afraid I'd have to turn it down."

"Not the sort of thing an Avalonian gentleman does?" she teased.

"Definitely not," I agreed, relieved that she found the whole thing so amusing. "Avalonian ladies, on the other hand . . ." Tinkie had never made any secret of her escapades while on leave, many of which seemed to have involved paid participants, although whether she'd been entirely truthful, or embroidering these accounts because my disapproval amused her so much, I had no idea. The thought of my sister was a poignant one, not least because we'd parted on such bad terms, and I found myself casting about for something to banish the sudden sensation of loss which threatened to overwhelm me. "Let's walk from here."

"Good idea," Clio said, instructing the cab to pull over.

We disembarked on a damp and crowded sidewalk, the sled rising and pulling away in search of fresh customers as soon as the door closed behind us. I debated with my conscience about whether I should mesh back in briefly to inflate the fare, to compensate for the additional wear and tear I'd inflicted on the little vehicle's systems, but for once I won: no point in leaving any anomalous traces of meddling which might lead to trouble later on.

For a mercy, the persistent drizzle we'd set out in had moderated to a thin Scottish mist, hazing the air between the hovering lights, and the garish illumination spilling from food emporia, tavern, and brothel alike. If there was any other kind of business on the street I didn't see it, although I suppose some of the rooms on the upper floors could easily have been offices of some kind rather than the apartments I assumed at the time.

The first thing which struck me, apart from the noise, was the smell: damp air, of course, but intermingled with the odors of sizzling meat and fish from the open-air stalls, and spicier aromas from the more permanent premises. Ozone, from the power plants of the sleds and drones hurrying by, and the sickly sweet smell of too many people in too little space who haven't had a chance to dry out yet.

"Which way?" I asked, and to my complete lack of surprise, Clio began to stroll off down the street in the direction we'd been going aboard the cab.

"It's not far," she assured me, after I'd trotted a couple of steps to catch up.

Not that I minded. Even constricted as it was, the thoroughfare seemed huge and open after the narrow corridors of the *Stacked Deck*, the constant bubble and hum of humanity around us curiously invigorating. I was, of course, reminded of the streets I'd followed my aunt along on Skyhaven, but here there was no initial sense of order, like the one I'd experienced on first leaving her apartment. Even the miserable weather seemed there to remind me of the random nature of the world, a raw, vibrant presence, instead of the omnipresent blandness of the residential sectors of the orbital.

"Pardon me." A young transgener, his purple fur, bisected by a vertical blue stripe down the center of his face, and matted against his skin by the rain, shot me an apologetic look as our shoulders bumped, forced together by the press of the crowd.

I nodded politely, trying not to gag at the smell, which reminded me rather too strongly of a wet dog. "You're welcome," I said, shooting a hand into my pocket. Sure enough I grabbed a wriggling tail, trifurcated at the tip into rudimentary fingers, which I squeezed tightly until my would-be pickpocket's lips compressed into a thin line. My point made, I released it, feeling the extraneous limb withdraw back to the open air. "We all make mistakes."

I half expected some thinly veiled threat in response, but the fellow just beat a hasty retreat, disappearing into the crowd with an expression in which relief, resentment and contempt seemed curiously intermingled.

"Nicely done," Clio said. "I wondered if you'd spot what he was up to."

"I didn't," I admitted. "I've just got a nasty suspicious mind."

"And good reflexes," Clio said, with what seemed to be a hint of admiration.

I shrugged. "Athlete, remember?"

To my relief we were coming to a block consisting mainly of bars and diners, with fewer of the less reputable businesses (and their distracting employees) to be seen. Though many of the passersby were dressed like cargo handlers and other port employees, Clio and I were far from being the only ships' crew visible: clearly the local recreation industry was flourishing because it catered to their needs as well as to the locals. Which made sense—when you were only going to be around for as long as it took to unload one cargo and find another, you wouldn't want to spend too much time travelling to find your entertainment. Most of the starfarers wore Guild patches somewhere on their clothing, although a minority didn't, sporting the logo of a non-Guild shipping line instead, or, in a couple of cases, nothing at all.

"Freebooters," Clio said when I asked, with an expression of deep disapproval. "Non-Guilders who've got hold of a ship somehow, and scrape a living hustling what work they can."

"Sounds tough," I said, neutrally. If Rennau had lost the *Stacked Deck* to financial misfortune, with the resources of the Guild behind him, I could barely imagine how hard an independent trader would find it to keep their ship in the sky.

"Better believe it," Clio said, with a venomous glare at the oblivious back of a photosynthesising transgener, whose usual lack of clothing was augmented by a tattooed ship's patch on her upper arm. "The only way they can compete with the Guild is by cutting their margins so much they can barely break even on a run. Unless they just steal the cargo instead."

"Does that happen often?" I asked. Getting a reputation for that sort of thing didn't sound like good business to me, and I suspected she might be exaggerating. Clearly there was no love lost between Guilders and the Freebooters.

"Now and again," Clio said. "Not so often you won't find a shipper willing to take the risk. Or threatening to, to get the price down." She watched the green woman undulate into a tavern, accompanied by a couple of her shipmates, and sighed. "Damn. We'll have to find a different bar now."

"Really?" I wasn't just surprised, I was faintly shocked. "Just because there are a few Freebooters in there?"

"There'll be more than a few," she said. "They stick together. Walk in there wearing that—" she indicated my Guild patch—"and we'll be fighting our way out again."

"I can take care of myself," I said, with more confidence than I felt.

"Right." Clio seemed unconvinced. "But we're still finding a different bar."

I glanced up and down the street. They all looked pretty much the same from where I was standing.

"Pardon me," a voice said at my elbow, in the slightly nasal tones I generally associated with citizens of the League. I stepped aside reflexively, making room for a blond fellow of about my age and height to slip past on the crowded sidewalk, arm in arm with a brunette. Both wore Toniden Line livery, and I glanced at the ship patches on their shoulders as they moved past, moved by no more than idle curiosity— then fought to keep my expression neutral. They were both from the *Eddie Fitz*.

"How about this one, then?" I suggested, indicating the doorway into which they'd disappeared.

Clio shrugged. "Guess it'll do," she agreed.

I'd feared the bar would be too crowded to keep my quarry in sight, but it was still too early in the evening to be really packed; a few of the locals were occupying tables, nursing tankards of ale, having just completed shifts in the nearby warehouses judging by their clothing and general air of fatigue, and the two deckhands from the *Eddie Fitz* were turning away from the bar counter, similar mugs in their hands. I spotted five or six other little groups of starfarers in there as well, mainly from Toniden Line vessels, although there were a few Guild patches at a couple of other tables. No Freebooters, though, much to my relief, as I strongly suspected that if there had been, Clio would simply have turned and walked back out again.

"What'll you have?" I asked, as we approached the counter, slipping my hand into my jacket pocket for my purse. We wouldn't be getting our full wages until the cargo had been signed and paid for, but Remington had handed out a small advance in the local currency as soon as we'd landed: a Guild custom I heartily appreciated, as my own stock of cash had run seriously low.

"I'm getting the first one," Clio said. "I promised you a drink, remember?"

"Far be it from me to make a Guilder break her word," I said, not quite so much in jest as I was pretending.

"Men have died for less," she agreed, in the sort of voice people use when they're making a joke out of something which might be literally true. She turned to the bar, which seemed to have been put together from preformed plastic units imprinted with an unconvincing wood grain effect, and spoke to the man behind it. "Two beers, warm enough to taste." She glanced back at me. "That is how you like it, right? Not how they ruin it on Skyhaven?"

"Perfect," I said, as she returned her attention to the bartender. He kept up a continual stream of small talk as he drew the drinks, to which she responded with a fair degree of animation; which was fine by me, as it was keeping her nicely distracted. As I'd reached for the purse, my fingers had encountered something else in the bottom of my pocket which had definitely not been there when we left the *Stacked Deck*; something I wanted to investigate at once.

Finding a vacant table to sit at, I slipped the small hard object out of my pocket and looked at it, with my eyes, and through my datasphere: a small, single-use memory cache, pulsing with pent-up information.

There was only one way it could have got there: clearly there had been more to my encounter with the would-be pickpocket than had at first met the eye. But whether he'd left the cache there on purpose, or dropped it by accident when I interrupted him, I had no idea. If it was the former, then why? Chances were it had something to do with my clandestine commission from Aunt Jenny: she'd told me that her local asset would get in touch with me, and perhaps this was his way of doing it. On the other hand, furboy might be an enemy, not an ally, and the tempting payload glittering in the corner of my 'sphere a malign piece of sucker bait, intended to do anything from strip-mining whatever it could from my own 'ware, to pureeing my frontal lobes.

I probed the packet cautiously, but none of the antibodies I'd stacked around it activated, so, somewhat reassured, I slit it open.

Good morning, Simon. My aunt's virtual image hovered on the fringes of my 'sphere, fragmenting and spluttering in the manner of most riftcom transmissions. *If it really is morning when you get this. I've asked Peter to record it and pass it on to you, but he has his own way of going about things.* At the mention of the name I received a brief image of my furry friend from the street, along with a datablurt, listing his surname (Mallow), where he could be contacted (Farland Freight Forwarding, a brokerage which, to my quiet satisfaction, had been close to the top of my self-generated list of possible fronts for her covert communications post), and rather more than I felt I needed to know about his genetweaks, sexual preferences, and taste in fast food. Which just went to show how green I was—only later did I realize that, if I read between the lines, I'd been given all the information required to track him down in a hurry if I needed to.

He's the contact I told you about, Aunt Jenny went on. *If you find anything of interest, channel it back through him.* There was a short pause while I waited for the message to end, then her businesslike demeanor fell away, revealing the woman I'd always thought I knew. *I hope playing spies is as much fun as you thought it would be.*

Its job done, the cache discharged the remaining power in its battery through the circuits in a single electromagnetic pulse, frying its synapses, and making any attempt to reconstruct the message it had carried completely futile.

"What have you got there?" Clio asked, joining me at the table, and placing the tankards between us.

"Piece of junk," I told her truthfully. "Just found it." I dropped it on the tabletop, among the litter of snack wrappers and discarded glasses left by its previous occupants. Like the counter, the furniture was made of lightweight plastic failing to masquerade as wood, which seemed somehow appropriate for my new life. I wasn't quite sure who or what I was any more, or even what I was doing here; I'd followed the couple from the *Eddie Fitz* more or less on impulse, but now I came to think about it, I couldn't see any good reason to have done so. They were drinking, and holding hands, and acting pretty much like everyone else in the place, even Clio and me (apart from the hand-holding). All right, their ship was a little unusual, but it was hardly the first fleet auxiliary to end up in private hands, and they definitely didn't look as though they were planning to invade Rockhall. In fact, if the kiss they were sharing was anything to go by, right about now they probably wouldn't even notice if someone invaded Numarkut.

"Congratulations." Clio raised her mug in an exaggerated toast. "You're now an honorary Guilder. Long may you remain one of us."

"Amen." I clinked my mug against hers, and took an appreciative swallow. Then the exact meaning of her words made its way through the fog of confusion still clouding my synapses. "Honorary? How does that work?"

"You're a full member when you finish your apprenticeship," Clio said, as though explaining to a kindergartner that the sky was blue. "Unless you're Guild born, like me. But you're a dirtwalker. You have to earn it."

"Fair enough," I said, savoring another mouthful of the ale. It seemed we had at least one taste in common. "So that means . . ."

Clio shrugged. "It's academic, really. You're a Guilder for as long as you stick to the rules, but if you screw up badly enough before you finish the apprenticeship, John can turf you out again. Or one of the Guild Masters can."

Great. Given my track record so far, it seemed my days as a Guilder were numbered.

Clio spluttered into her drink. "Don't look like that. It hardly ever happens."

"Glad to hear it." I tried to push the thought to the back of my head, but it bounced straight back to the front again. I shrugged, with a fine show of the nonchalance I couldn't really make myself feel. "I suppose I could always see if the Freebooters were hiring."

The moment the words left my mouth, I knew I'd put my foot in it again. Clio took a slow, deliberate swallow from her tankard, and placed it carefully on the tabletop.

"Don't even joke about it." The tightness of her voice belied the lightness of her words. "Their ships are fatal accidents waiting to happen, and the only Freebooters not in jail are the ones who haven't been caught yet. I wouldn't wish that on my worst enemy."

"Just kidding," I said carefully, feeling as though I was cutting the red wire in a thriller virt. "Anyhow, it's not going to happen." Not if

I could help it, anyway. I'd already had more than my share of second chances, and I wasn't about to squander this one, however my errand for Aunt Jenny turned out. I drained my tankard. "Same again?"

"Why not?" Clio seemed happy to accept a liquid olive branch, so I made my way back to the bar, pulling the leather bag of coins out of my pocket.

The barman smiled at me, the easy professional grin of a man to whom all the faces on the other side of the counter look the same after a while, and made momentary eye contact: just long enough to let me know that he'd registered my presence, and would deal with me as soon as he could. "Be right with you." Then he returned his attention to the customer he was serving.

It was the blond crewman from the *Eddie Fitz*.

"Hi." The word slipped out before I even realized I was speaking. The man turned and looked at me, with an expression of polite curiosity, probably wondering where I knew him from, or if I was about to try and borrow money. "We're docked a couple of cradles away from you. Saw your ship on the way in."

"Did you?" The words were politely neutral, but the intonation said "Piss off." I nodded, pretending to miss the subtext, and deployed the ingenuous expression I'd used at soirees on Avalon to let dull women think they were cleverer than me.

"Unusual design," I said.

"I wouldn't know. I just load the cargo." Then a belated concession to my apparent guilelessness, and a blatant lie, neatly rolled into one. "Nice to have met you."

"You too." I watched him return to his girlfriend, and say something I didn't catch; whatever it was, it made her glance in my direction, and laugh. I began to wonder if gathering intelligence was really my forte.

"What'll it be?" the barman asked, and I dumped the empty mugs on the counter top.

"Two more of these."

"Coming right up." The first mug began to fill. "Been down long?"

"Couple of hours," I said, wondering why he was bothering to repeat the conversation he'd just had with Clio only a few minutes ago, practically verbatim. Perhaps he never listened to the replies. "Just got into town."

"Hope you're having a good time." He placed the second drink on the counter, next to the first. "Anything else?"

Snack to go with it? I sent.

Clio glanced up, and nodded. *Nuts. Roasted.*

"Roasted nuts," I said, craning my neck to get a look at the rest of the selection. "And a packet of beet chips."

"Don't sell many of those," the barman said, dropping the selection next to the drinks. "Not all that popular." There seemed to be faint edge of hostility in his voice now, held carefully in check, and for the first time I remembered Plubek's warning about the locals picking sides. "Except with Commonwealthers."

"That'll be because it's a popular snack there," I said neutrally, locking eyes with him. "How much?"

"Four talents eighty-five." He broke eye contact first, and busied himself with the till.

I pulled out a handful of change, and sorted through it, a couple of coins dropping to the counter, where they rolled and fell sideways in a pool of something sticky. One was a piece of local currency, a five talent piece, the other a Commonwealth guinea, which the barman picked up between finger and thumb, and regarded as if he'd just found a mouse dropping on the counter. I nodded to the five talent piece, and held my hand out for the guinea. "There's five. Keep the change."

"Keep the lot." He picked up the local coin too, and dropped them both into my outstretched palm. "We don't serve your kind in here."

"My kind?" I messaged Clio. *I think we're leaving.*

Why? Then she looked across at us, reading the hostile body language.

"You're Commonwealth. I can smell it on you."

"We've just arrived from Avalon," I said levelly. "Guild ships get around." I pointed, in a slightly exaggerated manner at the Guild patch on my jacket.

"You expect me to believe that? It's just been sewn on."

"Trouble, Dev?" A couple of burly men in Toniden Line livery materialized at my elbow, addressing the barman in friendly tones, which hinted heavily that they were hoping for an affirmative answer.

"Commonwealther stinking the place up." The barman's scowl intensified, as something else belatedly occurred to him. "And he was asking Jaq questions. About his ship."

"Was he?" The burlier of the two digested this, and turned to me, in what he probably imagined was an intimidating manner. "Now why would you do that?"

"We're in an adjacent berth. Just being neighborly." I shifted my weight as unobtrusively as possible, redistributing it, ready for a rapid sidestep. This clown would be the first to swing, while the other tried to get behind me and grab my arms. With the counter impeding them, they could only move one way—if I was quick enough I'd get out from between them, and away while they were still entangled. If I wasn't, on the other hand . . .

"Problem?" Clio asked, in tones of polite enquiry. Preoccupied, I hadn't noticed her approach, or taken much notice of the flicker of message traffic in her datasphere.

"Apparently my money isn't good enough," I said, relieved to have her support, but concerned for her safety. None of the other Guilders in the place seemed inclined to get involved, which didn't surprise me, as there wasn't anything immediately apparent in it for them, and the Leaguers outnumbered them by at least two to one.

"Guilders' money's good everywhere," Clio said, in a brittle tone.

"If he really is one." The barman wasn't about to let it go. "He talks like a Commonwealther."

"I just told you he's a Guilder. Where he was from before that doesn't count."

"So you say." The tone was still skeptical. Clio's jaw clenched, and her face flushed; I wasn't entirely sure, but I thought I heard a collective, sharp inhalation from the other Guilders scattered around the bar.

Before Clio could formulate a reply, the tavern door shivered on its hinges, admitting a blast of cool, damp air. Rolf ducked through, followed by his wife, who nodded an affable greeting to the room in general as she straightened up.

"Sorry we're late." The two of them strolled to the bar, affecting not to notice the little drama going on there, although I had no doubt that Clio had already let them know precisely what was happening. Lena smiled down at Clio and I. "The sidewalks were a little crowded."

"Did we miss much?" Rolf added. The two men flanking me were suddenly a great deal further away.

"Just the first round," I said. "And a debate about snacks."

"And this piece of sewage calling me a liar," Clio added, with a venomous glare at the barman. Rolf and Lena narrowed their eyes, and loomed forward.

"I never said that." The words began to tumble over one another. "Wouldn't doubt a Guilder's word, no one would. Just a small misunderstanding."

"Which I'm sure you're eager to make amends for," Rolf prompted.

"Absolutely." The fellow wilted even more, if that were possible. He turned to Clio. "Profound apologies, milady."

It was probably the honorific that did it—the frown left her face, and she nodded judiciously, biting her lower lip to suppress a smile. "No harm done."

"Your drinks." The barman pushed them across the counter. "And something for your friends. No charge."

"That's very decent of you," I said, exaggerating my Commonwealth accent just enough to rub it in. I raised my voice, so it carried to the corners of the room. "Guilders drink free tonight."

"I didn't mean—" The barman looked horrified, no doubt calculating the financial loss he was about to incur.

"I know," I said quietly, with a meaningful nod at Rolf and Lena. "But you're not about to make a Guilder break his word in front of his friends, are you? That never ends well."

"Of course not." Idiot as he was, he wasn't that much of one.

Clio took my arm. With her free hand she indicated our shipmates, the rest of the Guilders closing on the bar counter, and a handful of others hurrying onto the premises as the word spread. "Looks like you got your party after all," she said.

"Looks like I did," I agreed, although neither of us seemed all that happy about it.

CHAPTER FOURTEEN
In which I receive some unsolicited advice.

I can't honestly remember much about the rest of that evening, although I'm pretty sure the bar was still crowded with Guilders when Clio and I staggered out of a cab onto the *Stacked Deck*'s cradle platform a couple of hours before dawn. Needless to say I'd not been tempted to start playing with this one's guidance system—with my reaction time seriously impeded, the automated systems had been welcome to do all the hard work. I'd half expected Rennau to still be lurking in the hatchway, but there was no sign of him—which probably meant he was asleep. At least I hoped so, after keeping his daughter out most of the night.

"That's what I call a welcoming drink." Clio stumbled against the cab's door sill as she disembarked, and I grabbed her by reflex, fearful of the vertiginous plunge into the darkness only a few feet away. Certain it was now unoccupied, the sled rose, turned, and dropped away into the depths, to become a blinking mote among the innumerable other metallic fireflies streaming around the cradles.

"Careful." I half steered, half carried her a few paces back from the abyss, our progress illuminated by the floodlights spaced around the platform. Drones were still buzzing around the *Eddie Fitz*, a few hundred yards away, disgorging crate after crate into her holds, and I found myself wondering idly what they contained before dismissing the thought. No point in becoming fixated with the wretched barge.

"Um, you can put me down now. If you like." I suddenly became aware that Clio was still pressed to my chest, and loosened my hold. Even so, she seemed to take a few seconds to peel away.

"I'm sorry. I just thought you might . . ."

"Fall. Yes." She looked at me appraisingly. "And we wouldn't want that. Would we?"

"God, no." I pictured the ground so far below. "That would be . . ."

"Messy."

"Very."

"Night, then." Clio waved a slightly unsteady hand in farewell, and made her way to the open hatch in a moderately straight line.

"Quite an evening you two seem to have had." Remington strolled out of the shadows, his hands in his pockets. I started, feeling unaccountably guilty, as though I'd been caught sneaking home after visiting a girl Mother thought was "unsuitable." (Not something that had happened very often, and I'd usually been able to lie my way out of it, citing a training session: which hadn't been so far from the truth, come to think of it, since vigorous physical exercise had almost certainly featured somewhere among the evening's diversions.)

"You heard about that," I said, trying to gauge just how much trouble I was in, if any. I certainly didn't recall any mention of a curfew, although I suppose in the excitement of setting off for my first bout of shore leave, I might have missed something.

"Me, and every other Guilder in the hemisphere. Word gets around fast when there are free drinks involved." He leaned against a nearby stanchion. "Besides, Rolf and Lena got back a short while ago. I got the details from them."

"Oh," I said. "But there weren't any, really. Details, I mean."

"Sounds like you handled it well," Remington said, to my complete surprise. "It'll be a long time before any dirtwalker dregs talk back to a Guilder round here. Hitting a Numarkuteer in the pocket's the best way to get his attention, believe me."

"He deserved it," I said, letting a little of my suppressed anger seep out. "Mouthing off to Clio like that."

"Clio, was it?" Remington said, with a wry half smile. "Way I heard it, he was having a go at you."

"I can take care of myself," I said.

"So can she." The skipper pulled a hip flask from his pocket, and took a swallow. "And if she does, you'd better make sure you're on the same side." He proffered the flask. "Nightcap? Helps keep the cold out."

I shrugged, and took it. Why not? I thought. I'd already drunk so much another mouthful or two wouldn't make a lot of difference. "Thanks." I took a tentative swallow, and found it full of a mellow local spirit I hadn't quite caught the name of earlier in the evening. Lena had tried to tell me, but by that point the bar had become so crowded that it had been almost impossible to make out anything being said to me, even without the alcohol in my system adding its own contribution to the fog.

"Better get some sleep," Remington advised, retrieving the flask. "It's going to be a busy morning."

"Is it?" I followed him inside the ship, our footsteps echoing as we entered the packed hold, weaving our way in between the towering crates towards the central stairwell. "Are we starting to unload the cargo?"

"Most of us." Remington turned, apparently trying to gauge my reaction. "But I'm off to meet one of the local brokers, and find a new one. You're coming too."

"Am I?" I was too surprised to say any more.

Remington nodded. "In the light of this evening's escapade, it's probably best I keep an eye on you, at least until you look more like an old hand. Besides, it'll be useful experience."

"Right," I said. "Thanks."

The skipper grinned. "Thank me in the morning, when the hangover cuts in." He sent a clock reading to my 'sphere, the local time adjusted to the one we kept aboard ship. "You've got about five hours to sleep it off."

CHAPTER FIFTEEN
In which I unexpectedly renew a previous acquaintance.

In the event, I had far less than five hours rest: stray thoughts kept colliding like icebergs, and when I did manage to fall asleep at last it was in fitful, dream-haunted snatches, punctuated by trips to the head to relieve my aching bladder. When I finally gave it up as a bad job, rolled my pounding head off the pillow, and staggered down to the galley, it was scant comfort to find that most of my shipmates seemed hardly better off than I was.

"Drink this," Sowerby said, handing me a mug full of something which looked and smelled as though it had just leaked from a pipe somewhere on the lower decks.

I took it, in a hand that hardly trembled at all. "What is it?"

"Better you don't ask," Remington told me cheerfully, sitting down next to the engineer with a plate full of bacon and eggs, which, to my hypersensitive stomach, hardly smelled any better than Sowerby's mug full of glop.

"If you don't want it, I do." Clio lurched in looking even worse than I felt, grabbed the beverage, and downed it in one, not even pausing for breath. She pulled a nauseated expression as she put the mug down on the tabletop, waited expectantly for a heartbeat or two, then visibly relaxed. So, I noticed, did everyone else in the immediate vicinity. My puzzlement must have shown on my face, because as she sat down next to me, she explained. "If you're going to throw up, it'll be in the first couple of seconds."

"Lovely," I said, resolving to stick to my habitual hangover diet of toast and black coffee. But Remington had other ideas.

"Drink it," he said, handing me another mug of the stuff. "I want you sharp this morning." He looked me up and down, thoughtfully. "Or at least not tripping over your own tongue."

"Aye aye, skipper." The sarcasm was, perhaps, unwarranted, but you have to remember I wasn't exactly at my most chipper. Following Clio's example, I gulped it down before the gag reflex had a chance to kick in; though I have to admit it did its best, trotting up panting as soon as the thick sludge had disappeared down my gullet. It wasn't the taste so much, although that was foul enough, but the texture, and the way it seemed to wriggle on the way down.

I held my breath, waiting to feel it on the way up again, but to my relief it stayed put, gradually filling my stomach with a warm, contented glow, as though I'd just finished a satisfying meal. Even the drumming in my temples seemed to quieten a little, and my eyes felt slightly less as though someone had spent the night diligently filling the sockets with sand.

"Feel any better?" Sowerby asked, and I nodded reflexively, without feeling as though the floor was shifting beneath my feet for the first time that morning.

"Much," I admitted, to my honest surprise. Even Remington's breakfast seemed less nauseating than it had done, although I wasn't sure I wanted to tackle a similar plateful myself.

The engineer nodded. "It'll soak up the toxins. Couple of hours and you'll feel like a new man."

"I quite liked the old one," Clio said, and grinned at me, with more than a trace of her old insouciance. "He certainly knew how to show a girl a good time."

"Did he?" Rennau asked, appearing at my elbow with a similar breakfast to the Captain, although augmented with a thick slice of black pudding and a couple of pieces of fried bread, glistening with fat. My newly pacified stomach thought about rebelling again, decided it couldn't be bothered, and subsided into quiescence. He regarded me thoughtfully. "You seem to have a Guilder's knack of twisting trouble your way, I'll say that for you."

"Thanks," I said, unsure if it had been meant as a compliment, but determined to take it as one. I smiled at Clio. "I've had a good mentor."

"I'm sure you have," Rennau said, eyeing me narrowly, before moving to a less crowded table.

By the time Remington and I set off into town I was feeling almost normal, apart from the faint echoes of a headache, and a persistent fluttering in my inner ear, which left me concentrating a little harder than usual on the business of maintaining my balance. Even our cab's typically erratic maneuvering did little to affect my equanimity, although that might have been helped by its relatively sedate progress compared to the wild ride I'd been on the night before. The weather had improved, too, which probably went some of the way towards lightening my mood, the cloud cover moderating to a blanket of white and lighter gray, through which a faint haze of sunlight seeped in intermittent patches.

To my relief, Remington seemed disinclined to conversation, spending most of the journey meshed-in, and dealing with messages. As he was connecting to the wider datascape through the cab's node I could quite easily have eavesdropped, but decided not to; for all I knew he was waiting for me to try it, and although I'd only promised not to muck around with the node on the *Stacked Deck* he might not see it quite like that. After all, I was a Guilder now, and my word was supposed to be a sacred trust.

"Here's where we're going," Remington said at last, punting the data over to my 'sphere. I glanced at it, noting the position on the city map—not too far from the area Clio had taken me to the previous night. That made sense—most of the brokerages would be close to the docks, where the cargoes they traded came and went, and the skippers of the ships they dealt with could find them easily. "Farland Freight Forwarding." I tried to keep my expression neutral, although this was an unexpected development I meant to take full advantage of. All right, by now I'd managed to convince myself there was nothing particularly sinister in the presence of the *Eddie Fitz*, but I could at least mention it to Mallow, and ask him to pass the information on to Aunt Jenny. She might notice signs of a wider pattern that was invisible to me, and it would show her I hadn't yet gone sufficiently Guilder to neglect the commission she'd given me. "They're small, but they get cargoes from all over."

Which, thanks to my earlier researches, I already knew. As well as Numarkut and Avalon, they had offices in a couple of the neighboring systems, and even handled cargoes bound for a few of the nearer League worlds. If we got one of those next, there was no telling what I might be able to ferret out within the borders of the League itself; although I tried not to get my hopes up too much. Remington would go with whatever he could make the most money on, and I was sure Farland wasn't the only firm of brokers he was talking to.

"Sounds good for us," I said, doing my best to project naive enthusiasm.

The city looked different in daylight, though no less crowded, a steady stream of vehicles moving above, below, and around us in all directions. It was more colorful than it had seemed the previous night, when I'd seen it washed out by the artificial lighting and the haze of water droplets hanging in the air, many of the buildings turning out to be faced in subtle pastel washes which had merely seemed drab in the rain. The warehousing district was even busier than before, laden cargo sleds arriving and departing every second or two, and the cab slowed to a crawl for a while before rising into a clearer lane, skimming over a few of the lower-lying rooftops as it did so; to my surprise, most of them were filled with neatly laid-out gardens. From directly above, the city would look like a patchwork of smallholdings, arranged in an unusually regular pattern.

"Are they ornamental, or for food crops?" I asked, and Remington shrugged.

"Depends on the owners. Either way, this is Numarkut; no one's going to grow anything they can't sell to someone."

"Of course." That went without saying. The cab skimmed a roof full of grape vines, startling a small flock of chickens scratching around their roots, and dived back into the traffic stream.

"Here will do," Remington said, a couple of blocks from our eventual destination, and the cab pulled over, dropping to the sidewalk in a quieter side street, over which the backs of two huge storage facilities loomed. "Bit of fresh air to help clear your head before we get there."

"Right," I agreed, clambering out while he fed coins into the payment slot, and taking a deep breath of the nearest equivalent to fresh air the city had to offer. The tang of ozone from the passing traffic sliced into my sinuses, scattering the residual headache, and I swayed a little on my feet, feeling faintly light-headed.

Remington looked at me critically. "If you're not up for this . . ."

"Of course I am," I said. I took another deep breath, and set off with a purposeful stride, which elicited a small smile from Remington.

"Oh, you look raring to go."

Once we'd passed the blank walls of the warehouses, we found ourselves in what was clearly a business district. Almost every door we passed was graced by a polished metal plaque, or something meant to look like one, although the mixture of architectural styles was even more eclectic than the one I'd noted on my first visit to the city the night before. Some appeared to be old town houses, abandoned as the well-heeled began to put as much distance as possible between themselves and the wellsprings of their wealth, others newer, purpose-built temples of commerce, proclaiming their tenants' material success by outdoing their neighbors in either blocky functionalism or garish over-ostentation, according to taste (or lack of it). The cafes and food stalls scattered amongst them were pale shadows of their exuberant counterparts in the area I'd visited with Clio, being not so much a place to enjoy a meal with friends as a necessary refueling stop for the battalions of clerks infesting the surrounding buildings like termites swarming through a collection of mounds.

And there were plenty of office drones on the streets, all soberly dressed, even the transgeners, in clothes of formal cut, no doubt intended to add an air of probity to whatever deals they were conducting. Many appeared to be transacting business in the street, meshed-in even as they scurried from meeting to meeting, or grabbed coffees and bun-wrapped sausages of dubious provenance from the street stalls and vending drones impeding their progress. Of course there were plenty of starfarers among them as well, easily identifiable by their more casual mode of dress and the ship's patches on their sleeves. Most, though not all, wore Guild insignia, a few bore the symbols of a bewildering variety of shipping lines, and one or two had neither.

"Freebooters?" I asked quietly, and Remington looked at me sharply.

"What do you know about Freebooters?" he asked.

"Just what Clio told me." I shrugged. "Best avoided."

"Clio's right. Follow her advice and you won't be an apprentice for long." He noticed my attention beginning to wander. "Someone you know?"

"Not exactly," I said.

A photosynthesising transgener was approaching us from the other direction, weaving easily though the crowd, many of whom were turning to look after her as she passed. And not without reason. Though considerably older than me, almost double my age by my estimate, her muscles were trim, and her feminine attributes disdained gravity, as if it was something that only happened to other people. Typically for that type of transgener she'd dressed in the barest minimum required by public decency, then cut it by half, maximizing the area of skin through which to draw energy from the ambient light. I'd only caught the briefest of glimpses the previous evening, but she had a familiar-looking tattoo on her upper arm, and I was fairly certain that this was the woman who'd prompted Clio to opt for a different bar than the one she'd originally intended.

"Wind your tongue in, lad," Remington chuckled, misreading my interest completely, although under the circumstances I could hardly blame him for that. "She'd eat you alive."

"I wasn't . . ." I felt my face reddening, from shirt collar to hair line.

"Really?" Remington seemed honestly surprised. "I was."

The green woman seemed unaware of our scrutiny, however, which wasn't that much of a surprise, come to think of it, as she was attracting the attention of the majority of the men on the sidewalk—and a few women too. Not all of it welcome, either, as a few of her admirers made ribald remarks a kindergarten child with poor social skills might have considered witty, although she seemed to have selective deafness down to a fine art, giving no sign of having heard.

"Hey, snotskin, I'm talking to you!" As she drew almost abreast of us, one of her interlocutors, whose good looks matched his mastery of sophisticated repartee, reached out and grabbed her arm, just below the tattooed ship's patch—which I was now close enough to see was of three vaguely heart-shaped leaves growing in a cluster, above the name *Poison 4,* the number rendered in Roman numerals.

I stepped forward instinctively to intervene—but before I could say or do anything the fellow let go, howling and grabbing his hand, which was erupting in angry, weeping blisters. He looked as if he'd taken hold of the wrong end of a welding torch, rather than a petite woman in her early middle years. Who was now regarding me with a distinct *froideur*, as though she suspected me of intending further incivilities.

"What do you want?" she asked, in clipped, self-possessed tones, which would have sounded more at home in a drawing room.

"I thought that ruffian was attacking you," I said, with a contemptuous glance in his direction. Which may have redirected a little of his barrage of invective towards me, although his voice was so choked it was hard to be certain.

"You thought right." The transgener looked at me coolly. "But I don't need a Guilder's help. Can't afford it. Shut up, you tiresome little man." This last addressed to the ruffian who'd accosted her. He didn't sound as though he was going to stop yelling any time soon, but suddenly did so abruptly, as she kicked out hard and accurately at the center of his groin.

"No charge intended, I can assure you," Remington cut in. "Simon here's still young enough to believe in doing the right thing for its own sake."

"I'm sure you'll knock that out of him soon enough." She turned back to me, her expression softening almost imperceptibly. "Thank you for your concern. But you don't go out looking like this without some defensive tweaks as well."

"You shouldn't need them," I said, with a venomous look at her would-be assailant, now curled up on the sidewalk making a noise like a sackful of small rodents, and impeding the progress of the passersby. None of whom seemed inclined to offer him assistance, or enquire politely of us what was going on. "I thought Numarkut was supposed to be a civilized world."

"Did you really?" She turned to Remington. "I'm surprised you let him out without a leash." Then she turned, and strolled away without another word.

"I see what you mean about Freebooters," I said.

"What?" Remington dragged himself away from the retreating view with a clear effort. "Yes, well. Most of them aren't quite as sociable as that."

The offices of Farland Freight Forwarding were only a block or two from where we left the whimpering detritus of the altercation, and by the time we arrived, I was feeling about as well as I ever did: possibly because the jolt of adrenalin I'd got while stepping forward thinking I was about to get into a fight was still sloshing around my system. The offices were larger than I'd expected, occupying an entire floor of one of the newest and ugliest of the modern blocks; although I suppose, since I already knew the brokerage was large enough to maintain its own riftcom, their size shouldn't have come as all that big a surprise.

We entered through a lobby consisting mainly of glass and unhappy-looking plants, carpeted in some kind of transgene moss that felt uncomfortably springy underfoot. Several yards in, we found a reception desk manned by a pale little fellow who clearly didn't get out much, and who looked at us suspiciously as we approached.

"Captain Remington, to see the senior logistics manager," the skipper announced. He glanced briefly in my direction, in case I'd somehow escaped notice. "And an apprentice from my crew."

"Have you got an appointment?" the receptionist asked, and Remington nodded, a little curtly.

"Of course I've got a bloody appointment. You don't think I'd just turn up, do you?"

"You'd be surprised who does." A prissy little sniff of disapproval, then the receptionist's eyes unfocused as he meshed with the building's datanode. Remington shot me another quick glance, tilted his head almost imperceptibly, and I suddenly realized why he'd been so keen to bring me along.

To think was to act, and within a heartbeat I was meshing in too, integrating the sneakware as I did so. There were several subnodes in the immediate vicinity, each heavily protected by antibodies which would have stripped the datanomes out of my 'ware in nanos if I went anywhere near them without a lot of preliminary work I didn't have time for, but the receptionist's desk was bulging with fresh data, so I had a quick trawl through that instead.

Lot of other skippers on the appointments list, I told Remington. *Looks like they're trying to shift a bottleneck, and bringing in anyone they can.* An item suddenly jumped out at me, an appointment a little earlier that morning: not the name itself, Captain Ertica, which meant nothing to me, but the ship it was attached to. The *Poison 4.* Interesting. *Even Freebooters.*

They really must be desperate. Remington suppressed a sudden smile. *We'll get a good deal on this. Well done.*

Buoyed by the unexpected praise, I debated trying to crack one of the shielded subnodes, but, perhaps fortunately, the receptionist forestalled me, looking up as a fresh message arrived in his 'sphere. "She's expecting you," he told us, as though mortally offended at the idea. A floor plan suddenly appeared in our shared dataspace. "You go—"

"I know the way," Remington said, moving off before the receptionist had finished speaking. He glanced back at me, urging me to follow with a tilt of the head. "I've been here often enough."

"I suppose you must have," I said, falling into place at his shoulder.

Despite Remington's confidence I kept the floor plan near the front of my 'sphere, so I could keep track of our progress for myself. I might need to come here alone some time, if I ever found a particularly juicy nugget of information to pass on to my contact, and under those circumstances I wouldn't want to be wasting any time trying to find the way to where he worked.

Which wouldn't be all that difficult, according to the map. The riftcom suite was at the center of the floor, as close as possible to the greatest number of offices. Not that the actual equipment was there, of course, just a lot of data-handling kit, where clerks like Mallow would encode the outgoing messages into a form suitable for transmission: the actual hardware would be somewhere in orbit, where it could direct the resulting modulated graviton beams into the mouth of whichever rift led to the intended recipient. Incoming messages would be cleaned up, and rendered into something electronic or neuroware compatible, before being passed on to whichever Farland employees needed to know; either directly, or, in the case of particularly commercially sensitive information, in single-use memory units like the one Mallow had slipped into my pocket, delivered directly to their offices.

The mossy corridors were full of employees hurrying about their business, most of them so engrossed in actual or virtual conversation I could probably have walked through the place in Tinkie's orbital deployment armor without any of them noticing. Certainly none of them gave a couple of Guilders a second glance, which was fine by me; I was too busy being mildly surprised at my surroundings to take much notice of them either.

The walls were made of living wood, transgened to grow rapidly in place then simply stop once the ceiling had been reached; a technique, I gathered from a quick dip into the datastore I'd purloined from the reception desk, that was quite common on League worlds, and was becoming fashionable on Numarkut for those who could afford it. The effect was a little creepy, as though someone had ironed a couple of trees flat and plonked them down on either side of us. Crevices in the bark had been colonized by small, brightly colored orchids, and a few equally garish butterflies flapped about the place, feeding on them presumably, if they weren't being blown off-course by the air conditioning. At least the ceiling looked relatively normal, what I could see of it between the lianas coiled around the light fittings.

"It's like being in a hothouse," I grumbled. The effect was supposed to be relaxing, bringing a touch of the outdoors indoors, but, paradoxically, I found it claustrophobic, in a way the much narrower corridors of the *Stacked Deck* had never been.

Remington shrugged. "Dirtwalkers. Go figure." Which I found mildly flattering, as it implied that I'd moved out of that category, at least in his mind.

Before I had time to formulate a suitable reply he stopped outside a door, which looked, to me, no different from any of the others lining the passageway, rapped once on the milled and polished wood (which jarred hideously with the bark surrounding it, like a lump of scar tissue), and pushed it open.

"John." A plump, middle-aged woman, looking vaguely like a well-groomed version of my aunt, rose from behind a desk, smiling an insincere welcome. "It's been ages."

"Ellie. It certainly has." Remington returned the smile, with every bit as much feeling as had gone into the original. The room was large, with an outside window, which went some way towards relieving the sensation of having got lost in the woods, although the rest of the decor was of a piece with the corridors outside.

"Who's this?" Ellie looked at me, and raised an immaculate eyebrow. Her tone was cordial, but her body language unmistakable. I was most definitely an unwelcome surprise.

"Simon Forrester." Remington waved a perfunctory hand in my direction. "New apprentice. Thought it would do him good to sit in and see how a deal's made."

"An excellent idea. Let me know how it went when you've tried it." She glanced at me again, and waved dismissively. "Now you are here, do something useful. There's a staff room in the next corridor, with a kettle. Cherry tea, and whatever it is he wants." This last with a nod to Remington.

Sorry, Si. Better luck next time. Remington pretended to consider for a moment, before adding, "Coffee. You know how I like it," verbally.

"Coming right up," I said, masking my real feelings with an ease born of a lifetime spent being bossed about by most of the women I'd ever encountered; although having got used to being taken seriously by the female crew members of the *Stacked Deck,* it seemed particularly galling in this instance. The kitchen was clear enough on the floor plan still floating in my 'sphere, so I strolled to the door without any further hesitation.

The flash of peevishness I'd felt at being so summarily dismissed evaporated the moment I was back in the corridor, however, as I suddenly realized I'd just been handed a golden opportunity to go and look for Mallow, without having to come up with some excuse to get away from Remington first. The comms center wasn't far from here, and if I headed on down to it I was sure I'd be able to invent some spurious errand allowing me access. And if I couldn't, I ought to be able to mesh in and pass him a message. All right, the system would have been secured against unauthorized access, but I was pretty sure I could deal with that somehow—it certainly hadn't stopped me at Summerhall, or the Naval Academy back on Avalon. (And look how well they turned out, a voice I was determined to ignore whispered in the back of my head.)

But first things first. Ellie and Remington would be expecting me back with the drinks they'd asked for in about ten minutes—which I could probably stretch to fifteen by acting dumb and pretending I'd got lost, but any more than that and they might start asking questions. So, find the kitchen and put the kettle on, then start looking for Mallow. Not much of a plan, but it was the only one I had.

With the floor plan to guide me I made my way into the next corridor, which was just as *faux* sylvan as the one I'd left behind. The doors lining it were of noticeably lower quality timber, however, indicating that this was the region where more of the actual work got done, and fewer decisions were made. This time I got a few curious glances from the clerks I passed, there being no other ships' crew about, but no one seemed concerned enough to challenge me. The kitchen was about halfway along, the door slightly open; as I approached it a young woman came out carrying a steaming mug of something, and walked off in the opposite direction.

I pushed the door open, and found myself alone in a utilitarian room, once again carpeted by the ubiquitous moss. Here, however, it seemed a bit the worse for wear, a few brown patches marking the sites of old spillages of stuff it couldn't readily metabolize. A couple of cheap plastic tables, surrounded by cheap plastic chairs, stood in the middle, one of them holding a couple of grubby plates, an empty sandwich wrapping, and a trio of mugs containing nothing but dregs. More plates and mugs were stacked in the sink, which was half full of dirty water.

The kettle was still warm, and more than half full, so I set it boiling again and began rummaging in the cupboards above the work surface, unearthing a cache of mugs and an assortment of beverages. Great. As soon as I made the drinks I'd been sent for I could head off in search of Mallow.

But I didn't have to. As I turned away from the cupboard, the door to the corridor swung open, to reveal the transgener standing on the threshold gawping at me, his face, so far as I could tell under its covering of particolored fur, a picture of stunned astonishment.

"What the hell are you doing here?" He recovered quickly, I'll say that for him, pushing the door closed, and advancing into the room, an empty coffee mug held out in a faintly defensive posture.

"My skipper's got a meeting with—" I realized I didn't know the woman's full name. "Ellie something, over in the next corridor. He asked me to sit in, for the experience. She sent me out for tea."

"She would." He looked at me, with what seemed like genuine sympathy. "And she won't thank you for it either."

Which didn't surprise me, given what I'd seen of her. "I was just on my way to find you," I said.

"What for?" He placed the mug he'd been carrying on the uncluttered table, and looked at me searchingly, his tail waving in the air behind him. It began to dawn on me that he wasn't quite as self-assured as he looked.

"I found something. Not sure if it's significant, but as I was here I thought I'd pass it on." The kettle boiled at last, and I made the drinks I'd been sent for.

"Lucky coincidence," Mallow said, sounding as if he thought it was anything but.

I nodded, unable to see how it could be anything else. Remington had contacts out all over the city; it was just my good luck that Farland had called him in today. "Guess so." I held out the kettle. "Want a refill?"

"You have no idea," Mallow said, sounding a little less suspicious. "I always need one around this time." He busied himself with the routine of caffeine production. "So, what's this possibly significant thing you've got?"

"There's a League ship a couple of cradles from ours." Or there had been: for all I knew, the activity I'd seen in the small hours had been a prelude to departure. "The *Eddie Fitz*. It's an old fleet auxiliary, sold on to the Toniden Line." I kicked across the information I'd gathered to his 'sphere.

Mallow shrugged. "I'll pass it on. But it's not the first one of these we've seen. The League fleet decommissioned a whole bunch of auxiliaries a while back, and most of them are on the Numarkut run."

"Oh." I felt vaguely deflated. "And you checked them out already, right?"

"Thoroughly," Mallow agreed, sipping his coffee. "Otherwise you'll always get some paranoid analyst thinking the weapons are still on board."

"Which they're not, of course," I said.

"And waste all that cargo space? Don't be daft." He shrugged. "Besides, that would violate so many treaties and customs regulations you'd have to be insane to try it."

I thought of Plubek, who Remington seemed to think was relatively honest for a Numarkut customs officer. "Or offer a huge bribe to turn a blind eye," I said.

"Wouldn't work," Mallow said. "You'd need to do that every time, and the word would get out. Besides, our customs inspectors are corrupt, not unpatriotic. Taking a backhander's one thing, endangering the security of the system quite another."

"I suppose so," I conceded, collecting up the drinks. I'd done what I could.

"It could still be useful," Mallow said, although I suspected that was more to spare my feelings than because it was true. "Building up patterns, that kind of thing. I'll pass it along, and let Commander Worricker decide." His tail flicked out, opening the door for me. "Mind how you go."

CHAPTER SIXTEEN
In which a spontaneous celebration has unforeseen consequences.

Mallow was right: I got no thanks from Ellie when I delivered the drinks, although Remington did glance up from their negotiations just long enough to nod an acknowledgement. On the plus side, she seemed too engrossed to tell me to piss off again, so I settled on an overstuffed sofa in the corner and tried to copy Dad's knack of becoming invisible.

Very little of the negotiation was going on verbally: their 'spheres were deeply meshed, and exchanging data at an astonishing rate. I stuck out a cautious tendril, meshing in through Remington's 'sphere, and was encouraged by a reasonably welcoming greeting.

Just watch. Don't distract me. Not wanting to break his concentration with a reply, I did as I was instructed, seeing a bewildering array of schedules, bills of lading, and cost breakdowns skimming back and forth, being constantly amended, along with curt comments like *Too high*, or *Not fast enough*, occasionally supplemented with an ironic laugh, or a verbal "You're joking, right?"

In truth, neither of them looked particularly amused; I was reminded of the faces of my fellow competitors when only a couple of points separated us on the leader board, and everything depended on the final round.

With nothing useful to contribute, I suppose it was inevitable that I started to poke around the local datascape, discovering almost at once that Ellie was connected to one of the secure nodes I'd detected at the reception desk; which, in turn, meant that I had access to it too, through the overlap of her 'sphere with Remington's. Too good a chance not to take advantage of, I thought, marshalling my sneakware once again. This was going to be tricky: companies with that much money to spend, and protect, wouldn't stint on security—not if they meant to keep it. But, before long, I'd seen enough to be sure of her encryption key, and swapped enough datanomes to be reasonably certain that my probe would pass for something she'd authorized.

Of course, reasonably certain isn't quite the same thing as absolutely certain, so I have to admit to holding my breath a little as I infiltrated it into the datastream: but no alarms went off, no roadblocks descended, and no virulent antibodies swarmed to puree my synapses. Great. I now had a few seconds before I had to withdraw, or run the risk of discovery. Which, in data time, was more than long enough to take a leisurely look round, and find something really interesting.

They've been offered a premium, I told Remington. *Five per cent extra if they can shift the entire consignment before the end of the month.* Which was only a few days away. And, if I was reading the manifests right, it was touch and go whether they'd make it. For an extra quarter of a million Talents, I was pretty sure Farland was willing to cut a few corners.

To his credit, Remington didn't waste any time asking how I knew, or whether I was sure. He just sighed heavily, and stood.

"I'm sorry, Ellie, but the margins are just too tight on this one. You'll have to get somebody else." He turned to me, as though suddenly remembering my presence. "Come on, Si."

"I'm sorry you feel that way," Ellie said, outwardly cool, as she stood too, and extended a hand. Only the minutest tremor of her voice betrayed her agitation. "Is there anything that might tempt you to reconsider?"

"An extra percentage point. Across the board." Remington was suddenly clipped and decisive. "You can afford that." And a lot more besides, with a quarter of a million in the balance.

"Can we?" Ellie was stonewalling, clearly wondering what he'd heard, and where he'd heard it from.

Remington nodded. "Word is, you're even hiring Freebooters to keep things moving." Ellie didn't quite flinch, but it was a close run thing. "If there's that much at stake, you can pay full Guild rates, no haggling, plus a bonus for my crew. Otherwise we're done."

"Half a percent." She didn't even bother to deny it. "Still a good earner for you."

"Not as good as three quarters."

"Three quarters, then." A faint half smile, almost instantly suppressed, although I'm sure Remington noticed it too. She thought she'd got one over on us.

"Why didn't you press for the one percent?" I asked, as we broke free of the synthetic forest at last and I found myself standing once again on honest pavement which didn't feel the need to masquerade as anything other than what it really was. "It would still have been a good deal for her."

"Three quarters is fine," Remington told me. "And she thinks she's played us. Means she won't think too much about how we knew as much as we did. Can you get back into that system again?"

"Probably," I said, although in truth I had absolutely no doubt of it.

Remington smiled. "Then that's got to be worth a quarter percent."

I thought about it. Over the long term, the extra leverage the knowledge I could extract for him during negotiations, and the concessions we'd be able to get from exploiting it, would be worth far more than the extra money we could have made on this contract. "Easily," I agreed. Then something else occurred to me. I'd been so busy ferreting out Farland's secrets, I had no idea where the cargo we'd just secured was bound for. "Where are we off to, anyway?"

"Freedom," Remington said casually.

I knew the name, of course. The nearest major system in the League of Democracies. Commercial hub, and a naval dockyard.

I was going right to the heart of the enemy.

After a coup like that, the only possible thing to do was celebrate it. So instead of hailing a cab we walked to the pleasure district Clio had taken me to the night before, in search of a drink or two; and that, I told myself, was all I'd have, a single dose of Sowerby's hangover cure being more than enough for one week.

The whole area seemed different in daylight, less garish and more tawdry at the same time, and curiously subdued, as though suffering from a hangover itself. The diners and bars were still doing a brisk trade, workers from the landing grounds and warehouses for the most part, although a few of the more salubrious had clerks among their clientele. Not to mention the inevitable starfarers, doggedly attempting to prolong a night out as far as possible into the following day, or freshly arrived on planet and desperate to squander their landing pay as soon as they could.

To my quiet relief most of the dollymops had disappeared, no doubt as a result of their nocturnal lifestyle, and the bordellos were shuttered and silent; although I was pretty sure any of my fellow starfarers in search of negotiable affection would still be unlikely to leave the quarter disappointed.

Most of the food stalls were still in business, however, and finding my appetite returning I exchanged a few coins for a sausage in a bun; it briefly crossed my mind to ask what kind of animal had provided the filling, but after my encounter with the Skyhaven pie merchant I was by no means sure that I wanted to know.

"You're braver than you look," Remington commented, his tone sufficiently dry to leave me wondering for a moment if he was serious.

I chewed and swallowed. "I've tasted worse," I said, which was true enough; though not all that often.

"When?" Remington sounded skeptical.

"This morning," I replied, without hesitation. "Sarah's hangover cure." I paused for a moment, then curiosity got the better of me. "What is it, anyway?"

"Beats me." The skipper shrugged. "Something she picked up on one of the League worlds. Technically it's a living organism." For a moment the sausage I'd just eaten considered completing the round trip, then settled down again. Remington studied my face with interest. "Sort of a slime mould," he added.

"Seems like a remarkably useful one," I said casually. Once you've spent a childhood playing competitive gross-out with Tinkie, not a lot gets to you.

If Remington was at all bemused or disappointed at my lack of a reaction, he didn't show it. "Guess that's why somebody made it," he said. "Just keep throwing nutrient in the tank, and you get all you can eat. She tells me it's good for clearing out the recycling pipes too."

"I can believe that," I said, having held wrenches for her while the system was serviced. A faintly disquieting thought occurred to me. "She doesn't put it back in the tank afterwards, does she?"

"Wouldn't surprise me." Now it was Remington's turn to look a little disconcerted. "Nothing she does surprises me any more." Then he smiled. "But in a good way."

We turned a corner, and I found myself on a street I recognized. Over there was where the cab had dropped us off, this was the bar Clio had been intending to visit, and over there—

"Bugger." I couldn't help glancing at the bar we'd ended up in, where I'd got into an argument with the owner; and, sure enough, there he was, sweeping up what looked like a small heap of broken glass. He must have felt my eyes on him, because he glanced up and glared at me, his pupils twin gun muzzles blasting hatred and resentment in my direction. "It's the tosser from last night."

"Where?" Remington followed my gaze, smiled, and waved a cheery greeting. The bartender went back inside, and slammed the door, on which a hand-scrawled notice announced *Closed for renovation*. Remington read it, and his smile spread. "Oh dear. Looks like your party got a bit out of hand."

"Maybe." I furrowed my forehead with the effort to remember. "It's all a bit blurred, to be honest. But everyone seemed to be having a good time." At least they still were when Clio and I had left. Okay, it had been a bit crowded, and maybe one or two things got broken in the crush, but that was hardly my fault.

"I thought Clio liked this one." Remington indicated the bar we'd originally been making for.

"It was full of Freebooters," I explained.

"Good call." He nodded thoughtfully, a faint edge of sarcasm entering his voice. "We wouldn't want you getting into any trouble, now, would we?"

Though trouble was precisely what we found ourselves in an hour or so later, when we left the hostelry we'd chosen. I could see why Clio liked it; the decor was clean and sparse, vaguely reminiscent of being shipboard, but with a few softer touches, like the brightly patterned abstract tapestries on the walls, which made it feel welcoming. It had been almost deserted, the only other patrons being a ship's crew with Guild patches enjoying a final drink before lifting, and who left soon after we arrived. Remington and I had settled at a table near the big picture window, through which we could keep a casual eye on the bustle of the street, as watching other people scurrying around while you're skiving makes putting your own feet up even more enjoyable, and kept the serving drone busy conveying several more drinks over to our corner than the two I'd promised myself before coming in. Despite that, though, it seemed Sowerby's pet slime mould was still doing its thing in the depths of my stomach, and I'd still felt completely sober by the time we'd left. Which was rather disappointing, really.

Remington, too, seemed completely unaffected by the whisky he'd drunk, although whether he'd taken a dose of the mould before setting out from the *Stacked Deck*, or was just well practiced at holding his liquor, I had no idea.

"Great." He punted a small piece of data over to my 'sphere; the estimated arrival time of the cab he'd just ordered. "Ten minutes." Which didn't seem all that long to me, but I suppose after leaving the bar he felt he was back on the clock, and ought to be using his time more productively. "I forgot about the shift change." Now he came to mention it, there were noticeably more people on the street than there had been a short while before, either tired and weary-looking, or trotting along purposefully, intent on arriving at a specific place at a specific time.

"Can we meet it halfway?" I asked: the sled's AI would be homing in on Remington's neuroware by now, and would find us wherever he was, so there was no point in hanging around here if we didn't have to.

"Might as well," he agreed, after a moment's thought. It would take us a little further away from the *Stacked Deck* initially, but not so far as to make any appreciable difference to the cab's travel time, and it felt like we'd be doing something instead of just wasting our time.

"This way." Remington set off confidently, and I trailed after him. "I know a short cut."

"Lucky for us," I said sarcastically, as something unpleasant squished beneath my boot. The skipper's short cut turned out to be an alleyway, carpeted with garbage in varying stages of decomposition, faced by the rear walls of assorted businesses on one side, and the looming concrete cliff of a warehouse on the other. Something squeaked, and scuttled away from my footfalls. "Fragrant little spot."

"Apart from the wildlife," Remington said. For a moment I thought he was referring to the rodent I'd just disturbed: then I noticed the fellow leaning against the wall of the warehouse ahead of us. He was trying to look casual, but there was a tenseness about him which belied his relaxed posture; I had no doubt at all he was waiting for us.

"Two more behind," Remington said, having come to the same conclusion. "Don't look back."

I forestalled the instinctive reaction just in time. "How do you know?"

"Let's just say it's not the first time I've taken a short cut I probably shouldn't have," Remington said. "Can you tell who they are?"

I expanded my 'sphere, picking up the residual echoes of neuroware in the buildings around us, and the faint buzzing of the vehicle nodes in the surrounding streets, but apart from Remington and myself, I couldn't find any traces of 'ware anywhere in the alley. "They're not meshed," I said. "No 'ware." An uncomfortable thought struck me. "Think they're Leaguers?"

"Maybe. Or locals. Lot of them follow the League line on neuroware." Which, to be honest, I'd never quite got my head around. How being able to mesh was supposed to erode your humanity, or even your soul according to the real crackpots, was beyond me. "Why would any Leaguers have it in for you? You're a Guilder."

"Not according to the wanker last night," I said. "My accent was a bit too Commonwealth for him." And the penny dropped. He must have seen where we'd gone, and got some of his mates over to lay in wait for us. This was supposed to be payback time.

A surge of anger ripped through me at the realization, and I damped it down, honing it, hoarding it for later.

"Cab's still three minutes away," Remington said calmly. "I don't suppose you're carrying any weapons?"

"Why would I be?" Perhaps it was the casualness of the question which had surprised me so much.

"No, of course not. You're the one who thought Numarkut was supposed to be civilized." His bantering tone drew the sting of the sarcasm.

"Does that mean you are?" I asked hopefully. If he had a gun, or a knife, or even a pointy stick . . .

"With the bribes you have to pay here to carry anything?" Remington sounded amused. "Dream on."

"Just have to deal with it the old-fashioned way," I said, picking up my pace a little, and making my gait a tiny bit unsteady, so that to the casual eye I'd look a little drunk. If you're going to have to fight, it never hurts to have your opponent feeling overconfident. I raised my voice waving, as if trying to attract the attention of the fellow lying in wait for us. "Oi! Mate! You Hugo?" Why Hugo I couldn't have told you, although we had a dog called that once: it was just the first name that popped into my head. At least I didn't ask if he was Skippy.

"No." An edge of uncertainty entered his voice; this wasn't how the script in his head had mapped things out. I should have been edgy, not pleased to see him, and I'd apparently got friends around here—or at least someone I was expecting to meet, who was probably in the immediate vicinity. "Never heard of him."

"Course you haven't," I said jovially, taking my money out. His eyes narrowed a little, instantly focusing on the leather bag of coins, which still bulged quite temptingly, despite me having bought most of the drinks in the bar we'd just left. Just as I'd intended. His little rodent mind would be focusing on the money now, wondering how much was there, what he could get with it after robbing me, not how much of a threat I represented. I winked, theatrically. "Katinka sent me. Said you could sort us out. Didn't she?" I asked Remington.

"That's right." He nodded, his voice suddenly slurred. "Said you had the best stuff."

He nudged my 'sphere. *Are you seriously trying to buy drugs from this tosser?*

He thinks I am, I sent back.

"You've got the wrong bloke," the lurker said, glancing back over our shoulders to see where his mates had got to. Close enough, evidently, as he suddenly pushed off from the wall and rushed at me, one hand already reaching out to grab my purse.

Which wasn't there. As he lunged forward, I pivoted out of the way, grabbed his outstretched arm, and pulled forward and down. His face met my rising knee with a satisfying crack of breaking nasal cartilage, and I brought the heavy bag of coins down hard on the back of his neck. He folded without a sound, collapsing into the filth beneath our feet, where, right now, I felt he belonged in any case.

I turned to meet the charge of his friends, who, by now, were too committed to the attack to either assimilate or be deflected by this unexpected setback. Remington had been wrong: there were three of them, not two. Other than that, though, I felt we still had the initiative. All of them, like the one I'd just dispatched, were young, lean, and desperate to seem dangerous, which probably accounted for the number of facial tattoos, although if their friend was anything to go by they just relied on sheer force of numbers rather than any actual fighting ability.

I slipped the drawstring of my purse around my wrist, to make sure I wouldn't drop it, and moved forward into the attack. *Go left*, Remington sent. *I'll break right.* He took his own advice instantly, blocking a clumsy punch to the face with a rising forearm, and counterattacking instantly with a head butt to the bridge of his assailant's nose. It looked like there would be a lot of mouth breathers in the neighborhood tonight. The thug fell back, and Remington followed up with a couple of solid punches to the gut which doubled him over.

Ignoring the skipper's advice, I stepped out to the right as well, taking advantage of the gap he'd opened up; they'd expect me to go left, in an attempt to get behind them, and were already turning in that direction, which meant they were getting in each other's way very nicely, and giving me a free shot at their backs. I pivoted in behind them, neat as you please, and grabbed the top of the head of the nearest, hooking two of my fingers into his eye sockets and yanking back as hard as I could. Off balance and blinded by tears, he fell backwards, howling, landing supine in the stinking debris, and I drove a heel into his groin with all my weight behind it. Something crunched and squished at the same time, and he went very quiet, apart from a series of long, indrawn breaths, which sounded uncannily like wind in a stovepipe.

Remington's target hit the mulch, not much better off, and the two of us turned as one to confront the sole survivor. By my reckoning, the whole thing had taken well over five seconds. Which is what happens when you neglect your training, you slow down and get soft—although, in my defense, there hadn't been that much opportunity for a proper workout aboard the *Stacked Deck*.

"Back off." It seemed the last man standing was too stupid to take his own advice. "Or I'll cut you, I swear." He waved a knife uncertainly back and forth, trying to work out which of us presented the greater threat.

"Try it," I said, doing my best to sound calm and dangerous, and wishing I couldn't remember what Tinkie had once told me about her unarmed combat training. Even an expert gets cut more often than not taking a knife from a determined opponent. "And the minute you go for one of us, you'll have the other one behind you."

I stepped forward, hoping to intimidate him into running away, but unfortunately it seemed to have the opposite effect, triggering the wrong part of the fight or flight reflex. Instead, he came at me in a banzai charge, thrusting at the center of my stomach with all the strength he could summon. Fortunately, I'd had enough punches thrown there in both sparring and competition to respond by reflex, ignoring the blade entirely, simply stepping in behind the outstretched arm and seizing his wrist. My knee came up on the outside of the elbow joint, which cracked like a dry stick in a fire, and his hand came open, dropping the knife. The squealing that came along with the broken arm was repetitive and annoying, so I swung the heavy purse a final time, connecting solidly with his temple, and he went down to join his friends.

"I thought you said you weren't armed," Remington said, with a glance at the purse as I stowed it safely away in my pocket again.

"I'm not," I said. "I was improvising."

"That was some pretty smart improvisation all round," Remington said skeptically. He looked pointedly at the three scofflaws I'd felled. "Is there something you haven't bothered to tell me about?"

"I don't think so." I shrugged. "I told you, I'm an athlete."

"That you did." He turned, and began to lead the way towards the alley mouth. "But I had you down more as a sprinter. Something like that."

"I run too," I said. "And swim, and fence, and shoot. I'm a pentathlete." We broke out into another crowded street, where, thank the Lady, our cab was just beginning to descend towards the sidewalk.

"And the fifth event?" Remington asked, as he ducked through the door.

"Self defense," I said. "Although there are a few rules in the sporting version."

"Most of which you just broke, I suppose," Remington said, as our ride rose into the traffic stream, taking the alley mouth out of my line of sight. I tried not to think about what we'd left there, and the snapping sound of cartilage and bone.

"Among other things," I said.

CHAPTER SEVENTEEN
In which I'm sent to pick up a package.

Though I pretended that the violent encounter had been a trivial affair, it disturbed me a good deal more than I liked to admit. True, I'd been fighting competitively for several years, but all those bouts had been strictly controlled, and I'd never inflicted more serious injury on an opponent than a few bruises. (Or suffered it, either, apart from the time I'd fallen flat on my back in a training session and had the wind knocked out of me—not a sensation I'd recommend.) For several days I found myself reliving moments of the melee, feeling my heart pound from a sudden surge of adrenaline, the jar of fist and knee against solid flesh, and hearing the snap and crack of bodies breaking under the impact of my blows. After which, I'd feel sick and trembling, fighting to get my breathing back under control. But the thing I found hardest to accept was that, in retrospect, I'd found myself rather enjoying the experience. Not that I'm a savage or a sadist, far from it, but the atavistic simplicity of fighting in earnest, knowing I'd be injured or worse if I let my guard down even for an instant, had been an undeniable rush. I could see how some people could get addicted to that, even to the extent of deliberately picking fights to repeat the experience.

I have to admit, too, that I was quite proud of myself; after all, I'd taken out three of the dregs without suffering so much as a scratch, and it's kind of hard not to feel good about something like that. (Remington hadn't been quite so lucky with the one he'd tackled, skinning a knuckle on a belt buckle or something, but otherwise emerging as unscathed as I did.)

It didn't exactly help matters that the skipper had begun to spread the story almost as soon as we'd got back to the ship, no doubt embroidering things to make me sound like a focused and skillful warrior, rather than a hobby athlete who'd reacted without thinking and been incredibly lucky not to get stabbed in the gut. Exaggerated or not, though, his account of the incident had definitely raised my status aboard the *Stacked Deck;* even Rennau seemed to look on me with a little less disapproval than before, while many of my shipmates went out of their way to talk to me about the brawl, and ask me to demonstrate the moves I'd used. (Which I was perfectly happy to do, as they were simple enough.)

None of them seemed quite as impressed as Clio, though, who seemed to have no other topic of conversation for several days.

"Weren't you scared?" she asked for the umpteenth time, guiding a drone into the hold, where it dropped its load in the spot vacated only seconds before by one of its fellows unloading the cargo we'd brought to Numarkut. Time was definitely of the essence on the Farland contract, so we were clearing and loading our holds at the same time: much to the annoyance of Rennau, who had to sort out the inevitable complications, and Rolf and Lena, who were effectively stuck with two jobs at once, and having to juggle the paperwork accordingly. "I would have been."

"No, you wouldn't," I said. "You'd have had far more sense than to get into a situation like that in the first place."

"True, I would." Clio shrugged. "But it sounds more like John got you into it, and then you got him out."

"Sounds about right," Rennau said, appearing on the catwalk above our heads. "That's John for you." He dumped a load of files in my datasphere. "Case in point."

"What are these?" I asked, skimming rapidly through a stack of the manifests from Farland. They all looked fine to me. "What's the problem?"

"That." Rennau highlighted a section of the paperwork. "To get to Freedom, we need to pass through the Iceball system. Right?"

"Right," I agreed, still not getting it. The very nature of rift shooting meant that you couldn't get anywhere apart from an immediately adjacent system without going the long way round; even detours through three or four intermediate destinations weren't all that uncommon.

"So we need a transit waiver," Rennau prompted.

I must have looked blank for a moment, because Clio cut in with a quick message.

A document for Iceball customs, showing we're just passing through. Otherwise we'll be boarded and inspected, like we were when we arrived in system here.

"And we can't afford the delay of another inspection," I said, hoping my momentary hesitation would be taken for careful consideration, rather than a quick pause for his daughter to bail me out.

"Or another unnecessary bribe," Rennau said, not giving anything away. He leaned on the catwalk rail, more or less where Clio had fixed it, and glanced down at me. "The Iceballers insist on transit waivers being accompanied by a sample of the signatory's DNA, which John forgot to get. You're the least useful person aboard, and you know your way to Farland, so you get to go pick it up. Lucky you."

"Lucky me, indeed," I said, with a smile at Clio, who returned it with a trace of envy; which I must admit I'd probably have felt in her place, watching someone go gallivanting off on an unsupervised errand in the middle of a hard and tedious job.

"Don't go wandering down any dark alleys," she said, and went back to work.

"Are you sure it was just a coincidence?" Mallow asked. Somehow he'd discovered I was on my way over to pick up a package (well, he was a spy, after all), and had contrived to be leaving the building for a coffee break just as I was signing the docket the supercilious receptionist had waved in my direction. It seemed the denizens of Iceball were firm believers in physical paperwork, which, given my gift for data manipulation, I could hardly fault them for; although to most people it was an irritating eccentricity at best. The Sanctified Brethren had been among the first to colonize the system, which, as the name implied, wasn't exactly the most prepossessing piece of real estate in the spiral arm, and their sensibilities still prevailed, even among the substantial minority of the local population who followed other faiths, or none at all.

"You mean like running into you was?" I asked pointedly, as we picked up drinks from a nearby stall; it was hot, and wet, and tasted vaguely like it was supposed to, which probably made it as good as anything else I was likely to find around here.

I glanced at Mallow to see if the shaft had hit home, but just as I did so a sudden puff of chill wind ruffled the particolored pelt on his face, obscuring the expression beneath it. Amusement? Impatience? Not that I cared anyway. I sipped at my coffee, grateful for the warmth it provided.

"I mean, did they say anything about what happened in the bar? Demand your money? Anything like that?"

"They didn't really say anything," I said, thinking back to the incident as dispassionately as I could. "One of them made a few threats about the knife he was waving around, and another one said he wasn't Hugo. That was about it." Unless you counted groans and screaming as polite conversation, of course.

"Hugo? Hugo who?"

I must have been getting better at reading him, despite the fuzz on his face: that was definitely puzzlement. "It doesn't matter," I said.

"So you're only assuming it was attempted revenge for the incident in the bar." Mallow drank a little more of his beverage, and nodded thoughtfully.

I tried not to laugh, and almost succeeded. "You think the League sent them?" Maybe I should have been flattered, and would have been if the suggestion hadn't been so ludicrous. Or worrying, depending on how you looked at it. "I'd have thought their field agents would be a bit better at skullduggery than that."

"They would be. But they wouldn't bother coming after you, either." He glanced around at the hurrying crowds surrounding us, perhaps having made himself a little nervous at the thought: after all, he'd be a much higher priority target for a League hit squad than I was. "They might get some of the local dregs to try their luck, though."

"Why would they do that?" I asked.

Mallow plucked a napkin from the stall with the tip of his tail, and wiped the fur around his mouth with it, a sight I found vaguely disturbing, although no one else around us even seemed to notice. "The DIR must know there are Commonwealth networks active on Numarkut; we certainly know about some of theirs." I took another sip of my rapidly cooling coffee, trying not to seem spooked by the mention of the Department of Information Retrieval, the League's most notorious secret service branch, which heretofore I'd only encountered as the perennial antagonist of Commonwealth spy fiction. According to the books and virts I'd seen, its agents were either fanatical psychopaths or bumbling incompetents, backed up by an inexhaustible supply of gun-toting dregs who couldn't hit a barn from the inside, and whose main occupation seemed to be dying in droves at the hands of an omnicompetent heroine. "And they'd know you're Jenny Worricker's nephew. They might not know quite what you're up to, but they're bound to think you're running some kind of errand for her."

"So they set up an attack," I said, "to stop me from doing whatever it is I'm doing, even though they don't know what it is?"

"Something like that." He pitched the napkin into the stall's waste disposal, where it flashed into plasma, powering the heating coils for a few microseconds. His cup followed. "Or to see if anyone came to your rescue."

"I didn't need anyone to rescue me," I said, following suit.

"No, you didn't." Mallow looked at me with what I suspected was an expression of mild concern. "You just showed them you're a lot more dangerous than they expected."

"If it was the League in the first place," I said, determined to restore a little perspective to the conversation. This was all getting needlessly paranoid if you asked me. "My money's still on the bar owner." Or the even more mundane explanation Remington seemed to believe, and which informed his version of the event every time he recounted it. Wrong place, wrong time: one of the gang had simply seen us in the bar, and noticed the weight of my purse.

"Let's hope you're right," Mallow said, turning away. "Although in this game you can't count on anything being the way it looks."

"I haven't yet," I agreed, trying to sound casual. But as my cab whirled me up into the maelstrom of the Dullingham traffic system and set course for the *Stacked Deck*'s cradle, I found my thoughts as chaotic as the streets and air lanes around me. In the end, I decided there was no point in trying to second guess everything, as I simply didn't need the stress, and resolved to take things the only way I could: just as they came.

Our departure from Numarkut seemed oddly undramatic, compared to casting off from Skyhaven; although, as in most things, I suppose that was just a matter of perspective. The planet was so vast in comparison to the orbital that, though we were falling up through the atmosphere far faster than we'd been able to repel the relatively tiny mass of the void station, we hardly seemed to be moving at all. I hadn't been invited to the bridge this time, but I remembered enough about the architecture of the *Stacked Deck*'s datanode to mesh in from my stateroom, find the displays I'd been privy to before, and even locate the external imager which had provided such dramatic pictures of our undocking and subsequent slingshot around Avalon.

As I'd hoped, it was still operating, providing me with a ringside seat as we rose from the docking cradle and plummeted skywards. I wasn't the only member of the crew enjoying the show either, I noted idly; there were half a dozen other 'spheres meshed in adjacent to mine, although none were close enough to overlap. Quite deliberately—the respect for one another's physical space, so necessary for harmony aboard a starship, seemed to extend to the datasphere, although whether this was a general Guild custom or peculiar to the *Stacked Deck* I had no idea.

Night had fallen while we finalized our departure, and the virtual image was crowded with lights, falling away beneath us into what seemed like a bottomless void. At first our field of vision had been filled with the bright lamps of the landing field, defining and illuminating the cradles in harsh floods and knife-edged shadows; but the higher we rose the more they mellowed, slowly seeping into one another, until they finally merged with the lights of the nearby city to form a single constellation of staggering complexity. Then this, too, shrank into a single, diffuse patch, to be joined by other miniature galaxies, all hazed with distance, altitude, and intervening cloud, each diminishing in turn to a single pinpoint, which combined to sketch the outlines of the major land masses in twinkling pointillism. The oceans were patches of stygian darkness by comparison, sparsely flecked with the glowing stigmata of the occasional island or offshore industrial facility.

As the area covered by the image widened, a glowing crimson crescent, fading through purple to blue, betrayed the position of the sun, which was just beginning to emerge from behind the dayside limb of the planet. For the most part, however, the freckling of lights across the darkened globe began to merge almost seamlessly with the backdrop of stars behind it, seeming remarkable only for their number and density, and slightly more yellowish cast. Then the sun appeared more clearly as Sowerby trimmed our course a little, rising from behind the planet to bathe everything in warm, golden light.

"We're on our way," she reported, a little redundantly. Once we'd left the atmosphere, there really wasn't anywhere else to go.

I found the right beacon, marking the rift to Iceball, and the border of the League; we were off to a good start, our boost against the mass of the planet leaving us with no real need to increase our velocity by pinballing off any other celestial objects. By my reckoning we'd be there and through in a couple of days. Add a few more, say three or four, to cross the Iceball system, if we didn't lose too much velocity on the other side, and another couple to coast into Freedom after shooting the second rift, and I'd be feeling the soil of a League world under my boots within a week.

Idly, I noted the traffic patterns, finding them oddly similar to the vehicle routes I'd traversed in Dullingham. We'd joined a steady stream of vessels heading for the Iceball rift, while just as many were inbound; the main difference was that, unlike the ceaseless torrent of conveyances swarming the streets of the city, each one was separated by several hundred miles, rather than the mildly worrying foot or so around the fenders of the cabs I'd used. The Avalon route was equally congested, if that was quite the right term given the vast distances between ships, as were the two rift points leading to neutral systems and the Rimward Way beyond; only the rift to Rockhall seemed sparsely travelled, which I suppose was to be expected. With the situation as tense as it was, there was little trade to speak of; only a couple of Freebooter ships and a Guild mailboat were inbound from there, and only a single Guild freighter was heading for the disputed world.

Of course, once the Commonwealth claim was recognized, all that would change: Rockhall would become our second gateway port for the Rimward Way, as prominent and wealthy as Avalon, funneling trade and economic growth into most of the neighboring systems.

Something about that thought disturbed me, and it took a second or two of ratiocination before I realized what it was; I'd thought *our* gateway port, instead of *theirs*. I was a Guilder now; Commonwealth born, it was true, but no longer a part of it—but a lifetime of ingrained loyalties takes time to replace with new ones. Which, perhaps, explained why I was persisting with the commission I'd had from Aunt Jenny.

I pushed the thought to the back of my mind. Right now, I could be a Guilder and still keep my promises to my aunt: in fact, I was pretty much obliged to. With any luck, the two sets of loyalties would never come into conflict: and if they did, I'd just have to make a choice between them. Though, given my track record at that, I wished I could be more confident about making the right one.

CHAPTER EIGHTEEN
In which Remington gives and receives a blessing.

The journey to the rift point was just as uneventful as I'd expected, filled with the same mixture of fetching, carrying, and broom-piloting as before. I must admit that I was a lot more nervous than I tried to appear as we came closer to shooting it, unable to shake the memory of the incident with the incoming freighter when we were making the transit from Avalon: but this time round there were no telltale bow waves to make us hesitate, and we shot through neat as you please, Sowerby reporting green lights right across the board. (Even though the physical instrumentation was about as much use to a woman monitoring the ship's systems through her neuroware as a quill pen would have been.)

Once we were through, the constellations shifting almost imperceptibly apart from the subtraction of Iceball and the equally sudden addition of Numarkut, we continued our long trajectory towards the Freedom rift. I'd long since given up looking at the external view, in favor of the status displays Sowerby continued to monitor, as to the naked eye we might just as well have been completely motionless against the starfield. The gravitational readouts, however, told a different story, one of constant trimming against the gravity fields of every major body in the system, as she continued to squeeze the last possible iota of advantage from the space surrounding us. We'd be going nowhere near Iceball itself on this run, remaining locked in the stream of ships heading deeper into the League, although roughly a third of our fellow travelers were peeling off to make the run in towards the main center of habitation; the *Eddie Fitz* among them, I noted, with a sense of wry amusement. Instead, we'd make a slingshot maneuver around the largest gas giant, currently well placed to correct our course and give us a welcome velocity boost into the bargain.

"What'cha doing?" Clio asked, pausing in the task of painting over the repair she'd made to the handrail. Pointless pretending I was still sweeping up, as I'd been engrossed enough to stand completely still for several seconds.

"Watching the course change," I admitted, sharing the data with her 'sphere.

She nodded. "Good. You're meant to be learning." She poked at the tangle of trajectories, linking the two rift points and the world of Iceball in a roughly triangular skein. *So what are these?*

"Customs cutters," I said, looking at the small, fast-moving dots she'd indicated. They were maneuvering far too freely to be relying entirely on gravity repulsion, although, unlike the one which had intercepted us off Numarkut, they clearly had graviton generators on board as well: which probably meant weapon systems. I isolated a small group of vessels, lying off the gas giant in a clearly defensive formation. *And those are warships.* To a Navy brat, their profiles and orientation, able to support one another with overlapping fire arcs, was unmistakable.

"Warships?" Clio was clearly surprised. "What are they doing there?"

"Not a lot." I shrugged, although the answer seemed obvious enough to me. This was effectively the frontier of League space, and they'd be insane not to station at least a squadron close enough to the Numarkut rift to discourage an incursion through it. Not that the Commonwealth would ever be stupid enough to try moving any of their assets through the neutral system, as pissing off the Numarkuteers would cut them off from the Rimward Way as effectively as annoying the Guild enough to provoke a trade embargo—and however arrogant the saber-rattlers got, the Queen and her ministers were sufficiently pragmatic to avoid committing economic suicide. Though few, there were enough instances on record of governments incautious or arrogant enough to antagonize the

Guild, most of which had lasted no longer than the first food riots, to provide salutary reminders of why that sort of thing was a very bad idea.

Interesting: I was back to thinking of the Commonwealth as *they*. My inner Guilder clearly had the upper hand at the moment.

I focused my attention on the nearest cutter, just disengaging from the vessel in front of us and firing up its reaction drive. Sure enough, it was heading in our direction.

"Looks like the pirates are on their way," I said.

Clio laughed. "Not in this system. Preachers, more like."

If I'd been puzzled at the remark, her meaning became clear as soon as we were boarded. There were two of them this time; an earnest young man with a neatly trimmed beard, dressed in a black suit with a high collar which, judging by the tidemark of psoriasis on the back of his neck, chafed more than a little, and an older woman, whose neatly knotted tie and mirror-polished shoes positively screamed *career bureaucrat*. Both wore a small lapel pin in the shape of an open book, in case there could be any possible doubt that they were members of the Congregation of the Sanctified Brethren, and the woman had a small laminated card identifying her as an employee of the Tithing Bureau of Iceball clipped to her left breast pocket. Despite the local title, I noticed, it also carried the seal of the League of Democracies, a salutary reminder that my Commonwealth persona was now in enemy territory; which was all the more reason to be as visibly Guild as possible. The young man produced a similar identity tag from somewhere inside his jacket, and hung it around his neck on a lanyard, which probably did his rash no good at all.

"We have a transit waiver," Remington said, producing a piece of paper with the Farland logo clearly visible at the top, and a scrawled signature at the bottom.

The woman glanced at it, and nodded. "That seems to be in order. You have DNA confirmation of the signatory?"

"Of course." Remington handed over the scraping of skin cells I'd been sent to collect. The young man took a small device from his jacket pocket, into which he inserted the slide. It beeped, and something scrolled up the tiny screen inset into its surface: though what it might have been I had no idea, being too far away to see it clearly. Remembering Plubek's handheld, I tried poking it with my sneakware, but it wasn't meshed into anything—judging by the socket on the side, it had to be physically connected to a terminal to exchange data with the wider world. Come to that, the datascape was completely blank around the pair of them: no neuroware at all, and no fuzzy ball of information betraying the presence of a data handling device of any kind.

"That seems to be in order." He read a little more from the screen, and frowned. "But your file sample doesn't seem to match the recipient."

"Because it was collected by my apprentice here." Remington gestured in my direction, and produced a copy of the docket I'd signed at the Farland reception desk.

The bureaucrat's face took on a solemn expression. "That's highly irregular."

"I'm the Captain of this vessel. I'm entitled to delegate whatever tasks I see fit," Remington said patiently.

"I'm not disputing that," the woman replied evenly. "I merely pointed out that delegating such an important task to the most junior member of your crew was more than a little unusual."

"He's meant to be learning," Remington said, "and the earlier he comes to appreciate the importance of following the correct procedures the better." Somehow he kept his face straight, and a tone of earnest practicality in his voice, for the entire sentence.

"Quite true." She nodded briskly, taking everything he'd said entirely at face value. "A creditable attitude, which all too many of your peers would do well to emulate." She turned to me. "I'll need confirmation of that, young man."

"Of course," I said; that was, after all, why I was there in the first place. I held out my palm, for her colleague to press his device against; it turned out to have a wooden casing, which felt warm against my hand. Something stung my palm, and he removed it, revealing a small needle mark, already beginning to fade. He consulted the screen again.

"That seems perfectly satisfactory." He nodded to his companion.

"Then I believe we're finished." She inclined her head, in brusque dismissal. "Captain Remington. May your voyage be blessed."

"And your endeavors likewise." He returned the nod solemnly, holding his hands together, then spreading them as if opening a book.

The Iceballers looked faintly surprised, and repeated the gesture, the young man juggling his genereader a little awkwardly in the process. Then they disappeared through the docking port, which ground closed behind them.

"I didn't know you'd been Sanctified," I said, referring to the sign of the book he'd just made.

"I'm not." The skipper grinned. "But I gather it's good manners among the God-botherers to return a blessing when you're given one. And it sometimes makes them drop things." He hesitated, glancing at me. "No offence. If you're that way inclined, I mean."

I shrugged. "I don't bother God, She doesn't bother me. We're not exactly on speaking terms." Although I'd never quite been able to shake the faith I was raised in either. A universe without Her guiding hand seemed a bit too cold and random to feel comfortable in.

"Fine." Remington seemed to have lost all interest in the topic. He handed me the wodge of paperwork. "Go and put these somewhere, will you? I need to talk to Sarah."

"And that was all there was to it," I concluded, after filling Clio in on all the excitement she hadn't missed while I'd been talking to the Iceball bureaucrats. "Is it always that easy?"

"Depends which system you're in," she said carefully. "I've been a few places where they board and search anyway, but most worlds don't even bother docking a cutter when you've got a transit waiver. They just link nodes, and exchange the data directly." Then she grinned. "Why would a Numarkut inspector bother coming aboard when there's nothing to legally confiscate?"

"Good point," I agreed, and returned to pretending to work.

We coasted on through the Iceball system without any further incident, leaving it through the Freedom rift a little over three days after we'd first entered. By this point I was beginning to feel something of an old hand at the business of rift shooting, so this time my nervousness was a little less pronounced as we went through: but I was still interested enough to be meshed in during the process, which meant I was probably one of the first people aboard to realize that things were starting to go very wrong indeed.

Not that there was any sign of trouble to begin with. We came through the rift at a fair clip, and at a good angle, which ought to have taken us to Freedom (or at any rate the orbital docks above it) comfortably within the couple of days I'd originally estimated, after some minimal course correction. The line of ships we'd followed was falling into the center of the system, or peeling off to continue their voyage through the second or third rifts to somewhere deeper within the League, shepherded by customs cutters; which, in the case of those vessels passing through, seemed just as content not to board as Clio had intimated.

Which reminded me, we should be due a visit from the local inspectors any time soon. Moved more by idle curiosity than anything else, I took a closer look at the steady stream of vessels inbound for Freedom, wondering if I could pick out the cutter heading in our direction from the mass of shipping ahead of us.

Skipper, I sent, as mental alarm bells started going off, *something's not right.*

To his credit, Remington didn't waste time telling me to sod off, he was busy, despite the obvious temptation to do so; his own 'sphere was a blizzard of data, cascading in from the ship's systems in the aftermath of our rift shot. *Nothing ever is. Be more specific.*

I meshed directly with his 'sphere, drawing his attention to the anomalies I'd spotted. A couple of the vessels ahead of us had League ships matching their course and velocity exactly. Moreover, they weren't just customs cutters if I was any judge: they had at least twice as much mass, and their gravitic signature hinted very strongly at heavier armament than a patrol boat would normally carry. *Those freighters are under escort. By something the size of a corvette.*

Which you'd know how, exactly? Despite his manifest skepticism, he focused in on them at once, filleting the data for confirmation.

You mean apart from growing up surrounded by Naval officers? Damn it, the sarcasm seemed to be contagious, and there was really no time to indulge in it. I tried to appear conciliatory. *They look like system defense boats to me.*

Better and better, Remington replied dryly. As their name implied, system defense boats were never intended to travel through a rift, their entire gravitic output being channeled through their weapons arrays, which made them formidable opponents size for size; the one heading in our direction could probably go toe-to-toe with a light cruiser, like the one my mother commanded, let alone an unarmed cargo ship like the *Stacked Deck*.

I started trying to make sense of the pattern I was looking at. Nearly all the ships heading in to Freedom were being boarded and inspected by customs cutters in the usual way; even as I looked, one undocked from a Guild merchantman, and came about to intercept the next vessel on its list. Nothing out of the ordinary there. There must be something in particular about the ships the SDBs were targeting.

Origin was the most obvious; a quick rummage back through the sensor logs was enough to confirm that they'd all left Numarkut a little ahead of us, and sailed on through the Iceball system without so much as slowing down. Just as we had. But then so had the Guild ship that had just passed its inspection, and the majority of the other ships around us too. It must be something more specific than that.

Isn't that your Freebooter friend? Remington asked, pointing out one of the vessels ahead of us.

Could be, I conceded, pulling up the data from its ident beacon. Sure enough, it was the *Poison 4*, Captain Ertica commanding. *So what?*

So she's on the shit list too, Remington sent, highlighting the system defense boat closing with the Freebooter vessel. A terse exchange of messages followed, too tenuous at this distance for me to eavesdrop on, however much I'd have liked to: it would have answered all my questions then and there. One thing was certain, however, neither party to the conversation was getting the answers they wanted: without warning, the *Poison 4* swung out of the shipping lane, reversing its course back towards the Iceball rift.

Neat trick, Remington commented. *Wonder how she did it?*

Took a boost directly off the sun, Sowerby cut in, having noticed Remington's distraction and meshed in to see what had taken so much of his attention. *It's the biggest mass in the system to push against.* Which I suppose must have accounted for the Freebooter's astonishing rate of acceleration—far more than most skippers would ever have countenanced, as it would have left the crew as little more than an unpleasant stain on the bulkheads if the internal field had failed. *Don't feel you have to try it.*

Can't see that I'd ever be that desperate, Remington agreed.

It certainly was a desperate gamble; the SDB came about and set off in pursuit, working hard to make up the lead the Freebooter had established. I started running the numbers. At that speed she'd be back to the rift point in a couple of hours, and away through it before any of the scattered customs cutters could move to intercept, although hopping from one League system to another without the proper paperwork didn't seem to offer much in the way of a long-term solution that I could see. One riftcom message, and they'd be run down before they had a chance to shoot the rift back to Numarkut.

Anyhow, the question soon became a purely academic one. The pursuing boat was suddenly surrounded by a nimbus of charged gravitons, which could have only one explanation: I'd been right about the weapons suite.

They're firing, Sowerby confirmed, no doubt after checking her own, more highly tuned, instruments.

Space rippled as the defense boat lashed out at the fleeing Freebooter, engulfing the fugitive ship in a dense pocket of increased mass, then tore open for an instant too short to measure. The *Poison 4* vanished into one of the uncountable dead-end rifts riddling the system, then popped back into existence looking much the worse for wear.

"Rift bounce," I said aloud, involuntarily. The extra velocity the Freebooter had put on to escape the pursuing defense boat had worked against her now, massively increasing the amount of damage she'd suffered from ricocheting off the closed end.

She's leaking atmo, Sowerby sent, pushing the cleaned-up data she was gleaning into the wider 'sphere, where Remington and I could see it more clearly. *And that doesn't look too good either.* She focused in on one of the readouts. The crippled vessel's core temperature was climbing exponentially. *Power plant's redlining.*

Why don't they shut it down? I asked.

I imagine they're trying, Remington commented dryly. *Wouldn't you?*

Then they'd better be quick about it, Sowerby added, self-evidently. Even to me, with only the most cursory knowledge of such things, it was obvious we were watching a runaway fusion reaction; and I'd heard enough dinner-table talk about naval engagements to know that those seldom ended well. A skilled, dedicated, and cool-headed engineer might be able to damp one, vent the plasma, and leave a crippled hulk to limp its way home or await rescue, but they'd need a healthy side-order of luck into the bargain: and I somehow doubted that a Freebooter crew would have anyone of that caliber aboard.

But I was wrong. *There she goes*, Sowerby commented, as a plume of concentrated star-stuff erupted from the crippled Freebooter; but instead of converting the whole vessel instantly into a cloud of expanding vapor, as I'd expected, it bled off harmlessly into the void, merely taking a section of hull plating along with it. *Now that was impressive.*

A comment I couldn't help but agree with, although the surviving crew was still in serious trouble. There wasn't much air leaking out any more, which implied that someone had got to the pressure doors in time, but without power they'd start to suffocate and freeze before too much time elapsed. *Can we help them?*

Help them? Somehow, Remington managed to inject a tone of surprise into the neutral message. *They're not Guild. And even if they were, I don't think now's a good time to break formation.*

Besides, the pursuit ship'll be there long before we could arrive, Sowerby added. Which was a good point. It was already maneuvering to match course and velocity with the drifting wreck. *And we've got troubles of our own.* Which was an even better one. The system defense boat I'd noticed before was approaching on a course, and at a speed, which could only be intended to intercept us. An assumption that was confirmed almost instantly, as a voice burst suddenly from every speaker aboard.

"Commerce Guild vessel *Stacked Deck*, this is the System Defense Force vessel *Presumption of Innocence*. Please maintain your current speed and heading, and prepare to be boarded."

"*Presumption of Innocence*, this is Captain John Remington responding." The skipper's voice was on every channel too, no doubt intended to reassure the rest of the crew; although, mercifully, no one else would be aware of the destruction of the Freebooter yet. "Maintaining course and speed as requested." This was a nice touch, reminding the *Presumption*'s skipper that we were Guilders, and not to be ordered around, or threatened with force. Potting Freebooters was one thing, but firing on a Guild vessel without a very good reason could escalate uncontrollably, damnably fast, with career-terminating consequences for the trigger-happy captain. Of course that would be scant comfort to us, if our flash-frozen corpses were on a leisurely cometary orbit around Freedom. "We'll have our manifests ready for customs inspection."

"That won't be required at this time," the *Presumption*'s skipper replied evenly. "Your vessel is hereby impounded, on suspicion of engagement in espionage against the League of Democracies."

CHAPTER NINETEEN
In which our delivery is indefinitely delayed.

"This is completely ridiculous," Remington expostulated, for about the hundredth time. The young officer in the uniform of the League Navy inclined his head, with the expression of someone who'd heard it all before and wasn't about to believe it this time either, but was determined to be courteous in any case. I assumed his name was Neville, as that was stenciled on his light grey body armor, beneath the single star and thin line denoting his rank. If I remembered League insignia correctly, that meant he was an ensign, barely an officer at all, probably on his first posting after graduation; but the novelty of seeing a man in uniform in a real position of authority, being trusted to act independently of his immediate superiors, shook me more than I'd expected. If I'm honest, I also felt a faint pang of jealousy—it was like being brought face to face with myself in a couple of years time, if I hadn't screwed up so badly at the Academy on Avalon. "We're on a contracted cargo run, for a broker on Numarkut."

"That would be Farland Freight Forwarding, correct?" The young ensign smoothed his moustache, which failed utterly to impart an air of gravitas and maturity to his faintly cherubic face. Clio seemed fascinated by him, though, gazing in his direction at every opportunity, occasionally glancing briefly at me to see if I'd spotted whatever it was about him that was so compelling: although so far I hadn't, unless it was the party of armed matelots accompanying him, most of whom were wandering around the hold poking at things, apparently in the vague hope that something incriminating would fall on their heads. Unsurprisingly, the talk of espionage had me thoroughly spooked, and I found myself wondering if Mallow had been right, and the League's intelligence agencies had become aware of my mission after all. But in that case, why hadn't they simply arrested me, instead of impounding a whole handful of ships, and blowing the *Poison 4* to kingdom come?

"It would," Remington confirmed, quite pointlessly, as their logo was all over the paperwork.

"Which turns out to have been employing an undercover agent of the Commonwealth Security Service." Neville paused, although whether for dramatic effect, or to see if any of the members of the *Stacked Deck*'s crew who'd turned up to enjoy the show were suddenly and visibly stricken with guilt, was beyond me. Drawing on the experience of years of hiding large segments of my social life from Mother, I continued to present a largely unruffled exterior to the world. I did, however, find myself wondering how Mallow was faring, and hoped he'd made a clean getaway. I had no idea what the penalty for espionage was on Numarkut, although from what I'd seen of the place I rather suspected it depended on how much money changed hands. "The broker, in fact, who contracted you for your present delivery."

"Ellie's a spy? Really?" Remington asked, in the tone of voice peculiar to a polite simulation of interest. "Well, she certainly fooled me."

"She seems to have fooled a lot of people," the young ensign said. "But our people on Numarkut are certain she used her position to engage agents among merchant crews to gather information on their trips into the League. Several of them, in fact."

"Lets us out, then," Remington said easily. "We've been in the Commonwealth for the last few months. Hauling supplies for their Fleet Auxiliary."

Neville's upper lip quivered, in what might have been a smile, but looked more like a tap-dancing caterpillar. "Hardly good reason for us to trust you," he pointed out. "Although I'm sure my superiors will be happy to debrief you about that."

"I'm open to offers," Remington replied, making it clear that any information about his earlier contract for Aunt Jenny would have to be paid for: although I was pretty sure that, knowing Guilders as well as she did, she would have been careful not to let him know much of any use to the League's intelligence analysts in any case.

Of course I hadn't just been standing idly by while this exchange was going on. Typically for Leaguers, none of the boarding party had any neuroware, which left nothing for my sneakware to exploit; but Neville had a handheld with him, gravid with data, which hung there like a ripe fruit just out of my reach. The problem was, he wasn't using it to link to the node aboard the defense boat, which meant there was no obvious way into it. Although I'd incorporated some military grade datanomes into my skeleton keys, filched from Tinkie while we were rummaging through Mother's forgotten message, they were for Commonwealth protocols, and attempting to use them on a League system would simply be asking for trouble. I'd just have to bide my time, and hope for an opportunity before the boarding party left the *Stacked Deck*.

"Everyone seems to be taking this remarkably calmly," I said, as Clio ambled over in my direction, her gaze still fixed on the young ensign.

"Why wouldn't they?" She seemed honestly surprised. "These things happen every now and then. Pretty much every government issues information-gathering contracts to Guilders, so they just take it for granted that a few of the Guild ships in their space are doing the same thing for other powers. Sometimes they think they've found one, and move in on it."

"And the Guild just lets them?" I asked, not quite believing that. The Guild's power depended on everybody else being too scared of a trade embargo to confront them, at least directly. Impounding a ship looked pretty much like confrontation to me.

"So long as they stick to the rules," Clio said.

"Right. There are rules." Of course there were rules. Rules and custom seemed to dictate pretty much any interaction between the Guild and the rest of the galaxy.

"They'll just escort us to a secure location," Clio said, "while they investigate. When they find out they're wasting their time, they'll let us complete our run, so we don't break our word on delivery."

"And pay us a nice big sum of money to compensate for the earnings we've lost while we're twiddling our thumbs," Remington added, looking remarkably cheerful at the prospect. He spoke a little louder than normal, intending the League officer to overhear. "So it's in everybody's interest to get this nonsense sorted out as quickly as possible."

"Right," I agreed. I tried to make my next question sound casual. "And what happens if they do find a ship's been spying?"

"Not a lot," Remington said, his voice returning to normal. "Just keep it impounded until the information's too out of date to be useful, so the crew don't renege on their contract." That made sense. Completely preventing a Guilder from fulfilling a promise would definitely have serious consequences, but most of them would be perfectly happy to live up to the letter of an agreement while letting the spirit fend for itself. "And if there's an actual shooting war going on, we'd have to sign an undertaking not to return to either side's territory until the dust settles."

"Well, that doesn't sound too bad," I said, trying to sound as casual as everyone else did about the situation. Things might be tense between the Commonwealth and the League at the moment, but they hadn't escalated to open conflict just yet, and if the diplomats on both sides did their jobs, with any luck it never would. I tried not to think about the consequences if they failed to, but a series of vivid mental images exploded in my mind anyway: Mother's lone cruiser drifting through the desolation of an uninhabited system, venting air and plasma like the *Poison 4*, while wave after wave of League ships poured through the rift towards Rockhall; Tinkie plummeting through the atmosphere in her deployment armor, while the ground defenses filled the air around her with lethal countermeasures, dying before she even hit the ground; Dad alone at the funerals, deprived by my selfishness and stupidity of even the presence of a son to help him grieve.

"It's bad enough." Rennau appeared with a small datacache, which he handed unceremoniously to the nearest matelot, who promptly shouldered her small arm and went trotting off with it towards the officer. "Always a lot of money to be made in a war zone, and we'd miss out."

"Which wouldn't be good." Remington nodded in agreement. "Moving supplies, evacuating wounded, all kinds of contracts. Hazard rates, good bonuses—"

"Getting shot at," I added, perhaps a little more sourly than I'd intended—if I'm honest, I found their casual attitude rather callous.

But then, I suppose, neither of them had people they cared about in the firing line.

"Fire on a Guild ship?" Clio actually laughed at that, and both the men smiled at me tolerantly. "No one would dare."

Her father nodded. "All the Guilders in their own logistics chain would regard that as a breach of contract, and pull out at once." Which would hand victory to the enemy overnight. An even better guarantor of good behavior than the threat of a trade embargo.

"I can see that," I said cautiously. A thought occurred to me. "What if one of the combatants pretends to be a Guilder? So as not to be shot at?"

"Same result," Remington said. "Any violation of Guild neutrality would be taken as an act of bad faith, and we'd unilaterally rescind the contract." Thereby letting the other side win *and* risking an embargo. Definitely not a strategy worth taking a chance on.

"Besides," Clio added, "you couldn't disguise a warship as an ordinary Guilder, the weapons would be too obvious. And any privateers in the warzone would already be accounted for."

"As well as having very specific contracts," Rennau added. Which was also true. The handful of armed merchantmen on the Guild registry tended to take commissions which weren't entirely legal according to the local governments; which probably accounted for them, or their neighbors, being the privateers' biggest clients.

Though it was undeniably interesting, my attention hadn't been entirely on the conversation. While it was going on, I'd been eyeing the datacache through my 'sphere, following the little sparks of information as the matelot carried it over to the young ensign with the comely facial hair. They conferred for a moment, the League sailor gesticulating in Rennau's direction, then, as I'd hoped, Neville meshed his handheld with the cache.

I watched the whole process avidly, recording everything as our manifests, crew list, and Sowerby's maintenance records drained into the ensign's device in less than a second. There wasn't time to try piggybacking on the transfer, and I was by no means sure I'd have dared to in any case; there were bound to be traps and countermeasures in place to prevent that kind of thing, and even in data time I'd have to react almost instantly to what I found there. Far better to take my time, and what I'd learned, to craft a piece of sneakware which would be taken for a legitimate mesh right from the start: it certainly sounded as if I'd have plenty of time to practice.

Any luck? Remington asked, having noticed my momentary distraction, and I shook my head, almost imperceptibly.

Too well protected. But I've seen enough to get started.

And I really thought I had. But, of course, the Leaguers knew about neuroware, even if they didn't use it themselves, and they were bright enough to have take precautions against it.

Eventually, the Leaguers seemed to decide that they'd wasted enough time rummaging around the *Stacked Deck* in search of nonexistent contraband or evidence of spying, and retreated to their ship, leaving us to our own devices. No one was particularly sorry to see them go, although Clio took a little longer than seemed strictly necessary in escorting Ensign Neville to the personnel lock, and assuring him of our full cooperation. I may have remarked on the fact, because Rennau looked at me in what I can only describe as a faintly pitying manner.

"Well, what did you expect?" he said. "You've had your chance," but before I could respond to that, Clio returned, looking faintly flushed, and he quickly changed the subject.

It took us the better part of two days to reach our destination, which, despite what I'd expected, was nowhere near Freedom itself. We left the main shipping lane an hour our so after being boarded, the *Presumption of Innocence* remaining alongside the whole time to ensure our compliance; although, after having witnessed the crippling of the *Poison 4*, I have to confess that her presence made me feel more than a little uneasy. Not that there was any need for force in our case, or even the threat of it; there was apparently a protocol for this sort of thing, which Remington and his crew seemed happy enough to follow.

So it was that we found ourselves coasting in to dock at a military void station hanging just above the Freedom system's biggest gas giant, an ominous, looming presence, striated in shades of blood and bile, and pockmarked with storms the size of the world I grew up on. If it had been very much larger it would have collapsed into a small protostar, a dim binary companion to Freedom itself, but as it was it remained nothing more than a planet of prodigious size. Which made it the perfect place to site a naval base, of course: departing ships would have all that mass to boost against, letting them accelerate quickly towards any of the rift points in the system, without having to slingshot around anything to build up momentum. Not to mention the dozens of moons, hundreds of smaller rocks, and millions of tiny objects orbiting the place, which would confuse the sensors of any enemy attempting to attack it, and which provided an almost inexhaustible supply of raw materials for the shipyard hanging in the same orbit. Coasting in, I spotted half a dozen vessels undergoing refit, surrounded by work drones and void-suited hulljacks, although with their beacons powered down there was no obvious indication of their names and classes; judging by their mass readings, however, most were about the same size as the *Stacked Deck*.

From which you'll probably infer that I was meshed-in as we approached the station, observing all that I could, and recording it too: I'd no doubt that Aunt Jenny would be more than a little interested in a first hand look at a major League naval installation. To my relief, as before, nearly all the off-duty crew were doing the same (apart, I presumed, from the recording part), which would act as a useful smokescreen for my intelligence-gathering: if I'd been the only one meshing in on our approach, I might as well be walking around in a T shirt saying *Commonwealth Spy*. If, indeed, that's what I was any more. I found myself remembering Aunt Jenny trying to explain how her two roles intermingled; a conversation which made a great deal more sense to me now. These days I felt more like a Guild apprentice than her eyes and ears, although the promises I'd made, and a residue of familial loyalty, kept me working at the commission she'd given me.

My first sight of the station itself, through the hull-mounted cameras, came as a surprise. I'd been expecting something like Skyhaven, though not quite on the same scale, but this looked completely different. One of the countless fragments of orbital flotsam had been built on and burrowed into, about a third of its grey, rocky surface encrusted with pressure domes, antennae, and docking cradles. Much of the rest was pocked with viewports and exterior hatches, leaking light out into the void, as if the whole thing had been turned into a gigantic halloween lantern.

And gigantic was the word. As the *Stacked Deck* swooped lower, the *Presumption of Innocence* maintaining her station at our side, I began to pick out a few details which enabled me to gauge the scale of things; the rock, and the base it contained, must have been roughly half a mile from end to end, and two thirds that across the middle, tapering slightly towards roughly rounded ends. Absurdly, I was reminded of a baked potato, left too long in the oven, to shrivel in its own skin.

"Kincora Base, this is the Guild merchantman *Stacked Deck* requesting permission to land," Remington transmitted, as if we had any choice in the matter, never slow to take the initiative in reminding our hosts of our privileged status.

"Acknowledged, *Stacked Deck*. Proceed to docking cradle delta zero niner." So, there were at least four different clusters of cradles on the surface of the rock. Or Kincora Base, as I supposed I'd have to start thinking of it from now on. For different types of vessels, or just to minimize the movement of goods and personnel around the interior? I made a mental note to find out.

I returned my attention to the visual image, while Sowerby's feedback from the power plant and the gravitics streamed through my wider 'sphere more or less unnoticed; to my inexpert eye they both looked pretty much optimal, which was hardly surprising for an engineer of her caliber. We were slowing, drifting over the base's surface, gradually descending towards what, for a moment, I'd taken for a cluster of craters, in shadow from the gas giant's baleful red glow. A moment later I realized they were too regular, and too regularly spaced, to be natural, an impression enhanced by the metal lining which became clearly visible as we began to drop into one. In an almost complete reversal of our undocking from Skyhaven, the field of view gradually narrowed and darkened, to finally disappear altogether.

"Down and docked," Rennau reported from his station. "Engaging clamps." Not that they ought to be needed, the local gravity field would be focused on the cradle, so the *Stacked Deck* would feel it was resting comfortably on the ground (which would actually have put intolerable stresses on the hull, but you know what I mean). But in the event of a power failure or some similar emergency the rock's miniscule natural gravity field wouldn't be sufficient to keep her in place, so a physical connection made a good deal of sense.

"Powering down," Sowerby said, and the readouts I was monitoring from her station started tending towards zero. "Initiating standby mode."

That was when it hit me just how long we were likely to be here. While we'd laid over on Numarkut, the power plant had been running on a reduced load, but shutting it down almost entirely, producing a mere trickle of energy to keep the onboard systems ticking over, implied that we'd be away from the ship for weeks, if not months.

"All hands, stand by to disembark," Remington ordered over the *Stacked Deck*'s internal speakers. "And don't forget to pick up your kit. Anything you leave behind, you'll just have to do without."

Forewarned, I'd packed my kitbag on the journey here; all I had to do was pick it up off the bed. I did so, and stood, feeling the space of my cabin all around me, wondering why I was suddenly so reluctant to leave it—then it struck me, this was the first real home I'd ever had. The house I'd grown up in was Mother's, suffused with her presence even in her long and frequent absences, and my dorm room at Summerhall had been just that, somewhere to sleep, between more interesting activities. (And the odd tedious lecture on estate management.) But this cramped stateroom aboard the *Stacked Deck* was entirely mine.

After a moment I got a grip, and opened the door, only to step back inside again almost at once as Rolf and Lena strode past, sweeping all before them like a flesh tsunami.

As soon as the corridor was clear again, I stepped out into it, pausing only to grab the white cloth from my door handle; even if the Leaguers knew what it meant, I didn't imagine for one moment that they'd respect it. I wadded it into a ball, and turned back momentarily to chuck it onto the bed, taking the opportunity for one last look round.

Of course I had no idea at the time that I'd never set foot in that room again.

CHAPTER TWENTY
In which Clio makes a new friend.

I wasn't quite sure what to expect as my shipmates and I assembled in one of the mid-level cargo holds, never having been interned as a suspected enemy agent before, but no one else seemed particularly worried. If anything, there was something of a party atmosphere, most of the crew treating it as a break in their normal routine; a couple were passing round bottles ("I'm not leaving the good stuff for some thieving squaddie to nick"): a quick gulp of one went a long way towards restoring my own good humour, not to mention providing a quick object lesson in the subjectivity of what constituted the "good stuff."

Not all the conversation was verbal, of course, the constant exchanges blizzarding through the datasphere neatly counterpointing the background hum of chatter echoing round the cavernous storage space.

Simon. A message from Remington cut through the babble, marked urgent, and layered with privacy protocols. I glanced round automatically, despite knowing he wasn't there yet, still locking down the bridge with Rennau, while Sowerby and her assistants did much the same thing in engineering. *Any luck with that thing you've been working on?* He didn't need, or dare, to be any more specific than that—the Leaguers might not use or approve of neuroware, but that didn't mean they couldn't find other ways to monitor our exchanges.

Needless to say, I'd spent much of our journey across the system tweaking and fiddling with datanomes, trying to put something together which would let me get into the next handheld I came across; or, better still, into a full node, if the opportunity presented itself.

A bit, I sent, keeping things simple. In truth, I was pretty confident, but I liked to sound less so than I actually was—mainly because it wasn't so embarrassing if I turned out to be wrong. *I won't really know how well it works until I try to get into something, though.*

Then don't try, Remington warned. *The last thing we need now is for one of the crew to look like they really are spying. It'd take forever to sort out, and we'd lose a fortune.* In truth, the compensation payment for a delay in completing our contract wouldn't be quite as generous as all that, but it would certainly come in handy—and, if the League wanted to play by the letter of the Guild agreement, keeping the *Stacked Deck* impounded until details of an operational military base were no longer of immediate use to an enemy would effectively maroon us all here for life. Of course it wouldn't come to that, the local Guildhall would send an intermediary, who would broker some sort of compromise—but that would take time, and undoubtedly involve an undertaking not to set foot in Commonwealth space again for the foreseeable future, neither of which was going to sit well with my commission from my aunt. Come to that, I didn't suppose it would win me many friends among the crew either.

Got it, I sent back, careful not to make any actual promises: I really was starting to think like a Guilder.

"I hope so," Remington said, materializing at my shoulder. "Because pissing off people with guns seldom ends well."

"Neither does shooting Guilders," I said, trying to sound a lot more casual than I felt.

"True." Remington nodded, conceding the point. "But retribution after the fact's not much good to a corpse."

"Someone's cheerful this morning," Rennau said, hefting a bulging kitbag onto his shoulder as he approached us. He glanced meaningfully in my direction. "But if this conversation's about what I think it is, you'd better be listening. Because if I find out you've been doing anything at all to complicate matters, I'll get to you long before our hosts do. Are we clear?"

"Pellucid," I assured him. Quite what he proposed to do if he caught me prying into areas I wasn't supposed to I had no idea, but I knew him well enough by now to be sure that I never wanted to find out.

"Good." He turned to Remington. "And talking of our hosts—"

He never got to make whatever disparaging remark he'd prepared about their tardiness, though, as, with a *thunk!* of disengaging bolts, and a faint hiss of equalizing pressure, the main hatch began to grind open. Through it stepped Neville, and what looked to me like the same boarding party which had accompanied him before: although it was hard to be entirely sure, as people in uniform pointing guns at you tend to look pretty much alike. Behind them hovered a dozen or so drones, bristling with sensor gear, peering into every corner of the electromagnetic spectrum: I tried to take a peek at what they were seeing, but their integral processors shrugged me off with some heavy duty encryption. Which, to be honest, was pretty much what I'd expected; nevertheless, I recorded the attempt, particularly some promising datanomes I just might be able to reverse engineer a key from. A moment later they'd scattered, no doubt to examine every square inch of the vessel for nonexistent evidence.

"Ensign Neville." Remington stepped forward, his hand extended for a shake, neatly wrong-footing the young officer, whose own right hand had been hovering unobtrusively next to his sidearm. The inadvisability of shooting Guilders notwithstanding, it seemed, Neville wasn't one to take anything for granted, particularly the goodwill of people whose home and livelihood he'd just impounded. (Well, not him personally, of course, he'd been acting under orders from his captain, who'd got hers—or possibly his, given the League's much-vaunted egalitarianism—from somewhere a great deal further up the chain of command.) "Nice to see you again." After a moment, Neville took the proffered hand and shook it as though he suspected it concealed something squishy.

"It certainly is," Clio agreed, with rather more enthusiasm than I thought was warranted under the circumstances.

"If you'll all follow me," Neville replied, speaking directly to Clio for some reason, as though she, rather than Remington, was in charge, "I'll show you to your quarters."

"Thank you." Clio smiled at the ensign, which seemed to disconcert him even more than Remington's handshake had, and held out a bulging kitbag. "If you wouldn't mind? It's rather heavy."

"Not at all." Neville was clearly losing the initiative, much to the inadequately concealed amusement of the men and women under his command. He hefted Clio's bag, which was, in truth, far lighter than loads I'd seen her lugging around the holds without a second thought, and began to lead the way towards the cargo hatch.

"She's quick off the mark, I'll give her that," Remington remarked, as the rest of us lined up to follow, the members of the boarding party considerately not quite pointing their guns in our direction.

"Takes after her mother," Rennau said, with a fond paternal smile.

My first impression on stepping through the hatch was of a smaller version of the docking ports on Skyhaven—although in this case "smaller" was something of a relative term. A broad plain of flat gray rock, broken by the smooth metal domes of the docking ports, stretched across a vast cavern, illuminated by floodlights depending from the ceiling. Ours wasn't the only berth occupied, of course, but whether entirely by other impounded merchantmen, or a mixed bag of those and other vessels, I couldn't be sure. The latter seemed more likely, though, given the number of drones and light vehicles buzzing around one of the docked ships in the distance, which seemed to be in the process of unloading: I was fairly certain that the cargo aboard the *Stacked Deck* would be considered under the protection of the Commerce Guild, and that the League would therefore leave it alone. Of course any non-Guild freighters that had had the misfortune to be seized could be looted with impunity, but it still seemed more likely that I was seeing the arrival of a regularly scheduled cargo run. And it went without saying that Neville's presence meant that one of the adjacent domes was certain to be concealing the *Presumption of Innocence*.

I glanced around, wondering which of them it was. Which was a stupid question: it just had to be the next docking port over, Neville's captain apparently having taken his or her instructions to keep a close eye on us more or less literally. It wasn't that hard to spot, given the number of people in League naval uniform milling around its gaping hatches, although what errands they might be on I didn't have a clue.

I stretched out my 'sphere, searching for anyone in the vicinity who might be out of my line of sight, but, as I'd expected, the only neuroware interfaces I could detect were those of my shipmates. Many of the hurrying figures had bright flashes of data hovering around them, though, indicating the presence of handhelds, or other information-handling devices, but none of them seemed linked to a node anywhere in the vicinity, which effectively shut me out of any attempt to get into them. And even if I had seen an opening, I'm not sure I would have taken it, with Remington and Rennau's warnings still fresh in my mind: I was pretty sure they were both keeping a wary eye on my own 'sphere, to make sure I complied, and I wasn't stupid enough to test the hypothesis the hard way.

The biggest difference I could see from the docks on the orbital was that everything was on the same plane, all the gravity in the chamber pointing in the same direction: which was hardly a surprise, now I came to think about it. Unlike the Skyhaven docking arm, which was free to add cradles on any edge, this gash in the rock only had one side directly facing the void. The other three would be surrounded by solid rock, or, more likely, whatever other passageways and chambers had been burrowed into it. I made a firm resolve to find and access a detailed plan as soon as I could—not just for its intelligence value, although I was sure that would be considerable, but to satisfy my curiosity about our surroundings.

Which was only piqued by Neville, who escorted us to a waiting utility sled, hovering a few inches off the floor. It was a heavy duty model, about twenty feet long, the kind of flatbed I was more used to seeing scurrying around under an open sky in the streets of a city, or hovering over the fields at harvest time while the drones piled it high with root vegetables. Bench seats had been installed, temporarily, judging by the finish, and the way they'd been locked into place with the retainers normally used to secure cargo pallets.

"This looks comfortable," Lena said, with patent insincerity, climbing easily over the tailgate. The power plant hummed as the sled began to tilt, and the onboard system fed a little more energy into the emitters on that corner to compensate. The buzzing went on, rising and falling in pitch, for several seconds while she found a seat, stowed her kit under it, and her husband joined her. I couldn't be entirely sure, but it looked to me as if the sled's nose had tilted up about a quarter of an inch by the time the two of them had settled.

"I'm sorry it's so basic," Neville said, still apparently talking to Clio rather than the rest of us, as he extended an arm to help her up. She slipped, and, to my surprise, he took her weight easily, clearly a good deal stronger than he looked. "There wasn't much time to make the arrangements."

"I can appreciate that," Clio said, with a disarming smile. "Having to accommodate what, half a dozen ships' crews on a couple of days notice?"

"Five," Neville said, without thinking, and paused, as the belated realization that he might have been a little indiscreet began to sink in.

"That many?" Remington stepped into the awkward silence. "Ellie was a busy girl." He fixed the young ensign with an affable grin, through which the underlying steel barely showed. "But of course we're not all part of her network. I think you'll find most people undertook contracts with her entirely in good faith."

"Damn right." Rennau didn't bother even pretending to affability. "And I'll thank you not to flirt with my daughter while you're waving a gun in my face."

"I wasn't—I'm not—" Neville flushed, taken completely aback, much to the almost-concealed amusement of his subordinates.

"What are you going to do, ground me?" Clio shot back. "And he's not waving a gun, it's still in his holster."

"It's a metaphorical gun," Rennau snapped, throwing his kitbag aboard the sled, and vaulting over the tailgate.

I followed, feeling faintly bemused. I'd heard Rennau raising his voice often enough since joining the crew of the *Stacked Deck*, but never to Clio, and, come to that, I'd never heard her argue with her father before either. Pointedly turning her back on him, she smiled at Neville. "Are you going to be docked here for long?"

"Just a few hours." He answered automatically, still looking vaguely stunned at this unexpected turn of events. "We're going back out on patrol once we've finished the paperwork."

"But you will be back?" Clio persisted, holding eye contact for just a fraction of a second longer than necessary.

"In about a week." He stepped back from the sled, maintaining eye contact in his turn, and grinned.

"Maybe we'll see you then," Clio said breezily, and settled into a seat at the side of the sled, where she could rest her arm more easily. A second later the driver fed power to the emitters, and the vehicle began to move. She turned to wave to Neville, and then back to Rennau. "What the hell was all that about?"

"Just smoothing the path," Rennau said.

"By dropping a boulder in it?"

Rennau smiled lazily. "Trust me. Lad like that, he's going to be twice as keen if he thinks I don't approve."

"Thanks for nothing," Clio said. An uncomfortable silence descended as we crossed the docking bay, a foot or two above head height, and I found myself thankful for a human driver, instead of the AIs of the Numarkut cabs. The ride was certainly a great deal smoother, which, considering how close I was sitting to Rolf and Lena, came as something of a relief.

As the silence stretched, I found myself searching for a fresh topic of conversation. Clio's love life certainly seemed a lot more complicated than I'd hitherto suspected, but now really didn't seem like a good time to ask her about that, even if it had been the sort of thing I felt comfortable discussing.

"Do you think any of the ships they've impounded really do have Commonwealth agents aboard?" I asked instead. I suppose, technically, ours did, but since I'd had nothing to do with Ellie at all, apart from fetching her a drink, I was quite confident of escaping any lines of enquiry focusing on her associates.

"Who knows?" Remington said.

"Who cares?" added Rennau. "So long as they sort it all out quickly and send us on our way."

"It'll be the Freebooters," Clio put in. "Why else would they cut and run like they did?"

"Could be lots of reasons," Remington said. "Freebooters are always up to something dodgy."

While we were talking, the sled had reached the edge of the docking area, and moved into a long tunnel, wide as a city street, which others intersected with at intervals in neat right angles, both horizontal and vertical. Several times we climbed or dived into these shafts, finding the local gravity swinging around with us, so that after a brief altercation with our inner ears we found ourselves moving along a subjectively level surface again.

Wherever we went, drones and other sleds were skimming along around us, either keeping pace, or heading in the other direction.

There were innumerable pedestrians too, most of them in uniform, passing in and out of doorways, or the mouths of narrower corridors too small to navigate a vehicle down. One or two seemed to be on guard in front of particularly solid-seeming portals, but we were past too quickly to try and see whatever it was they might have been protecting. Several times we passed through pressure doors, intended to seal off sections of the base in case of a breach, but I couldn't really see the point: by this time we were so deep within the rock that any accident or attack which threatened to vent the atmosphere would have been so catastrophic there would probably have been no survivors left to breathe it anyway.

At first I tried to memorize our route, in case I needed to find my way back to the *Stacked Deck*, but soon gave up the attempt; even my neuroware's tracking program found the frequent twists and turns hard to follow, so I simply let it record our progress, resolving to sort it out later when I had the chance.

"You'd think they'd have found us some quarters a bit nearer the ship," Sowerby complained. "It's going to be really inconvenient getting back to run the systems checks."

"That's the military mind for you," I said, with the authority of long familiarity. "They want us a long way away from the docking bay, so we can't just steal the ship and make a run for it."

"Through a squadron of warships, and whatever else they've got defending this place." Clio rolled her eyes. "Oh, please. Like we're that stupid."

"Quite." Remington nodded. "All we've got to do is sit tight, and everything'll be fine."

CHAPTER TWENTY-ONE
In which a fountain makes an unexpected appearance.

Our new quarters turned out to be comfortable enough, and quite different from what I'd expected; after several more twists and turns, the sled pulled up next to a heavy pressure door, sealing off another section of the base, and sank gently to the floor. (Or, to be a little more accurate, came to rest a inch or two above it.) A small squad of Naval Infantry was waiting for us, in different uniforms than the ones the boarding party had worn: dull green fatigues, instead of the deep blue Neville and his people had sported, with the same color body armor over the top of it, rather than grey. They were, however, carrying short-barreled small arms, with folding stocks, as though they knew how to use them, and wouldn't mind proving it if we gave them enough reason to.

"First the Navy, then the Marines," Clio said disdainfully. "I suppose we ought to be flattered."

"They're not Marines, they're Naval Infantry," I said, without thinking. Tinkie would have had a conniption if she'd overheard that mistake, and, not for the first time, I found myself missing my sister; far more than I did the rest of my family. We'd not been that close as adults, but a shared childhood with a largely absent mother had forged a strong bond I'd always felt able to rely on, and although she'd undoubtedly become a good friend since our initial meeting, I still couldn't see Clio in quite the same light.

"If you say so." Clio shrugged, apparently indifferent to the distinction, then relented, as curiosity got the better of her. "All right, I'll buy it. What's the difference?"

"Marines are trained to operate in space as well as on the ground," I said, "and deploy directly from orbit. NI just hitch a lift aboard starships, and use landing craft to get to the surface." At least the Commonwealth ones did; I was beginning to realize just how much I didn't know about the way everybody else went about things. Apart from the Guild, of course; I was pretty sure I was starting to get my head around some of their customs and practices, even if I still didn't understand a lot of them.

"Captain Remington?" The corporal in charge stepped forward, searching the line of faces staring at him for some sign of seniority, and settled on Rennau.

Who indicated the skipper with a perfunctory jerk of his head. "Him."

"That's me," Remington confirmed, climbing out of the sled, and proffering a hand to shake. "John Tobias Remington, Commerce Guild, master of the *Stacked Deck*." The corporal was too wary, or constrained by military protocol, to shake hands, however, simply nodding curtly in acknowledgement. "And you are?"

"Corporal Fledge." A simple statement, giving nothing away. I tried reaching out with my 'ware again, but, just as before, I found nothing I could latch on to; none of the League soldiers had a personal datasphere, though they all seemed to be carrying handhelds of one sort or another. "If you'll come with us, please."

"Of course." Remington continued to act as though he was completely at his ease. "I take it the Guild representative is on their way from Freedom?"

"I've no information about that, sir." The final honorific was delivered in a flat tone which made it clear it was purely for convention's sake.

"No, of course, you wouldn't. I'll just have to talk to someone more senior." Remington's nod in return was a mere hair's-breadth on the right side of patronizing. He turned back to the rest of us, who had all remained in our seats aboard the sled, watching the conversation unfold. "Come on, then, down you get. I'm sure the nice lady driving us has a job to get back to." Having established that we took our orders from him, not a League non-com, to everyone's satisfaction (except possibly that of Corporal Fledge), he turned to the driver, who'd not budged an inch since coming to a halt. "Thank you for the lift."

"You're welcome, sir." Her tone was neutral, although it seemed plain from her expression that she couldn't have been much more surprised if a crate had expressed polite appreciation for her driving.

I jumped down after Clio and Rennau, and hefted my bulging kitbag onto my shoulder. It was a little heavier than I remembered, and I found myself stumbling sideways as I took the weight, bumping into someone I took at first for one of my own shipmates. "Oops. Sorry."

"Don't mention it." One of the troopers, a young woman with skin a shade or two darker than my own, smiled at me in what looked like genuine amusement. "If you were trying for my gun, it's the worst attempt I ever saw."

"I wouldn't dream of it," I assured her. "Not unless I had a buyer lined up."

Her smile spread. "You must be a real Guilder with an attitude like that."

"Why would there be any doubt?" I asked, already anticipating the answer. Which, of course, was precisely the one I was expecting.

"An accent like that, and you have to ask?" But, unlike the idiot barman back on Numarkut, it was said with a smile.

"He's Guild. Does it matter where he was from before that?" Clio asked, with a little more heat than seemed strictly necessary, probably expecting the same kind of trouble we'd run into before.

"Not to me." The trooper looked faintly surprised, glancing from one of us to the other with an appraising expression.

"Mokole!" Corporal Fledge nailed her with a glare only a fraction of a degree above the temperature of open space. "Are we interrupting your hectic social schedule?"

"No, Corporal." She began to turn away from us, pulling a face, while he was still only able to see the back of her head. I began to suspect that Corporal Fledge didn't exactly enjoy the unqualified respect and confidence of the people under his command. Not all of them, anyway.

"Yikes!" A sudden yell snatched at my attention, and I whirled round to face the sled. Lena had slipped in the process of disembarking, and was toppling towards us like an avalanche of transgene muscle. Clio and I both flinched reflexively, and I barged her aside without conscious thought, shoving her unceremoniously out of the way. Had I not done so, I'm pretty sure I'd have been able to avoid the falling woman with ease, but pushing Clio out of danger had eaten my margin for error; now, it seemed, I was about to pay for my moment of gallantry by being crushed myself.

Even as I began my desperate leap, however, Mokole was there, in a blur of motion, her arm upraised. "I've got you," she said cheerfully, arresting Lena's fall with one hand, while the transgene giantess got her feet back under her again.

"Thanks." Lena regained her balance, and looked at her with an air of faint bemusement. "You're stronger than you look."

"We don't all go for the visible tweaks," Mokole said, and I remembered Neville helping Clio into the sled a short while before. It seemed a lot of our new hosts had subtle enhancements of one kind or another, which I suppose shouldn't have come as all that much of a surprise. The League had taken to transgenics as enthusiastically as the Commonwealth had to neuroware, and tweaks were probably just as ubiquitous here as the ability to sense dataflow was back on Avalon. I found myself gagging reflexively at the memory of Sowerby's hangover cure—that had come from a League world, or void station, somewhere, hadn't it? If the Leaguers could throw something like that together, God alone knew what else they were capable of brewing up.

"Why not?" Rolf asked, seeming genuinely curious.

Mokole smiled. "Why play your aces face up?" she asked.

I thought about that. Enhanced strength would be a popular tweak, if she and Neville were anything go by; pretty much a no brainer for any Leaguer joining their military. It might even be a perk of the job. (As it happened it was; I found out later that one of the inducements to enlist was a complete set of tweaks intended to enhance their effectiveness in the field, which they could keep when they returned to civilian life.) Her reflexes were a lot faster than the baseline too, I'd just seen that for myself. As to what else had been worked on, I'd simply have to keep my eye on the people around us, and see what I could deduce.

"Now who's thinking like a Guilder?" I said, in a bantering tone.

"I take it you think that's a compliment," Mokole said, as though she wouldn't mind at all if I did.

"Pay attention." Fledge cleared his throat, with a hint of self-importance, and glared at everyone from the *Stacked Deck*. He gestured towards the bulkhead behind him. "Through here are your quarters. The rest of the base is strictly off limits. If you wander off," he directed a cynical glance at Remington, who returned it with a bland smile, "we cannot be responsible for your safety."

"In other words, stay put or get shot," Rennau muttered, just loud enough to be heard.

"In other words, we prefer our guests not to have any unfortunate accidents," Fledge said, meeting Rennau's eyes. A moment of quiet understanding seemed to pass between them.

"How very reassuring," Remington said, as the bulkhead door began to grind open in response to a rapid, and encoded, data pulse from Fledge's handheld, which I watched carefully through my 'sphere. The basic principle seemed simple enough, but the encryption appeared to be based on the Corporal's own genetic code, which made it very secure indeed; only a pulse from a device being held by an authorized person would open that door, and that was probably true for most of the others on Kincora Base into the bargain.

"It should be," Mokole said to Clio and me, in a conversational undertone. "Any of you lot get hurt, and we have to explain it to the Guild. Could get very messy."

"Would get very messy," Clio corrected her.

After a little more shuffling around, and retrieval of baggage from the sled, we all coalesced into a loose group in front of the bulkhead, the troopers on the outside, and the crew of the *Stacked Deck* in the middle. After a word from Fledge, and a confirmatory nod from Remington without which none of the Guilders were going anywhere, we set off together, the formation now a little lopsided from the heartbeat's delay between the troopers' response and our own.

After passing through the portal, which looked intimidatingly solid to me as it ground closed behind us, we found ourselves in a completely different environment from the one I'd anticipated.

"This looks . . . comfortable," Clio conceded, a little grudgingly.

"It'll do," Rennau agreed, glancing round at our surroundings.

I suppose I'd been expecting something spartan, or utilitarian, but we'd entered a wide cavern, the center of which was floored with grass; a wide, lush lawn, like an urban park, broken up with shrubs and flower beds, filled with bright blossoms. Scattered bench seats were artfully placed to make the most of the vistas thus created, all of them converging on a fountain in the middle, the spray from which fluoresced into rainbows whenever the light from the overhead lamps caught it at the right angle.

Around this central garden area ran a wide, paved walkway on which a number of people were strolling, in civilian clothing, a good deal of which was adorned by Guild patches. The few exceptions were wearing the uniforms of non-Guild shipping companies, although I didn't recognize either of them offhand. Most of the strollers lacked any visible tweaks, although one or two had tails, or the enhanced musculature Rolf and Lena had gone for, presumably for much the same reason.

Many of the internees nodded a greeting as they passed our group, or bade us welcome with a few words, though no one lingered; there would be plenty of time for introductions later, without the League troopers around to overhear. The main thing I noticed, however, was that most of the people in the cavern were surrounded by personal dataspheres, which I immediately found reassuring.

At least we can find out what's going on, I sent to Clio. *As soon as we find a node—*

Good luck with that, she rejoined. Perturbed, I expanded my 'sphere right to its limits, finding nothing other than the personal 'spheres of my companions and fellow prisoners to mesh with. My rising spirits immediately plummeted again. *You didn't really expect them to leave a node within easy reach, did you? Leaguers are paranoid about 'ware.*

Of course they were; everyone knew that. They thought it made you less human, although how anyone willing to muck about with their own biology on a molecular level as casually as changing their socks could think that, I had no idea. For my money, if God had intended people to have tails and paisley fur She'd have made them like that in the first place.

"Here we are." Fledge smiled as sincerely as he could, and waved a hand at one of the building fronts facing the garden; although I use the word "building" only in its loosest sense. On the outside of the walkway enclosing the open space, living quarters had been carved out of the cavern wall, the stone being dressed to resemble a freestanding structure. "Your home away from home."

"I'm sure it'll do fine until we can return to our ship," Remington said courteously, managing to sound as though the quarters weren't quite up to the standard he'd expected, but he was willing to make the best of it.

"Which I'll need to do every couple of days," Sowerby put in. "Unless you want an unexpected plasma vent in your docking bay."

"This is a Naval base, ma'am." Now it was Fledge's turn to sound faintly patronizing. "I'm sure we can find someone qualified to maintain your systems for you until you've been cleared for departure."

Sowerby bristled. "Now wait just a minute," she said, her voice rising, until Remington put out a hand and took her arm.

"Sarah." His voice was calm, with an unmistakable undercurrent of warning. "The quicker these people can get on with their jobs, the quicker we'll be on our way. I'm sure they're well aware of what any damage at all to the *Stacked Deck* will mean."

But they're my *engines. No one knows the systems like I do.*

Exactly. Remington gave a faintly self-satisfied smile. *So when you find something's not been done right, and we complain our ship's not been looked after properly, they'll have to take your word for it. And pay us. If they don't want the Guild arbitrator in.*

Sowerby nodded, a little grudgingly. *Take your point.*

Rennau shook his head, in rueful admiration. *You're unbelievable. I swear to God you could find an angle in a straight line.*

Remington acknowledged this with the faintest of nods. *It all depends how straight you want the line to be, Mik. If you'd been willing to bend things a bit more a couple of years back, you might still be the skipper.*

I doubt it. The expression of bonhomie was gone from Rennau's eyes now. *You'd still have found a way to bend it just that little bit more.*

What can I say. It's a gift. Remington turned his attention to the rest of the group. "OK, let's make ourselves comfortable while we wait for the Guild representative to turn up."

And comfortable, I have to admit, we made ourselves. The building, or set of tunnels to be more accurate, was more than large enough for all seventeen of us, even with Rolf and Lena among our number; though they did have to duck a lot more than they were used to aboard the *Stacked Deck*. I found a room for myself about three times the size of my cabin aboard the ship, which actually gave me room to walk round the bed and get to the closets, and spent a few minutes throwing things onto hangers and into drawers. Then I sat down on the bed, dived into my 'sphere, and called up all the data I'd archived that might help me crack a handheld. If there wasn't a node in the vicinity, that was the only way I was ever going to get hold of any useful information.

I began with the way I'd got into Plubek's, back in the Numarkut system. That was a promising start, but I'd never be able repeat so simple a trick here; for one thing there wasn't a constant stream of data going in that I could watch for weaknesses. I'd picked up a few promising datanomes from Neville, but reverse engineering them into a key I could plug into my sneakware wasn't going to be an easy job; and even when that was done, I was still going to need the genetic code of an authorized user, which I didn't have a clue how to go about obtaining.

Well, I'd just have to worry about that one later; for now I'd get on with everything else I could, so that if an opportunity presented itself later, I'd be ready to exploit it. So thinking, I started teasing out the datanomes I'd recorded while Neville was using his handheld, and began modifying them.

"Getting comfortable?" My concentration shattered as Clio stuck her head round the door.

"Settling in." I stuck the sneakware away, behind my strongest datawall, and stood up. "How's your room?"

"Identical to this one, surprisingly." She smiled, quietly. "It is a military base, after all."

"Quite." I made for the door, and she stood aside to let me out into the corridor, which was decorated in standard Institutional Bland. Though there was a lock next to the handle, it never occurred to me to trip it. I'd been a Guilder long enough to trust my shipmates not to go in there without an invitation, and any Leaguers checking up might realize how unusual a locked room was, and assume I had something to hide. Which I most definitely did.

The bedrooms had been arranged around a large communal area, which opened out into the square, providing an excellent view of the garden across the walkway. Comfortable chairs and sofas were scattered around the space, many of them flanked by a few strategically placed tables, and a well-stocked kitchen area occupied one corner; a facility several of the *Stacked Deck*'s crew had already availed themselves of, judging by the steaming mugs in their hands. Seeing Clio and me enter, Rennau waved us over from behind the counter. "Want anything?"

"Not right now," Clio said. "We were just going for a walk around. Get orientated." Which was news to me, but news I was happy to go along with. There might just possibly be a node around here I could find if I looked hard enough, and with the two of us apparently wandering aimlessly, the risk of discovery and challenge would be greatly reduced.

I nodded. "Might as well find out if any of the other crews know anything," I added.

"Nothing more than we do," Remington cut in, from the sofa he was sharing with Sowerby. "I've been talking to some of the other skippers already. Same story. They took a contract from Ellie, good deal because it was a rush job, and the next thing they know they're being boarded and brought here."

"Are they really sure she's a Commonwealth agent?" I asked, trying to look ingenuous. "She didn't look like one to me." And Mallow definitely was. Perhaps he'd realized the Numarkut authorities were on to him, and deflected the finger of suspicion to point at an innocent co-worker.

"I think that's the point, Simon," Remington said, trying not to look too amused. "Spies who look like spies tend not to be ones for very long."

"I guess not," I said, trying not to think too hard about that. "But you know her . . ."

"As a cargo broker," Remington said, "nothing more." Then he shrugged. "But I wouldn't put it past her to have a little something going on the side. She'd just see it as another deal to be made."

He pinged a laconic message to my 'sphere.

You do realize they're probably listening to this.

And monitoring our 'spheres, I added, more in the spirit of mischief than because I thought it was actually likely. If I really believed they were capable of doing that, I'd have purged the sneakware, and everything else incriminating I'd been collecting since my conversation with Aunt Jenny. But if Remington realized I was pulling his leg, he didn't let on.

"Enjoy your walk," he said, as Clio and I walked past. "And if you can't be good, be careful."

CHAPTER TWENTY-TWO

In which I make some ill-advised remarks
about my family history.

Leaving our temporary quarters behind, Clio and I wandered around
the square in a desultory spiral. As Neville had let slip earlier, there
seemed to be four other crews already in residence; two Guild, and one
each from a pair of Numarkut-registered shipping lines, who seemed to
be having as little to do with the Guilders and each another as possible.
As well as the five occupied sets of living quarters, which, at first glance,
appeared to be identical (so far as we could tell without being invited in
to see for ourselves), there were another fifteen ranged around the
square, all shuttered and locked. Whether this meant the Leaguers were
expecting a great many more unwilling guests, or simply started stowing
us here because they found it convenient for some reason, I couldn't tell,
and could see no point in speculating about.

We also found a small commissary, staffed by serving drones,
where a few of our fellow guests were eating—but as neither of us felt
particularly hungry, and Rennau had been banging pots and pans
around before we set out, we politely declined their invitation to join
them, and carried on walking after a brief exchange of pleasantries.

"No hurry," one of our new acquaintances, who'd introduced
himself as Deeks of the *Ebon Flow*, said, with a philosophical shrug.
"We'll have plenty of time to get to know each other."

Everyone else seated around the table laughed, without much trace of humor. "Got that right," one of them agreed. "Not a lot else to do around here except talk."

"Be seeing you." Deeks waved us off with a cheery salute, and returned his attention to what might have been a steak sandwich.

"They seemed nice," Clio said, as we wandered across the grass.

I nodded, my mind not entirely on the conversation. There was the hatch we'd come in by, and there was another, diametrically opposite, which presumably led deeper into the base. A couple of bored-looking NI troopers were standing next to both of them, but in the kind of desultory fashion that made it all too plain they'd given up expecting trouble a long time ago. That might work to my advantage in some way, but I couldn't see how at the moment.

At any event, the two pressure hatches seemed the only routes in and out of the cavern we were being held in. I wondered if they might be opened from time to time to admit the serving drones from the commissary, but there was no sign of any entering or leaving that way. Which wasn't all that much of a surprise; given their size, they probably just delivered any meals that had been ordered through a network of service pipes. Which would, of course, be far too narrow to crawl down, whatever you might have seen in the virts.

"Looks like we're stuck here," I said, as we struck out across the lawn towards the fountain.

"For a while," Clio agreed, seating herself unhurriedly on one of the benches. She turned her head slowly, taking in our surroundings. "But I suppose there are worse places to be stuck."

An opinion I found myself progressively less inclined to agree with as the next few days crawled past in a haze of monotony. A few of the crew found old friends among the other Guilders interned with us, and took the opportunity to renew their acquaintance, but that wasn't an option open to me; though I socialized with the other crews, lunching with Deeks and his cronies a couple of times, I never hit it off with anyone sufficiently well to establish a real friendship. Accordingly, I spent a lot of time in my own room, a rag across the handle, fiddling with datanomes, just in case I managed to find a way of accessing a handheld without the cooperation of its owner—hardly the most likely of prospects.

Periodically, Clio would drag me from my lair, expressing concern about the amount of time I was spending alone, and chivvy me into taking a walk across the garden with her, which at least gave me some exercise; absorbed in the problem of cracking the handsets, I'd begun to neglect my training regime again.

"The thing is, I'm bored," I admitted, as we sat on one of the seats together, watching the rainbows ripple in the fountain. "There was always something to do aboard the ship." Heaven help me, I was even beginning to miss the broom.

"Well, the way I see it, you've got two choices," she said briskly. "You can sit around feeling sorry for yourself, or you can find something else to do. If you're supposed to be an athlete, don't you need exercise?"

"You're right." I looked around the wide open space surrounding us, really seeing its potential for the first time. "I could start running again here." Something impossible aboard the *Stacked Deck*, and which would give me the perfect excuse to cover every inch of the place, trying to detect a node. "You're amazing." Buoyed with a sudden surge of optimism, I put my arm around her shoulders and hugged her briefly, the way I used to do with Tinkie.

"You're welcome." She flushed, far more taken aback than I'd expected, and I disengaged a little awkwardly, conscious of having crossed an unspoken line. Since ruling her out as a romantic prospect I'd grown used to thinking of her purely as a friend, and she seemed to have made the same decision about me: now she'd started taking an interest in Neville, it would hardly be fair to complicate things for her. She cleared her throat. "Enjoy yourself."

Which I'm bound to say I did, adding several circuits of the cavern's perimeter to my daily routine from then on; a habit which was to have far-reaching repercussions.

Of course our captors hadn't left us entirely to our own devices; every one of us was interviewed several times by polite men and women, generally in the uniforms of officers, and, on a couple of occasions, in the kind of sober civilian garb more suited to mid-level bureaucrats. They asked a lot of questions, which all boiled down to variations on two basic ones ("Are you a spy?" and "Do you think anyone else in your crew might be one?"), both of which I batted away with bland assurances of innocence, which seemed to be believed. In truth, I think, my lowly status aboard the *Stacked Deck* worked in my favor here, as the general dogsbody was hardly the most promising candidate for Ellie to have recruited for a covert mission into the heart of the League. I was also lucky in that my interrogators seemed convinced that anyone aboard the *Stacked Deck* working for the Commonwealth must have been recruited by Ellie on Numarkut, and once they'd been convinced that the only contact I'd had with their prime suspect had been boiling a kettle on her behalf, they seemed happy enough to cross me off their list.

From time to time the inquisitors arrived accompanied by a white-haired man of indeterminate age, who turned out to be the long-awaited representative from the Guildhall on Freedom. Not that I ever found out much more about him than that: every time he turned up, he immediately disappeared into a private room with Remington and the other Guilder captains, though what they found to talk about I had no idea. How much money all this was going to end up costing the League, probably.

Even Sowerby began to relax a little, although she continued to fret about the *Stacked Deck*'s power plant, until a petty officer turned up one morning to talk to her about some maintenance issues; after that she seemed a good deal happier. Particularly as he would pop by every few days thereafter, and the two of them would disappear into a corner of the communal space to discuss readouts from his handheld with great animation. Not unnaturally, I took a more than casual interest in this arrangement, feeling it would be the closest I was likely to come to one of the devices, but I never found an opportunity to try to crack it. Though I loitered hopefully in their vicinity for as long as I could without attracting attention, waiting for him to open a data channel I could exploit, he never did; and even if he had done so there was still the open ditch of the genetic tag to leap over.

So musing, and seething with frustration, I began another run, hoping the physical activity would jar something loose in my brain. As always, I found the rhythm of running calmed me down, the familiar routine allowing me to lose myself in the moment.

"Hey there," called a vaguely familiar voice. By this time I'd become used to casual greetings from my fellow internees, a group which had since been supplemented by two more crews who'd been picked up not long after us; I'd become The Running Guy, a sight so familiar that most people barely even noticed me any more. "How's it going?"

"All good," I began to respond reflexively, before it dawned on me that I was being addressed by one of the guards at the gate leading deeper into the body of the base. Which was unprecedented. Since we'd arrived, they'd been courteous enough, but from across a clearly defined divide; an easy assumption of authority on their part, and a faintly disdainful refusal to recognize it on ours. Then the penny dropped. It was Mokole, the trooper who'd saved me from being laminated to the carriageway when Lena had slipped getting out of the sled just after our arrival. I slowed, and began jogging in place. "How's things with you?"

"You know." She shrugged. "Same old same old."

"Jas." Her companion shot her a warning glance; it was hard to tell behind the visor obscuring his eyes, which was bleeding a small amount of dataflow into my 'sphere from its connection to the targeting 'ware embedded in his gun, but he looked a little older than she was. "You know what the Corporal said about fraternizing."

"Who's fraternizing? I'm winning hearts and minds," Mokole said, her teeth flashing white as she grinned at me.

"You'll have your work cut out with this lot," I warned her. That trickle of data, running between weapon and eyeware, fascinated me, and I began recording it, looking for crackable datanomes. It was hardly a handheld, just a simple, functional link, but it might be a start. I smiled back, prolonging the conversation. "Unless you win them in a card game."

"Now there's an idea." The grin spread. "Found a buyer for my gun yet?"

I shook my head, tracing the path between the weapon and her visor. Both of them were carrying handhelds, little beacons of fizzing information in the middle of my 'sphere, but still impossible to get at. There was probably some interface between the three systems; I knew Tinkie had a head-up display built into her helmet, in case her neuroware link went down in the middle of a battle zone, and that was tied in to her company command net. The Leaguers probably had something similar, which meant the visors would be capable of receiving signals—but that still wouldn't get me into a handheld, or, through one of those, into a node.

"Too many around," I said. "Not enough profit." I tried poking her visor input, sneaking in along with the feedback from her weapon, but none of the datanomes quite fitted.

She tapped the side of the eyeware irritably, and I abandoned the attempt, withdrawing the tendril.

"What is it?" The other trooper was eyeing me suspiciously. "Is he doing something with that crap in his head?"

"Don't be daft." Mokole looked at him scornfully, then back to me, with the first faint trace of suspicion beginning to appear on her face. "Are you?"

"Of course not," I assured her, truthfully enough. I'd stopped trying seconds before, which was almost a geological age in data time.

"Just a glitch," she told her companion. Her eyes unfocussed for a moment, as she concentrated on the inside of the visor. "Cleared now."

"It had better have." The trooper glared at me suspiciously, and adjusted the weight of his weapon.

"Nice running into you," I said to Mokole, picking up my pace, preparatory to moving on. Now I came to think about it, the visor might be a lot easier to crack than a handheld—no genetic code to worry about, for one thing. And if it really did have a battlefield commo system built in, maybe I could leapfrog to a node on that, bypassing the handheld entirely. Definitely worth thinking about. "Maybe I'll see you again."

"Maybe you will." She smiled at me, in what seemed like a genuinely friendly manner. "It's not as if I don't know where to find you."

Of course that worked both ways; I knew where to find her too, at least when she was on duty, and managed to contrive a few more casual meetings, during which I continued to probe her visor interface, tweaking and refining the sneakware in the light of what seemed to work and what didn't. At least that was the theory. In practice, I found myself enjoying the conversation a little too much to remain entirely focused on my objective. It turned out we had a similar sense of humor, and since I'd had precious little to laugh about for quite some time now, her company was a good deal more congenial than I'd bargained for. It also didn't hurt that the other trooper assigned to guard the gate with her continued to make his disapproval more than evident, which added a faintly heady whiff of the illicit to our burgeoning friendship.

I'd braced myself for the disapproval of my shipmates, since I could hardly tell them what I was up to, and there was absolutely no chance of keeping my conversations with Mokole a secret; after all, they were taking place in full view of the entire compound. For the most part, however, their reactions ranged from the indifferent to the positively encouraging; I got a nudge in the ribs from Rolf which nearly cracked a couple one morning, as Mokole took up her station by the gate. "Better comb your hair, Si. Your girlfriend's arrived."

"She's not my girlfriend," I protested, provoking the inevitable wave of banter and surreptitious kissing noises from all corners of the living area, although a part of me couldn't help wistfully wondering if that would still have been true if we'd met under more propitious circumstances. She had a sharp mind and a ready wit, both qualities I'd always found attractive, and she wasn't bad looking either, which is always a bonus where women are concerned. Men too, I suppose, although I'd never considered one of those as a romantic prospect.

"No. Simon doesn't go in for that kind of thing," Clio said, coming unexpectedly to my defense, although there seemed to be more of an edge to her voice than a bit of mild teasing would normally warrant.

"Chance would be a fine thing," I said ruefully, trying to keep the conversation light, and receiving a plasma torch glare in return.

"Then you'd better get over there and practice," Clio said shortly.

"Sound advice." Remington glanced up from a private conversation with Sowerby. "Practice makes perfect."

"You wish," Sowerby said, elbowing him in the ribs almost as hard as Rolf had nudged me.

"Just haven't had enough practice yet," Remington said cheerfully.

Feeling the gaze of my shipmates on my back, I jogged around the cavern's perimeter, following my usual route. Mokole saw me coming, of course, and we both pretended not to have noticed one another until I was almost at the pressure hatch.

"Hello, stranger," she greeted me, as though it had been far longer than a mere three days since we'd last spoken. "How's it going?"

"Oh, you know." I shrugged. "The fun around here just never begins."

"And there I was thinking you enjoyed our little chats." The teasing tone I'd come to appreciate was in her voice, but overlaid with a faintly wistful quality, as if she thought I really might be resenting her presence.

"I do, very much." I hastened to reassure her, which was clearly the reaction she'd been hoping for, judging by the faint twitch at the corner of her mouth. "I'll miss them when I move on."

"Me too." She sighed faintly. "But it's the life. Makes it hard to put down roots."

"Tell me about it," I said, cautiously extending a tendril towards her visor's comms port. I'd given up trying to break into the link between the visor and her gun, having belatedly realized it would be a prime target for battlefield countermeasures, and therefore hardened far beyond anything I'd be able to crack with a bit of homemade sneakware and a talent for digital mischief. At least in the time I had available. "Only in port long enough to drop off one cargo and pick up another."

"At least I get to stay put for a whole tour," Mokole said, but her voice barely registered. My 'sphere was suddenly overlaid with a series of graphics; a targeting reticle in which my face was centered, a free-floating dot wavering around the vicinity of my feet, apart from occasional forays in the direction of the fountain (which after a moment's thought I realized represented the point of aim of the gun slung casually at her side), and some numbers, which I assumed were confirming the weapon's state of readiness. Nothing to indicate an outgoing communication link, though.

"There is that," I said, forcing myself to follow the verbal conversation as if I had nothing else at all on my mind. "If you don't mind being away from your family for so long. I hardly saw my mother while I was growing up." I hesitated for a moment, before honesty impelled me to add, "Which suited us both fine, as it happens."

"Your mom's in the military?" She sounded surprised, and I nodded without thinking, still rummaging through the visor's rudimentary 'ware in search of a communications protocol. Easiest just to snag everything I could, and analyze it at my leisure, I decided. "The Commonwealth military?"

"Navy," I said. "Bit of a family tradition."

"Really?" Mokole was looking at me with an odd expression on her face, as though I'd just produced a coin from her ear without warning. "Then why aren't you in uniform?"

"Wrong chromosome," I said shortly, then relented a little. "Actually, I tried. Screwed it up big time."

"How big?" She was looking at me with frank curiosity now, and the trooper with her seemed hardly less interested: maybe he was waiting for me to hand over the Commonwealth Navy's battle plans, or, given most people's perception of Guilders, at least open the bidding on them.

"Disowned by my family big," I said. I'd never verbalized it before, and was faintly surprised by the way the words seemed slightly too large for my larynx. "Unwelcome back in the Commonwealth big."

"That sounds pretty big, all right." Mokole nodded slowly, her tone sympathetic. "But these things blow over. They can't stay mad at you forever."

"That might be true," I said, "but my mother will still give it her best shot."

"Hmph," Mokole said. "The worst thing mine ever did was call me Jasmine."

"Jasmine?" I seized on the change of subject gratefully, and, my virtual booty secure, cut the link to her visor. The faintly disorientating image of myself apparently standing three feet in front of my own eyeline, superimposed on the woman I was talking to, disappeared, and I found I was able to concentrate more fully on the conversation again. When I did, I immediately regretted my indiscretion. If the Leaguers were looking for spies, which I knew full well they were, I'd just made myself look like the prime candidate. And I wasn't naive enough to believe for a moment that Mokole wouldn't report it, however much she enjoyed our little chats. "I like it. It suits you."

"I'd rather you stuck to Jas. The full version's a bit too floral for the military."

I smiled, as casually as I could, hoping it didn't look too forced and sickly. "I've always preferred Si to Simon, as it happens."

"Then it's a deal. Si." She stuck out her hand.

"Deal it is. Jas." I shook it, in the time honored fashion of Guilders throughout the Human Sphere, thinking just how insane this was. I'd just put myself in imminent danger of exposure, and suddenly we were on first name terms.

"I'll say this for you, you're certainly full of surprises." Jas grinned at me. "Any idea what your mom's up to now?"

I kept my face as blank as I could, wishing I'd kept my nose out of the data packet Tinkie and I had found in the node back home. If the

League ever discovered she'd gone to Sodallagain, despite it being off limits to both sides while the diplomats played their interminable games of syntactical chess, they'd send a warship of their own to confront her. At the very least the results would be hugely embarrassing to the Commonwealth; at worst, it could tip the whole situation over into outright war, and in either case it was more than likely that my mother would be killed in the first exchange of fire.

"Like I said, we don't talk," I replied, truthfully enough.

"That's a shame." Jas looked me square in the eye, with what seemed to be real sympathy. "Mine's always been there for me. Dad too."

"Then you're lucky," I said. All of a sudden I wanted nothing more than to be somewhere, anywhere, else. I began jogging on the spot. "Guess I'd better get moving again. Before I stiffen up."

"And we'd both really hate that, right?" She waited for a reaction, but the flirtatious innuendo didn't get the laugh it normally would have done. Her eyes narrowed, as if she could see what was going on inside my head, but that was impossible, even with neuroware, let alone the relatively crude technology of the visor. "Be seeing you."

"That you will," I said, trying to sound carefree, but probably not succeeding nearly as well as I'd hoped.

It took a good deal longer than usual to run my doubts and fears away, and achieve something akin to a clear head.

Once again, it seemed, I'd put myself squarely in the crosshairs, by letting my mouth get away from my brain. Of course I could still brazen it out, deny any connection with the Commonwealth military, but the fact remained that now I'd been stupid enough to bring it up, the DIR would hardly take any time at all to confirm that I was indeed the son of a warship captain in the Royal Navy. Of course, on the bright side, their agents on Avalon (and there were bound to be a few) would also report back on the scandal I'd unleashed, the disgrace I'd brought on my family, and the fact that (to polite society, at any rate) I'd disappeared into the galaxy, hopefully never to be seen again. Which, now I came to think about it, was exactly the kind of elaborate cover story secret agents in the virts seemed to construct all the time.

I needed to talk it over with someone, I decided, and to my vague surprise the name which immediately sprang to mind was Clio's. I suppose Remington would have been a more logical choice, since he was the one who'd taken me on as an apprentice in the first place, but confiding in him could get very complicated, very fast. Though I only intended to discuss the fact that I'd let some of my family background slip, rather than reveal the whole story, he'd worked for Aunt Jenny before, and was far from stupid; he could easily have deduced something of her less public role, and come to his own conclusions about why I was aboard. If that was true, the last thing I needed was to confirm any suspicions he might have in that regard.

No, Clio it would have to be.

As I came to that conclusion my spirits rose, and I redirected my aimless orbiting of the compound towards our living quarters. Only to slow down again, as I approached them. Something wasn't right. Instead of being scattered more or less randomly around the communal area as usual, everyone was loosely clustered together in the half adjoining the kitchen counter.

"What's going on?" I asked, as I made my way inside.

Sowerby looked up, and grinned at me. "Clio's got a visitor. He just dropped by to . . ." her fingers crooked into air quotes ". . . see how we were settling in. But the only one he's spoken to for more than thirty seconds is her." She smiled indulgently, but from where I was standing all I could see was Lena's back, which this close to her was eclipsing half the room.

I shuffled around the transgene deckhand, and got a glimpse of a familiar profile. Clio was leaning forward in her seat, apparently fascinated, while someone told what I assumed was intended to be an amusing anecdote, judging by her reaction—which seemed to consist of an astonishing amount of wide-eyed giggling, so utterly different to her usual behavior I had to look twice to confirm that it was indeed the same woman. Rennau seemed as nonplussed as I felt, radiating a slightly theatrical hostility in the direction of her companion; and when I saw who it was, I could hardly blame him. League Navy uniform, exaggerated moustache: Ensign Neville had indeed come to call.

CHAPTER TWENTY-THREE
In which I recall a childhood pet,
and a kiss seems less than pleasant.

"I really don't see why you like him so much," I admitted, a couple of hours later, after Neville had disappeared back to his ship—which was apparently going to be in dock for another week or so, for resupply and a bit of downtime for her crew. Which apparently meant, in turn, that we could look forward to the pleasure of his company several more times in the interim. Or Clio could, anyway: Sowerby was right, he hadn't seemed all that interested in anybody else. He'd conversed briefly with Remington, because protocol demanded it, deflecting questions about how long we were going to be stuck here with unshakable, and apparently genuine, ignorance, but the rest of the time he'd spent strolling in the garden with Clio, who seemed to bypass about twenty percent of her neurons every time she so much as glanced in his direction.

"No, I don't suppose you do." She tilted her head, indicating Jas and her companion, who seemed to be killing time until they were relieved by gazing idly around the cavern, keeping an unobtrusive eye on the movements of every internee who was out in the open. As we glanced in their direction, Jas nodded an almost imperceptible greeting. "Small clue. Why do you spend so much time hanging around Soldier Girl like a puppy hoping for a biscuit?"

"Well . . ." I hedged, trying to find an acceptable answer. I had a pretty strong suspicion that "I've been trying to sneak a link to one of the base nodes through her eyeware" wouldn't be one, and was certain to result in a very uncomfortable conversation with Remington, not to mention an even more unpleasant time with Rennau shortly thereafter, if she didn't keep it to herself. "We seem to have hit it off . . ."

"How nice for you." Clio's voice positively dripped with sarcasm. "Then why do you find it so hard to believe that I've hit it off with Ronnie Neville?"

"His name's Ronnie?" I asked involuntarily. "I had a hamster called Ronnie once." Which was true, when I was about seven, but not particularly relevant. "He died." I wasn't sure why I'd added that, either, as hamsters weren't exactly renowned for their longevity, and Clio could hardly have thought he might still be around somewhere. We'd buried him in the broccoli bed of the kitchen garden, and Mother had rebuked me for sniveling.

"Did you?" Clio looked taken aback for a moment, then rallied, returning to the subject at hand with renewed vigor. "If you can make friends with one of the knuckle-draggers here, I don't see why I can't. At least Ronnie's an officer, which proves he's got some intelligence. What's it even got to do with you, anyway?" She concluded her peroration with a short, expectant pause.

"Nothing," I said, with the faintest of shrugs, hoping to mollify her, and failing completely. It hardly seemed a propitious moment to raise the subject I wanted to discuss with her, but I felt I was running out of time. Jas would be going off duty soon, and I was certain that as soon as she did, she'd report what she'd learned about me to her commanding officer: she was too good a soldier not to realize what it might mean to have a family member of one of the enemy forces in custody. (All right, technically the Commonwealth was a rival rather than an enemy at this point, but tensions between the two powers were at the highest they'd been in a generation: since the Commonwealth had first annexed Rockhall, in fact.) The DIR would want to wring me dry of anything I might possibly have picked up from my mother and sister, and the longer they tried, the more likely it was that they'd find some indication of my covert commission from my aunt. Not to mention the big secret I carried, that the *Queen Kylie's Revenge* had been deployed in a neutral system while the negotiations were still going on, in clear contravention of the agreed conditions.

Of course I was still a Guilder, which should offer me some protection, but I couldn't entirely rely on that. I was a very junior member indeed, and if the Commerce Guild had a single overriding principle, other than "grab what you can," it was expediency.

"Exactly," Clio said flatly. "Do I ask you what you see in Soldier Girl?" Which she pretty much had, a few moments before, but it hardly seemed tactful to point that out under the circumstances.

"Actually, it was Jas I wanted to talk to you about," I said. "I told her—"

"Jas?" Clio snorted derisively. "What sort of a name's that?"

"It's short for Jasmine," I said, "but that's not—"

"Kind of suits her, though," Clio conceded, with another glance at the pair of League troopers guarding the pressure hatch. "A bit androgynous. Masculine, even."

"Is it?" I hadn't really thought about it like that. To me, names were just a handy way of knowing who you were talking about to someone else: when I thought about Jas it wasn't the sound of her name which came to mind, it was the way she smiled, and the tone of her voice, which had always struck me as decidedly feminine. True, she was a warrior, but so were my mother and my sister, so that didn't exactly label her unfeminine in my eyes; though I was prepared to concede that, since the League had an unshakable ideological commitment to gender equality, the men and women serving together in their military might merge their characteristics into some kind of androgynous soldier archetype. Possibly quite literally, in a few cases, given their penchant for transgenic mucking about.

"Definitely," Clio said. She might have said more, but if she did I failed to hear it, as that was the moment I noticed some unfamiliar activity in my datasphere. While we were talking I'd meshed briefly with Jas's visor again, partly just to see if I still could at this distance, and partly out of a paranoid conviction that her eyeware might be able to magnify an image, and have some datanomes built into it to help her lip read at this sort of distance: after all, being able to tell what an enemy was saying could be very useful if you were trying to sneak up on them. She had been looking in our direction, but not very much more than at anyone else, and I'd been relieved to note that if she did have any image intensifying 'ware available, it wasn't being used to spy on Clio and I. "So what's the problem? Lovers' tiff?"

"I told her about my mother," I said, my mind, once again, only half on the conversation. It seemed as though Jas's visor was equipped with a comms package after all, and she'd started to receive a message through it. I rifled frantically through the datanomes I'd scavenged, trying to find something that matched the protocols.

"You did what?" Clio stared at me in astonishment: so much so that she seemed to have forgotten she was mad at me. "Why would you do something as stupid as that?"

"I don't know," I said, sounding a bit lame even to myself. "It just sort of came up while I was talking to her." I could hardly admit I was distracted by having successfully merged with Jas's eyeware for the first time.

Then I finally found a set of datanomes which meshed with the incoming communication she was receiving, and the datastream resolved at last. It was a simple voice message, nothing more, clipped, and so riddled with jargon and acronyms it might as well have been in Ancient English for all the sense it made to me. I could have kicked the fountain with frustration, but all I'd gain by that was a throbbing foot, and Clio would probably notice, so I restrained the impulse.

"I'll just bet it did," Clio said grimly.

"We were just talking about our families," I explained, still trying to make sense of the strange voice in my dataflow. But before I could extract any kind of meaning from it, the transmission abruptly ceased.

"Roger that," Jas said in response, her voice crisp and efficient. "We'll be waiting."

I infiltrated a tendril into the outgoing message, and felt it being carried deep into the heart of the base. There was a node nearby, a big one, I could feel the crackle of concentrated data pulsing like the heart of a distant sun, but before I could reach out towards it, she cut the link. I snapped back into myself, feeling momentarily disorientated, as I had done when the roadblocks descended in the examination hall back at the Naval Academy on Avalon.

"So you just happened to mention to a League squaddie that your mom's the captain of a Commonwealth warship, and your sister commands a platoon of Marines? God in heaven, Simon, what were you thinking?"

"I wasn't thinking anything," I admitted, glancing across to the gate in what I hoped was a casual manner. Something was going on, I'd overheard enough to be sure of that, and if it was going to happen before Jas went off duty, it was going to be soon. But nothing looked any different from the way it had before. Jas and the other trooper were still mooching about like school teachers in the lunch break, keeping a desultory eye on us all, and their counterparts by the other hatchway seemed no more engaged than they were.

Clio snorted. "No change there, then."

"And I never mentioned Tinkie," I added, acutely conscious that I sounded as though I was clutching at straws. Which was fair enough, as essentially I was. "Do you think I should tell John?"

"Absolutely not," Clio said emphatically. "It might not come to anything," although she didn't sound as though she thought that was any more likely than I did, "and if it does, everyone'll just assume they found out about your family through regular background checks."

"You're probably right," I agreed, with a faint sense of relief. I'd been beginning to make a new life for myself aboard the *Stacked Deck*, and if it wasn't too late, I wanted to carry on doing so when we left here. There was certainly nothing to be gained by undermining whatever good opinion Remington may have had of me by jumping the gun on confessing.

"What's going on over there?" Clio asked, abruptly, and I seized on the sudden change of subject with alacrity. Jas and the trooper with her were turning to face the pressure hatch, and bringing their weapons up; not on aim, but with the air of people who knew what to do with them, and liked to have them ready just in case they needed to prove it. Clearly, whatever the message I'd overheard the end of had been about, it was starting to happen.

"Only one way to find out," I said, and began strolling casually in that direction, my sneakware poised to exploit any further communication through Jas's visor. To my faint, and welcome, surprise, Clio fell in at my elbow, no doubt as curious as I was about what was going on. And we weren't the only ones. By the time we got to the hatchway, over a dozen people had drifted over there to see what was happening. Remington was among them, and greeted us cheerfully.

"Any idea what this is all about?" he asked, addressing me as we approached.

"No." I shook my head, wondering if he'd deduced anything about my attempts to access a node. He probably hadn't really expected me not to try, despite his and Rennau's orders to the contrary; but to anyone else in the cavern with neuroware there simply wasn't a node within reach, and that was that, so he'd have no real reason to suspect that I'd persevered. "Why would I?"

"I thought you might have a little inside information," Remington said, glancing in Jas's direction with a meaningful nod, and a faint smile.

"Step back, please," Jas said, in a tone of voice which made it perfectly clear that this wasn't a request. To my relief, everyone complied, with a shuffling of feet and some exaggerated slouching which made it very clear that they were treating it as one anyway, and acceding to it purely because they felt like it, not because they recognized the authority of her uniform or were intimidated in any way by the weapon she carried. Once she seemed satisfied that we'd all moved far enough away not to be underfoot, she turned to the other trooper and nodded. "OK. Send them through." The last in a quick transmission, which, like the previous one, was too brief for me to tap into the distant node, although it certainly confirmed that it was there.

"On their way," the voice at the other end responded, and the thick metal hatch began to crank open. I craned my neck to see what was behind it, but, somewhat anticlimactically, saw nothing more exciting than a long, dimly lit corridor, pretty much identical to the ones I'd seen on the way here, with a sled parked at the other end. There were people walking down it, about halfway along, and the first thing to catch my eye was a glimpse of Naval Infantry uniforms. I'd just made up my mind that it was nothing more exciting than Fledge and his people swinging by for a snap inspection and an early guard change, when Clio nudged me, apparently forgetting she was supposed to be mad.

"Isn't that the Freebooters?" she asked.

I nodded. "I think you're right," I agreed, becoming more certain by the second. "Some of them, anyway." There were three civilians in the middle of the group, none of them looking particularly happy, and one of whom I definitely recognized: the green woman Remington and I had met on our way to our meeting with Ellie at Farland Freight Forwarding. I tried to recall if either of her companions, a burly man with short graying hair and no visible tweaks, or a younger fellow, whose eyes glowed green in the reduced light of the corridor and had the vertical slit pupils of a cat, had been with her when Clio and I first caught sight of her entering the bar in Dullingham, but I couldn't remember. Maybe I'd ask Clio later, if it seemed important.

"Where have they been all this time?" Clio asked. We'd seen the System Defense Boat which had crippled the *Poison 4* moving in to pick up the survivors shortly before Neville and his team had boarded us, so they couldn't have been in transit for as long as we'd been here: the Guild representative had made the round trip from Freedom two or three times in the interim. The only possible explanation was that they'd been held somewhere else on the base; where and why I'd have to try to find out.

"The hospital, probably," Remington said. "At least to start with." Which made sense—hardly anyone came out of a rift bounce feeling entirely chipper, and serious injuries were common. "After that . . ." He trailed off, and shrugged. "I don't imagine our hosts were quite as concerned about their welfare as they have been with us."

I nodded, feeling a tight knot growing in the pit of my stomach. Cutting and running, as the *Poison 4* had attempted to do, would be taken as a tacit admission of guilt from the outset, and a Freebooter crew didn't have the economic and political clout of the Guild standing behind them. No doubt their interrogation had been a good deal more rigorous than ours, and I had no desire to find out how much so: but if the Leaguers ever got wind of the secrets I was carrying around with me, I wouldn't get any choice in the matter.

"So why are they putting them in with us now?" I asked.

"Because they finally got tired of asking the same stupid questions, and they can't be bothered to shoot us," the green woman said, overhearing, and turning to glare at me. Clearly a couple of weeks of sustained interrogation, not to mention having her ship shot out from under her, had done little to improve her disposition. Then she looked at my face properly, and her expression softened a little. "Simon something, right?"

"Forrester," I said, introducing my companions. "This is Clio Rennau, and—"

"John Remington, master of the *Stacked Deck*." Remington stepped forward, nodded a greeting, and smiled a little tightly. "Forgive me if I don't shake hands."

"I never shake hands with Guilders. I need all my fingers." She returned the nod coolly. "Carolyn Ertica, mistress of a gutted hulk." She indicated the older of the two men accompanying her. "Baines was my engineer." That made sense: he was the only one of the three with neuroware, his datasphere shrunken and closed off with privacy protocols. He nodded slightly, regarding us all with suspicion, and an almost-healed flash burn became visible on the side of his face as he turned in our direction. Ertica tilted her head towards the young man with the cats' eyes. "And that's Rollo. Does a bit of everything."

"Don't we all," I said, faintly surprised to receive a friendly grin from him in return.

"What about the rest of your crew?" Clio asked, with a glance back down the empty corridor. "Where are they?"

"I suppose that depends on what their religions were," Ertica said shortly.

"Some of 'em'll be lucky to make cockroach next time round," Rollo added cheerfully, before being silenced by a glare from his captain.

"That's enough." Corporal Fledge stepped in to exert a little of his fondly imagined authority. He gestured with the barrel of his gun. "Your quarters are this way."

"Not too close to ours, I hope," Deeks said, shouldering his way through the crowd, a couple of his shipmates tagging along behind him. "Don't want 'booters stinking up the place." Which pretty much explains why I'd never really taken to him, despite his affable greeting the first time we'd met. I'd never quite been able to shake the feeling that it was my Guild patch he was being friendly to, rather than the person wearing it.

"Ooh, aren't you adorable?" Ertica said, with a patently insincere smile. Before anyone could react she leaned in, and planted a flirtatious kiss on his cheek. "I could just eat you alive."

"What?" Utterly taken aback, Deeks stood in stupefied astonishment for a moment, before his hand went up to his face. "Aaagh!" Blisters began erupting across the skin, just as they had done when she'd been accosted in the street back on Numarkut. But it seemed to me that the effect was far less pronounced than it had been on that occasion, when Ertica's would-be attacker had been completely and instantly incapacitated. "What did you do?"

Fledge barely glanced at the spreading lesions, before gesturing to one of the guard detail. "Holby. Take him to the infirmary."

"Corporal." She saluted, in a fairly perfunctory manner if I was any judge, and led the loudly complaining Deeks away up the corridor, passing through the cordon of guards blocking the open hatch in case anyone was bored or stir crazy enough to try making a completely pointless run for it.

"This way, please." Jas took Ertica by the elbow, and got her moving with polite but insistent pressure. Once more reminded of the incident in Dullingham I began to shout a warning, before turning it into a face-saving cough as I realized that Jas seemed completely unaffected by whatever toxin Ertica had in her skin. Another of her invisible tweaks, perhaps, or was Ertica able to control its potency by an act of will? Another question to try and find the answer to.

But at least I'd have time to do that. I raised a hand in farewell, as Ertica and her friends were escorted away.

"Be seeing you," I said.

CHAPTER TWENTY-FOUR
In which I reveal a secret in order to keep one.

And of course I did, although it took longer than I expected. I'd already resolved to wait a day or two before contriving a chance meeting with one of the Freebooters, which would be difficult enough to begin with; they kept themselves to themselves as assiduously as Freebooters always did, ostentatiously ignoring Guilders and shipping line crews alike. To be fair, the antipathy was mutual; word about what had happened to Deeks got around almost at once, growing in the telling to those who hadn't seen it, and no one seemed at all keen to attract Ertica's attention after that. Which had probably been the point in the first place.

The one exception to the Freebooters' universal disdain, surprisingly, was me, perhaps because our meeting on Numarkut had convinced Ertica of my good nature—or possibly naivety, which in her view was pretty much the same thing. At any event, on the rare occasions we caught sight of one another, she would nod, almost imperceptibly, instead of pretending I was a human-shaped hole in the air, as she and her companions did with everyone else.

Something which hadn't escaped Clio's notice. "You'll have to watch that," she remarked, a little frostily, after one such exchange. "Soldier Girl will be getting jealous."

I had no idea why she'd think so. I had to admit I found Ertica attractive in the abstract, although I could hardly be blamed for that:

like most men, and quite a few girls, I was biologically programmed to respond in certain ways to the sight of a scantily clad woman, however corrosive her personality. I was hardly in a position to do anything about it, though, even if I'd wanted to: I'd seen what the consequences of getting too close would be, even if I didn't annoy her. And it wasn't as if there was anything romantic in my friendship with Jas either, come to that; although, if I was entirely honest with myself, she was precisely the kind of girl I'd have had those kinds of feelings for under more propitious circumstances.

And the circumstances were far from propitious. As I'd expected, her sense of duty far outweighed whatever value she might have put on our fledgling friendship, and she lost no time in reporting my family connections to her superiors. Something which became almost immediately apparent the following morning, with the arrival of a lieutenant commander in the League Navy, whose uniform was tellingly devoid of any insignia denoting his service branch.

"Simon Forrester, isn't it?" he asked, as I entered the room in our quarters which had become so familiar through previous interviews. It had obviously been intended as a conference room, containing a table, lined with chairs on both sides, with a single, more generously padded, one at the head. My interlocutor had seated himself about halfway down one of the long edges, facing the door, and smiled affably as I came in.

"Don't you know?" I asked, as I took the seat opposite, and placed a mug of coffee and a plate of cookies on the table in front of me. He had a similar plate in front of him, next to his own beverage, which came as no surprise; if this interview followed the pattern of the previous ones I'd sat through, his next move would have been to offer me one, to put me at my ease and persuade me to open up. Bringing my own was supposed to send the clear message that I realized that, and wasn't going to be quite so crudely psychologically manipulated. I really was beginning to think like a Guilder. "That doesn't say a lot for the League's intelligence service."

"I'll take that as a yes." The polite smile congealed a little, although his voice remained relaxed. "I'm Paul Wymes. With a y, not double e." He waited for a conventional polite response, like "Pleased to meet you," or something like that.

"You're expecting me to write it down, then?" I said. "Am I going to have to report your conduct to the Guild?" Although if I did, I wouldn't have to write anything down, of course: my neuroware was recording the entire conversation.

"I sincerely hope not," Wymes said, the pose of affability getting steadily more frayed around the edges. He smiled, a little disingenuously. "And speaking of the Guild, I gather that the intermediary appointed by the system Guildhall to deal with this unfortunate situation has had to return to Freedom." Of course he had: the DIR, or whoever else this clown reported to, wouldn't want a senior member of the Guild getting wind of this latest development. It would complicate things far too much. "Perhaps you'd like to have your captain sitting in on our discussion instead."

"Not really." I shrugged, to his evident surprise, and bit into one of the cookies—chocolate chip, which I've always thought goes particularly well with coffee. "I don't want to have to pay him a cut if we reach an agreement." I pushed the plate across the table. "Help yourself."

"An agreement," Wymes repeated, taking a cookie with the air of a chess player reaching for a sacrificial pawn. "And what kind of an agreement would you have in mind, Mr. Forrester?"

"A business one, of course," I said. I'd had some time to think, since inadvertently revealing part of my family history to Jas, and I'd come up with what I hoped was a workable strategy to limit the damage. The key was to play up the fact that I was a Guilder, rather than a former Commonwealth citizen, and play that role to the hilt. "You think I might have some information you can use. I'm willing to talk it over, and find out if you're right. And how much you're prepared to pay for it if I do."

"Pay for it?" Wymes looked at me a little quizzically, the half-eaten cookie pinched between his finger and thumb. "I must say I'm a little surprised at your attitude."

"Are you?" I sipped at my coffee, trying to project an air of easy unconcern. "It seems simple enough to me. My mother's a Commonwealth naval officer, which means I might know a few things about where she's been and what she's been up to. You'd have found that out eventually, even if I hadn't mentioned it to Private Mokole, but I thought it wouldn't hurt to speed things up a bit." I shook my head dismissively. "I kept expecting the topic to come up in one of my earlier chats with you people, but I suppose your networks on Avalon aren't quite as efficient as I thought."

"So you told her on purpose, to get our attention?" Wymes took a small, precise bite of his cookie, and brushed a nonexistent crumb from his upper lip, his voice reeking of skepticism. "Why would you do something like that? Betray everything you ever believed in?"

"Why do you think?" I shrugged again, and picked up another cookie. "If you've done any digging at all, you'll know why I left the Commonwealth. I don't owe it anything."

"I see." Wymes nodded slowly, dismally failing to counterfeit sympathy. "This is about revenge." So he had been checking up.

"Bollocks it is," I said. "It's about money. I've spent my entire life around Commonwealth naval personnel, and probably picked up a lot of information you can use. But the older it gets, the less it's worth. I want to cash it in while it's still valuable enough to get a good price."

"And that doesn't bother you at all?" Wymes asked, a faint edge of distrust elbowing its way past his carefully modulated vowels. "Committing treason against the Commonwealth?"

"I'm not committing treason against anybody," I said firmly. "I'm a Guilder now, a free agent, and I'm doing what any Guilder would do with confidential information. Selling it for as much as I can get." I paused momentarily, wondering whether to twist the knife, and decided I might as well. If I didn't want him taking me seriously, it wouldn't hurt to come across as a bit of a tosser. "Pity you never did find that Commonwealth spy you keep insisting is somewhere around here. The price would go a lot higher with someone else to bid against."

"When we find them, we'll ask if they're interested." Wymes permitted himself a thin smile, about as warm as a midwinter frost. "Although they'll have quite a lot of pressing business to consider by that point, so I suggest you prepare yourself for some disappointment in that regard." He looked at me narrowly over the rim of his coffee cup. "And how much were you thinking of asking for this invaluable information?"

I sipped my own drink, refusing to be hurried. "Make me an offer." Heaven help me, I was starting to enjoy this. "Then I'll tell you it's an insult, double it, and we'll negotiate from there."

"That's all very well," Wymes said, leaning forward across the table, and looking seriously engaged for the first time, "but you can hardly expect me to bid for information you may or may not have. Tell me what you know, and I'll give you an honest estimation of what it's worth."

To my pleased surprise, my chuckle of amusement sounded completely spontaneous. "We both know that'll be nothing at all," I said. "As soon as I tell you anything, I've nothing left to sell."

"Then we seem to have reached an impasse." Wymes leant back in his chair, and took a self-satisfied sip of his coffee. "If you won't tell me anything, I can't assess how valuable your information might be."

"Fair enough." I leaned back too, trying to look equally unconcerned. "How about the location of the Commonwealth task force preparing to relieve Rockhall if it all goes pear-shaped?"

"That would be worth a lot," Wymes said, "if we didn't already know." He studied my face for a flicker of expression, but the practice I'd already had insulating large areas of my life from Mother's interference paid off yet again, and I didn't react at all.

"How much?" I asked levelly. This was skating on very thin ice—I was sure they already knew what I was about to tell him, but if they didn't, I'd be putting Mother and Tinkie directly in harm's way. But if they did, that would convince Wymes beyond all possible doubt that I was precisely the kind of amoral chancer Guilders were popularly supposed to be, with no lingering loyalties to the Commonwealth. His attention, and that of the agency he worked for, would move on, leaving the secrets of my covert assignment from Aunt Jenny, and my mother's presence in the Sodallagain system, comfortably preserved.

"Ten thousand," Wymes said, in the kind of take it or leave it tone that made it plain to any Guilder that there was still plenty of room for negotiation.

"Ten thousand what?" I asked. "Ducats?" I'd assumed he meant the League's own currency, but there were so many monetary systems even in this relatively tiny part of the Human Sphere that it paid to be cautious. Ten thousand ducats was a respectable sum, right enough, but worth only about two thirds that number of Commonwealth guineas, or half of it in Numarkut talents. And on some worlds, ten thousand of the local denomination would just about buy you a meal, and cup of coffee afterwards to wash it down.

"I was going to say guineas, as I thought you'd be more used to that." Wymes smirked a little. "But ducats would be perfectly acceptable."

"Thirty thousand of them would," I agreed.

"Twenty." Wymes' temper was beginning to fray, and he was making less of an effort to hide it. "If the intelligence is good."

"It's good," I said. "We just need to work out a way of doing this that makes sure I get paid."

"Of course." A sarcastic tone began to creep into Wymes' voice. "I take it my word as a representative of the League of Democracies will be sufficient guarantee?"

"Don't be ridiculous," I said cheerfully. "But I'm happy to give you my word as a member of the Commerce Guild that I believe the information I'm selling you to be sound." Which raised the stakes nicely. However skeptical he might be about me, personally, Wymes could hardly fail to be aware of the binding nature of a Guilder's oath. At the very least he'd have to believe I was in earnest about trying to cut a deal now.

"Then what do you suggest?" he asked, his demeanor becoming instantly more businesslike.

"A double blind," I said. I fished a small notebook out of my pocket, tore out one of the pages, and skimmed it across the table, along with a pen. I deliberately aimed them wide, but, to my complete lack of surprise, Wymes caught them both easily, his tweaked reflexes as highly tuned as Jas's. "You write down where you think the Commonwealth task force is being assembled, and I'll write down where I know it is. If they match, you're right, I've got nothing to sell, and we're wasting each others' time. If they don't, you pay me the thirty grand."

"Twenty," Wymes said, without missing a beat.

"Twenty," I agreed, with a shrug and a smile I felt sure was guaranteed to irritate him. "Can't blame me for trying."

"You're a Guilder. I expect it," Wymes said, and my heart skipped. Unless he'd said that to play me, which I certainly couldn't discount, it sounded as though he was halfway convinced already. "I take it you want this agreement notarized?"

"No need," I said blithely. "I've been recording this ever since I entered the room, and so have you." I gestured towards the bulge in his jacket pocket. "I can see the datastream from the cameras to your handheld."

Which I'd been very careful not to try and infiltrate, despite the obvious temptation to do so. Wymes was clearly a spook of some kind, although quite possibly not entitled to the uniform he was wearing, and I had no doubt that his handheld would be very comprehensively protected. Possibly by the kind of countermeasures which would scramble any intruding neuroware badly enough to puree my brain, and leave it leaking out of my nose. Quite apart from killing me, that would make an unconscionable mess of my favorite jacket, neither of which I considered an acceptable outcome. Even if it didn't come to that, and all I did was trip an alarm, that would pretty much put an end to any attempt at bamboozling Wymes into concluding I was harmless, and shoving off to look for his nonexistent spy somewhere else.

"Very well." He looked at me narrowly, probably wondering what else I'd been doing with my 'ware since the start of our meeting. "Let's get this over with."

He scribbled briefly on the piece of paper, and skimmed the pen back to me. It came hard and fast, but I caught it anyway, and he stared at me for a moment; he'd clearly expected me to fumble it, but my athlete's reflexes were quite good for non-tweaked ones, and, though I'd never be able to match a transgener with the right modifications, I was a fair bit faster than most. For some reason I found myself remembering the fight in the alley back on Numarkut, and Mallow's remark that if we were under observation I'd just shown myself to be more dangerous than anyone expected; well, even if the dregs hadn't been sent by Wymes's people, he was probably getting the idea that there was more to me than met the eye by now. Time for a bit of distraction, so I pretended to fumble with the pen as I scribbled in turn, and held up the scrap of paper where he could see it.

"Tintagel," I said.

"Snap." Wymes permitted himself a wintery smile as he held up his own, across which *Tintagel* was emblazoned in a curiously untidy scrawl.

"Lucky guess," I said, trying to look disappointed, in spite of a sudden surge of elation.

"You were right," Wymes said, getting to his feet. "We are wasting each other's time." He walked round the table and looked down at me on his way to the door; another cheap psychological trick. "Unless you've got anything else you want to sell."

"That was the big thing," I admitted. I tried to sound a little desperate. "I know some other stuff . . ."

"I'm afraid we aren't in the market for out of date gossip." His voice was flat with finality, and I realized I'd actually pulled it off. He thought I was trying to hustle him, and had had enough. "I don't think we can do business."

"Guess not," I agreed. "Ah well. Easy come, easy go." I waited until the door had clicked closed behind him, then sighed with relief, hardly able to believe that I'd got away with it. My desperate gamble had worked, and my secrets were safe.

Even better, I'd got his plateful of cookies.

CHAPTER TWENTY-FIVE

In which I listen to an appeal for help, and learn something to my advantage.

When I went for my habitual run that afternoon, Jas seemed a little embarrassed at the sight of me, if it's possible to look embarrassed while holding a gun and keeping a watchful eye out for potential trouble. Nevertheless, I smiled a friendly greeting, and slowed, jogging on my accustomed spot in front of the pressure hatch she was guarding as though nothing had changed between us.

"Hi." I poked at her visor with my sneakware, but, as usual, there was no comms traffic I could exploit; which I found even more frustrating than ever, since I'd come so close to tapping a node through it the day before.

"Hi." She smiled back, but seemed to be having trouble meeting my eyes; a suspicion I swiftly confirmed by accessing her targeting display. Her gaze was hovering around my face like a bee round a flower, focusing on it for a second or so before skittering away again. "How are you?"

"A bit disappointed, actually," I said, and her posture stiffened, becoming noticeably more defensive.

"I really didn't have a choice," she said, and the other trooper on guard with her drifted a little closer, clearly getting ready to intervene if I felt like making trouble. "I've a duty to report—"

"I know that," I said, trying to sound as reasonable and relaxed as possible. "And I really don't have a problem with you doing it. To be honest, I'd have thought a lot less of you if you hadn't."

"You would?" She seemed genuinely surprised, and I smiled in response, as disingenuously as I knew how.

"Navy brat, remember? I know the kind of oath you must have taken when you enlisted, and I know how important it is to live up to something like that. I knew if you were the kind of person I thought—hoped—you were, you wouldn't be able to go against it, even for a friend. If that's what we actually are."

"I've been wondering that too," she admitted. Her eyes flickered over me, the scattering of other internees within her field of vision, and the trooper beside her, lingering for a moment on his gun. "It's kind of complicated."

"Exactly," I said.

"Then what are you so disappointed about?"

"Honestly?" I asked, as if hoping to be coaxed. I was pretty sure Wymes had bought my hastily improvised story, but just in case he checked back down the line, I needed to cover myself with Jas. Too bad if that meant she decided I was a duplicitous creep, best kept at arm's length from now on: I still had hopes of getting to a node through her eyeware, and, if I was honest with myself, I'd miss our conversations too. "I was hoping to sell some information to your intelligence people, but it turned out they already knew it."

"You were hoping—" then the coin dropped. Her voice hardened a little. "So that's why you told me about your mom. So I'd set them up for the pitch."

"It seemed like a good idea at the time," I said, trying to sound contrite. "And we were talking about our families anyway, so—"

"Typical bloody Guilder." She sounded pissed off and amused at the same time, neither emotion quite managing to gain the upper hand. "Always an angle."

"So," I said after a moment. "Are we good?"

"I don't know." At least she was looking at my face again. "You're not the only one who's feeling a bit disappointed right now, to be honest."

"Fair enough." I knew pursuing the point would just be pushing my luck; the best thing I could do now would be to tactfully withdraw, and let her process this in her own time. I waved, probably trying a little too hard to sound cheerful and carefree. "Be seeing you."

"Yeah. Well, you know where to find me." She nodded, a little stiffly, and I resumed my run. Or, at least, that was the idea. I turned, jogging backwards as I waved goodbye, and cannoned into someone behind me. We both went sprawling.

"Ow. Smeg." The voice beneath me was unfamiliar, which came as a vague surprise; after so much time in enforced proximity, I could more or less recognize all my fellow internees by sound alone, even the ones I'd barely exchanged a sentence with (or none at all, in the case of the shipping line crews) since our arrival.

"Sorry. My fault entirely," I said automatically, scrambling up, and extending a helping hand downwards.

"You reckon?" Rollo, the cat-eyed Freebooter, glared at me for a moment, then sprang to his feet, with a litheness which made me suspect he'd acquired a few more feline characteristics than just the slit pupils. He staggered theatrically, one eye on the watching troopers, keeping all the weight on his left leg. "Ow. Ow. I've done my knee in." He stared at me again, waiting for me to take the hint. "A little help getting back to our quarters?"

"Oh. Right," I said, finally getting it. His leg looked fine to me, but I offered him a shoulder to lean on nevertheless. I'd been meaning to contrive a meeting with the Freebooters in any case, so if they'd had the same idea, I might as well go along with it. "I never even noticed you were there."

"No, people generally don't." Rollo looked smug for a moment. "Not until it's too late, anyway." He put his weight on my shoulder, and pointed to one of the accommodation units, which, until yesterday, had been closed up. It didn't look all that different now, but the main door was hanging open. "We're in that one."

"Having trouble, Si?" Rolf and Lena loomed up out of nowhere, and down at us. Rollo met their gaze unflinchingly.

"No. We just tripped over one another," I said. "I'm helping him back to his quarters."

"Need any help?" Lena asked, and I shook my head.

"He's not that heavy."

"Okay." Rolf nodded. *We know where you are.*

I'll be fine, I sent back, but I have to admit I felt a strong sense of relief as I did so. After everything I'd heard about Freebooters, it was nice to know I had backup if I needed it.

"You're limping on the wrong leg," I said, once I was certain my shipmates were out of earshot.

"Picky, picky." Rollo shifted his weight from right to left. "Whenever you're ready."

We must have made an incongruous sight as we staggered across the garden towards the Freebooters' quarters, which, either by coincidence or a hitherto unsuspected sense of humor on the part of Corporal Fledge, was situated next to the section occupied by Deeks and his friends from the *Ebon Flow*. A number of heads turned to watch us, with varying degrees of contempt or puzzlement, one of the latter being Clio's.

What are you doing with him? she sent.

He's hurt his leg, I replied. *Just helping out.*

Of course you are. Though the message was as blandly neutral as everything else in my 'sphere, her expression loaded it with exasperated amusement. *You want to be careful, or you'll be turning Freebooter before long.*

Never going to happen, I assured her. It seemed a marginal existence at the best of times, and I couldn't imagine anyone leaving the relative security of the Guild to get involved in it.

Relieved to hear it. Nevertheless, her head turned slowly, tracking us until I'd crossed the threshold of the Freebooters' quarters.

Rollo stopped limping as soon as we passed inside, although he kept his arm around me until we reached one of the sofas scattered through a communal area the same size as the one the crew of the *Stacked Deck* occupied. Ertica and Baines were already there, almost lost in a space meant for so many more people, and they both looked up as we entered.

Rollo dropped onto the couch with a contented sigh, and patted the upholstery next to him. "Plenty of room for a small one, if you want to keep on snuggling."

"I'm fine," I said, remaining on my feet.

Ertica looked daggers at her deckhand. "Give it a rest, Rollo, he's only interested in girls. Why else would he keep hanging around the bitch who dragged us in here?"

"I'm not prejudiced." Rollo shrugged, and grinned at me. "You know where I am if you ever change your mind."

But my attention was already entirely on Ertica, which, given that she apparently wore even less in the privacy of her own quarters than she did outside, was hardly surprising.

"She didn't react when she touched you," I said, remembering how Jas had intervened to lead her away after the altercation with Deeks. "Is she immune to your tweak, or can you control it?"

"Straight to the point," Baines said, the first time I'd actually heard him speak. His voice was deep and gravelly, with a trace of an accent I couldn't place—a legacy of whichever backwater world he'd left decades ago, in early adolescence. "Not something you often see in a Guilder."

"A bit of both," Ertica said, ignoring the pair of them. "League grunts have a broad spectrum antitoxin tweak, but I can vary the potency myself if I want to." She shrugged, which set up some briefly distracting oscillations. "I wouldn't have much of a love life otherwise, would I?"

"Well, there have been a couple of guys—" Rollo began, before falling silent again in response to a glare from his captain.

"If you can't say something relevant, don't say anything at all." She turned back to me, her voice becoming almost strangulated with the effort of trying to sound hospitable. "Can we offer you some tea? Or something?"

"Tea," I said. "Why not?" Whatever they wanted, or, more likely, Ertica wanted, it was clearly going to take some time before she came to the point. No reason not to be comfortable while I waited to find out what it was.

"Tea. Right." Baines sighed, and began to boil a kettle.

Simon. A message appeared in my 'sphere, from Clio if the tag was to be relied on. *What's happening? You've been in there five minutes already.*

Nothing, I sent back. *Just having tea.*

Tea with Freebooters? This time I had to imagine her incredulous expression for myself, which I did without too much difficulty. *Just don't let her stir it with her finger.*

I'll be careful, I promised.

"So." I seated myself at a vacant table, and tried to sound focused and businesslike, which was a lot harder than it sounds under the circumstances. "What did you want to talk to me about?"

Ertica smiled tightly. "You really are new to the Guild. Otherwise your first question would have been 'What's in it for me?'"

"You've already offered some tea," I said. "We can move on from there once I know exactly what you want, and how badly you want it."

Her smile became a little more genuine. "That's more like it," she said. "Spoken like a real Guilder." She glanced up as Baines put a couple of mugs of tea on the table between us; they were overly full, and slopped slightly, leaving rings on the fake wood grain of the plastic surface. "Thanks, Hiro."

"Cookie?" I asked, pulling the ones I'd scored from Wymes out of the pocket I'd stashed them in. They hadn't crumbled much, and weren't particularly fluffy. "No chocolate ones, I'm afraid. Too liable to melt."

"Aren't you full of surprises." Ertica looked at them suspiciously, and let them lie unmolested on the tabletop; a reaction which, now I came to consider their condition more carefully, I could hardly blame her for.

"Ooh, a jammy one." Rollo bounced up, grabbed it, and subsided onto the sofa again, in one fluid movement.

"Isn't everyone?" I asked, responding to Ertica's question, and ignoring her excitable subordinate; which seemed to be the strategy of choice among his shipmates.

"In my experience." Ertica nodded, and sipped at her tea. Somewhat reassured, I ventured to take a mouthful of my own, and found it no less drinkable than I'd expected.

"Then what's your surprise?" I asked. "Why am I here?"

"We need a favor," Ertica said, putting her mug on the table, next to her metaphorical cards. "What's left of our ship's been impounded; which is only a technical inconvenience, as it'll never fly again anyway. So when they let the rest of you go, we'll be stuck here. Indefinitely."

"Years, probably," Rollo put in. "Even if they don't press—" He went quiet at a glare from Ertica.

"What charges?" I asked. "You must have convinced them you're not the spies they're looking for, or they'd have sent you straight to Freedom for a detailed debrief instead of putting you in here with us. So why did you try to make a run for it?"

"Who says we tried to run?" Ertica asked.

"You did, when you arrived here. 'Mistress of a gutted hulk,' remember? They wouldn't have had any reason to open fire if you'd just let them board like the rest of us." I didn't see any point in admitting I'd watched the whole thing through the *Stacked Deck*'s sensor suite; if they thought I was more astute than I was, they'd be less likely to try something underhand for fear I'd spot it. Although these were Freebooters I was dealing with: pirates, liars and thieves, if Clio was to be believed, so underhand probably came with the job description.

"We weren't spying," Ertica said, after a moment's hesitation, "but we did have an extra item among the cargo. Two hundredweight of refined sugar."

"Which isn't exactly legal?" I asked. Some worlds regarded the stuff as a health hazard, particularly where a substantial part of the population had transgenic tweaks to speed up their metabolisms; overuse by a handful of them could even lead to addiction and psychosis.

"That's a bit of a grey area," Baines put in. "Some places it is, some places it isn't."

"One of the places it isn't being Freedom, I take it," I said. Unlike the Commonwealth, which had a one-size-fits-all approach to the legal code, the League let its member systems run their own affairs pretty much as they liked, so long as they subscribed to a few core principles, and paid their fair shares of the budget for things like the armed forces and the official riftcom network.

"Most of the League worlds, if you're going to get technical," Rollo said. "Which drives the price up nicely."

"Why take the risk?" I asked. "Farland were paying over the odds for this job anyway." And much good it had done them, as things turned out, with their precious cargo impounded as soon as it arrived. No doubt a platoon of lawyers would be on a nice little earner for the next few years sorting out the ensuing squabble about who was liable for the financial fallout.

Ertica shrugged, with the same disconcerting effect as on the previous occasion. "I'm a Freebooter. It's in my nature." She studied my face for a moment, realized I wasn't buying it, and sighed. "All right, then, the truth is we were desperate. The Farland contract came along just in time to keep our ship from being repossessed, but it would only have bought us a breathing space. A quick, clean smuggling run on top of that would have got us out from under. And it would have worked perfectly if that stupid bitch hadn't been exposed as a Commonwealth agent, and got us all caught up in a spy hunt."

"All right." I'd had enough practice at lies and misdirection in the last few weeks to be fairly sure there was a backbone of truth to that, at least. "You're busted, stranded, and probably looking at jail time. And I'm concerned about this because . . . ?"

"I don't know, actually." Ertica shrugged again, but this time I ignored the result; it was too erratic to be a genuine tic, and too frequent to be entirely unintentional, and I wasn't quite young or naive enough to be bamboozled into thinking with my hormones. But if she thought I was, fine; I'd grown up being underestimated, and knew how to turn that to my advantage. "Perhaps because you thought Numarkut was civilized."

"I won't make that mistake again," I said. "But I still don't see what I can do help you."

"It's simple enough. We need a ride. You've got a ship. Talk to your skipper, see what it'll take for him to give us passage. I'm sure we can work something out."

Which was more than I was. Given the amount of antipathy I'd already witnessed between Guilders and Freebooters, I couldn't see Remington exactly falling over himself to do her any favors: but, at that, the *Stacked Deck* probably represented the best chance they had of cutting a deal with someone. They certainly wouldn't get anywhere with Deeks and his chums, or the other Guilder crews interned here, and the shipping line employees were, if anything, even more hostile.

"I'll talk to him," I said, after pausing just long enough to look as though I'd been giving the absurd proposal some serious consideration, "but I can't promise anything."

"Good enough." Ertica nodded briskly. "Have you finished your tea?"

"More or less." I ignored the implicit dismissal, and sipped at it, finding it had gone cold while we talked, which hadn't exactly enhanced the flavor. "What's the rest of this rock like? You've seen a lot more of it than I have."

"Not that much," Rollo said. "Just the infirmary and the brig." He gestured expansively at our surroundings. "And this bit. Which I can assure you is way better than both."

"I can believe that," I said. I took another sip I didn't want. "So not much chance of getting orientated."

"None at all," Baines put in. "I tried tapping a node from the hospital, to get a map, but it's completely secure."

How secure? I sent. *There are usually holes if you know where to look.* So, it might be possible to tap a node, if I could somehow get myself sent to the infirmary. Which didn't sound like much of a plan, but it was the closest thing to one I'd been able to come up with since our arrival: unless you counted continuing to hang around Jas with my fingers crossed as a positive course of action.

Not here. Baines clearly felt the need to prove the point; perhaps his pride had been hurt by his failure to mesh. *It's got all this military grade stuff around it.* He kicked a file across to my 'sphere, and my heart leapt. He'd recorded his attempt to mesh in, and the security protocols which had prevented him from doing so.

Looks pretty solid, I conceded, with a nod. But he hadn't had my sneakware, or my knack for adapting datanomes on the fly. I'd need to take a long, careful look at this, but it was just possible he'd handed me the key to the node.

All I had to do now was find a way to get near the lock.

CHAPTER TWENTY-SIX

In which I become embroiled in a timely altercation.

As I'd expected, Remington didn't exactly leap at Ertica's proposal.

"What's in it for us?" he asked, and I found myself suppressing a smile at the echo of the Freebooter's words. There could be no doubt at all that John Remington was a typical Guilder.

"She was a bit vague on that side of the deal," I admitted. "But it pretty much boiled down to 'name your own price.'"

"Which pretty much guarantees she's got no intention of paying up once she's got what she wants," Remington said.

Rennau nodded in agreement. "Of course she hasn't, she's a Freebooter." The three of us were conferring in a quiet corner of our accommodation area, to which Remington had led the way as soon as I returned from the Freebooters' quarters, ignoring the curious glances of our shipmates. Clio, in particular, had seemed relieved at my safe return, although quite what she imagined might have happened to me I had no idea.

"Is there anything they can offer that we might want?" I asked. Not that I cared particularly either way: from where I was standing it looked as though they'd brought their misfortune entirely on themselves, and I didn't think I was going to lose much sleep at the idea of them finding out actions had consequences. Nevertheless, I felt grateful to Baines for the information he'd given me, even though he'd been unaware of its value, and I suppose I thought I owed them something in return.

"Like what?" Rennau snorted derisively. "They've only got the clothes on their backs. And damn few of those, in one case."

"Information, maybe?" I was reaching, I knew, and tried not to sound like it. "If they were smuggling, they must have connections, here and on Numarkut. Could any of those be useful to us?"

"Gangsters and organized criminals?" Remington shook his head, smiling at my naivety. "We only deal with those through the local Guild reps. Who'll have far better connections than a bunch of chancers like that."

"Fair enough." I nodded, unable to find a hole in his reasoning. "She made it pretty clear they think we're a long shot, anyway. I don't suppose they'll be all that surprised to find out we're not interested."

"Even if we were, they've broken the law here. We could hardly tell the League we're taking them with us in any case," Remington pointed out.

"Not without putting them under Guild protection," Rennau agreed. He exchanged a brief, amused glance with the skipper. "Like that'd ever happen. Guildhall would piss themselves laughing if we even asked."

"Even so." Remington looked thoughtful for a moment, wondering if there could possibly be an angle he'd missed, then shook his head. He turned to me. "Next time they invite you to tea, tell them they're on their own. Unless they can come up with a concrete proposal that's clearly to our advantage."

"Right." I nodded too, in complete agreement. But I couldn't help feeling a little regretful nevertheless.

I got very little sleep that night. I couldn't resist taking a quick look at the data I'd got from Baines as soon as I got back to my room, and, as I should have anticipated, quickly became so engrossed that the passage of time barely registered; it was almost morning by the time I'd finished examining it. Even so, I felt surprisingly energized as I grabbed some toast and coffee: every step felt as though I was back in Aunt Jenny's guest room, bouncing me off the floor a tiny bit higher than it should have done.

And with good reason. The more I'd worked on it, the more sure I'd become that I could actually get away with cracking a node if the opportunity presented itself. The sneakware I'd put together to get into

Jas's visor would mesh neatly with the outer protective layer, and I'd been able to construct some datanomes mirroring the protocols Baines had recorded lurking deeper inside the system with very little difficulty. I still might need to do some quick modifications on the fly, but I was good at that sort of thing, so it shouldn't be a problem. All I needed was some kind of excuse to visit the infirmary.

And that, of course, was where the whole thing fell down. I'd need to create some plausible-seeming accident, which would require my hospitalization, but still leave me well enough to function when I got there. And not have anyone suspect that I might be faking it, or raise any doubts about the seriousness of my injuries.

So I went for a run as soon as I'd finished breakfast, hoping that something might occur to me, and that even if it didn't I'd be able to dissipate some of the energy still coursing through my system. I'd been hoping Jas might be on guard duty, but there was no sign of her at either pressure door, and I completed a couple of circuits of the cavern completely wrapped up in my own thoughts.

The second time round I caught sight of Clio and Ensign Neville, who for some reason had become inextricably linked in my mind with the image of a hamster in a League Navy uniform, seated on a bench beside the fountain in the central garden. They seemed to be deep in conversation, although Clio wasn't quite engrossed enough to miss me as I passed through her peripheral vision.

Hi, I sent, not really expecting a reply. I wasn't disappointed either; she simply turned back to Neville and laughed at whatever inanity he'd just emitted. Fine, I wasn't exactly in the mood for conversation myself.

"Looking for your new best friend?" Recalled to my immediate surroundings, I realized I'd slowed down as I approached the Freebooters' quarters, and glanced at it automatically as I did so. Deeks was standing in my way, one side of his face still swollen and red where Ertica had kissed it. His eyes narrowed. "You seem to be spending a lot of time with the 'booters."

"They had a business proposition," I said, thinking it was none of his damn business, but determined to be polite anyway. One advantage of an Avalonian upbringing, at least in certain social circles, was the ability to seem affable to people you'd rather scrape off your shoes.

"Guilders don't do business with Freebooters."

"No, we don't." I nodded, in polite agreement. "Which is why we're not interested."

"Good." He relaxed a little, some of the hostility draining out of his posture, while curiosity gradually got the better of him. "What sort of business?"

"You know better than that," I said, keeping the tone light. As a rule, Guilders weren't that big on sharing job opportunities, unless there was something in it for them. "Besides, you wouldn't be any keener on taking them up on it than we were. Trust me."

"If you say so." He didn't seem all that convinced, but that wasn't my problem. "So you were just passing by, then?"

"Got a message to deliver." I caught a flicker of movement inside the Freebooters' quarters, and the first faint glimmering of an idea began to take shape. I allowed the merest hint of a challenge to enter my voice. "Unless you've got some objection to me having a quick word with your girlfriend."

"What's that supposed to mean?" He was rising to it, the unmarred side of his face darkening to match the part still inflamed from Ertica's toxin. Attracted by the disturbance, a few of his shipmates started wandering over to watch the show.

"Just kidding," I assured him, with patent insincerity, the trace of mockery in my voice belying the conciliatory words. "You know." I blew a couple of air kisses. "You seemed to be getting on with her much better than I did."

"Think that's funny, do you?" His ego must have been even more tender than his face, because he swung a punch at me without any warning at all. Unless, that is, like me, you've sparred long enough and often enough to be subconsciously aware of even the tiniest shift in the weight of the person in front of you.

Which meant I was probably aware of the attack even before he realized he was starting to make it, and ducked out of the way long before it could land. I made a big show of blocking it, though, far more slowly and clumsily than I normally would, which was surprisingly hard to do; when you're fighting you rely on instinct and muscle memory, which needs a lot of conscious thought to override.

"Quite funny," I admitted cheerfully, hoping there were a nice lot of witnesses around. I was pretty sure I could ride a couple of punches, make out I'd cracked a rib or something, and get hustled off to the infirmary in jig time.

Since I wasn't too bothered about getting hit, I risked a moment's distraction to see what was happening around me. A couple of the troopers guarding the pressure doors were already running towards us, leaving only one man or woman guarding each of them; the ones left behind were leveling their weapons, presumably in case the brawl was nothing more than a diversion, and they were about to be rushed by a group of suicidal would-be escapees.

"Simon!" Clio was running too, I noted absently, a bemused-looking Neville a few steps behind, drawing his sidearm—although what he thought he was going to do with it was beyond me, as I suspected gunning down a Guilder or two would turn out to be a seriously counter-productive career move.

Deeks lashed out again, and I planted myself where it would catch me on the side of the face, just at the fullest extent of his arm: the blow landed more lightly than I pretended, with an impact that jarred my jaw, compressing the cheek against my teeth, and, by great good fortune, opening up a minor cut that let me spit out some blooded saliva in a suitably dramatic fashion.

"Get off him!" Clio launched herself at Deeks, a compact bundle of ferocity which took the pair of us by complete surprise, headbutting him in the groin. Deeks howled, and collapsed, leaving Clio free to kneel on his chest and attempt to twist his ears off.

"Clio!" I took her by the arm, and tried to haul her back to her feet. The rest of the onlookers from the *Ebon Flow* were surging towards us, no longer passive spectators, and clearly intent on avenging their fallen comrade. "Back off!"

"When I'm good and ready!" I'd never seen her this angry. She gave Deeks' ears a final vengeful twist, and got back on her feet, glaring a challenge at his oncoming shipmates. "Come on then, if you think you're hard enough!"

"Will you calm down?" I tried to push her behind me, but she was having none of it, ducking under my elbow to stand at my shoulder, her fists cocked.

We're coming! In the distance I could see Rennau, Rolf and Lena boiling out of our own quarters, a handful of our shipmates behind them. Another Guilder thing, I belatedly realized; attack one member of a ship's crew and you attacked them all, irrespective of whose fault it had been to start with. But the crew of the *Ebon Flow* obviously felt the same way, and by the time our reinforcements arrived, Clio and I would have been pounded to mush.

At least that was probably what they thought; after the fight in the alley, I was feeling pretty confident that I could at least hold them off until our friends arrived. And I'd been hoping to contrive a trip to the hospital anyway . . .

"Be careful what you wish for," I muttered under my breath.

Clio glanced at me. "What?"

"Never mind." I braced myself for the charge. At least none of them seemed to be carrying weapons, so we'd be down to fists and feet, which suited me fine.

"Stop this at once!" Ertica's voice cracked across the open space, and I turned in surprise to find her striding towards us, a look of exasperated disdain on her face. "Or if you must squabble like children, take it somewhere else. People are trying to sleep in here."

"Think you can make us?" Clio turned on her at once, the lightning bolts of her fury finding a new conductor.

"Clio!" I took hold of her arm, trying to calm her, and she shook me off. "She's not our enemy."

"Of course she is, she's a sodding Freebooter. Which you'd have noticed if you ever listened to what she says, instead of staring at her all the time with your tongue hanging out!"

"Whereas your tongue seems to be getting quite the workout this morning," Ertica remarked, in the *faux* conversational manner which, in my old social circle, was the verbal equivalent of a stiletto between the ribs.

And Clio rose to it, swinging a punch at the Freebooter's face without pausing to think.

I'd like to claim it was quick wits which led me to intervene, but in all honesty there was no time to think, and I acted purely on instinct. Before Clio's fist could make contact I threw myself into the gap between the two women, receiving a right hook to the jaw which made my head ring, snapping me round towards Ertica; I just had time to register her impressively proportioned décolletage looming up in my field of vision before my face collided with it, and rebounded as Ertica took a belated step backwards.

For an instant, I staggered, regaining my balance, and, if I'm honest, enjoying the moment as much as any straight man would under the circumstances: then I clutched my face, screaming a good deal louder than seemed possible through a mouth now surrounded by soft tissue swelling up to what felt like double its natural size. It felt as though my entire face had been scorched with a blowtorch—I'd never felt such intense pain in my entire life, and sincerely hope never to do so again.

"Now look what you've made me do," Ertica said, sounding no more than mildly tetchy about the whole thing. I tried to focus on her face, but my eyes were swollen into narrow slits by now, and I could barely pick out anything around me.

"Do something!" Clio demanded. "You must have some sort of antidote!"

"Must I?" Ertica sounded amused. "And if I did, what are you prepared to offer me in exchange? That is how you people think, isn't it?"

"Get back, all of you." Of course, Neville was taking charge, whether anyone wanted him to or not. That's what junior officers did in a crisis. Started issuing orders, so everyone else would feel reassured. My datasphere began to hum with message traffic. "Medical emergency, internment area. Exposure to Captain Ertica's dermal toxin." A reply, through his handheld, too encrypted to read: fortunately I could still follow one end of the conversation by listening to his voice. "No, if he's breathing well enough to make that much noise we can pretty much rule out anaphylactic shock."

He was right about that, at any rate: I fired up the bio monitor in my neuroware, looking to check out how bad the damage was, and, to my relief, found it mostly superficial. If anything it seemed to be healing remarkably fast; Ertica must have given me a relatively low dose. Something to be thankful for, anyway: unless, of course, Neville realized I'd recover on my own before too long.

Baines, I sent, finding to my relief that the Freebooter engineer's 'sphere was so close he must have come out of their quarters to back up his skipper—or possibly just to enjoy the spectacle of Guilders brawling among themselves, which I'd no doubt he'd find highly entertaining. *Tell her to say it's serious.*

Why should I? He was quick off the mark, I'll give him that.

Skip says no deal. Play along, I might get you some leverage.

That your word as a Guilder? Sharp, as well as quick. Something I might have realized sooner if Ertica and Rollo hadn't done most of the talking.

Yes. There was no time to waste, even if I had been in the mood for a long conversation. Which I most emphatically wasn't, since my face still felt like it had been dipped in acid. (Which, come to think of it, was pretty much what had actually happened.)

"He'll be fine," Ertica said, apparently trying to reassure Clio now, although I was pretty sure that would be more to pre-empt any retaliation by the crew of the *Stacked Deck* than because she actually cared how the girl felt.

"If he gets to the infirmary fast enough," Baines added.

"Right," Ertica agreed, not missing a beat, which told me a good deal about how much her crew trusted one another.

"Otherwise he's a goner," Rollo added, not wanting to be left out. "Though they sometimes last for hours. Mind you, the way he's feeling now, he probably doesn't want to."

"Not helpful, Rollo," Ertica said waspishly.

"Make way," Neville said, probably waving his gun around or something, and the troopers who'd left their stations at the pressure doors took hold of my arms, providing some much-needed support. "Can you walk?" The last addressed to me, in the slightly exaggerated enunciation of someone trying not to let you know how bad things look.

"Just about," I managed to force past my swollen lips, and staggered a bit, to reinforce the point.

"Simon, I'm so sorry." Clio sounded really upset, far more so than I thought the accident warranted; which, at the time, I put down to embarrassment at having lost her temper so publicly. "This is all my fault."

"You think?" Ertica asked acidly.

No, it's not, I assured her. *This is all down to me.* Which happened to be true, even if she thought I was only saying it to make her feel better. The troopers began to half-lead, half-carry me away towards the pressure hatch.

"What about me?" Dazed and in pain as I was, it took me a moment to realize the querulous new voice was Deeks. "I need medical attention too!"

"Like me to kiss it better?" Ertica asked, and the ensuing argument lasted until the raised voices were finally cut off by the pressure hatch sliding closed behind me.

CHAPTER TWENTY-SEVEN
In which I find what I was looking for, and discuss politics.

To the Leaguers' credit, they got me to the infirmary pretty quickly, although for obvious reasons I don't remember much about the trip; I was bundled into a sled at the end of the corridor on the other side of the hatch, and then out again after a few minutes of rapid changes of direction in all three planes, but since I was effectively blind and in pain the whole time, that wasn't a lot of help in getting orientated. I was pretty sure from the echoes of our footsteps that we'd moved into a corridor, then on into a room, but other than that I didn't have a clue.

"This way," a reassuring voice said, as a hand took hold of my arm. "Can you sit up there for me?"

I emitted a strangulated gurgle of assent, which was the best my swollen mouth could manage, finding shortly thereafter that "up there" meant the kind of examination table common to doctor's surgeries throughout the Human Sphere.

"Close your eyes . . ." the voice went on, in the same soothing monotone. Which was the single most pointless request I'd ever had, since they were now swollen completely closed in any case. A moment later I heard the hiss of a spray, and something cool began to leach the heat from my burning face. Only as the pain receded, and my muscles spontaneously relaxed, did I realize how cramped and tense they'd become. "Does that feel any better?"

"Much," I mumbled. I tried opening my eyes, and felt a flare of panic as they refused to respond.

"Take it easy," the voice said. "It's not that quick. Although you should recover a lot faster than the other guy." For a moment I wondered who he was talking about, before the penny dropped: Deeks. "We synthesized a new antitoxin after treating him, once we knew what we were dealing with. Just in case anyone else"—a short, hesitant pause, while he searched for a tactful phrase, "um, came into contact with her."

"Lucky me," I slurred. I checked my biomonitor again, and found the traces of toxin in my system already noticeably reduced. At this rate I'd be clear of the stuff within a few hours. Which was both good news and bad. I needed to be here for a while if I was going to search for a node, and crack it if I found one, but if they knew how fast I was recovering they might just send me straight back to the internment area. I swayed a little, and put a hand down to steady myself against the surface of the couch. "Ough. Still feel a bit groggy."

"I'm not surprised." My eyes were open a slit now, and a blurry image of someone in a white coat suddenly filled them. I couldn't make out much in the way of facial features, but he seemed to have dark hair, and be mercifully free of any visible tweaks. He shone a light directly into each eye, and seemed pleased with my reaction. "Your pupils are dilating and contracting normally. That looks promising."

"Good." I might as well attack the problem head on, then, instead of hedging around it. "Does that mean I can go back to my friends now?"

"If you insist." Damn. It looked like I'd overplayed my hand; perhaps I could counterfeit a seizure or something. But before I could make a complete fool of myself, the medic carried on talking. "I'd rather keep you in for a few hours, though, for observation. Just in case there's an allergic reaction to the antitoxin."

"Sounds good to me," I said, hiding my relief. "You're the doctor."

"Just a corpsman." He held out a steadying hand as I hopped off the table, and stood, turning my head in an attempt to see more of the room despite the narrow field of vision left open to me by the swelling around my eyes. "You don't need that much in the way of treatment."

"Glad to hear it," I said, faintly surprised to find that it was true.

"This way." He led me out of the room and down the corridor

outside, steering me with a light pressure against my elbow. After a couple of dozen steps, he opened another door, and ushered me through. "You can rest up in here for a while."

"Thanks," I said, entering cautiously, and finding a small, utilitarian room, containing very little beyond a bed and a couple of chairs. Though I could just about make them out, I made a point of bumping into one of the chairs on the way to the bed anyway; it probably wouldn't hurt to look a bit more incapacitated than I actually was.

"Just call if you need anything. There are plenty of people about outside." He delivered the veiled warning pleasantly enough, as if it had been nothing more than a piece of casual conversation.

"Thanks. I will." I pretended to take the remark at face value, and stretched out on the bed. "But I'm going to try and sleep it off." I even managed a reasonably convincing yawn, which wasn't that surprising considering how little sleep I'd had the previous night.

"Good idea. I'll look in on you later." The door clicked behind him, leaving me alone in the heart of the enemy citadel. Or, if not the heart, one of its organs, at least.

Almost as soon as he left, I dived into the datasphere, immersing myself fully in the flow of information. Baines had been right, there was a node nearby, dense with data, pulsing with it like a dwarf star of undiluted knowledge. I reached out cautiously, fearful of being burned, and deployed the sneakware, meshing with the outer layers as easily as I'd become used to doing with Jas's visor. No alarms went off, and no roadblocks descended, so at least I'd managed to pass myself off as an authorized user. Heartened by this initial success, which I must admit I'd been expecting, albeit with a little more difficulty, I began trying to access some actual data, deploying the datanomes I'd reverse engineered from the recording of Baines' fruitless attempt to do the same.

This time it wasn't such plain sailing, and I had to modify a couple of things as I went along, but after a bit of cautious poking and fiddling I finally broke through into an index. The rush of elation which accompanied my success was so strong I was even able to forget the throbbing discomfort of my healing face.

Right. Time to see what I could find. Prudence dictated that I make the most of my limited time, as the longer I was meshed in the more likely it was that someone would notice my presence, so I'd have to prioritize. I swooped through a nebula of interlocking data trails, looking for something worth filching. Plans of the base seemed like a good place to start, and I snagged one into my 'sphere, realizing for the first time just how much you could cram into a hollowed-out rock this size.

The place was huge, a termite mound heaving with military personnel: though we'd only met a few in person, there must have been over ten thousand people living and working there, not counting the crews of the ships arriving and departing on an almost hourly basis. The whole moonlet was a honeycomb of living quarters, workshops, power plants, storage areas and weapon emplacements; not just graviton beams, but old-fashioned missile racks too, which could still be fired if the main generators went down. Freedom might be well within the League's borders these days, but this place had been built when it was a frontier fortress, and hadn't forgotten the lessons it had learned back then.

The cavern we were billeted in turned out to be surprisingly close to the surface, but almost the entire diameter of the base from the hangar bay where the *Stacked Deck* and the other impounded vessels were docked. Which made perfect sense to me. No one in their right mind would attempt to break out and recover their ships by force, but taking the precaution of making it as difficult as possible anyway certainly couldn't hurt.

Feeling that I'd got hold of a prize well worth the risk, which Aunt Jenny would be more than satisfied with, I briefly considered withdrawing, then went back to the main index anyway. While I was here, I might as well see what else I could get away with: after all, it wasn't as though I was likely to get another chance.

I hesitated, wasting precious nanoseconds trying to pick a likely target. The sheer quantity of information was working against me, and I was just about to grab a file at random and cross my fingers that it contained something worthwhile when I noticed a log of ship movements in and out of the base. That would be gold dust if I could get it back to my aunt; I had no doubt that an analyst of her caliber, and the people she worked for, would be able to deduce a vast amount about the League's strategic aims and state of preparedness from the raw data, especially if it included details of the vessels' destinations. I grabbed that too, and prepared to cut myself loose.

Then, at the last minute, I remembered my promise to Baines. There had to be something here I could give him to trade with Remington. I dithered again, then pounced on a list of cargo brokers in systems outside the League who were being paid substantial retainers to expedite shipments of materials the Navy wanted to get its hands on—which probably overlapped with parts of their intelligence gathering network too, come to think of it, another welcome surprise for Aunt Jenny. A few quiet words in their offices ought to ensure a steady stream of lucrative cargoes for the *Stacked Deck* if I was any judge of how the skipper liked to do business; something that was bound to occur to him if the list was waved under his nose.

Right, that would do: if I got caught now I'd be in serious trouble, and there was no sense in pushing my luck. I disengaged from the node, stretched out on the bed, and started to sort through my spoils.

As it turned out, I didn't get nearly as far as I'd expected before my body decided it had had more than enough to put up with for one day, and shut itself down while the toxins got on with working their way out of my system. After half an hour of sifting through the data I'd pilfered I was beginning to yawn in earnest, not just for effect when the corpsman stuck his head round the door to see how I was getting on, and my thoughts were running noticeably slower than they normally did. According to the biomonitor the levels of toxin in my blood were dropping rapidly, something I was able to empirically confirm by the way my jaw was opening more widely with every yawn, and the fact that I could see reasonably well out of both eyes by now. So I decided to give way to the inevitable, and allowed myself to doze off.

I was woken by the sound of the door opening, and sat up, expecting to see the corpsman again; though my eyes opened more or less fully this time, it still took me a moment to realize that it wasn't him.

"Hi," I said, blinking in perplexity. "What are you doing here?"

"Guess," Jas said, walking fully into the room. She stared at me for a moment, then suppressed a smile. "You look terrible."

"You should see me from this side," I said.

"Right." She sat on the end of the bed, and examined me critically. "They tell me you're on the mend."

"The corpsman gave me some sort of antidote," I said. "They had it all ready, just in case Ertica touched somebody else. Luckily for me."

"The way I heard it, you touched her," Jas said, her voice carefully neutral.

"Purely by accident," I said, a little more defensively than I'd intended.

"So I heard." Jas didn't sound all that convinced. "And just how do you accidentally get your face stuck down a woman's cleavage?"

"Believe me, it wasn't as much fun as it sounds," I said. "Clio punched me."

Jas nodded. "Getting a bit jealous, was she?"

"Of course not," I said, stunned by the absurdity of the idea. "We're just friends. Most of the time, anyway. What would she have to be jealous about?"

"Oh, Si." Jas shook her head pityingly. "You really shouldn't be allowed out on your own."

"Well, I'm not," I pointed out, with perhaps a little more asperity than I should have done. "That's what you're here for, isn't it?"

"To escort you back?" Jas nodded. "Do you want something to eat first?"

"Why not?" Now that she came to mention it, I found I was feeling a lot more hungry than I'd realized. I swung my feet to the floor, and stood; rather too quickly, apparently, as a wave of dizziness swept over me. For a moment I thought I was going to collapse back onto the bed, but Jas was suddenly there, moving with the preternatural swiftness I'd noticed before. An arm went round my waist, and she leaned her shoulder in beneath mine, so my own arm draped itself limply around her neck.

I was abruptly aware of the warmth of her body against mine, and the whisper of her breath against my ear. Then I found my balance, standing firmly on my feet again, but neither of us seemed particularly inclined to break free.

"Okay now?" Jas asked after a moment, her voice unnaturally brisk and businesslike.

"Fine." I could feel her heartbeat throbbing against my ribcage, in almost perfect synchronization with my own. If this was a virt, I thought, we'd stand there like that for moment or two, gazing into one another's eyes, then lean in for a kiss. But it wasn't, of course. What actually happened was that we stared at each other for a couple of seconds, then broke apart, looking at the air next to one another's faces in mutual embarrassment.

"Right. Food." Jas broke the awkward silence, and held the door open for me.

"Food. Good idea," I said, trying not to think about the way her body had felt pressed against my own. Once again I found myself wondering how things would have been between us if the circumstances of our meeting had been different, and regretting that we'd never get the chance to find out. I blinked the last of the blurring from my eyes, and belatedly realized that, though dressed in her usual fatigues, she wasn't wearing her body armor, or carrying a gun. "Are you off duty now?"

"Technically." She followed me into the corridor outside, and I turned left, back towards the examination room and the entrance I'd come in by. "But I thought you'd prefer to see a friendly face when your vision cleared, so I volunteered to pick you up."

"I appreciate it," I said, sincerely.

"Good. This way." She turned, and started off down the corridor in the opposite direction. I felt a sudden irrational impulse to make a break for it, but suppressed it firmly: there was no point in even trying. She was faster and stronger than I was, and even if she hadn't been, there were so many other service people around I'd be brought down within a matter of moments. Rather more cogently, though, it would shatter any trust that had started to grow between us, along with our nascent friendship. Which I really didn't want to think about too closely; it was true I'd started to cultivate her purely as a means to an end, to try to get to a node, but I'd quickly begun to like her, and enjoy her company. If she ever realized how duplicitous I'd been she'd be badly and justifiably hurt, and I didn't want that on my conscience, any more than I wanted to lose her friendship. And realizing that had just made me feel guilty about exploiting her in the first place.

I wondered how other agents in my position dealt with that kind of thing. Were they able to compartmentalize their own feelings and the needs of the mission, so they simply didn't affect each other, or were they unfeeling sociopaths, who just didn't give a damn? Either way, I didn't feel too comfortable about joining their ranks.

"We're here," Jas said, breaking into my thoughts. She cocked her head, looking at me curiously. "Penny for them?"

"They're not worth that much," I said.

Jas had led me to a commissary, crowded with men and women in uniform. No doubt I'd have learned a lot about what was going on in this part of the base if the variations and insignia had meant anything to me, but at the time I was too intent on keeping her in sight to take much notice of the people around me, or compare their shoulder flashes against the file I'd got stashed away somewhere in my 'sphere. For the most part, like Jas, their tweaks weren't visible to the naked eye, but one or two exceptions stood out; a few tails waved over the shoulders of seated diners, and a couple of people, their gender indeterminate, were little more than stocky slabs of muscle, who looked to me like collateral damage looking for someone to happen to.

My Guild patch and inflamed visage attracted a few curious glances, but, for the most part, we were left to find a quiet table with little fuss. I expanded my 'sphere out of habit, but, of course, the serving drones weren't designed with a neuroware interface in mind. "How do we order?" I asked.

"Through this." Jas pulled her handheld out of her pocket, and looked at me curiously for a moment, until realization dawned. "Oh. You don't use these, do you?"

"Not as a rule," I said. "But I can't mesh with the systems here." She looked a little uncomfortable as I said that, suddenly reminded of the cultural gulf between us. "Does it bother you?" I asked. "Knowing I've got neuroware in my head?"

"Not usually," she admitted, tapping the little device, and launching a blurt of information at one of the hovering drones. Buoyed up by my success with the node, I couldn't resist poking at it with my sneakware, but, just as before, the genetic code lock kept me out. "You look so normal, it's easy to forget."

"I am normal," I said. "But I know what you mean. When I look at you, I just see a person, not a tangle of transgener tweaks."

"Only a person?" She smiled wanly in response. "You really know how to flatter a girl."

"A lot more than just a person," I admitted. "A woman I'd really like to get to know better."

Her smile grew brighter, like the sun beginning to break through a layer of cloud, but retained a rueful edge. "Be careful what you wish for, Si. A League soldier and a Commonwealther—could get messy, especially now."

"I'm not Commonwealth," I said, "I'm a Guilder," although a small part of me was wondering how much of that was actually true. I'd certainly gone to a great deal of trouble to follow through on my promise to Aunt Jenny, although technically I should have set any previous allegiances aside the moment I became a Guild apprentice.

"You say that now," Jas said, as a drone descended, depositing plates and drinks on the table between us. "But I imagine you'll feel different when your mom's in the firing line."

"You think it'll come to that?" I asked, trying to keep the tone conversational. If she'd heard anything about the League's plans for mobilization, asking her flat out about it would be certain to close down the topic.

"I hope not," she said, digging in to her food. She chewed and swallowed. "Bacon sandwich okay? I thought you'd prefer something simple, under the circumstances."

"Perfect," I said, taking a bite of my own. I went on around a plug of masticated bread and pig flesh. "The League's been demanding a Commonwealth withdrawal from Rockhall longer than either of us have even been alive." Struck by a sudden thought, I gave her an appraising look. She might seem about the same age as me, but with all the tweaks I knew she'd had, it was hard to be sure: it was common knowledge even in the Commonwealth that it was possible to slow the aging process with the right transgenic modifications, and, despite the general disapproval of such things, there were always rumors about the rich and well-connected taking discreet trips to Numarkut to find out for themselves. "And the diplomats are still talking to each other."

"Yep." Jas took a sip of her coffee. "They're good at that. But if the Commonwealth won't give us our planet back willingly, we won't have much choice in the end."

"Your planet?" I asked. "Don't the people who live there get a say?"

Jas nodded. "I suppose they should do. Have a referendum or something. But the Commonwealth isn't that big on democracy, is it?"

"Of course it is," I said, feeling I ought to defend my old home, even if I didn't belong there any more. "We have elections."

"Do you?" Jas asked, sounding skeptical. "And how often did you vote? Oh, I forgot, men aren't allowed to."

"That's not true," I said, a trifle defensively. I didn't really feel comfortable discussing this. "Married men are. And widowers."

"And you really think that's fair?" Jas asked. "How many men are there in Parliament?"

"I don't know." I shrugged. "A few."

"And in government?"

I shrugged again. "A few less." I could see where she was heading with this, and decided to cut it off before we ended up arguing. "But it's nothing to do with me any more. The Guild has its own way of doing things."

"If you say so," Jas said, sounding less than convinced.

"Of course we do," I said, suddenly a good deal less sure than I sounded. Up until now I'd just gone along with things, picking up how they were done a piece at a time, but there was still a lot I didn't know about how the Guild actually managed its affairs. On the other hand, whatever they did seemed to have worked for centuries, so they must be getting something right.

So I shifted the conversation to safer topics, until the meal was over and it was time to return to the internment area.

CHAPTER TWENTY-EIGHT
In which I discover a deception.

I wasn't sure what sort of a reception would be waiting for me when I got back to our quarters, but it was rather less fraught than I'd feared. Someone, possibly Jas, had seen to it that I was expected, and Remington, flanked by Rolf and Lena, was waiting by the pressure hatch when Jas escorted me through it. The presence of the transgener deckhands effectively kept anyone from the *Ebon Flow* determined to exact revenge for my squabble with Deeks at arms' length, but in the event they seemed willing to let bygones be bygones; probably on the principle that nothing they could do to me could possibly be any worse than what I'd already gone through.

"He's all yours," Jas said cheerfully, although whether she was talking to Remington or the guards on duty I couldn't be sure. She grinned at me. "Be seeing you."

"You can count on that," I agreed, and fought down the impulse to wave as she turned and disappeared though the hatch.

"I'm sure she can," Clio said, a little sourly, as she moved out of Lena's shadow; until then I hadn't noticed her presence among the welcoming committee.

I stared at her in surprise, the conversation I'd had with Jas in the infirmary suddenly coming back to me. It was ridiculous, but, all the same. . . . "You're not jealous, are you?" I asked, trying to inflect it like a joke.

"Don't flatter yourself," Clio snapped, looking mortally offended. Rolf and Lena exchanged pitying looks, probably at my consequent embarrassment. Then her expression changed. "I'm sorry. I really came here to apologize." She raised a tentative hand, and touched my inflamed cheek for a moment. "Does it hurt much?"

"Hardly at all," I said. "They gave me a tailored antitoxin. I should be back to normal in a day or two."

"I suppose I should say thank you as well," Clio said, with a hint of reluctance. "If you hadn't got in the way, I'd have been stung instead."

"I suppose so." I shrugged. "But in that case I should say thanks to you, too, for rushing to my defense in the first place."

"I'd have done the same for any of my shipmates," she said, which I suppose was truthful enough.

But maybe not quite so fast, Rolf added, for my benefit alone.

"Glad to have you back," Remington said. "We had some news from the Guildhall while you were away."

"Good news?" I asked, although his expression was too sober for me to have much hope that it was.

"Not really." We began to walk back to our quarters. Out of the corner of my eye I caught sight of Baines, and inclined my head briefly, in a manner I hoped would go unnoticed by my companions; I'd have preferred to send him a copy of the file I'd filched for him straight away, but with Rolf's 'sphere still overlapping my own, I didn't want to take the chance of the transfer being noticed. That would lead to far too many questions. "The Leaguers are still convinced there's at least one Commonwealth agent among the crews with a Farland contract, and until they find them, or get some irrefutable evidence that there isn't, no one's going anywhere."

"Can they get away with that?" I asked, already knowing full well that they could. "Surely there's something the Guildhall can do about it?"

"Up to a point," Remington said. "But there's only so much pressure they're willing to exert. Imposing any real sanctions will damage the business of every Guild crew in the system, which means reducing the Guildhall's own tithes. And the Leaguers know that."

I nodded. "So we're stuffed, basically."

"In the short term, pretty much," Remington agreed. "They'll cut a deal sooner or later, and we'll get a nice big payoff for the time we've wasted kicking our heels here, but I'd be lying if I said this place is growing on me."

"Sooner we get to Freedom the better," Lena agreed.

Rolf nodded. "I'd kill for a night out at a decent opera house," he said.

"Right now I'd even settle for an evening at the burlesque," Lena added, then smiled at his horrified expression. "Just kidding, dear."

"So I should hope," Rolf said. "I grew out of being entertained by tricks with party balloons years ago."

"It's not the balloons," Remington said, with a faintly distant expression, "so much as what happens when they burst."

"Really don't want to know," Clio said firmly, leading the way into our quarters.

"What happened after I left?" I asked, a few moments later, finding the two of us alone in the communal area. Rolf and Lena had disappeared into their room almost as soon as our feet crossed the threshold, and Remington had gone into a huddle with Sowerby, who wanted to go over some of the finer points of the latest report about the state of the systems aboard the *Stacked Deck*.

"Not a lot," Clio said. "The green slut apologized for what had happened to you, which surprised everyone, and John said I should apologize for trying to hit her." I noted the careful phrasing, which left me in little doubt that any apology actually offered would have been grudging to the point of nonexistence, if she'd actually bothered to make one at all. "Deeks kept on whining until his skipper told him to shut up, then Ronnie threatened to arrest anyone who wouldn't go back to their own quarters."

"Well, at least that gave the two of you something to talk about for the rest of the evening," I said, trying to look on the bright side.

"Yeah, well, that's another thing," Clio said. "He left straight away, said he had reports to write, and was shipping out right after that. So it looks like I scared another one off."

"Really?" I tried to sound surprised, but I couldn't really blame him. If he'd thought she really was a giggling simpleton, the sight of her going all valkyrie on Deeks had probably come as a bit of a shock. "Then it's his loss if you did."

Clio smiled, a little more warmly. "Nice of you to say so, but, no, not just his. I'd been working on him ever since he first boarded, hoping to get a bit of information we could use as leverage to get out of here, but that's all wasted effort now."

"You were playing him?" I asked, surprised, although now I came to think about it, at least that explained her apparent personality flush every time he was around.

"Mostly, but I can't pretend it wasn't fun as well. He is quite good looking, after all." She shrugged. "You're not shocked, are you?"

"Why would I be?" I asked. "I've been doing the same thing with Jas, haven't I?"

"Oh, please." It was hard to tell which was the most scornful, her voice or her expression. "You're all over her every chance you get. Don't tell me you're only after info nuggets."

"I do genuinely like her," I admitted. "But I've been trying to crack her comm link with my sneakware too."

"Really?" Clio looked surprised. "I didn't think you had it in you. Guess you really are a natural born Guilder."

"I can be a lot sneakier than that," I said, not quite sure how I felt about the way the conversation was turning, but relieved to find that she seemed to approve of my actions anyway. "I managed to crack a node while I was in the infirmary."

"You did what?" Despite the number of times you read it, people's mouths very seldom drop open in surprise in real life, but if they ever did I imagine it would probably look a lot like Clio's expression at that moment.

"I got into the system," I said. "Not for very long, but I managed to get hold of some stuff."

"Like what?" I had her attention now, all right, and I must admit I rather liked the feeling: Clio wasn't exactly the easiest person in the galaxy to impress.

"Like this," I said, sending her a copy of the shipping movements I'd lifted. "Do you think John can use that for leverage?"

"He might." She nodded, turning the idea over in her mind. "Not directly, but it'll be catnip to the Guildhall. If he waves this in front of them, they'll do whatever it takes to get us out. As soon as they've analyzed what cargoes are moving in and out of here, they'll be able to corner the market in whatever the League Navy most wants, and set their own price."

"Good." I yawned, taken suddenly by surprise by how tired I felt. "I'll talk to him as soon as I can."

"Yeah. You look like you could do with some sleep." Clio nodded sympathetically. "Catch you later."

Sleep, however, was a long time coming. I couldn't resist starting to sift through the data I'd snaffled as soon as I was alone, and, as before, it wasn't long before I was completely absorbed. It was dry stuff, though, and I found myself stifling a yawn or two long before I reached the end. In fact I was beginning to doze, which was fortunate as it turned out; because it was in that half-waking state where the mind begins to free-associate that I spotted something seriously wrong, and sat bolt upright on the bed, suddenly completely awake.

One of the vessels listed on the schedule was the *Eddie Fitz*, which had apparently arrived from Numarkut the same day the *Stacked Deck* had been boarded and impounded. But that was impossible: I'd seen it breaking away from the transit lane in the first system we'd passed through, bound for Iceball. I was absolutely positive about that, because, doubting my own memory, I replayed the datastream I'd tapped from the *Stacked Deck*'s sensor suite—and there it was, large as life.

Perhaps the files I'd filched had been corrupted, or the wrong date entered by mistake—these things happened. I went back and checked, but the data was all clean, and verified by the ship's ident beacon. Which meant one of two things: either the *Eddie Fitz* was capable of being in two places at once, which I rather doubted, or another ship had been given her identity. The question was why.

Looking for a clue, I began to examine the file more carefully. The impostor was definitely a vessel of the same class, the attached visual made that perfectly clear, even down to the distinctive blisters on the hull which had once housed its defensive armament. Or perhaps still did: this was a Naval base, after all. I moved on to the maintenance schedule for the ship, and found my forebodings confirmed almost at once—the graviton beamers weren't just still mounted, they'd been upgraded. The not-*Eddie Fitz* wouldn't last long in a stand-up fight against a proper warship, but if she got the first shot in she wouldn't need to; and no one would expect a freighter to be armed in the first place. A cold chill began to work its way down my back. I still didn't know what this was all about, but I was beginning to have some very dark suspicions.

Which were confirmed the moment I looked at the manifest. Officially, the *Eddie Fitz* was about to leave Freedom for Rockhall with a mixed cargo of consumer goods and agricultural supplies, via Numarkut, with a transit waiver in place for the neutral system. But what was actually being loaded looked to me a lot more like the kind of supplies a company of Marines would need to establish a beachhead, and support themselves while they waited for reinforcements.

I digested this slowly, still not quite able to take it all in. As plans went, it was pretty neat in some respects; the *Eddie Fitz* and her sister ships were frequent enough visitors to Numarkut for no one to give them a second glance, and with a transit waiver she'd just pass straight through the system without even the most cursory of inspections. The League would be able to sneak its raiding party into Commonwealth space without the Numarkut authorities being any the wiser: or at least being able to claim they hadn't been. Having seen the place, though, I'd be very surprised if a substantial sum of money hadn't changed hands, to make absolutely sure the Trojan freighter would pass through without any hindrance from Plubek and his chums.

But parts of it still didn't make any sense. Even if you were able to pack a couple of hundred combat troops into a ship that size (which you just might, if they were all very friendly with one other), a planet's an awfully big place, and has far too many strategic objectives for such a small group of men and women to take unaided. Even if they took one each, which hardly seemed likely.

I was missing something, I was certain of it, something I'd half thought of a moment ago, and skipped over. Something about the ersatz *Eddie Fitz* going unnoticed . . .

Because the real one and her sister ships had been plying that route for years.

Sister ships.

Now I knew what I was looking for, I started trawling the data in earnest, looking for matches, and to my growing horror, I found a good half dozen. The league wasn't just planning to raid Rockhall, it was preparing to invade it. The latest Trojan was even docked here, the *Tom Shelby*, waiting to take on cargo as soon as the engineers finished working on it. Which, according to the schedule, would be in less than a day.

Of course the Commonwealth would retaliate as soon as they learned of the attack, but by that point it would be too late. The League fleet at Caprona would make their move at exactly the same time as the trojans, moving into the Sodallagain system to lie in wait for the relief force from Tintagel. Which would put my mother and sister smack in the middle of the firing line. . . .

I was still trying to digest all this when my bedroom door opened, and I belatedly remembered I'd forgotten to tie a rag to the handle before settling down to review the data I'd acquired.

"Clio says you've got something to tell me," Remington declared, without preamble.

"Yes." I nodded, the words practically falling over themselves in my sudden surge of relief. "We've got to get to the Guildhall right away, use their riftcom—" Which would only get a message as far as the next system, of course, but the Guildhall on Iceball would relay it to Numarkut, and thence to Avalon. Once the warning was coded it could be on Aunt Jenny's desk within a day or two, while the invasion fleet was still preparing to shoot the rift to Iceball, or possibly Numarkut, depending on how long it took us to get out of here. Long before it could get anywhere near Rockhall, anyway, which was the main thing.

"Slow down." Remington shook his head, and waved an expansive arm, which I assumed was meant to encompass not only my room, but the base beyond it as well. "In case you haven't noticed, we're not going anywhere."

"I got us some leverage," I said, dropping the file I'd been examining into his 'sphere. *Think the Guildhall will pull a few strings to get their hands on this?*

"Definitely," Remington said, after a moment of paging through the data, and coming to the same conclusions as I had; which was probably a lot easier than it had been for me, as the files I'd been looking at were still open. "The logistical contracts alone would be worth a fortune once the shooting starts." He glanced down at me, curiosity and respect mingling on his face. "How the hell did you manage to get hold of this?"

"I cracked a node," I said. "From the infirmary. They put us down here because it's too far away from the operational areas to mesh in to one, but the surgery isn't. I found I was close enough to use my sneakware, and I thought I might as well give it a try." I thought it best to sound as though I'd been acting purely on impulse; mentioning that I'd picked a fight with Deeks in a deliberate attempt to get myself sent there, so I could use some customized datanomes I'd spent days putting together, would raise all sorts of questions I didn't want to answer.

"I'll get on to the Guildhall," Remington said, "and tell them what we've got. Our hosts won't listen in to official Guild business." Not when pissing off the Guild could mean having their logistical and supply chains disrupted just before the shooting started; people had lost wars that way before. He looked at me curiously. "What do you want to use a riftcom for?"

"How much do you think the Commonwealth would be willing to pay to get a look at this stuff?" I asked, falling back on the default Guilder response to a difficult question. It was a reason he'd consider, whereas not wanting the next thing I heard from my family to be the news of Mother and Tinkie's deaths in action probably wouldn't have very much weight with him. "We'd make a fortune."

"Maybe. Or the League would pay us just as much to keep our mouths shut about it." He sighed heavily, and appeared to reach a decision. "Leave it with me, and I'll see what I can do."

"Fair enough," I said, and finally felt ready to get some sleep.

CHAPTER TWENTY-NINE
In which I move to less salubrious quarters.

I was woken an indeterminate time later by raised voices outside, one of which sounded like Clio's shouting my name. I just had time to throw back the duvet and plant my feet on the floor when the door of my room burst open, to admit Wymes, a couple of troopers whose fatigues and body armor were as devoid of insignia as his uniform, and a comet tail of my shipmates, headed up by Remington; perhaps fortunately, Rolf and Lena were next, which kept the rest bottled up in the corridor.

"Get your pants on, please," Wymes said, in a manner which made it abundantly clear that this wasn't a request despite the polite form of words. "You're under arrest."

"You can't do this," Clio's voice interrupted, tight with anger. I glanced around for a moment, wondering where it had come from, before I noticed her in the corridor, bobbing anxiously about, trying to get a look past the looming transgeners blocking the door. "He's a member of the Commerce Guild, and protected by charter."

"I'm afraid not." Remington looked a little uncomfortable for a moment, then rallied, and met my eyes with a resolute stare of his own. "I'm revoking your apprenticeship."

"You're doing what?" I asked, not sure if I was playing for time, or genuinely unable to get my head around this unexpected development.

"I'm cutting you loose." To be fair, he didn't seem all that happy about the situation, but having made up his mind he was determined to go through with it. "I warned you when you signed on that I'd do that if you let me down."

"That was before you took me on as an apprentice," I said. "And you can't expel me from the Guild without running it past the local Grand Master."

That's Grand Mistress on Freedom suddenly popped up in my 'sphere, with Clio's ident attached. *But you're on the right track.*

"Not exactly," Remington said. "An apprentice can be dismissed by whoever takes them on, but you're entitled to appeal to the head of the local Guildhall to get the decision reversed." He glanced pointedly at Wymes, and the two soldiers accompanying him. "Good luck with that."

"I can appeal it on your behalf," Clio said, her face appearing for a moment beneath Lena's elbow.

"You won't get the chance," Remington said. "We're undocking this afternoon, as soon as our clearance comes through. I gave my word we'd deliver our cargo as quickly as possible, and I intend to follow through on that."

"Then I'm staying behind, as his advocate." Clio's voice was as grimly determined as his own. "I'm leaving the *Stacked Deck* right now."

"You're doing what?" Rennau's voice carried clearly from somewhere near the back of the crush. "You're not doing anything of the kind before we talk about this properly."

"Fine, we'll talk." Clio returned her attention to the drama in the bedroom, and her glare to Remington. "You've got no grounds for expelling him."

"If you think you have, I'd like to hear them," I said, doing my best to keep my voice level. After all, I'd had a lifetime of practice at hiding how I felt.

"You've lied to me from the beginning," Remington said flatly. "You were planted in my crew by Commonwealth Naval Intelligence, and you've carried on working for them even after I granted you an apprenticeship. I should have realized something was going on after you swiped that data from the customs inspector in the Numarkut system."

"Data you were happy enough to have at the time," I reminded him evenly. "In fact, I seem to remember that was what persuaded you to offer me the apprenticeship in the first place."

"It was." Remington nodded. "And if I hadn't been so blinded by the business edge it gave me, I'd have asked a lot more questions. Like why an Avalonian social parasite had a headful of sneakware in the first place."

"I told you, it was just a hobby," I said.

"You told me a lot of things. Like your aunt's a logistics and supply officer."

"You know she is," I said, uncomfortable with the way this was going. "You've run cargoes for her. That's why you took me on, as a favor, because you thought it would give you some leverage the next time she offered you a contract."

"You never told me her day job's a front for gathering intelligence!"

"News to me," I lied, with an easy shrug of indifference.

"But not to me," Wymes chimed in. About time, I thought, much longer and we'd all forget he was there. "Jenny Worricker's been known to us as a senior network controller for a long time. When Captain Remington confided his suspicions to me a couple of hours ago, I must admit I was on the point of dismissing them, until he mentioned in passing that you were her nephew."

"Something else your background checks missed?" I asked, sarcastically, before going back on the attack. "But even if I did believe your absurd suggestion that Aunt Jenny is some kind of spy, that's no reason to assume I am as well."

"Do you deny you had a private meeting with Ellie Caldwell at Farland Freight Forwarding just before you lifted from Numarkut?" Wymes asked, as if he was going for the jugular. "Another known Commonwealth agent?"

"I was sent to pick up a package," I said. "We never even spoke."

"A package which contained your orders," Wymes said, with the air of a man laying four aces on the tabletop.

"This isn't fair!" Clio interrupted, from the far side of Rolf's buttocks. "Guilders are always taking information-gathering contracts! You can't expel him for doing what any one of us would do, given the chance!"

"That's the whole point," Remington said. "He wasn't a Guilder when he joined the *Stacked Deck*, he was a spy, using us for cover." He sighed, and shook his head, looking genuinely regretful as he addressed his next remark directly to me. "If you'd admitted that when I offered you the apprenticeship, we could have worked something out, converted it into a standard Guild contract with your aunt. But you were using me and my ship, and you betrayed us all."

"I betrayed you?" I couldn't believe what I was hearing. "How do you work that one out?"

"How long have we been stuck here?" There was an undercurrent of anger in his voice now. "If you'd been honest from the start, we could have cut a deal. Left you behind on Kincora while we made our delivery, and picked you up on the way outsystem, something like that. You'd have been under Guild protection the whole time, wouldn't even have been asked many questions—"

Wymes nodded. "Because we'd expect the same courtesies extended to any of our information contractors detained by the Commonwealth."

Remington went on as if he hadn't even heard the interruption— possibly because he hadn't. "Instead of which we've all lost time and money we couldn't afford."

Apart from the compensation payment, I sent dryly.

"Bugger the compensation payment!" Remington retorted, leaving Wymes looking faintly confused. "You've made us look like idiots! We're Guilders, we're supposed to be on top of every deal, and now every second-rate hustler we take a contract with is going to think they can put one over on the *Stacked Deck* because you did! There's no amount of money can buy back a dented reputation!"

"Who's going to know?" I asked.

"Everyone! You think the *Ebon Flow* mob are going to keep quiet about it after the way you picked a fight with one of them? Not to mention the Freebooters. They'll pass on anything that'll make the Guild look bad."

"They're letting the Freebooters go too?" I asked. Not exactly the most pressing concern I had right then, but my head was still reeling at this unexpected reversal, and I suppose I was grabbing at whatever piece of mental flotsam floated by in an attempt to regain my footing.

Wymes shook his head. "They still have charges to answer in the civil courts. We'll turn them over once the paperwork's done, and we've cleared the other ships. Shouldn't be more than a day or two." He shrugged indifferently. "I don't imagine they'll be in any hurry to leave, anyway; they won't find their next accommodation nearly so comfortable." He looked at me, like a hungry cat contemplating a rodent. "Neither, I'm afraid, will you."

Well, he was right about that, though perhaps not as much as he'd thought. Even though the cell they moved me to was a good deal smaller than the room I'd been staying in, my quarters aboard the *Stacked Deck* hadn't been all that much bigger, so I didn't find it as claustrophobic as I might have—although being unable to leave whenever I felt like it made a big difference, of course.

Wymes had, at least, granted me a degree of privacy in which to get dressed before leaving the internment area; since my old room had only one exit, which made trying to run for it impossible, and hiding in the wardrobe didn't look like much of a long-term strategy, he'd agreed to wait outside in the corridor for a few minutes while, as requested, I put on my pants.

By the time he and his escort came back inside, I was fully dressed, and had packed the few items I thought I might be allowed to take with me—spare clothes and toiletries, for the most part.

Wymes nodded approvingly as he rummaged through the bag. "I see you like to travel light."

"I didn't leave home with much," I said.

"So I gathered." He plucked out my shaving kit, and held it up. "This is a joke, right?"

"Do you see me laughing?" I asked, before it dawned on me he was actually serious. "You expect me to fight my way to a docking bay and hijack a ship with an inch-long blade?" I asked, incredulous.

"That's more than long enough to sever an artery." He tossed it on the bed. "Nice try."

"Is delusional paranoia a job requirement for you people," I asked, "or did you just decide to go with what you're good at?"

"You should know." He finished rummaging through my pack, and lobbed it at me; I caught it by reflex, and Wymes nodded, confirming the impression of my reaction time he'd gained during our duel of pens. Another mistake on my part; I should have fumbled it, and made myself seem less of a threat.

Fortunately, the crowd of my shipmates had left the corridor before we emerged, most of them busily collecting up their possessions in their own quarters. The few exceptions we encountered acknowledged me with what I can only describe as distant embarrassment, unsure how to engage with me, and by no means convinced that they actually wanted to.

The exception, of course, was Clio, who broke off from arguing with her father in the common area as we passed through, and hurried over to bar our way. She glared at Wymes. "You're making a big mistake," she said. "He's still protected until his appeal's been heard by the Guild Mistress."

"That's not my understanding," Wymes said levelly. "If he is reinstated following your appeal, we will, of course, pay appropriate compensation. But unless and until that happens, he's a Commonwealth intelligence agent—"

"Alleged agent," I interrupted.

"—and subject to the civil and military codes governing acts of espionage."

"If you hurt him," Clio said, with cold intensity, "I'll have the Guild embargo this entire system until the most sophisticated piece of technology still working on Freedom is the ox cart." Wymes began to smile, then hastily suppressed it. *Don't make threats you can't follow through on,* I sent her. *It makes you look weak.* Something I'd learned early on, growing up with a sister like Tinkie, although I imagine it wasn't exactly news to a Guilder either. But Clio wasn't all that big on hiding how she felt. "Right after I finish removing your testicles with a rusty spoon," she added for good measure, and suddenly Wymes wasn't amused at all.

"If you insist on staying behind to play out this ridiculous charade, I'll see to it you have access to the communications net," he said stiffly. "Under supervision, of course."

"Guild communications are privileged," Clio snapped back. "You'll give me full access to an outgoing channel through my neuroware, and if I even suspect my discussions with the Guildhall are being monitored you'll be spending the rest of your career cleaning the heads on a garbage scow."

"I'll see what I can do," Wymes said tightly, recognizing the first moderately credible threat for what it was.

"That's my girl," Rennau said fondly, ruffling her hair. He picked up his kitbag. "So there's really no chance of you changing your mind?"

Clio shook her head.

"Didn't think so." He sighed, resigning himself to the inevitable. "Look after yourself."

"You too," Clio said, her expression softening. "Love to mom, if you run into her first."

"Will do." Then he turned, resolutely, and hurried away, keeping his face averted.

"We'd better get moving too," Wymes said, and led the way out of our quarters.

Good news, it seemed, travelled fast—all my fellow internees seemed to have heard that the Commonwealth spy no one really believed in had been unmasked at last, and were feverishly preparing for departure. Which didn't stop a lot of them from pausing in the act of whatever they were doing to stare, glare, or, in one or two cases, catcall, depending on their temperament. I'd expected Deeks to be one of the most vocal, but in the event he just turned his head without comment to watch me go by, and resumed stacking boxes outside the *Ebon Flow* crew's quarters.

I glanced round, hoping to catch sight of the Freebooters, but they seemed to be staying in their quarters—which I could hardly blame them for. The ferment of activity in the rest of the cavern would only have reminded them that their stay here was coming to an end, along with the short period of relative liberty it represented. I could still detect Baines's datasphere, though, so I sent a quick farewell message: *Didn't work out. Sorry.* Which probably wasn't much in the way of consolation to a man facing jail time, but it was the best I could do under the circumstances. Of course it did cross my mind to kick over the file I'd swiped for him in any case, but with the crew of the *Stacked Deck* already on their way to the docking bay, and no chance of cutting a deal with anyone else, being caught in possession of it would only create more problems for him than it would solve.

As we approached the pressure hatch I'd passed through before, I glanced quickly at the guards on duty, finding, to my relief, that neither of them was Jas. I was never going to see her again, that much was certain, and I didn't want my last memories of her to be tainted with the embarrassment of being brought together again under these circumstances.

The rest of the journey was made in silence; I didn't feel much like talking, and Wymes seemed content to let me brood for a while, no doubt hoping that it would soften me up. In fact he didn't speak again until I was standing in my new cell, looking around at the spartan furnishings.

"Make yourself comfortable," he said sarcastically.

"Cozy." I walked the three paces from the door to the bed, and dropped my kitbag on it. "Interesting decor. Minimalism still fashionable in the League, is it?"

"Glad you like it. Because if it's up to me, you'll be in here till they take you out and shoot you." He paused for a moment, waiting for a reaction I was damned if I was going to give him the satisfaction of. "Unless you decide to cooperate."

"I'd be happy to." I sat down on the narrow bunk, finding it a little more comfortable than I'd expected; which, as I'd expected the mattress to feel like a bag of rocks, still wasn't saying much. "But I don't know what else I can tell you. Last time we had this conversation, you said you weren't interested."

"Not in the sacrificial data you knew we'd know already." Wymes nodded thoughtfully. "Smart move, by the way. I really had written you off as a small-time chancer after that, until Captain Remington started putting two and two together." He leaned casually against the door jamb, silently challenging me to try and get past him, but I had more sense than to rise to the bait. With his tweaked strength and reflexes he'd be more than a match for me, although my fighting skills might take him by surprise just long enough to give me an edge. Even if it did, though, the place was swarming with troopers, who'd bring me down long before I made it to the first security door—which I wouldn't be able to open in any case. All I'd succeed in doing by making the attempt would be to remind him that there was more to me than appeared on the surface, and I wanted to divert his attention from the physical side of that at least. Why play your cards face up, as Jas had once put it.

"Shame he made five," I said.

"I don't think he did," Wymes said matter-of-factly. "I think he was right on the money with everything he deduced. I think Jenny

Worricker put you on that contract-bender's barge to gather intelligence for her, and set you up with a handler on Numarkut you could channel it back to her through. And when you found you had a cargo for a League world, you thought you could really go to work." He paused again for effect, a habit I was already beginning to detest. "What do you think?"

"I think I'm as insulted by the phrase 'contract-bender' as any other Guilder would be, and you ought to apologize for using it," I said. To be honest I couldn't have cared less, but I knew it was a disparaging term common among non-Guild freighter crews, and anyone using it in a dockside tavern had better be as quick with their fists as they were with their tongue. If I was going to carry on playing the affronted innocent, I'd better be seen to react to it in a typically Guilderlike fashion: so I got slowly to my feet, clenching my fists. I paused. "Still waiting," I said.

I never even saw him coming: suddenly something slammed into my midriff, and my face met a rising knee. Fortunately, even winded, my reflexes cut in, letting me ride the blow to some extent, or he'd undoubtedly have broken my nose. As it was, it started bleeding so copiously he probably thought he had anyway. I collapsed back onto the bed behind me, and, to add insult to injury, cracked the back of my head against the wall. The biomonitor kicked into life, assuring me none of the damage was serious, so I ignored it in favor of the light show sparking and fizzing on the back of my retina.

Before my vision had time to clear Wymes was on me again, in a blur of motion, grabbing the front of my shirt and hauling me to my feet as effortlessly as I'd have lifted the pillow.

"You're not a Guilder, and I don't have to take that shit from you. Do we understand one another now?"

"We do." I nodded, still gauging his strength, which I'd underestimated as much as his speed. He could probably hold his own against Rolf, let alone me. "But you just made a big mistake." I had to regain the initiative now, or it would all be over; letting him gain the upper hand would be tantamount to admitting my guilt. "Two, in fact."

"Which are?" He didn't sound all that concerned, but I'd been to enough Avalonian cotillions to know underlying uncertainty when I heard it.

"My neuroware's recorded this assault, and I'll be relaying it to my advocate as soon as she visits. Who'll enter it as evidence at my appeal hearing." I twisted my features into a smug grin, which I was pretty sure would get under his skin. "Where we'll see how much the Grand Mistress appreciates your choice of language."

"And the second?" He did a pretty good job of appearing unconcerned, I'll give him that. He even shook me a little, to emphasize how in control he was—which he wouldn't have had to do if he really had been.

"You've just doubled the price of any information I do have that you might want," I told him.

CHAPTER THIRTY

In which an unexpected visitor makes a tempting proposition.

After that there was nowhere for the conversation to go, apart from a litany of half-hearted threats on his part, and increasingly snide comments on mine, so Wymes finally left me alone to drip blood on the sheets and brood. No doubt he was hoping that the chance to assess my position undisturbed would leave me dispirited, and I have to admit he wasn't wrong about that. From where I was sitting, it looked pretty dire, with only the remote possibility that Clio could somehow prevail on the local Guildhall standing between me and a firing squad.

Before they hauled me out to shoot me, though, Wymes would want to wring me dry of all the information he believed I possessed, and that clearly wasn't going to be pleasant. He'd already shown he was willing to get physical if he thought that would help, but I didn't imagine for one moment that he'd resort to methods that crude when there were plenty of other, more subtle, ones to hand. For one thing there was my ability to record everything that happened for posterity, which I was certain being reminded of had rattled him, however much he'd tried to hide it; there was still a remote possibility that my Guild protection would be restored, and if that happened he'd be held accountable for every step he took over the line. And, for another, simply battering the information he wanted out of me would be unreliable at best—we both knew I'd say pretty much anything to avoid that, whether it was true or not, and he, or his associates, would have to waste an inordinate amount of time verifying everything he got that way. It was far more likely they'd use some biotech glop to mess with my brain chemistry, twisting my perceptions to the point where I'd happily tell them everything I knew because it seemed like a good idea at the time.

The other possibility, I really didn't want to think about. Leaguers might have some weird cultural prejudice against neuroware, but they understood how it worked right enough, and their data nodes were just as compatible with it as anyone else's—as I'd recently found out for myself. It wouldn't take much to do in reverse what I'd done to gain access to their node, and strip-mine my 'ware for every last scrap of information it contained. If I was lucky, that would be no more harmful than meshing-in normally—but if I wasn't, the results could be dire, ripping enough holes in my neural network to leave me a drooling vegetable.

Then there was Mother and Tinkie to think about, potential casualties of the League's covert invasion of Rockhall. At the moment, it seemed, I was the only one able or willing to warn the Commonwealth that it was coming: although quite how I was going to manage that under the circumstances I didn't have a clue.

Such cheerful thoughts kept me occupied for several hours, which I tried to while away by running recreational 'ware, or taking a more detailed look at the data I'd swiped, although neither held my attention for as long as I'd hoped. I wasn't in the mood for taking refuge in virts, and there didn't seem much point in reviewing something the League would delete as soon as they managed to force their way into my head.

All of which meant I was at a pretty low ebb when the lock on the door disengaged, hardly bothering to raise my head as it was pushed open from the other side. Then I realized who it was, and jumped to my feet in astonishment.

"Jas! What are you doing here?"

"Shouldn't I be asking you that?" She looked at me quizzically, taking in my appearance, which, despite a wash after Wymes's departure, was still more than a little rumpled. "Are you all right?"

"Fine," I said. There was no point talking about it now; she was hardly likely to report him even if I did go into the gory details. I waved a hand at the bunk. "Can I offer you a seat?"

"I bet you say that to all the girls." She grinned, and accepted the invitation. I followed, settling next to her, feeling faintly uncomfortable. All right, fair enough, there was nowhere else to sit, but it was still a bed after all, and the subtext wasn't exactly lost on either of us.

"Only the cute ones," I said, returning the smile. The irony of the situation wasn't lost on me either; for the first time since we'd met we were free to flirt openly, away from the prying eyes of her squad mates and my fellow internees, and all I'd had to do to make it possible was get myself thrown in jail.

"We need to talk, Si." I'd never seen her eyes so close and clear, and they drew me in, until the rest of her face seemed to fill my entire field of vision. "You're in serious trouble."

"I believe I am," I said, although I wasn't entirely sure I was talking about my arrest any more. I could feel the warmth of her body, radiating against my own, a tingling precursor of the physical contact my imagination kept foreshadowing, despite my best efforts to concentrate on the grim realities of my precarious situation.

"I'm serious." She pulled away a little, and I found myself a bit more able to concentrate on her words. "Are you really a Commonwealth spy?"

"Everyone seems to think so," I said, finding myself curiously reluctant to lie to her outright. "But if I am, I'm obviously not a very good one."

"Don't play games, Si. Not with me." She shrugged, which had an interesting effect on her embonpoint. Though the body armor I'd usually seen her in had done it few favors, she had quite a full figure, which even the standard-issue fatigues she was wearing couldn't entirely conceal. "I'm the closest thing you've got here to a friend."

"Which is why they sent you in here to talk to me, isn't it?" I asked, facing the realization I'd been shoving to the back of my head since she walked through the door.

"Of course it is," she said briskly, "and before you ask, of course we're being monitored."

"I knew that already," I said. I could detect the datastream from the handheld in her pocket, and poked at it from force of habit, but the genetic code lock kept me out as effectively as ever.

"Of course you did," she agreed, a simple statement, devoid of sarcasm or judgment.

"Good." I felt vaguely wrong-footed. "So is this just a social call, or
. . ." I cocked my head interrogatively, reluctant to put what I was
certain her real purpose was into words. It could hardly have escaped
Wymes's notice, or at least the people he worked for, that the two of us
had hit it off, and leverage like that would be too good not to exploit.
However she felt about me, though, Jas was a League soldier first and
foremost: she'd already proved that by reporting my family connection
to the Commonwealth navy to her superiors as soon as I let it slip, and
that was the side she'd come down on if her loyalties were divided.

"They asked me to come see you," she admitted, then hesitated.
"But I would have tried anyway." I found myself believing her. "I really
don't want to see you executed."

"Neither do I. But it won't come to that," I assured her, wishing I
was as certain about that as I sounded. "Clio will get the Guild back on
side."

"And if she doesn't?" Jas asked, in a tone which somehow managed
to substitute "when" for "if."

"I'll still be okay," I said, blithely, "as soon as that idiot Wymes
realizes I'm not really a spy."

"Not much of a plan, is it?" she asked, and I shook my head in
rueful acknowledgement.

"Only one I've got, though."

"Then get a better one," Jas urged. "While you still can."

"Which would be?" I asked, pretty sure I already knew the answer.

"Defect," Jas said. "You don't owe the Commonwealth anything,
you said so yourself, and now the Guild have cut you off at the knees
too. But there'll always be a place in the League for people with your
talents."

"There will?" I asked. I'd been anticipating an appeal to co-operate
in exchange for a life sentence instead of a firing squad, but this
substantially raised the stakes. Simply turning my coat hadn't even
occurred to me.

"Definitely." She nodded. "There's a deal on the table, as a Guilder
would say, and you've got twelve hours to think it over. After that, the
interrogators make a start on you. Believe me, you don't want that to
happen."

"What kind of a deal?" I asked, intrigued in spite of myself.

"Immunity. League citizenship. Enough of a stipend to live on, if you don't spend too lavishly." She grinned. "And an ensign's commission, if you still want to put on a Navy uniform. Working on intelligence analysis."

"It's tempting," I hedged, while the realization slowly sunk in that I could get out of this. Easily. All I had to do was betray Mother and Tinkie, and live with that on my conscience if they died as a result. "Anything else?"

"Only this." She leaned across and kissed me, long and slow, and I found myself responding in kind, our tongues tangling, while my biomonitor went quietly crazy trying to classify her range of transgenic tweaks in terms it understood. The contrast with Carenza's drunken fumblings could hardly have been more marked, and I'm not ashamed to admit that I rather lost track of the time for a few moments. As our bodies touched, yielding against one another, I found the reality of the contact far exceeded anything I could have imagined.

"Quite an incentive," I agreed, as we finally came up for air.

"I'm not saying it would be easy," she cautioned, moving away a few inches, "but at least we'd have a chance to be together for a while. See how we get on when we can behave like normal people."

"I'd like that," I admitted.

"So would I." She stood, with what I hoped was genuine reluctance, and headed for the door. "Think about it. Do the right thing."

"I will," I said, wondering what the right thing was. She reached into her pocket, triggering the locking code from her handheld, which I recorded out of habit. The datastream seemed strangely clear all of a sudden, no more complex than Plubek's had been, and sudden understanding punched me in the sternum, almost as hard as Wymes had done. Our little game of tonsil hockey had given me access to her genetic code, through the biomonitor I'd barely noticed activating in the heat of the moment, and I could use that to crack her handheld, or anything encoded by it. If I was quick enough . . .

"Be seeing you," she said, pausing in the doorway for a final glance back in my direction. "I hope."

"Me too." I said, smiling, and gazing into her eyes, playing for time as I frantically stripped out datanomes from the sequence I'd constructed to get into Plubek's handheld, and melded what was left with the strips of her genecode my biomonitor had recorded. It was a long shot at best, I reminded myself, but it was the only one I had . . .

Jas turned away, and the door thunked to behind her. I could still detect the compacted datacloud around her handheld, however, and, crossing my fingers, tried meshing into it, sneaking in along the pulse she triggered to relock the door. To my surprise and relief it worked, and I suddenly found myself with full access, and the weird sensation of having stumbled through a door I'd just leaned on expecting it to be barred on the other side.

There was no time to explore all the data encoded there, so I simply grabbed whatever was immediately adjacent, and dumped it into my 'sphere.

Only to find I'd hit the jackpot: locking codes for all the areas of the base Jas was authorized to enter. Which was, of course, by no means all of it, some sections remaining classified well above a Naval Infantry private's clearance level, but since her right of access included my cell, more than good enough for me.

Of course, even if I could open the door whenever I felt like it, that wouldn't get me very far. I needed a proper plan of action if I was going to get out of here, and find some way of warning the Commonwealth of the impending invasion of Rockhall.

But I had a map of the base, and a fighting chance at last. I sat on the bed, and started to work something out, trying not to wonder if I should just take Jas up on her offer instead.

CHAPTER THIRTY-ONE

In which I go for a shower, and change my clothes.

Despite a growing sense of urgency with every passing minute, I forced myself to take my time. I was only going to get one shot at this, and if I screwed it up every trooper in the base was going to get a shot at me instead, so a bit of careful planning seemed in order. Not to mention the fact that the longer I stayed put, the more it would appear that I'd simply given up, and was on the verge of accepting Jas's offer to skip off together into a rosy future as a citizen of the League. Which, if I'm honest, I couldn't help seriously considering, especially as my body kept sparking with the tactile memory of hers pressed against it; which, in turn, wasn't exactly an aid to concentration.

After studying the map carefully, my first thought was to head for the riftcom at the heart of the base, and try to get a message to Aunt Jenny that way. I'd even plotted out a route, before the obvious flaws in that idea began to occur to me. For one thing, I had no idea how to encode a message for transmission, and for another, even if I somehow managed to figure it out or coerce an operator to do the job for me, the message would only get as far as Iceball before someone at the other end realized what it was and reported it, instead of sending it on. The only riftcom network any good to me would be the Guild one, and to access that I'd have to get to Clio. In theory, as my Guild advocate, she'd be visiting me in my cell at some point, but I was sure Wymes or one of his minions would be stalling her as long as possible, in the hope of getting me to crack before she could intervene.

Which meant I'd have to go to her.

That, of course, raised a whole new set of problems, not the least of which would be having to admit to her that Remington had been right. I couldn't be entirely sure how she'd react to that, but I strongly suspected it wouldn't be with a merry laugh at how easily I'd fooled her. She'd probably give up any idea of getting me readmitted to the Guild, and refuse to take the message, before calling the guards and getting me dragged back here to meet the interrogators Jas had warned me about.

But I couldn't see any other way of getting the message out, so I'd just have to take the chance.

After biding my time for several hours, I hoped I'd been quiet enough for any guards in the vicinity to have written me off as harmless, taking the edge off their vigilance. I'd certainly done all I could to foster that impression, accepting the meal I'd been given with a quiet word of thanks, and doing my best to look subdued and apprehensive—which, given what I was about to do, required less acting than you might think.

I'd paid careful attention to my surroundings when I arrived here with Wymes, so I was pretty confident I could find my way out again even without the aid of the map I'd purloined from the node I'd cracked, and I was able to visualize the corridor outside without too much difficulty. My cell was about halfway along a relatively narrow passage, lined with identical doors, and sealed at both ends by other, thicker ones. The one we'd come in by had a guard station on the other side of it, and beyond that was a lower security area, in which the detainees were able to associate in mess halls and recreation rooms, and do dull but useful jobs to help keep the base ticking over. I hadn't noticed anyone else in the corridor while I was being led in here; it was possible it had been cleared on purpose, but I hadn't heard much ambient noise from outside since my arrival, so I'd just have to take the chance that it was generally just as empty.

Unable to put it off any longer, as about half of the twelve-hour deadline I'd been given had already expired, I made my final preparations, stripping down to my undershorts, and grabbing a towel from my kitbag. This was probably the single most stupid idea I'd had since deciding to cheat in the Academy entrance exam, but, on the other hand, it was so spectacularly dumb no one could possibly be expecting me to try it. I hoped.

I let Jas's access code float in my datasphere for a moment, then, holding my breath, melded it with her genetic key and directed it at the door. I'd more than half expected nothing to happen, but the lock clicked obligingly open, and I stepped out into the corridor as if I had every right to be there. To my relief, no one else was around to challenge me, and I closed and locked the cell door again, just in case anyone decided to check. The passageway was being monitored, of course, but, armed with Jas's security clearance, I was able to mesh with the data recorders through the ceiling-mounted cameras, and replace the live feed with pictures of an empty corridor taken a few minutes before. By the time the delayed footage caught up with me leaving the cell, it would have gone back to the live feed, with no one any the wiser—just so long as no one had been looking at a screen before I managed to switch the images.

So far, so good. Now for the tricky bit. I approached the door barring the end of the corridor, the flow of data through the guard station console bright in the corner of my 'sphere. This was the make-or-break moment. I sent out a tentative tendril, and meshed with it, rummaging through the files I found there; as I'd expected, my own name popped up almost at once. It didn't take long for my sneakware to wriggle through the security protocols protecting it, and I snagged a copy, more for my own amusement than anything else. According to the paperwork I was a skilled and dangerous field agent, in possession of highly sensitive information, and only to be seen by a short list of specific individuals, all of whom, apart from Jas, had security clearances so high they were practically in the stratosphere. Even the guards had standing instructions not to engage me in conversation, and to report everything I said. My estimation of Wymes's level of paranoia rose a couple more notches.

Once I was in there, though, it didn't take me long to amend the records. I was now a minor felon, one of Ertica's crew, being segregated from the others for my own protection after agreeing to testify against my former shipmates on the smuggling charge they faced. That done, I skipped to the duty roster, and breathed a silent prayer of thanks to the Lady. As I'd hoped, the shift change had been the same as the one the guards in the cavern had followed, which was why I'd picked now to make my move; none of the ones currently on duty had seen me arrive, or brought me my meal. If they hadn't done any more than a cursory check of the paperwork after clocking on, I might just get away with this.

Only one way to find out, though, and waiting wouldn't make that any easier. I took a deep breath, and tripped the door lock.

"Thanks," I said, turning my head to address the empty corridor behind me as I stepped through, and closing it as I did so. "See you later." With any luck the woman at the guard station would assume I was talking to one of her colleagues, who had just opened it for me. And why wouldn't she? Prisoners didn't have handhelds, or a genetic code authorizing them to open locks.

"And you are?" Her eyes travelled slowly over my exposed skin, clearly enjoying the trip. I smiled, in a friendly manner, trying to look as though I was returning the complement.

"Si Forrester, from the *Poison 4*. What's left of it. Transferred in here earlier today on health grounds."

"Really." She pulled up the file on her console, and scanned it. I tried to keep the tension from my face. If she was going to smell a rat, now would be the time. She glanced up from the screen. "What are you doing out here?"

"Need a shower," I said, holding up the towel as evidence. "Next level down, right?"

"Up," she said, lulled by the deliberate slip, as I'd intended. If you want to get someone to take you at face value, it never hurts to let them feel slightly superior. "Next to the laundry."

"Up. Right. Thanks." I leaned in, pretending to take a look at the floor plan on her screen, and tried to look flirtatious. "How soon do you get off?"

"It depends on who I'm with." She smiled, more in amusement at my effrontery than because she was tempted. "But you're not my type."

"My loss, I'm sure," I said, stepping into the elevator, and punching the icon for the next floor up.

The corridor there was crowded, as I'd hoped, and I blended in nicely with the dozen or so other seminude inmates heading for the showers at the far end. A premonitory waft of warmth and steam was seeping out into the passageway, and I found myself tempted to take advantage of the facility for a few minutes after all—but the clock was still ticking, and I couldn't afford to waste a second. Accordingly I turned left, just before reaching the showers, and found myself in the laundry area.

This was another part of the plan I just had to take on trust—although it was marked on the map I'd got floating in one corner of my datasphere, that hadn't told me precisely which part of the process went on in that room. I'd been hoping it was storage for the freshly laundered garments, but instead I was met with the unmistakable reek of an unfeasible number of recently worn ones, stuffed into laundry bags, and awaiting cleaning. On the plus side, though, there was no one around to challenge me.

I rummaged through a couple of the bags before anyone could enter, finding a set of fatigues more or less my size, and not too malodorous. I have to admit that my skin crawled a little as I put them on, but I soon got used to the faintly clammy feeling of someone else's sweat, and I supposed that, on the plus side, looking a little rumpled would help me to blend in a bit more easily.

I walked casually back into the corridor, and regained the elevator, without attracting the notice of anyone. There was, of course, a security lockout on the panel, preventing any unauthorized access to the entrance level, but I cracked that easily enough with Jas's code, and arrived in a lobby where a couple of armed guards were mooching around looking bored, while a third manned a console a bit bigger and more impressive than the one I'd passed through downstairs.

"Log out, please." He barely so much as glanced at me, more interested in the images of scantily clad young men being projected by his handheld. He and Carenza would probably have got on like a house on fire.

"Be seeing you," I said, trying to inject a more nasal, League-sounding twang into my voice, and inputting Jas's code once again. The system tried to flag it as having already been used to leave, of course, but I was ready for that, and slipped in an error message confirmation which headed it off from tripping the alarm.

Then I was outside, in one of the main transport arteries, watching the sleds hurtle by.

CHAPTER THIRTY-TWO
In which I find transport, and some new allies.

Not wanting to attract undue attention to myself, I didn't waste any time looking around, but strolled unhurriedly away in a random direction, looking as casual as possible. I wasn't the only pedestrian in sight, but most of the traffic around me was sled-borne, and I'd need to get hold of one somehow if I was to get to the internment area and talk to Clio before somebody noticed I'd gone and sparked a manhunt.

The trouble was, unlike the sleds I'd hailed so casually on Numarkut, these were all manually controlled, the dim sparks of their onboard AIs concerned only with speed limitation and collision avoidance: another inconvenient consequence of the Leaguers' irrational prejudice against neuroware. But if I couldn't get one to come to me, I'd just have to go to where they were parked.

That involved a short hike along a network of service corridors, ducking, in a few cases, through utility conduits, which at least ought to make my trail harder to follow. After some twenty minutes of twisting and turning through the bowels of Kincora Base, during which my confidence rose every time I passed someone who didn't seem surprised to see me there, I found myself walking into a service bay on the edge of one of the main transport arteries. I'd briefly considered heading for a transport pool and attempting to requisition a sled, but that had struck me as a lot more potentially hazardous: I'd be dealing with professional clerks, who'd probably have PhDs in officious box-ticking, and even the tiniest anomalies in the credentials I'd have to forge were likely to be noticed at once. The mechanics in a place like this, on the other hand, would be more concerned with the vehicles themselves, quite likely overworked, or at least disposed to think of themselves that way, and consequently more casual about the paperwork.

At least that was the theory: time to put it into practice. I took a deep breath, and walked into the clamor of a busy repair shop.

"Yes?" A harassed-looking tech sergeant extracted himself from the bowels of a partially dismantled emitter array, and glanced in my direction, clearly hoping I'd take the hint and piss off.

I waved my arm in an approximation of a perfunctory salute, not entirely sure how it was supposed to go: even in the Commonwealth the different service branches liked to have their own ways of doing things, and though I'd never paid much attention to the interactions of our hosts, I'd got the impression the same thing held true for their counterparts in the League. The sergeant didn't seem all that bothered, though, simply acknowledging it with a nod, instead of bawling me out for sloppiness as I'd half expected.

"Private Mokole," I honked, ironically grateful to Wymes for the damage to my nose, which went a long way towards masking my Commonwealth accent. "Here to pick up Ensign Hamst—" quick recovery—"Neville's sled."

"Hamish Neville? Never heard of him." The sergeant shrugged, and poked something inside the emitters, which were clearly far more interesting than me or my problems.

"Wish I hadn't," I said, "he's a complete asshole. And he'll take it out on me if I go back without at least a progress report."

"Right." The sergeant glanced up again, with a scintilla more sympathy. "Grover," he called. "Officer's sled. Done yet?"

"Dunno." Another technician appeared from the recesses of the workshop, and glanced in my direction. "Let me check." He pulled out a handheld, and inspected it. "Could be."

"Then show him, and get him to sign for it." The sergeant went back to work, my existence already forgotten.

"Over here." Grover led me through an echoing cavern full of disemboweled sleds, some of which were being worked on by preoccupied technicians, and some of which looked as though they'd been abandoned as hopeless cases a long time before. He stopped beside one which looked barely more functional than Aunt Jenny's, but right about then I was happy to go with whatever I could get. "It'll run, but you'll need to get it back here for a proper service some time in the next few weeks. Otherwise you're going to lose focus on the rear left emitters again. And the cupholder's still rattling."

"I can live with that," I said.

"You won't if that emitter fails in the middle of a traffic stream," he said, although even I knew the chances of that happening were pretty remote. Grover, however, was clearly not one of life's little rays of sunshine. He got out his handheld. "But it's your funeral. Name?"

"James Mokole," I said, putting my hand in a pocket as though activating a handheld of my own, "but I usually go by Jas."

"Whatever." He opened a clear channel, which I meshed with straight away, using Jas's identity code again. If Grover double-checked it, and realized I was an X chromosome shy of who I was supposed to be, it would all be over, but, as I'd anticipated, he couldn't be bothered. The sled was signed for, and no longer his responsibility. He started to turn away, his mind already on more important things, like the job I'd interrupted, or the time remaining to his next tea break. "You can get it out of here on your own?"

"Sure," I said, with a confidence I didn't feel. I could drive a sled manually, after a fashion, but I wasn't exactly an expert at it; I was used to meshing with a neuroware interface for that sort of thing, and had never really felt the urge to master the physical controls. Besides, that sort of thing wasn't thought of as a suitable skill for an Avalonian gentleman to cultivate, being best left to the artisan classes. I slid into the driver's seat, and poked the starter.

The power came on with a smooth hum, and I felt a faint lurch in the pit of my stomach as the sled lifted a foot off the floor. I fed a little more power to the emitters, feeling the vehicle steady, and slide forwards, oversteering slightly and almost ramming a roof support before bringing the nose round and heading towards the large double door in the wall of the workshop. Just as I was beginning to panic slightly it began to slide open, triggered by a proximity sensor, and I found myself in the fast-moving traffic stream outside.

My first sensation, I have to admit, was one of alarm. Everything seemed to be moving a lot faster than I was, and I overcorrected wildly a few times in an attempt to avoid a collision, before I began to relax and accept that the AI, limited as it was, could do the job a great deal better than I could. After that my confidence increased, and I cranked up the speed to the maximum it would allow, following the twists and turns of the map in my datasphere with single-minded diligence. It would have been a lot easier if I could simply have fed the destination I wanted to the AI, and let it get on with the trip all by itself, but League sleds were a lot more basic than the ones I was used to, and relied on a human driver to handle the steering, braking, and acceleration.

Eventually, though, I reached the main thoroughfare I wanted without killing myself, and coasted to a halt outside the hatch leading to the cavern in which I'd been interned for so long.

I disembarked, and regarded it cautiously. There were no data hotspots on the other side, which would indicate the presence of troopers carrying handhelds, but that didn't necessarily mean there was no one around.

There was only one way to find out, and by now I'd got away with so much I was beginning to feel quite blasé about courting risk. I sent an unlocking pulse to the door, only to be met with a complete lack of response. After an initial surge of panic, during which I convinced myself that my escape had been discovered already, and Jas's security codes purged from the system, I realized it simply hadn't been locked in the first place, and pulled it open, feeling slightly foolish.

On the positive side, it had been a wake-up call, reminding me I wasn't untouchable, and could still make mistakes. And as I padded down the corridor towards the internment area, I couldn't help wondering if I was about to make my most catastrophic one yet.

To my faint surprise, I met no one on the way down the corridor, but then in retrospect I suppose I shouldn't have found that particularly strange. All the merchant crews who'd been interned here had left the base by now, boosting for Freedom with as much speed as kicking against the gas giant we were orbiting could give them, and no doubt vying to be the first to deliver their long-awaited cargoes. The only people still in residence here would be Clio and the trio of Freebooters, so there wouldn't be much point in anyone else hanging around.

I expanded my 'sphere about as far as it would go as I approached the pressure hatch, searching for the telltale glow of handhelds or eyeware beyond it, but I couldn't detect a thing. Which probably meant the guards had been withdrawn from inside the cavern too, as there was no one left in there worth keeping an eye on. I could pick up the distinctive signatures of two neuroware dataspheres, though, so I sent a message to one of them, hoping it would get through.

Clio. Are there any guards inside the cavern with you?

Simon? Not quite the crisp response I'd been hoping for. *How are you doing this? You should be well out of range.*

Long story, I replied. *Short version, jailbreak. I'm just the other side of the pressure hatch. Are there any guards there?*

No she isn't. The terse message managed to seem snapped, even though it arrived in my 'sphere in the same neutral manner as all such communications. *Try the barracks. Or wherever it is Soldier Girls go for fun around here.*

I'm here to see you, not Jas. Perhaps I'd better not mention I'd already spoken to her. And definitely not mention the kiss. It didn't sound as though there was anyone on the other side of the hatch ready to greet me with a gun butt to the head, however, so I used Jas's code once again, and stood back expectantly as it slid open, just in case I was wrong.

No one shot at me, or tried to part my hair with a bayonet, so I hurried through, and closed the hatch again, leaving it unlocked in the faint hope that I might be able to make a run for it once my business with Clio was concluded. I tried not to think about where I could run to, or for how long—big as the base was, sooner or later Wymes and his people would catch up with me, and when they did I was pretty certain that the offer Jas had made would no longer be open.

"Simon!" Clio was running towards me, and I had a sudden flash of *déjà vu*, wondering if this was how Deeks had felt just before she felled him. But instead of battering me to the ground, she hugged me, squeezing the breath from my lungs with such enthusiasm I began to fear for the structural integrity of my ribs.

"Good to see you too," I gasped, as she released her grip just in time to allow some air into me before I passed out.

"What do you mean, 'jailbreak'? Why are you dressed like that?" She paused delicately. "It's not exactly fragrant, you know."

"You should smell it from the inside," I said. "Have you heard anything from the Guildhall yet?"

"My request's in the system," she said. "I've asked for a personal meeting with the Grand Mistress to argue your case, which would mean the tossers here would have to let you come with me, but that was a pretty long shot even before you complicated things." She stared at me in perplexity. "How did you get out, anyway?"

"Cracked the security system with my 'ware," I said, deciding part of the truth would be simpler than lying. "Tripped the locks, got hold of the uniform, and walked out like I owned the place."

"You utter pillock," she said, which I must admit fell some way short of the awestruck admiration I'd been hoping for. "I've gone to all this trouble to be in with a chance of getting you out of here legitimately, and you've just blown it open to vacuum. What are you planning to do now, walk home?"

"I hadn't thought any further ahead than here," I admitted. "I never really expected to make it this far. But I had to see you."

"I suppose I ought to feel flattered," Clio said, eyeing me appraisingly, "but I know you too well for that. What do you want that's so urgent it's worth running the risk of getting shot for?"

This, I sent, dropping the file I'd shown Remington into her 'sphere. *You've got to get it to the Guildhall, and have them transmit it to Avalon.*

"Do I, hell," she said coldly, after taking a cursory look at it. "So, John was right about you after all."

"Sort of," I admitted. "But that's not important right now. If this invasion isn't stopped, people will die. Possibly people I care about." Which actually did include Mother, though possibly not as much as it should have done.

"Guilders don't take sides," Clio said flatly.

"Yes, we do," I said. "All the time."

"Only when we're paid to," she said.

"Fine," I snapped. "Then I'll pay you to deliver the message to my aunt, all right? You've just got to get it to the Guildhall riftcom."

"How much?" she asked, like any Guilder would under the circumstances, although I thought I could detect a hint of other motives for considering the request.

"Whatever the Commonwealth pays for the information," I said. "It's all yours." I thought I saw her wavering, and went in for the clincher. "Enough to get your dad his ship back, probably."

"Maybe John was right," she said, considering the matter. "You'll never be a real Guilder, if you're willing to give that much away."

"It's not like I'll ever get the chance to spend it," I pointed out.

"I suppose not." Clio sighed, with what sounded like genuine regret. "All right, how do you suggest I get the message to the Guildhall?"

"You're in touch with them," I said. "Wymes gave you access to the comms system, I heard him. Just transmit the data, and ask them to forward it."

She actually laughed. "Oh yeah, like that'll work." She began to count off points on her fingers. "We're twenty minutes transmission time from Freedom, so it's not like we're having a conversation. I send a few words, and wait an hour before anyone gets back to me. If I'm lucky, and whatever I say doesn't need too much discussion at the other end first. A datafile this size is going to stick out like a sore thumb on the system logs, and the bastards are bound to take a look at it, Guild privilege or not. Assuming it doesn't just trip some automatic filter they've got in place to pick up any classified data being sent out by someone who shouldn't even have seen it."

"Good points," I conceded, with a sigh. "Sorry to have wasted your time." I was, too. Conscious that this was probably the last time I'd ever see her, I leaned in, and kissed her lightly on the cheek in farewell. "Look after yourself."

"I always do. No other bugger will." She watched me appraisingly for a moment, as I turned to go back through the pressure hatch. "Where do you think you're going?"

"No idea," I said. There was still a remote possibility that I hadn't been missed yet, and could sneak back to my cell before anyone noticed I was gone, but my luck had already been stretched to breaking point, and I strongly suspected it would go *twang!* long before I managed to complete the return trip. "Just somewhere I won't make things any more difficult for you."

"So you're giving up," she said, with an edge of contempt in her voice. "Just like that."

"Unless you can come up with another way of getting off this rock," I said, "I can't see any alternative. It's not like the League are just going to lend me a ship, is it?"

Then the idea struck. All the pieces had been rattling around in my head for a while, I suppose, but they just hadn't collided up until now.

My sarcastic remark to Wymes about hijacking a ship with a shaving blade, the shipping schedule I'd pilfered, and my recently assumed false identity as one of Ertica's freebooters . . .

"What?" Clio watched me narrowly. "You're having ideas again, aren't you?"

I nodded. "Just how far would you go to deliver that message, and buy John out of his interest in the *Stacked Deck*?" I asked.

"Pretty far," Clio said, after a moment's thought. "But unless that's a rhetorical question, I draw the line at murder."

"No one needs to get killed," I assured her, hoping that was true, especially in my case. "But you've already accepted an information gathering contract from me. Are you willing to up the ante?"

"To what, exactly?" She'd been playing the negotiation game most of her adult life, and wasn't about to give anything away, even to me.

"Privateering," I said. "I want to commission you, on behalf of Commonwealth Naval Intelligence, to steal a ship from one of the docking bays, and deliver me to the Guildhall in it."

"All by myself?" She looked at me in astonishment. "They haven't been putting hallucinogenics in your food, have they?"

"I don't think so," I said, with an exaggeratedly serious frown, "but how would I know?"

"Because you're talking bollocks?" she suggested. Once again her fingers began counting the reasons I manifestly was. "They don't just leave ships lying around unattended, you know."

I meshed with her 'sphere again, and highlighted one of the ships currently in dock. "The *Tom Shelby*. Just finished refit, waiting to be loaded. Crew all on shore passes."

"That doesn't mean it won't be guarded, especially as it's a Q ship. But let's assume it isn't. That bay's too far to walk to before they definitely realize you're missing. By the time we arrive, it'll be locked down tight."

I grinned. "I've got a sled."

Clio grinned back. "Got a crew as well? Because it's a League ship, so it won't have a neuroware interface, and I can't fly it alone."

I shook my head. "No, I don't have a crew. But I know a woman who does."

Ertica proved surprisingly easy to convince, although I suppose from her point of view there wasn't much left to lose by joining our last desperate gamble. Her ship was gone, and with it her liberty, at least for the foreseeable future.

"What the hell?" She shrugged, with the usual effect, but by now I was used to it, and couldn't afford to get distracted anyway. "Might as well go down in a blaze of glory."

Baines nodded. "I'm in," he agreed, which was just as well, as we wouldn't get far without an engineer. He turned to Rollo, who, unusually, had listened to the entire proposal in silence. "What about you?"

"Forget it. I'm too young and pretty to die." He shook his head dolefully. "Prison can't be all that bad. At least you get someone to talk to. Not like a coffin." Then he burst out laughing. "Oh, your faces. Really had you going there, didn't I?"

"Keep that up, and I might not wait for the Leaguers to shoot you," Ertica said.

"Right. So what's the plan?" He hunched forward in his seat, bristling with eager anticipation.

"The plan's flexible," I told him.

He nodded, in instant understanding. "You don't actually have a plan, do you?"

"I've got the outline of one," I said. "Broad strokes, the big picture—"

"We're winging it," Clio said. "Get in the sled, see if we die when we get there. Or afterwards, when they bounce us."

"Been there, done that, still breathing," Rollo said. "Just so I know."

"Why are you doing this?" Ertica asked, turning to Clio with an air of faint puzzlement. "The rest of us are desperate, but you've got a choice. The Guild's got your back, you can just walk away any time you want."

"I took a contract," Clio said, staring at me in a way that made me feel distinctly uncomfortable. "And I made a promise. That's enough for any Guilder."

"Sure it is." Ertica couldn't have sounded less convinced if she'd tried. "You'd have put your neck out like this for anyone, right?"

"Simon's not just anyone," Clio said, and went a peculiar shade of red. "He's a . . . friend."

"And a damn sight luckier than he knows, apparently," Ertica said, getting to her feet. "Are we ready?"

"Ten minutes," Clio said, rising to hers. "Just need to pick up my kit."

"What's the point?" Rollo asked. "We're all going to die anyway."

"And if we don't, I'll be the one with clean underwear."

"Fine," I said, recognizing a tone of voice with which I'd become familiar aboard the *Stacked Deck*. "You've all got ten minutes to collect anything you want to take with you."

And after that, we'd be committed.

CHAPTER THIRTY-THREE
In which I take my farewell of a friend.

Against all the odds, and my expectations, my fraying luck held a little longer. No alarms went off as we left the internment area, and I locked the hatch behind us. Even Rollo seemed subdued as we made our way back to where I'd parked the sled, but he perked up as soon as he saw it, and vaulted straight into the driver's seat.

"Can I drive?"

"Why not?" I said, trying not to notice the look which passed between Baines and Ertica, and which began to make sense to me the moment we were all aboard. He wasn't exactly a reckless driver, but clearly enjoyed pushing machinery to its limits, and if I hadn't become so familiar with the AI's expertise at collision avoidance on the journey over here I would probably have been a lot more nervous than I actually felt. As it was, though, I simply took advantage of being able to delegate the driving to someone else to mesh-in to the communications grid. There wasn't time, or the lack of distraction, I needed to try breaking into any of the secure areas, but I was relieved to note that there still hadn't been a general alarm call to look out for a fugitive.

"Left, down, left, up, second right, left . . ." I called to Rollo, wishing he'd got some neuroware so I could simply have kicked him a copy of the map.

"Got it," he confirmed each time, and, to his credit, he did, however little warning I gave before the junction was upon us.

Are they going to start shooting at us soon? Clio sent. *Because it can't be any worse than his driving.* Which struck me as a little unfair. It was certainly no more unsettling than the traffic lanes of Numarkut had been, although the number of human drivers in the mix added an element of unpredictability, even with their transgenically enhanced reflexes.

You think this is bad, wait till you see him with something on wheels, Baines added.

"That's the bay up ahead," I said, indicating a line of heavy duty cargo haulers, their flatbeds loaded with crates and boxes, peeling off from the main artery. "See if you can follow them in."

"Okey dokey," Rollo said, the first real live person I'd ever heard actually using the phrase, and sideslipped us neatly into the stream of traffic. In a civilian facility, like the docks of Skyhaven, that would have put us in the queue for a battery of security checks, and I monitored the surrounding dataflow for something similar, but my luck was still hanging on by a thread which refused to part: since the entire base was effectively a secure area, the only things being checked were cargo manifests.

"Inspection crew for the *Tom Shelby*," I told a bored-looking corporal, who waved a handheld in our direction as Rollo slowed to pass through the checkpoint.

He sucked his teeth. "Personnel are supposed to go in through the lower gate."

I breathed a faint sigh of relief. I'd been banking on the assumption that the covert invasion of Rockhall was being conducted on a strictly need-to-know basis, and grunts this far down the food chain would expect the ersatz freighters to be crewed by civilians. Which meant the real crews would be dressed like them, rather than in uniform. If I'd been wrong, though, we'd all have been in serious trouble.

"Can you cut us a little slack?" Ertica asked, leaning over the side of the passenger compartment to give him a grandstand view of her décolletage. "It's such a long way round, and we're on a tight schedule."

"What the hell." The corporal shrugged, unwittingly consigning the rest of his career to oblivion, and waved us through. "Just this once."

"Nicely done," Clio commented acidly, as Rollo got us moving forward again.

"Works every time," Ertica said smugly. "Flash a bit of cleavage at a man and you can get away with murder." She glanced pointedly at Clio. "Assuming you have any."

"This'll do," I said hastily. "Put us down somewhere inconspicuous."

"Got it," Rollo confirmed, as we broke through the choke point to find ourselves in a cavern full of sleds, most of them parked, others landing and taking off in a continuous hive of activity. Drones buzzed around the stationary vehicles, lifting loaded pallets off, or replacing them with empty ones, while several dozen people milled around directing them, gesticulating at the drivers, or, in one or two cases, picking up particularly precious items of cargo to carry themselves. "How about over there?"

"Fine," I said, spotting the gap he'd noticed between a pile of unloaded crates and an air recirculator, which, judging by the sheen of sweat on some of the torsos on view, wasn't working quite as effectively as it might have been. To my surprise he judged it to a nicety, tucking the sled into the narrow space without touching the obstructions on either side.

"Right," I said, quite redundantly given the company I was keeping, who were probably even more used to skulking around than I was, "just walk away calmly, as though you've every right to be here. And try not to attract any attention."

"That'll be easy," Ertica said sarcastically.

Although she turned an inordinate number of heads on the way, however, we did manage to get through the loading bay without being challenged; probably because everyone we encountered automatically assumed that someone so clearly visible must have a right to be there, and the rest of us just faded into the background by comparison. I'd taken the precaution of preparing some idents, in case we were challenged, but didn't actually need them until we reached the docking bay itself, where the usual array of towering domes rose from the floor in front of us.

"Which ship?" A guard with a gun slung ready for use stepped forward to challenge us, handheld at the ready, while a couple of her colleagues stood a few paces away, not quite pointing their own weapons in our direction, but ready to do so in an instant if necessary. I put my hand in my pocket for an imaginary handheld, and meshed with hers.

"Guess," Rollo said cheerfully. "But if you need a hint, it's not a warship."

"The *Tom Shelby*," the guard said, reading the information I'd kicked over from the handheld's screen, and smiled at him. "Who'd have thought it." She turned back to me, automatically assuming that the one in uniform was the one in charge. "Number five."

"Thanks," I said, keeping the conversation to a minimum, and beginning to move off.

Then the guard stepped forward a pace, blocking Clio, and forcing her to stop. "Isn't that a Guild patch?" she asked, pointing to her jacket.

"Yes, it is." Clio nodded, keeping her voice noncommittal.

"I thought you were all Toniden Line crews." A faint edge of suspicion entered her voice, not quite hardening into certainty yet. I tensed, and tried to hide it.

"We are." Clio nodded again. "I won it."

"In a card game, I suppose." The undercurrent of suspicion was growing, I could feel it, and I tensed, ready to defend myself if necessary.

"In a fight," Clio said.

"Now that I can believe." The guard laughed, and stepped back, waving us through.

"Well done," I said, once I was certain we'd passed out of earshot.

Clio just nodded a sober acknowledgement, not bothering to comment. It was just as well she'd already removed the ship's patch for the *Stacked Deck*, I reflected, as Guild custom demanded on leaving a crew: I was fairly sure the news of the arrest of a Commonwealth spy had spread all over the base almost at once, along with the name of the ship which had brought me here, and if the guard had seen it on Clio's jacket, our little enterprise would have come to a rapid and ignominious end.

"That's the one," Baines said, pointing out one of the nearby domes. It looked almost identical to the others, and the cradle the *Stacked Deck* had settled into on our arrival; the only difference I could see was that seven of the equatorial cargo doors were closed, while an armed guard stood watch over the remaining open one.

"Leave the talking to me," I said, as we approached him, our forged credentials hovering in my 'sphere ready for use. But before I could transmit them to the waiting handheld, the communications band lit up with the message I'd been dreading. My face and description were being flashed to every visor and handheld in the base. "Sod talking, just run."

Out of the corner of my eye I could see the guard we'd been chatting with raise her weapon, the troopers with her following suit, and talking urgently into her comm. I felt the tug of passing graviton bolts as the soldiers opened fire, taking me off balance as they sped past, fortunately missing us by what felt like fractions of an inch. The guard on the ship raised his gun too, with the preternatural speed I'd noticed in Jas.

But Rollo, astonishingly, was even faster, dropping to all fours and barreling forward in a series of leaps even the guard's enhanced reflexes were too slow to follow. Before he could bring his weapon to bear, Rollo was on him, crashing into his chest and knocking him off his feet.

"Come on!" I yelled, although no one else needed any encouragement. I was a few paces ahead of the pack, but Clio was hard on my heels, running with the easy athleticism I'd first noticed in the cargo hold of the *Stacked Deck*, and Baines was lumbering forward, his head down, with the unstoppable momentum of a landslide. Ertica was lagging a little, but not by much, and as soon as I'd reassured myself of that I looked away; not all her motion was entirely forward, and I really couldn't afford to be distracted right now.

I charged into the cargo bay and took refuge behind the thick metal wall, finding my surroundings almost identical to the mid level of the *Stacked Deck*; a flurry of graviton bolts followed me, and left a series of dents in the far bulkhead. Clio followed, hurdling Rollo and the guard, who were both thrashing about on the floor outside trying to damage one another, and sprinting for the panel controlling the hatch as soon as she was aboard. Baines was next, disappearing straight into the bowels of the ship. *I'll take the power plant*, he sent, as the cargo elevator began to descend, and I kicked back a brief acknowledgement.

Ertica followed an instant later, ducking behind one of the crates, and began to make her way more cautiously towards the steps to the catwalk leading to the central stairwell. "I need to get to the bridge," she called, although climbing up there would leave her dangerously exposed.

Simon, Clio sent. *Security lockout.*

Damn. I probed the panel she was at with my sneakware, and began frantically switching datanomes. Jas's security code wasn't on the ship's system, unsurprisingly, and even if it had been, chances were it had been disabled by now.

The guard stopped moving, and Rollo got up, scuttling inside the ship on his hands and knees, trying to present as low a profile as possible to the incoming fire.

"Is he dead?" I asked, and Rollo shrugged.

"Maybe a bit. Hope not. They tend to hang you for that sort of thing around here." Then he grinned. "But on the bright side, they'll probably shoot me before they get the chance. And talking of which . . ." He held out the guard's gun. "Any idea how to use this? They're about to rush us."

"Some," I said, throwing myself flat on the deck plates, and snuggling the stock into my shoulder. I'd spent plenty of time on the firing range training and competing as a pentathlete, although I'd never expected to use those skills in anger. Well, I hadn't counted on my brawling skills coming in handy either, but that had worked out all right on Numarkut. Giving up on the security panel for now, I kicked the sneakware over to Clio. *Keep cycling through the substitutions,* I sent, hoping I'd done enough of the preliminary work. It would undoubtedly be quicker if I did it myself, but right now I needed to concentrate on other things.

Fortunately, the gun was both simple and robust, which is what you wanted in a military weapon, rather more so than the ones I was used to, which fired steel pellets along an acceleration coil. It had a trigger, a safety catch, and a power setting, currently set to a medium output: which, if I remembered Tinkie's enthusiastic descriptions of the kit she was allowed to play with at work, was more than enough to put someone down hard, even with body armor to absorb the impact. Judging by the dents in the bulkheads, though, the Leaguers weren't too bothered about conserving power, or taking us alive; a clean hit from one of those grav bolts would be enough to pulverize an unprotected ribcage, or crack a skull like a breakfast egg.

I risked a quick glance round the rim of the hatch, and saw that Rollo hadn't been exaggerating for once: the guards we'd already seen had been reinforced by others, and more were arriving all the time. The blizzard of bolts was supposed to keep our heads down, and was more than doing its job, while a second team prepared to rush the hatch.

Well, fine, two could play the discouragement game. I squeezed the trigger, momentarily surprised by the lack of recoil, and the trooper I'd centered in my sights obligingly toppled over backwards. A couple of his squad mates grabbed him and dragged him into the cover of a pallet mover. He was still twitching, to my great relief, so at least I wasn't a murderer. Yet.

"You got one!" Rollo yelled superfluously, and slapped me on the back.

"Go help Ertica," I said.

"You're no fun." But he scuttled off anyway, keeping his head down, leaving me free to concentrate on picking the fleas off our backs. I downed two more before they got the message, and began trying to flank us instead, staying behind the cover of a couple of loaded cargo sleds, which crept forwards across the docking bay floor at a steady walking pace. The drivers were keeping their heads well down, hunkered low inside the cabs, for which I could hardly blame them, but which didn't leave me much of a target.

"Lock down the other doors!" Ertica shouted. "Otherwise they'll be in through the rest of the bays!"

"What do you think I'm trying to do?" Clio snapped back, while the security system continued to repel every attempt she made to mesh with it.

We've got power, Baines sent from Engineering. *We can lift any time.*

Any time we got the hatches sealed, and Ertica to the bridge, anyway.

Got it! Clio sent at last, and the hatch began to grind closed. Sensing the initiative slipping away from them, the troopers behind the nearest of the advancing sleds began to lean cautiously around it, snapping off what shots they could. I shot one of them, who fell back, dropping his weapon, then shifted my aim to the next.

And froze. It was Jas, I was certain of it, despite the distance and the obscuring effect of her helmet and visor. She had a clear line of sight on me, too.

We stared at one another for a split second which felt like a lifetime, then she squeezed the trigger.

CHAPTER THIRTY-FOUR
In which a starship is embarrassingly rechristened.

The bolt impacted on the edge of the closing hatch, inches from my head, leaving me stunned by the nearness of the miss. Had she hesitated deliberately, waiting until the thick metal intervened, or was she genuinely trying to kill me? Under the circumstances I could hardly blame her if she was, but I'd like to think her offer back in my cell had been at least partially genuine—and part of me still regretted not taking her up on it.

There was no time to brood, though: no sooner had the hatch thudded into place than Ertica and Rollo were sprinting up the staircase, their footsteps echoing on the open metal treads.

"Rollo, gunnery. Guilder, you're with me."

"You bet I am," Clio muttered, sprinting towards the foot of the stairs. "If that viridescent tart thinks I'm letting her out of my sight—" She broke off, and glanced over to where I was scrambling, a trifle unsteadily, to my feet. "Are you all right?"

"Fine," I said hastily. "Bit of a near miss, that's all." I trotted across to join her, still feeling a little nauseous from the narrowness of my escape. "But you're right. Better keep an eye on Ertica."

"You hardly do anything else," she said, but for once there was no heat in her voice. "Come on."

The bridge of the *Tom Shelby*, or whatever the ship was really called, seemed very different from the one on the *Stacked Deck*. For one thing there was no steady stream of data cascading through my 'sphere, everything being routed through the array of consoles in the center of the room. There were half a dozen of these, all facing inwards, where the operators could best exchange information verbally, and by the time Clio and I arrived, Ertica had already installed herself at the largest, where small screens repeated and summarized the data being displayed on all the others. Clio bristled at the sight of the Freebooter in the Captain's chair, but let it go for now, settling herself in front of the communications board instead.

"Good, you're ahead of me." Ertica nodded, in a brisk and businesslike fashion. "Start yelling for help to the Guild, and hope they're listening."

"Even if they are, they won't hear anything for twenty minutes," Clio reminded her. "We'll probably be dead by then."

"Then at least we won't be forgotten. Hiro, I want full power to the emitters, I'll route it from here." Her fingers danced rapidly across the board, slaving the conn to her station, and I began to feel a little more confident in my choice of allies. "You, cloak-and-dagger boy, sit down before I have to scrape you off a bulkhead."

Not needing to be told twice, I dived for the nearest chair, and found myself at the conn station Ertica had just remotely taken over. Which was probably just as well, as I'd no idea what any of the physical controls around me actually did, and would probably have precipitated a disaster if I'd tried poking any. There were a couple of screens there, though, relaying images from outside the ship, so at least I'd be able to get some idea of what was just about to kill us.

"Is this going to take long?" I asked, trying to keep my voice level. "Because the Leaguers outside don't seem to be giving up." One of the images I could see was the inside of the hangar bay, and the number of soldiers out there had increased by an order of magnitude, rather too many of them setting up heavy weapons on tripods for my liking.

"They've overridden the docking clamps," Ertica said tightly. "I'm still trying to disengage."

"Allow me," I said, relieved to finally find something I could do to help, and meshing directly into the ship's node as I spoke, my sneakware at the ready. The override signal stood out like the proverbial sore thumb, bristling with security protocols, most of which

I'd already circumvented while cracking the node back in the infirmary. After several nanos of swapping datanomes I managed to get round the rest, and overrode the override. "Done."

"Thanks." Ertica nodded curtly. "Green across the board."

"Well, I guess you'd know." Rollo looked up from the gunnery station, and grinned, in a manner I didn't find entirely reassuring.

"Do you know how to use those things?" I asked.

"Not a clue," he said cheerfully. "But I'm sure I can figure it out as we go along."

"Lifting," Ertica said, without any of the reporting between stations I'd heard aboard the *Stacked Deck*. Nevertheless, I remembered enough of our departure from Avalon to be able to follow what was happening around me. The ship was detaching itself from the docking port, rather more rapidly than the *Stacked Deck* had separated from Skyhaven, but still painfully slowly from where I was sitting. The base's feeble gravity didn't give us much to push against, but even so, I'd expected the gap to widen a little more quickly than it was doing. I was just about to remark on the fact when Ertica did something to the controls which sent us spinning wildly across the surface of the rock, what seemed like no more than a few yards above it, then off into space.

"What the hell?" I asked, as the image in my screen tumbled wildly, stars, gas giant and bleak grey rock alternating in a nausea-inducing blur.

"We've just blown out an emitter," she said calmly, and smiled at my expression of shock. "Or we look as if we have." She glanced at Clio. "If you wouldn't mind?"

Clio nodded. "Mayday, Mayday, Mayday, this is the Guild prize vessel *Simon Says*." She glanced across at me, and grinned. "Got to call it something."

"Anything but that," I said.

"Disabled and under attack. Requesting immediate assistance." She concentrated, meshing with the ship's node for a moment, then shook her head. "I'm trying to send our contract to the Guildhall, but the Leaguers are jamming us. Big surprise there."

"Why aren't they shooting?" I asked, and Rollo shrugged.

"Why bother? We're already crippled. And oh, look, we're just about to die." Another of the uncountable pieces of orbital debris was looming up ahead of us, a dirty chunk of ice about a quarter of a mile across. I found myself wondering if this was what a bug felt like, watching a windshield approach. Even though I was sure Ertica had something up her sleeve, or would have had if she wore any, I couldn't help tensing.

At what seemed to me to be the very last possible second she manipulated the controls again, and we skipped sideways, clipping the top off an outcrop of ice in a spray of crystalline shrapnel. Realizing too late that we were able to maneuver after all, the graviton batteries on the base opened up, but by that time we were safely behind a megaton of dirty snow; which flickered for a moment as it vanished into a rift, before bouncing back as an expanding nebula of fist-sized chunks, neatly shielding us from a follow-up barrage.

"Neat trick," I said, with genuine admiration.

"Missiles launching," Rollo said from the tactical board. "And ships. You think we pissed them off?"

"With impeccable manners like yours?" Ertica asked. "Of course we did."

"Can't take him anywhere," Baines put in from the power plant, his voice attenuated by the speaker, "Unless it's back to apologize. We're running at about eighty-five per cent, by the way. Trying to squeeze a little more out of it."

"That should be enough," Ertica assured him.

"Enough for what?" I asked. I was pretty sure we could outrun the pursuing ships, given the start we'd had, but the missiles were something else again. They were propelled by fusion torches, didn't need a mass to kick against, and were closing like piranha birds scenting blood.

"This, for a start." Rollo called up a targeting display, and sent a burst of gravitons from three of our weapon blisters at once, concentrating the fire on the leading warhead. It tumbled into a rift, bounced, and reemerged, the warhead detonating as its outer casing disintegrated. The rest of the spread exploded too, as their proximity fuses registered the sudden presence of the metallic debris all around them.

"Looks like you figured it out after all," I said.

"Okay, so I lied a bit for dramatic effect." Rollo shrugged. "Five years on an Outworlds convoy escort." I'd never heard of the Outworlds, but I don't suppose many of its citizens would have heard of the Rimward Commonwealth either, so I guess that made us even.

"Till I fell in love with a pirate and switched sides." He sighed. "It was very romantic."

"Especially the bit where he ran for it, and left you for dead," Ertica said acidly.

"I never said he was perfect," Rollo said. "Oh look, another salvo. Persistent, aren't they?"

"A bit too much for my liking," I agreed. "Can you do that again?"

"Can a Guilder bend a contract?" He glanced at Clio. "No offence."

"None taken," she assured him, through gritted teeth, and he triggered the weapons again, with the same result as before. The pursuing missiles vanished in a hail of detonating munitions, leaving the sky around us clear, unless you counted enough pieces of cosmic flotsam to form a respectable ring system. And a trio of warships dogging our heels. "Can you do anything about those ships?"

"Too much stuff in the way," Rollo said. "But on the bright side, they can't shoot at us either."

"Until we're out of the rings," I said. We had a good lead on them, but we'd still be well within range on the long fall in towards Freedom. We were already more than halfway out of the debris belt, on the most direct course for the system's capital world, and the Guildhall in orbit around it, and by my estimation our pursuers would have a clear shot at us in less than two minutes.

"That depends on how we leave them," Ertica said, poking the controls again, and sending us soaring up and out of the plane of the rings, in a long parabola back towards the gas giant. The pursuing warships continued on their old course for a moment, then began to follow, but by that time we'd opened up an impressive lead. "And how quickly we can get you to the Guildhall." She adjusted our course again, sending us diving towards the huge ball of roiling gas, on what was clearly the approach to a slingshot maneuver. She smiled tightly at the sensor echoes of the warships, which were curving back to follow us. "Which rather depends on how badly these fellows want us."

"I'd say pretty badly," Rollo said. "I forgot to tip room service before we left."

"Are we still being jammed?" I asked, and Clio shook her head.

"They're trying, but I've got a clear Guild channel. Transmitting my contracts with you now." A second later she nodded in satisfaction. "Done. When they pick it up, they'll consider this ship the legitimate prize of a privateering contract, and we'll be protected." Then she shrugged. "Not that it'll do us much good if we get blown out of the sky in the next twenty minutes."

"We won't," Ertica said confidently, as the gas giant loomed larger in the screen in front of me, blotting out the rest of the sky. I'd found my first slingshot around Avalon unnerving enough, but this was far worse; I was beginning to feel confident enough in Ertica's piloting skill, but the slightest miscalculation now, or the minutest fluctuation in the internal gravity field, and we'd be crushed like an egg by the huge world's vast gravity well and dense atmosphere. "We'll be too far ahead for that."

"The warships are slingshotting too," I warned her, spotting their sensor echoes following our course, and Ertica snorted in derision.

"Let them. They'll go wide."

"They don't look like they're going to," I said, after a moment. So far as I could tell they were in our wake as though nailed to it.

"Then we'll go narrow." Ertica worked the controls again, and the ship shuddered, beginning to dive through the outer reaches of the atmosphere. A few red lights appeared on the control panels, but I didn't know what they meant, and wasn't sure I wanted to. The external screens were no help at all now, showing nothing but shifting murk, in various shades of unpleasant.

"They're still with us," I said after a moment, as the pursuing echoes adjusted their courses to follow.

"Not for long," Ertica said, making another adjustment. More red lights came on, the booming groan of overstressed metal began to resonate through the hull, and I wondered if I was looking as worried as Clio did. Even more so, probably. "This'll work. One way or the other."

"One way or the other?" I asked, and she nodded grimly.

"We'll lose them, or die. Probably."

"Probably lose them, or probably die?" Rollo enquired. "Just asking."

"Flip a coin," Ertica said.

"Getting a lot of stress on the hull," Baines put in from the power plant. "I'm compensating, as best I can, but it's not easy. Too much fluctuation to keep up with."

"Not long now," Ertica assured him, looking a slightly paler shade of green than usual.

"They're breaking off," I said, with a sudden surge of relief. "Maintaining their course."

"Good." Ertica nodded, with quiet satisfaction.

Then all of a sudden we were free of the atmosphere again, hurtling out of the gas giant's pull like a slug from my old competition gun, with a hefty kick from our emitters against its mass to boost our velocity still further. The image in the external screens cleared, showing a bright, clean starfield, and the sullen mass of the gas giant, bisected by its glowing ring, receding rapidly into the distance.

An instant later the pursuing ships broke clear of the atmosphere too, dropping further and further behind with every passing second.

"We made it," I said, in stunned disbelief.

CHAPTER THIRTY-FIVE
In which many matters are resolved.

Of course it wasn't quite as clear cut as that. We had an inordinate amount of velocity to kill when we got to Freedom, which took some tricky maneuvering around the planet and both its moons to dissipate, to the eloquently expressed displeasure of the local traffic control. Fortunately, Clio's message had preceded us, and the flotilla of League Navy vessels awaiting our arrival had to sit on their hands and watch us dock at the Guildhall without interfering, however much they may have wished to blow us out of the sky.

At least the docking bay was reassuringly familiar, though smaller than any I'd seen so far, with only six cradles set into the station arm, three each on the floor and ceiling; although, like the one I'd embarked from on Skyhaven, which of them was which depended entirely on where you happened to be standing at the time.

To everyone's surprise, our welcoming committee of half a dozen Guilders included Rennau, who was waiting outside the hatch for us to disembark, and promptly embarrassed Clio by enveloping her in a hug as soon as our boots hit the deck plates.

"What were you thinking?" He demanded as they broke apart. "You could have been killed!"

"But I wasn't." She was fizzing with excitement. "I got a contract, Dad. Two, actually. And I need to get to the riftcom right away."

"What for?" Rennau's attention switched suddenly to me, becoming a glare that would have reduced me to a scorch mark on the floor if my ability to be intimidated hadn't been pretty much burned out by the events of the last few hours. "What's he got you mixed up in this time?"

"He's got some intelligence to sell to the Commonwealth. Worth a fortune. And the fee's all mine." She hesitated. "Enough to pay John off, and get you the *Sleepy Jean* back."

"If it's the plan to invade Rockhall with Q ships, you're a bit late." Remington appeared from behind a couple of men who looked like stevedores, if you ignored the pistols holstered at their hips, and the woman they were escorting, who was middle aged, quite striking, and looked vaguely familiar. Her clothing was as utilitarian as most Guilders favored, but seemed of noticeably higher quality. Given her obvious status I merely clenched my fists at the sight of my former captain, and fought down the urge to deck him on the spot. There'd be plenty of time for that later. "Your aunt contracted me to find out what the Leaguers were up to before we left Avalon, and I reported back to her as soon as we docked."

"You set me up." Despite my best efforts to fight it down, the anger was swelling inside me, growing exponentially as it became clear just how comprehensively I'd been played. "The pair of you."

"Not really." He shook his head. "She didn't tell me she'd recruited you, but I suspected it. I wasn't really sure until you gave me that file you'd filched, though. Then I just did whatever was necessary to fulfill the contract." He smiled, in what he probably thought was an ingratiating manner. "You'll get a good percentage. You were the one who found the information for me, after all."

"So you were the spy the Leaguers were looking for all along," I said, my voice tight.

"Sort of. I knew I needed to get on to Kincora to find out what the League was up to, so I made it look as if Ellie was a Commonwealth asset, knowing they'd impound all the ships she'd been dealing with. I was pretty sure you'd be able to ferret out whatever they were hiding once we were there, and I was right."

"And as soon as I did, you cut me loose and hung me out to dry," I said bitterly.

"You had Clio to look after you." He nodded to the woman he'd arrived with. "And I knew the Grand Mistress would grant your appeal if she was the one to present it."

"Not entirely true," the woman said dryly, "but I'd certainly have listened." She smiled at Clio, stepped forward, and embraced her with even more enthusiasm than Rennau had done. "Hello, sweetie."

Clio returned the hug, with equal warmth, and an even wider smile. "Hi, mom."

"So all you had to do was sit tight for a while," Remington concluded, with an admiring glance at the ship behind us, "and everything would have been fine. I never expected you to be quite so . . . enterprising."

"I'm full of surprises," I said.

After that, of course, my appeal was just a formality. Clio's mom rescinded the cancellation of my apprenticeship without even bothering to convene a formal hearing, and smiled at me across the polished wooden table of the conference room she'd requisitioned to interview me in. Beyond the wide viewport behind her, Freedom rotated, looking uncannily like Avalon, if someone had dropped it and scrambled the continents a bit.

"I imagine you'll want to consider your future," she said, relaxing back into her chair now the formal part of our talk had been concluded. "Captain Remington's more than willing to have you back in his crew, but I'm not entirely sure you'd be so happy with that."

"Neither am I," I said, forcing down the flare of resentment before it could seep into my voice. I'd certainly never feel able to trust him again, however many assurances he gave. "But will he even have one now? If Mik's paying off his debt with the money I gave to Clio, he'll get the ship back, won't he?"

"He would." She nodded. "But we've been talking since he arrived. There's a job going here, in the Guildhall, and we'd like to see a bit more of each other. At least until one of us gets itchy feet again. So John gets to keep the *Stacked Deck* for a while, with the Rennau family as equal partners."

"At least you'll have Clio to keep an eye on him," I said sourly.

"Ah, yes, Clio. I think she's rather hoping for a berth on your ship, to be honest."

"My ship?" I frowned in perplexity. "I haven't found a skipper to take me on yet."

"The *Simon Says*." The Grand Mistress looked at me, with a hint of amusement. "You contracted Clio as a privateer to steal it for you. Under Guild rules, that makes you the owner, unless you want to sell it on, or back to the League. And you still owe her a third of its market value, by the way."

I sat still for a moment, gazing at the planet below, and the starfield it was embedded in, speckled with the moving motes of distant ships. Astonishingly, this simply hadn't occurred to me before; I'd been thinking of the vessel we'd stolen simply as a means of escape, without a thought of what to do with it afterwards.

"That's an interesting thought," I said. "We could run cargoes . . ."

"You could do a lot more than that," Clio's mom said. "She's armed, don't forget. There'll be plenty of work for a privateer when the League and Commonwealth start shooting at one other."

"That's true," I said, heavily. The Commonwealth would be certain to react to the information I'd found by moving a task force into the Rockhall system ahead of the League infiltrators, and the diplomatic wrangling would end in accusations of bad faith on both sides, followed shortly by a bloodbath. Accusations which would be perfectly justified, unfortunately. Unless, of course, they both needed to save face. . . .

"You've got some nerve, I'll give you that," Wymes greeted me, as he stepped through the airlock from an external docking port, and glanced round at the reception area the Guild maintained for visitors it needed to do business with, but preferred to keep at arm's length. Comfortable chairs surrounded islands of coffee tables, marooned in the middle of a carpet the deep purple color of the upper atmosphere, and I waved a perfunctory greeting from the nearest.

"Coffee?" I asked, as a serving drone deposited a tray containing two cups, a steaming pot, and a plate of cookies in front of me, before buzzing away to take an order from the far side of the room, where Clio and the Freebooters were huddled in earnest consultation.

"Why not?" Wymes dropped into the seat opposite me, pretending to ignore the faint sound of flatulence emitted by the deforming upholstery. He waited while I poured, and handed him a cup. "What do you want?"

"Strangely enough," I said, "I wanted to talk to someone on your side I trust." He raised an eyebrow, but said nothing, just sipping his coffee. "You want to do what's best for the League, and in this case so do I."

"Pardon my skepticism," Wymes said, "but you're a Commonwealth agent. Which inclines me to doubt that."

"I'm a Guilder," I said, indicating the patch on my jacket, both of which were new. "I wouldn't be here, otherwise. And I've a proposition for you."

"I'm listening."

"Good. I have proof that the Commonwealth's been planning a preemptive strike on Rockhall, just like you were." Which was stretching what I'd deduced of Mother's brief a little, but not all that much. "Show them you know, and you've both got a chance to save face, stand down, and go back to the negotiating table. Otherwise you'll both lose a lot of ships and people. Am I making sense?"

To my relief, Wymes nodded. "And this proof would be . . ."

I held up a memory cache, like the one Mallow had slipped into my pocket at our first meeting on Numarkut, into which I'd loaded a copy of the file Tinkie and I had found in the node at home. "Movement orders for a Commonwealth warship. My mother's, in fact. To Sodallagain." He reached out reflexively, and I twitched it away. "So let's talk about the price."

For the first time I saw a smile of genuine amusement on Wymes's face.

"It seems I owe you an apology," he said, taking a cookie from my plate, and chewing with what seemed like genuine relish. "You're clearly a Guilder to the bone."

My business at last concluded, probably on less advantageous terms than Clio would have managed, but satisfactory nevertheless, I wandered over to join her. "How's it going?" I asked.

"I want to hear this from you," Ertica said with a scowl, before she had a chance to reply. "She says the two of you own the ship we stole."

"Technically, under Guild rules, Clio owns a third of it," I said. "The rest's mine. For the moment."

"And you want to cut us in too."

"It seems fair," I said. "We'd never have got away without you." I turned to Clio. "You've explained the proposition?"

She nodded tightly. "Till I'm blue in the face."

"Then what's the problem?" I asked. "We need a crew, you need a ship. And you'll have a third share between you, to divide up however you want." How Ertica wanted, anyway; I was fairly sure the division wouldn't exactly be equal. "And you'll have the Guild behind you as well. That's got to be worth something."

"That seems to be the sticking point," Clio said.

"I'm not going to be anyone's apprentice at my age," Ertica said. "Least of all a child." She glared at Clio, as if mortally offended.

"That's just a technicality," I explained. "I'm her apprentice too, at least on paper."

"That makes me feel so much better," Ertica said.

"We can pay you off instead, if you prefer," I offered. Wymes had promised me enough for that, and we hadn't even started taking bids on the list of compromised cargo brokers yet.

"Well, I'm in," Rollo said, unexpectedly. "I've missed being on a ship with guns. Big guns are fun."

Baines was nodding too. "A chance to join the Guild's a huge opportunity, Carolyn. We won't get another."

"I suppose not," she admitted grudgingly. "Or another chance at a share in a ship." She sighed. "All right. But I'm not taking orders from her. Unless I agree with them."

"The same goes for me," Clio said, "but otherwise you're the skipper." She signaled to a loitering drone, which promptly dropped to the table, and deposited five glasses she must have ordered earlier in front of us. She lifted one in salute, which we all echoed a moment later after picking up our own. "A toast then. To the *Simon Says*, and all who sail in her."

The former Freebooters drained their glasses in unison. "The *Simon Says*."

"We're changing the name," I said.

END

ACKNOWLEDGEMENTS
Those without whom, etc . . .

Novels, alas, don't spring straight from the mind of the author to the shelves of Barnes and Noble (or Waterstone's, if you live on this side of the Atlantic.) The intermediate process involves a lot of hard work, and occasional profanity.

Fortunately, most of us get help and encouragement from a variety of sources. In this case I'd particularly like to thank David Drake, for first suggesting I'd be a good fit for the Baen list; Toni Weisskopf for listening, and inviting me to pitch something; Kelly Marshall, my agent, for contractual I dotting and T crossing; Duncan Lunan and others on the Milford email list for help with the diagrams on page 3, any technical errors in which are entirely due to my own scientific illiteracy; John Lambshead, for much invaluable advice on being English and writing for Americans, which turned out to involve a lot more than simply omitting the occasional vowel; and, most importantly of all, Judith, for remaining married to a writer for so long in spite of the obvious drawbacks.